JEANNIE LAIRD COLTER SPEAKS:

"First of all . . . defeat the homosexual rights bill. But that's only the beginning. Then bring back all the old laws. Make it illegal for homosexuals to appear on the street or in public places in women's dresses, or leather, or any of the other shocking costumes they wear. Make it a felony for consenting adults, give them twenty years, the way they do it in some other states . . .

"Make it explicitly illegal to hire them or rent housing to them, especially in situations where they will have contact with children . . .

"I'll carry my campaign to national TV if I have to."

Her eyes were blazing as she rapped out the words.

Bantam Books by Patricia Nell Warren
Ask your bookseller for the books you have missed

THE BEAUTY QUEEN
THE FANCY DANCER
THE FRONT RUNNER

theBeauty Queen

by Patricia Nell Warren

BANTAM BOOKS
TORONTO · NEW YORK · LONDON

*This low-priced Bantam Book
has been completely reset in a type face
designed for easy reading, and was printed
from new plates. It contains the complete
text of the original hard-cover edition.*
NOT ONE WORD HAS BEEN OMITTED.

THE BEAUTY QUEEN

*A Bantam Book / published by arrangement with
William Morrow & Company, Inc.*

PRINTING HISTORY
*William Morrow edition published July 1978
Bantam edition / July 1979*

ISBN 0-553-12094-8

Published simultaneously in the United States and Canada

Bantam Books are published by Bantam Books, Inc. Its trademark, consisting of the words "Bantam Books" and the por-
trayal of a bantam, is Registered in U.S. Patent and Trademark
Office and in other countries. Marca Registrada. Bantam
Books, Inc., 666 Fifth Avenue, New York, New York 10019.

PRINTED IN THE UNITED STATES OF AMERICA

To Bud and Carol

the Beauty Queen

One

It was going to be a beautiful June day, Jeannie Laird Colter thought.

Another God-given day for her to pray, and then to agonize about when, and if, God would answer her prayer.

It was one of those summer days in Manhattan when you could sit in a penthouse garden, as she was doing now, and have the illusion that you could see forever. That you could see to the Second Coming, and the fiery end of the world. In reality, the smog had lifted today so that a person could see out across Manhattan to the Jersey flats, and the nearest shores of Long Island, and the green rolling country of upstate New York.

But in this life, things were never what they seemed, were they? God had made the real world, and Satan had made illusions. So a nice day like this had to be one of Satan's tricks. She did not dare put too much stock in this nice day.

Her father's penthouse garden, on top of the high-rise apartment building on East 69th Street, was one of her favorite places, and it certainly did give her a good view of the most amazing and frightening city on earth.

From where she sat at the wrought-iron breakfast table, toying restlessly with her empty juice glass, she could let her eyes leap along the horizon and see all the great suspension bridges—the Triborough, the Queensboro, the Brooklyn, the Verrazano, the George Washington, even the little Willis Ave. bridge up in Harlem—that linked Manhattan Island's insanities with the rest of the world. Psychiatrists, in their godless and detached scientific way, agreed with believers that big cities like New York were a magnet for psychotics. Sometimes she wondered why she still linked her life with this evil place. Maybe it had something to do with her mother, who had managed to keep her innocence in this valley of the shadow of death.

It was 9 A.M. that summer day. The morning sunlight struck fiery reflections from the windows of tall buildings facing the sun. On the East Side the FDR Drive was a river of fire, as sunlight ricocheted off the thousands of cars jammed there. Down in the streets, people teemed like ants—her husband Sidney was down there somewhere, on his way to the New York *News* building downtown. And every one of those antlike persons carried a staggering burden of sin, and had to be saved.

She raised her eyes to the west. Far out in Jersey, where industries dotted the flats, a black column of smoke rose, filling the whole sky there. In reality it was probably a fire at a tank farm, near one of the refineries. But the menacing cloud made her think of doomsday—her imagination swept her closer to it, so that she could hear the rumble of flames and the screams of sinners. Thank heavens this would never happen to her.

"More juice, sweetheart?"

Her father's deep voice broke in on her apocalyptic reverie.

"No thanks, Dad, this is fine," she said, forcing a smile.

"You won't gain any weight back that way," he said.

"Maybe God wants me to be skinny now," she said,

giving the smile another try. "Anyway, I weigh the same now as I did when I was nineteen."

Her father returned her fake smile with a real one. Sitting across from her, William Laird was reading *Barron's* with all the attention that one of Manhattan's biggest real-estate executives would give it. *The New York Times* and the *Wall Street Journal* lay already read and folded carelessly on top of *Fortune* and *Dun's*, beside his half-empty cup of coffee.

At sixty-one, with a net worth of over forty million dollars (mostly in real estate), she thought, her father could allow himself the luxury of morning coffee, and a 10 A.M. arrival at his downtown office. Bill Laird was not your typical businessman with relentless drive and a cardiac arrest coming up. He knew how to soften up a little and enjoy life—a quality that was somehow un-Baptist and un-Christian, Jeannie thought. Yet she had never actually known him to backslide. He was, well, a gentle and low-key Christian. That was all right, wasn't it?

Her father was dressed up this morning—he was wearing the black pinstriped suit that she had always admired. Often he slopped around the city in old slacks and sweaters with the elbows falling out, carrying blueprints, and his horn-rimmed glasses sliding down his nose, looking half in a dream. His face, still faintly tanned from a week in the Florida Keys a month ago, was lined in all the right places, giving him an air of one of those dignified handsome middle-aged models in the *New Yorker* ads. Standing six foot one, he had the rugged look and lonely eye of a yachtsman, and in fact he did have a silly thing about the sea.

In a few minutes, he would leave for the office, and then she would have to go home and decide what to do with her day. She would have to sit in her suddenly hushed study, and read what was left of her mail, and brood on all the things still undone.

"You're quiet today," said her father.

3

Jeannie sighed.

"It's starting to get to me a little," she said. "I really have to get myself together. I pray and pray. I read the Bible like it's going out of style. But somehow . . . nothing happens. That has to be my fault, of course."

Her father put down his *Barron's*, and refilled his cup from the sterling antique coffeepot on the table.

"After what you've been through, there's no need to rush things," he said.

She rested her eyes on him thoughtfully. Taking it easy was not really a Christian concept, was it? It was curious that she should find herself questioning him.

"I've drifted long enough," she said, a little sharply.

Her father's frank brown eyes, which had mesmerized so many New York clients and politicians into doing what he wanted, now fixed firmly on her. She found that she could not meet his gaze, and dropped her eyes.

"Sometimes," he said softly, "you think you're drifting. But God sees the river, and all the bends it takes, and the ocean where it's heading."

A rush of warmth went through Jeannie. How could she have doubted her father's faith? She smiled—a real smile this time.

"Now you know why I come trotting over here for breakfast every morning," she said, grinning. "To pick up some crumbs of wisdom from your plate."

Her father threw back his head and laughed his hearty laugh—she had always called it his bear laugh.

"Why don't you come with me today," he said. "Today's the big day—we close on the South Street property. Maybe I could tempt you to taste just a drop of champagne with me."

Jeannie considered. The thought of shuffling papers down on South Street, about which her father had talked just a little too much, didn't fit with her doomsday mood.

"Oh, I just feel like being quiet and thinking today," she said. "How about dinner tonight?"

"Not tonight," he said. "I've got a dinner engagement."

"A lovely lady, I suppose?" she said.

She was always jealous that some other woman would replace her mother. God should have put the word "remarriage" in the seventh commandment along with the word "adultery."

Her father laughed again, not so heartily this time.

"No," he said, "a client."

Jeannie shrugged and picked up his copy of *The New York Times*. She never asked about the clients he had dinner with. They were always dull people who talked about zoning and sewers.

She scanned the front page quickly, expertly. The *Times* was an infidel rag. But she would have to get back into the old routine of reading it, as well as other papers, and briefing herself on the news. And if things started going well for her again, she'd have aides who would brief her. Good aides were the key to everything these days.

In the lower right-hand corner of the front page, there was a modest headline that read, GAY RIGHTS TO BE REVIVED IN CITY COUNCIL.

Jeannie knew very well what "gay" meant. And it did not mean "happy."

A slow prickling rush went over her—the kind of rush she thought she might feel if she ever saw Satan face to face. She had the feeling that Satan did not look like the pictures in books—a fierce-looking android with horns and bat wings. No. Satan was legion, the way the Bible said. He was a mass of lost souls, seething like maggots, as huge and as dead as the moon spinning through space. And many of those lost souls were homosexuals—more and more of them, these days, sucked into that dead mass by the forces of gravity peculiar to their condition—liquor, drugs, the evil dances in their bars, and most of all by their own perverse willfulness to ignore the written Word of God.

5

Jeannie shook her head slowly. "The homosexuals never give up," she said. "They're starting it again, right here in town."

Her father looked engrossed in *Barron's*, and for several moments he did not look up. Suddenly he did look up, and said mildly, "What, sweetheart?"

Jeannie's mind was already off and running.

"The pervert bill," she said. "Councilman Matthews is introducing it again. How that pervert-lover got elected, I'll never know. You know, that's the bill that gives them the right to teach in schools, and live where they please, and so forth."

"Why worry about it?" said her father, burying his face in *Barron's* again. "It always got voted down."

"Dad, did you ever knowingly sell a building to homosexuals?" she said.

Barron's came down slowly, and her father stared at her.

"What?" he said.

"Well, did you?"

He put the paper down on the table. "Sweetheart, I don't pry into the sexual secrets of my clients. I'm sure that even my, uh, heterosexual clients have secrets that wouldn't bear examination."

"If every decent person refused to sell to them, or rent to them," she said, "they'd have to leave town. They'd even have to leave the country."

"Sweetheart, many homosexuals aren't identifiable as such. How would you know them?" He sipped at his coffee. "What got you off on this tangent?"

"*Tangent?*" she said. "This is no tangent, Dad. The sexual perverts *never* give up. That's the fourth time they've tried to get that bill through the city council."

She was still skimming the article. "It says here that the homosexuals have been doing a lot of lobbying with the unions and the police force and the firemen, and that this time they are optimistic about getting the bill passed, if one can believe the *Times*."

Her father looked engrossed in *Barron's* again. But suddenly he said, "They're very stubborn, aren't they?"

"Who? The homosexuals or the firemen?"

"The . . . homosexuals. If only they could be true Christians, they'd be very staunch soldiers for Christ, wouldn't they?"

"Well," said Jeannie crisply, "they'd have to give up their perversions first, and be born again."

Her father was riveting her with his eyes again. "That goes without saying." Suddenly he smiled. "I haven't heard you use your speechifying tone of voice in a long time. Good to hear it."

"Well, the news item just got me stirred up," she said. "Honestly, I don't know why we go on living in the city. There's so many perverts here that they even talk about the gay vote now."

Her father's smile had vanished perceptibly, as if a cloud shadow had passed over his face.

"If you go back into politics," he said, "you'll have to consider that vote."

Jeannie was sitting bolt upright. "Maybe there *is* a gay vote. But if that bill was voted on by the *people* of New York, it'd be defeated by a landslide. All the homosexual lobbying would be for nothing."

Her father was laughing again. Suddenly Jeannie had to laugh, too.

"You think," she teased, "that I am thinking of running for office again, don't you?"

"All I think," he said, "is that my little girl is getting back to her old self again."

He returned to his *Barron's* again. Jeannie went back to her gazing around.

The penthouse garden was a picture of affluent peace and quiet. Graceful white birches, weeping willows and flowering crab-apple trees grew in giant granite containers. Along the gravel paths, hybrid tea roses and tuberous begonias spilled their red, pink and yellow velvet flowers everywhere. Near the slid-

7

ing glass doors of the living room, a moss-stained antique marble fountain dripped serenely into a small pool where a few butter-yellow water lilies floated. Her father had put in the garden two years ago when he moved here. He was so fussy about his garden that every day a greenhouse crew came up to spray or wipe the pollution particles from every single leaf. She loved this garden, and wished her father would never give it up. There was definitely something unstable in the way her father moved all the time.

The morning sunlight came down on her with a peculiar force. She had prayed, and waited for God's call, but He had made her wait. When He did send her the call, in her mind, she would see plainly that it was *His* call and not something of her own impatient making.

All during this past year, as she struggled to put her life back together, she had wondered what lay next. The brush with drinking, and the nervous breakdown, and her decision not to run for state senator again, had all made her realize how far she had drifted from the simple faith of her childhood, when her mother was alive to guide her. She had refused to enter a clinic for treatment, because she was afraid it would hurt her political career. Both Sidney and her father had been amazingly understanding and helpful, considering how difficult she had been. And then had come the rush of light, the renewal of faith, the conviction that she had been born again, the offering of her life to Jesus Christ.

Suddenly a thought came flaming down into her vacant mind with the force and light of a meteorite.

"Dad, what about politics again?" she said suddenly. "Do you think I have a chance?"

"Why not?" he said, taking out a silver cigarette case, extracting a Camel, and lighting it with his silver lighter.

"I mean," she faltered, "if Nixon could make a comeback . . . and I have a *good* record. I fought everything in the world. I fought gambling and off-track betting and drugs and pornography and prostitution . . ." She wrinkled her nose at the cigarette smoke.

"You even got the disco across the street closed," said her father.

She smiled. "Don't tease me, now," she said. "I'm very serious. I'm not thinking of running for the legislature again. I'm thinking of running for governor."

Her father put the paper down again. This time she had his full attention. He looked straight at her, and this time she met his eyes unflinchingly.

"Why shouldn't I think about it?" she said. "Heavens, Jimmy Carter's staff *seriously* considered a woman for vice-presidential nominee. There are a lot of women mayors. Men have made such a mess of city politics and state politics that maybe I'd succeed where they failed. Besides, my experience is here, not in Washington. I have an edge over people who have been in Washington and then want to come back and run for governor. Finally I'm from New York City, so maybe I could end the feud between New York and Albany!"

She leaned back in her chair, stretching luxuriously into the warm sunshine.

"And maybe, after I've been a good governor of New York, I'll think seriously about running for President. You need five of the eight big states, and I'd have this big state right in my apron pocket."

Her father was grinning, showing all his even white teeth. It was the way he smiled when he had closed a big real-estate deal.

Jeannie felt herself sinking down into a sensuous warmth of well-being.

"And I think I'll start my comeback," she said, "by working to defeat that disgusting homosexual bill."

Her father was suddenly looking at his watch, and folding up his newspapers, and sliding them into his black pigskin Gucci briefcase.

"That's an odd issue to make a start with, isn't it?" he said.

"No time like the present," she said crisply. "It's something that's going to be in the news for the next two weeks. They'll vote at the next meeting. The people of the city are going to be up in arms about it. Besides, people know exactly where I stand on every other moral issue. That's the big difference between Jimmy Carter and me. Besides the fact I'm a woman and a Yankee. I've never been the *least* bit fuzzy on issues."

Her father was looking at her intently as he shut his briefcase.

"No," he said. "That's true. Not in the least."

Bill Laird studied his daughter's face from across the breakfast table. It was a round, soft face, and it was framed—as if in a Victorian watercolor portrait —by the graceful trailing branches of the weeping willow on the uptown side of the garden. But the expression in her brown eyes was anything but soft and sweet.

She had always been like that, ever since she was a little girl. She always knew exactly what she thought and exactly what she should do, and she was far more stubborn and intransigent than the homosexuals she talked about. The one exception had been that period starting two years ago, when the pressures of trying to be a successful wife, successful mother and successful politician had gotten to her. She had faltered, cracked a little, like an old building wall from heavy stresses. She had started drinking a little too much—not an alcoholic, mind you, but definitely too much. She hadn't been sick enough to be hospitalized, but she had closeted herself at home, and she had expressed doubts to him that she didn't express even to Sidney.

That strength of hers, that stubbornness, that drive, had always been disturbing. Now he was actually frightened at the way this new resolve might affect his life.

How clearly he remembered her, skipping rope on

the sidewalk outside the Good Shepherd Baptist mission on Joralemon Street where her mother had worked long days as a volunteer. She had always brought home A's from school. Then suddenly she was a high-school student, queen of the prom, one of the few girls in her class who didn't smoke pot and who wasn't pregnant at graduation time. Suddenly she was a senior with the lead in the senior play, talking about a career as an actress—a *nice* actress, mind you, like Dale Evans or Debbie Reynolds. Suddenly she was working days as a secretary and going to acting school at night, and he would meet her outside the school to drive her home no matter how late it was. Suddenly she was Miss Subways, and her round sweet face was smiling down from the ad racks on every subway car in the metropolitan area, competing with the cigarette ads and the gang graffiti for the passengers' attention. After that, she was Miss New York, and landed a job in a TV series where she played a very nice nurse. And after that, runner-up to Miss America, and movie actress. She had wanted to make a career in family pictures, and refused to play any sexy roles. But family pictures hadn't done too well, so she finally left acting.

That was when Nixon's 1972 Presidential campaign moved her to get into politics. Besides, her mother had finally made her ashamed of living amid glitter and innuendo.

She brought into politics the speaking skill and the vital presence onstage that she had learned before the cameras and on the beauty contest runway. From volunteer fund-raising work in New York State for Nixon's campaign, she had risen swiftly to two successful terms in the state senate. She was one of that new race of politicians who were bred in the media, and one of the youngest women state senators in the country. Even now, at thirty-nine, she looked more like twenty-nine or thirty. Even now she was the darling of the New York *News,* who had loved her ever since

11

the Miss Subways days, for the wholesomeness and innocence of her arch-conservatism. In fact, Sidney, a refugee from the *Life* staff when the magazine folded, had gotten his first job at the *News* largely because he was her husband.

Looking at her now, Bill Laird had the uneasy feeling that he had created a beautiful and beguiling monster. And monsters always took a few swipes at their creators before the last reel of the movie.

Of course, he had nothing to reproach himself for. He had lived *mostly* according to his lights. He had been an attentive and loving father, and he had been —as far as he knew—a devoted husband to Cora. Even in the business world, he had tried to conduct himself according to the family's Baptist faith, although he was a liberal Baptist and had never really felt born again. He had acquired his modest fortune (modest if you compared him to J. Paul Getty) by shrewd but legal business dealings, and he always paid his taxes.

It was strange to look back over the years and see it all beginning—he with his dad's little real-estate office in Brooklyn Heights, and Jeannie skipping rope in front of the Baptist mission. He could actually sit here on his rooftop, and look down the East River on a clear day, and fancy that he could make out the rooftop that had sheltered their third-floor apartment in the old brownstone shadowed by the Gothic towers of the Brooklyn Bridge.

No, he had not built grandly in that city. He had not raised any World Trade Center on that horizon. But he had saved many modest and beautiful rooftops, for he had pioneered the trend of recycling old commercial and factory buildings and turning them into living space. He had built well and God knew that. Surely he had nothing to fear from God.

But he had much to fear from Jeannie, and this sudden new idea of hers.

At the end of the movie, just in the nick of time, the creator always managed to destroy his monster. But he didn't want to do Jeannie in. After all, how could he?

He got up from the table, zipping his briefcase shut, and forced a smile.

"If I linger any longer with my darling daughter," he said. "I'll be late, and Mrs. Voeller will be mad at me." Mrs. Voeller was his secretary.

Jeannie got up and kissed him softly on his cheek. He kissed her back. "Can I drop anything at the cleaners for you on my way home?" she said.

"No," he said. "Will I see you this afternoon?"

She appeared lost in thought.

"I miss the children terribly," she said. "And God knows what unholy mischief they're getting into. I might drive upstate and see them for a few hours. Sid and I could come over after dinner, though."

She always talked as if Sidney never had any plans of his own, Bill thought.

"All right," he said. "Drive carefully, sweetheart."

As he strode toward the glass sliding doors of the living room, he thought about the home he was going to make for himself on the South Street property. Soon he could finally move out of this soul-less glass apartment tower. All his life he had moved around the city like a nomad, and finally he was going to have a house that was truly his own.

He looked across to New Jersey, and noticed the immense cloud of black smoke for the first time. *Fire,* he thought, and flinched all over. Right away, the only thing he could think about was Marion pinned in the wreck of the Lotus at Le Mans.

Marion was the "client" he was having dinner with tonight. He wished he was having lunch with Marion instead. Maybe he would call Marion from the office, and try to change their meeting to noon. He was anxious to talk about the new development with Marion,

13

who had colder nerves than he did. Maybe Marion would tell him that everything would be all right.

Far downtown, on Bedford Street, in the west side of Greenwich Village, Mary Ellen Frampton and Liv Lavransson were sitting in their more modest rooftop garden, enjoying a grittier glimpse of the same view.

The old brick tenement was only six stories, but it did give you a peek at the tops of the towers on the Manhattan and Brooklyn bridges, as well as a closeup of the gloomy crowded Wall Street skyline just to the south. As Mary Ellen stirred her instant coffee and added a little more raw sugar, she sadly studied the neighboring rooftops with their crumbling brick chimneys and flues, and their similar efforts at little gardens.

Mary Ellen and Liv had lived on Bedford Street for a year now. The whole building was gay, as were many buildings in this part of Manhattan. All the tenants, both men and women, had worked at fixing up the garden. With the New Yorker's thrift and skill at scavenging, the tenants had found some old unmatching ironwork chairs and a low table, which had been left at various curbs to be carted away. Mary Ellen and Liv had painted the furniture in blue, red and yellow. Barry and Phil, on the fourth floor, had found some old wooden milk-delivery boxes, which now spilled geraniums and petunias brought from the garden shop where Phil worked. Magda, on the second floor, worked in a decorator fabric shop, and had contributed the rainbow-striped canvas, which was now stretched on tall frames around the garden's edge. The frames cut off the depressing view of the nearby tarpaper roofs, with their dust, pigeon shit and broken glass. Even Jerry, on the ground floor—thought he was a little richer than the other tenants and had his own tiny back-court garden—had contributed an extra garden hose, and everybody used it to water the flowers and keep the dust sprayed off them.

Barry and Phil had just left for work, clattering off down the stairs, so Mary Ellen and Liv were left to enjoy the rooftop morning by themselves.

Mary Ellen *had* been enjoying it, till she picked up her *Times* and saw the article about the gay rights bill.

It was an exercise in futility, she thought—the bill would get voted down again.

She slumped back into the blue ironwork chair and stretched out her long lean legs in their ripped-off denim shorts and blue sneakers. She was off duty today, so she wouldn't have to pull the hot blue uniform pants up over them. She and Liv had picked this apartment, because it was close to the Twelfth Street post office where Liv worked as a mail sorter. It was also comfortably far from the boundaries of her police precinct on the East Side, where Mary Ellen was known as Sergeant Mary Ellen Frampton, AKA "Sarge" and "Cuffs." Her .38 Smith and Wesson service revolver and her smaller off-duty hand-gun were downstairs in the bedroom drawer.

The two of them had lived together for over two years now, and Mary Ellen was always amazed at how loving someone got better and better. Right now, the only thing wrong with her life was that she couldn't be open with her superiors about being a lesbian, and that she was not officially welcome in the American society whose law and order she had formally sworn to help uphold. That was a large thing to be wrong in her life.

She had met Liv while still a rookie. She was on a weekend upstate with three other women, visiting a woman who had a lovely old house in Rhinebeck overlooking the Hudson. That morning, Mary Ellen had gone out to get a gallon of milk, and Liv had come striding up the shady street, carrying her heavy mailbag like it was nothing. Her uniform was crisply pressed. Her mailperson's visored hat set off her white-blonde hair in its strict little bun, and her baby-blue eyes. Her sweet Scandinavian face with its china-white skin was trying hard to tan.

She swiftly looked Mary Ellen up and down with a look there was no mistaking.

By the time Mary Ellen was able to get her breath back, Liv had gone striding on up the street.

But the next morning, Mary Ellen waylaid the smiling young mailperson and struck up a conversation. This led to her contriving to be invited to Rhinebeck another time.

She learned that Liv had come to the United States as an exchange student in psychology, decided to stay, and become a citizen, but had been unable to get a job because of over-crowding in her field. She was staying in Rhinebeck with an aunt and uncle, also Swedish-born, who were good somber churchgoing Lutherans. She was neither butch nor femme—but a kiki, in her naturalness and dislike of role-playing. And Mary Ellen, under her own uniform, was also a kiki.

One thing led to another, and Liv left her quiet upstate town and moved to New York with Mary Ellen. There, she found the U.S. Post Office unwilling to put her on the street as a mail carrier again. So she took the next best thing, working on the noisy high-pressure mail sorter. Mary Ellen was so dizzied by love that she barely passed her exam for sergeant.

Liv and the police force—they made things almost perfect. Mary Ellen loved her work on the force with a passion that was almost physical. As a rookie she had made her mark—her first arrest was eight white males with a stolen car and drugs. She had handcuffed the boys in pairs and brought them all in. In court, as each perpetrator admitted that he, too, had been arrested by Police Officer Frampton, the judge was unable to suppress a smile. After that, Captain Bader had nicknamed her "Cuffs." She had never yet killed a person in the line of duty. Police Commissioner Benny Manuella had told her that she was one of the main reasons why he had (grudgingly, of course) changed his mind about putting women officers on the New York streets. Mary Ellen liked to remember that moment in the PC's office, and how she had nearly burst with pride. Too bad her dad was no longer alive, to be proud in his own way. It would have made two generations of police sergeants in the Frampton family.

But now Mary Ellen sat frowning at *The New York Times*, and some of the pleasure was going out of her day off.

"Law and order," she thought. "Oh, how I believe in that. But law and order doesn't include me and Liv. On me and Liv, it's open season. It's a personhunt."

Sitting on the other side of the table, Liv was fluffing her long hair out in the sun, drying it after her morning shower. The hair dryer was going, with the extension cords that led down to an outlet in the apartment —that hair dryer that, often, at night, wore ribbons and feathers and became an instrument of love. Liv was a fanatic about cleanliness, and showered and dried her hair two or three times a day. "What is it, Mary Ellen?" she asked.

Liv was so sensitive to Mary Ellen's moods that Mary Ellen often had the sensation that her thoughts were being read. This was usually a nice sensation, not at all scary. But today, somehow, it gave her an eerie feeling. She recognized that someday, she might think a thought that she'd want to hide from Liv.

Instead of answering, Mary Ellen tossed the paper across the table, making their tabby cat, Kikan, jump down. She pointed at the article.

Liv studied it briefly, then shrugged.

"Someday it will pass," she said in her soft, correct, accented voice.

"I'm not so sure about that," said Mary Ellen.

Liv picked Kikan up and the cat relaxed in her arms. Kikan, too, had been scavenged off the street as a starving kitten with huge eyes and legs like toothpicks. Now she was a great solemn adult mackerel tabby. Liv loved cats fiercely, and always said that they were aloof because "they know most people believe cats cannot show love, and they don't want to exert themselves."

"But it is a question of the Bill of Rights, no?" said Liv.

"Most Americans interpret the Bill of Rights as applying only to themselves personally," said Mary Ellen, just a little bitterly.

"But so many American cities now have such a bill, no?" said Liv.

"Sure," said Mary Ellen. "But now the backlash is starting. We'll have to fight like bastards just to defend those laws. Those laws can always be repealed, you know."

She sipped at her coffee slowly.

"It's ironic," she said. "When the force sends me out on the street, they give me a gun, right? If some person tries to blow me away, I can blow him away." She said this reminding herself that, as yet, she had never killed another human being. "But supposing some perpetrator tries to blow me away on the *moral* plane, right? Not take my life, but take my dignity and my career and my money and maybe my lover, too, right? And I can't do anything. I'm supposed to turn the other cheek. I'm supposed to be like a lamb led to the slaughter."

Liv's eyes were shadowed with pain. She had absorbed much of the somber steady churchiness of her family, and on coming to New York and gravitated to the Metropolitan Community Church on Seventh Avenue, as there was no gay Lutheran church group in the city yet. Mary Ellen, for her part, had retained much of her family's somber Presbyterian faith, especially that of her father, though she wasn't as churchy and spiritual as Liv. The two women's strong belief in their own dignity had led them, quite naturally, to attend the MCC's gay worship services.

But now Liv's answer was not a theological one, but a practical one.

"Mary Ellen," she said, "if you think so much about this, you will go crazy."

"I know," said Mary Ellen. "I know."

They sat silent for a moment. Mary Ellen's eyes drifted along the Wall Street skyline, and noted the great black smoke haze rising over New Jersey. An oil fire, she thought. Part of her mind was instantly in her cruiser, taking the radio run, tearing along the streets at Code One speed, responding to such a scene. Part of her was directing traffic at the fire, assisting firemen, helping injured people, holding back crowds.

"You know," she said, "it's incredible that no lesbians ever get really violent about this. Or gay men either, for that matter. I mean, *really* violent. Not just yelling and demonstrations and stuff."

"What do you mean?" asked Liv suspiciously.

"I mean, straights get violent with us. Straight gangs beating up gay people coming out of bars. And all the quiet violence, like firing us from jobs, and not giving us insurance. And all the verbal violence. Calling us human garbage, and so on. And we yell a lot, and we march, and we write letters to the editor, and we take out our hostilities by fighting a lot among ourselves. But we don't hand that *real* violence back."

Liv shrugged. "God says not to kill," she said. "Just because they kill doesn't give us the right to kill. Why should we stoop to be on their level? We should be better than they are."

"That's true," said Mary Ellen. "All I'm saying is, sometimes I'm surprised that gays don't go bananas and take a little revenge."

Liv was looking straight into Mary Ellen's eyes. "That is very dangerous thinking, Mary Ellen."

Mary Ellen flushed a little. She was not even sure why she was flushed. But she felt curiously like a little kid caught beforehand, in the premeditation of doing something naughty. In fact, she didn't even know what that naughty thing was. Liv had divined the thought, whatever it was, before she herself had thought it.

"I'm not thinking anything," she said. "I'm just saying that I'm surprised I never catch a squeal to go to such and such a block, and some gay perpetrator is sitting on the roof playing sniper because she or he's fed up. With all the fed-up *homosexuals* in this town, you'd think it would happen all the time. But it doesn't."

To cover her mysterious embarrassment, she got up to water the plants.

Very industriously, she turned on the faucet and started to spray the geraniums gently. It made Mary Ellen feel a little better, washing the city pollution off the flowers.

But Liv wasn't through with her yet. With Kikan now sleeping in her arms, she looked at Mary Ellen as steadily as a clairvoyant and said, "Tell me, Mary Ellen, looove. You have the pistol downstairs. When you lose control, who will you shoot?"

Mary Ellen stopped dead with the garden hose in her hands. The stream wet the striped canvas screen behind the geraniums. She stared at Liv, shocked out of her mind.

"Are you crazy?" she said. "*Me* lose control?"

Then she recovered herself, on seeing a mischievous sparkle in Liv's blue eyes.

"Well, let's see," she said. "Uh, I'd have to make a long long list. Who would I shoot first? I dunno. But I'd go down the list one by one."

Mary Ellen scratched her head, burlesquing the moment with an attempt at low comedy. She stood pigeon-toed, and let the hose spray on her sneakers. Liv started to giggle.

Suddenly Mary Ellen swooped at Liv, yanked her up out of the red iron chair and hugged her, lifting her right off the deck. This was no easy feat, because Liv was as tall as she—five foot nine and weighing 135 pounds. Live screamed with laughter, and let the cat fall gently from her arms. Mildly offended, Kikan stalked off and sat in the shade of the geraniums. Then the two women stood hugging each other, a lesbian hug, breasts between breasts, groins grinding softly, as they rocked warmly back and forth.

"I do not think," said Liv, "that we should spoil our day off by planning assassinations."

They held each other's faces, and gave each other a kiss on the lips.

"Neither do I," said Mary Ellen. "How about something special for breakfast? Strawberries are forty-nine a pint at Gable's."

Jeannie Colter strode out of the elevator, carrying her mail. Her heeled patent-leather sandals clicked on the marble floor of the tiny fifth-floor foyer. She unlocked the door of her apartment.

It was that rare thing—a *sunny* New York apartment. The beautiful old building on East 68th Street was tall enough that it rose above its relatives, and it was narrow. So the windows on both sides of the big living room poured in sun all day long, instead of giving you a closeup look at the dingy old brick wall of the next building. She had bought the apartment after she and Sid got married, with a tax-free money gift from her father, and Sid had said he liked it okay.

Now the sun slanted in strongly from the east, across the sofa and chairs upholstered in a prim brocade of tiny flowers. An antique American china clock sat ticking on the mantel of the green marble fireplace. By the windows stood Sid's contribution to the room—several huge plants that he had bought at Terrestris—ferns, palms. Jeannie hated potted plants, because they were always dropping dead leaves on the floor. But she had decorated the room, so she had to let Sid have something, at least.

Her tall antique secretary desk stood against the

21

north wall, beside the sofa. Moving with swift ease, she sat down on the plain Shaker chair, and sorted through her mail. Usually her aide Gertrude Utley did it. Gertrude still came up for a few hours a week, usually in the morning. But today she was looking for something specific.

The usual—fan letters, bills, letters requesting political support, junk mail addressed to Occupant. Her small neat well-manicured hand ripped open the envelopes, jerked out the letters, tossed them impatiently aside when read.

Just what she'd been looking for: three invitations to speak. For months now, she had refused all such invitations. But now she needed one that would provide the perfect occasion for the speech she wanted to make—the speech that would launch her comeback.

Then she picked up the little white Trim-Line phone and punched the musical numbered buttons.

"Mrs. Haley? This is Jeannie Colter, calling about your invitation. Oh, why, thank you. Yes, of course . . ."

Mrs. Haley's voice bored in her ear, apologizing for the last-minute nature of the invitation. They had invited someone else months ago, and the dignitary had been taken ill.

"That's quite all right," said Jeannie. "I happen to have the date free, and the Y.W.C.A. has always been very close to my heart."

When she'd hung up, she sat thrilling in every nerve with a strange excitement.

Events had been set in motion. All she had to do now was write the speech, and of course discuss it with Tom Winkler, her old campaign manager, and with Reverend Irving too, and her father and her other advisers. The *News* would cover the opening of the new Y.W.C.A. in Queens, of course, and Jeannie would contact her old PR man to stir up the other media. A week from now, her name would once again be all over the newspapers and the TV news.

A few minutes later, she was striding out the door again, a little silk plaid scarf tied over her hair, dark glasses in place. Her heels clicked more purposefully than ever on the marble floor, and her car keys jingled in her hand.

It was a beautiful God-given day, and her children had better be angels, up there in the country.

Bill Laird was telephoning, too.

He was behind the massive captain's desk in his office on Canal Street. His face was set as he dialed the familiar numbers. As he waited for the call to click through, he was so tense that he didn't even doodle on his memo pad.

"Rolls-Royce, good morning," said a female switchboard operator voice.

"Marion Rhodes, please," he said.

Another click, then the so-familiar English voice.

"Rhodes here," said Marion.

"Hi, it's me," said Bill. "Are you free for lunch today?"

"Afraid not." A slight pause. "Is it important?"

"Yes."

"I can cancel then." Another slight pause. "You sound rather upset."

"I am. It's Jean."

"Oh dear. Not drinking again, I hope?"

"No, nothing like that. I'll tell you at lunch."

"All right. The usual?"

"Twelve-thirty, at the Sumptuary," said Bill.

Mary Ellen and Liv were walking along Christopher Street, arm linked warmly through arm. Since they were in the West Side gay ghetto, no one even so much as glanced at them—people just brushed by.

Walking arm in arm was a reckless thing to do.

The two women had just browsed through the streetside vegetable market, Gable's, and had lingered lovingly over the display of melons, artichokes, even

23

sun-ripened tomatoes. Liv was wearing faded jeans, huaraches and a plaid Indian cotton shirt, and carrying a brown paper bag with two pints of strawberries in it. Mary Ellen was wearing brown slacks. Inside the pants leg, strapped to her ankle in its small neat holster, was the short-barreled .32 automatic that she was required to carry off duty, in case some emergency might require her to act as a police officer. But, devoted as Mary Ellen was to her job, she liked to draw a fine clean line between her on-duty self and her off-duty self. Here in the West Village, far from the boundaries of her East Side precinct, she could be herself.

Mary Ellen had always worried a lot about running into police officers from her precinct while she had her arm around Liv. Only three of her colleagues knew she was a lesbian. One of them was her partner, PO Danny Blackburn, who was gay himself. She knew about PO Blackburn because she had run into him at a Metropolitan Community Church coffee hour. Their first reaction to each other was deep suspicion—each thought the other could be a "shoofly," or police internal-security agent. Then after a little spirited kidding around, during which they threatened to bust each other on morals charges, there was a tacit agreement to keep each other's secret. Danny became her partner on patrol. With time, Mary Ellen grew to feel a deep bond with Danny. He was like a kid brother and she had never had a brother. He was among the very few men that she and Liv knew well and trusted, and invited to their home for socializing.

Now Mary Ellen and Liv strolled west on Christopher Street, looking into the windows of shops, admiring a book cover here, a leather vest there.

Then, in front of a small antique shop, Liv stopped and gave a little cry of delight. Sitting amid dusty Wedgwood plates and small junky andirons was a small primitive oil painting of a cat, unframed. The cat was a dignified solemn tabby, sitting up very straight, with round yellow eyes like an owl's. Liv liked to collect antique cat things, though her $183 a week made it hard to afford anything made before 1930.

"You like that, huh?" said Mary Ellen.

"I loooove it," said Liv. She had a way of saying looooove that always tore at Mary Ellen's heart. "It is Kikan, no?"

"Sure looks like Kikan."

"It knew I would be walking by," said Liv. "It was in another store, and it flew here so I would see it."

They went into the shop. A few minutes later, they came out again. The painting was circa 1800, and the shop owner wanted $750 for it. Liv had a small tear in her eye, and she looked at the painting again before they walked on.

Mary Ellen hugged Liv against her side, trying to comfort her.

"Someday we'll be filthy rich," she said, "and I'll buy it for you. Because at the price that perpetrator is asking, it's still gonna be there ten years from now."

She hoped that no shoofly had seen her hug Liv. But life wasn't worth living if you had to be that scared.

At the station house, she had cultivated the image of a super-cool young woman who gave her all to her job and didn't entertain at home. The straight officers had never visited her apartment, and they knew only that she lived with another working girl—a thing so common in New York that it didn't arouse suspicion in itself. On top of that, she and Danny let them think that they were dating each other.

Often the two of them were convulsed with laughter when the men in the locker room and the women at desk jobs hinted fondly that they were waiting for wedding bells to ring for PO Frampton and PO Blackburn.

Two

Her scarf snapping smartly in the wind, Jeannie drove north on Route 684, at seventy-five miles an hour. Her left elbow stuck tensely out the open window of her white Lincoln Continental, and she drove skillfully with her right hand. A love of driving fast was one of the things she shared with her father, and she often eschewed chauffeurs to indulge in it.

It was possibly just a little un-Christian to drive so fast. On her way out of the city, Jeannie had weaved and shot her way along the East River Drive, then the Major Deegan Expressway, like a salmon fighting its way upstream. But she always drove fast. She was always in a hurry—had been in a hurry all her life, gulping down her food as a child, rushing off to church, to school, to her marriage, to beauty contests and acting school. She couldn't help it. "I was *born* going seventy miles an hour," she liked to say, referring to the fact that her mother had delivered her in exactly three minutes. "And," she'd add, "I'll get a speeding ticket on the way to Heaven."

Now she was safely out of that city that sometimes terrified her with its sinfulness and violence. Out here, as the car flew along through the soft wooded Westchester County estate country, she could breathe more deeply. There was a kind of innocence here, even though she reminded herself that sin could flourish as well in a country mansion as it could in a 42nd Street massage parlor.

She was just reaching the Westchester-Putnam county line, where the six-lane Route 684 narrowed down into old Route 22, when she saw the state trooper's red lights flashing in her rearview mirror.

She pulled over, heaved a weary sigh, put her hand over her eyes and waited while the trooper swaggered up to her car.

"Your driver's license, please."

She handed it to him without a word. It already had one other speeding violation recorded on it within the three-year limit. She'd have to be more careful.

"*Senator* Jean Colter?" he asked, grinning.

"That's right," she said shortly.

The trooper seemed to take a perverse pleasure in writing out a ticket for a woman politician.

She drove on, and when the trooper was out of sight, the speedometer inched up to seventy-five again. Once she was on the winding old Route 22, however, she had to slow down to fifty-five. "I owe it to my children," she thought, "not to get myself killed. They need me."

Now she was out of suburbia, and into the real farm country of upstate New York. The rolling hills were crowned with soft woodlands and apple orchards. Holstein cows dotted the pastures, beyond the low tumbledown stone walls that bespoke the colonial past of this area. Here and there, pastures were growing up with cedar and birch brush, and the barns were badly weathered—hints that the local agricultural economy was hard pressed by rising costs and taxes.

In contrast were the splendid motels and restaurants with names like Heidi, L'Auberge Breton, the Elms, Bel Aire, that lured the tired vacationer. Little shops along the road offered crafts, homemade pies, farm-fresh eggs, antiques.

The children. The thought of them made her stom-

27

ach clench a little. During each school year, she sheltered them from the vicious realities of the city as much as possible—private schools, tutors, rides to and from school. During the summer, she sent them upstate to Quaker Hill, where her Auntie Mary stayed full-time in her father's country home. There, too, the watchful eyes of Reverend Irving could be on them, at Sunday school. She called them several times a day, and drove up two or three times a week. When they'd been smaller, she had knocked herself out making time to be with them. But somehow, someway, it had not been enough.

The fact was that three of Jeannie Colter's children were growing up as wild as young mustang colts. However successful she had been as a politician, as someone fearlessly carrying the word of God into public life (where it was so sorely needed), she seemed to have been less successful as a mother.

She slowed a little. Ahead just off 22 on the right, hidden by trees and on a little hill, drenched in sunlight, was the snow-white First Baptist Church. Her church. It was one of the oldest churches in North America. It had been built in 1790, by Roger Tobias and his little group of those first Baptists who came to America from England seeking freedom from savage persecution by both Catholics and Protestants.

She turned off 22 onto the little drive that wound through the trees up a little hill to the church. The church was plain and simple as the Word of God itself. It was built on a foundation of fieldstone dragged from the land around it. Its honest clapboard walls were hewn from the long-vanished virgin forests. The first congregation members had planted four sapling elms beside the fieldstone steps, to shade the tall double doors. Two of the elms were still there, tall and old now, shading the square tower with its little Gothic pinnacles. The other two had died of the elm disease, which the present pastor, Reverend Frank Irving, was fond of comparing to the moral decay of America today.

The church was still owned by the local Baptist society, who had declined to have it named a national historical landmark because they didn't believe in tracing back authority. But the congregation cared for the building lovingly, donating time and materials. The men kept it painted and repaired, and the women planted and tended flowers around it.

Nearby lay the little cemetery, which was also immaculate. The chipped old tombstones stood up straight as soldiers, and the grass was clipped as neat as a golf course. A few big old hemlocks and cedars shaded it. One of the newer shiny granite gravestones belonged to Jeannie's mother.

As usual, she detoured to the cemetery, picked her way among the graves, and stood looking down at the dark granite plaque. Cora Swan Laird, born August 3, 1922, Died January 28, 1977. As usual, the fist of deep regret clenched in her stomach. Her mother had insisted on being buried unembalmed, in a plain pine coffin. By now she must be moldering hideously there, the earth caving in through the rotting coffin lid, onto her skelton and rotted clothes, the earthworms playing hide and seek in her hair. Jeannie shuddered at the thought—her mother had always been so fussy about cleanliness, always smelling faintly of lavender sachet, never a drop of coffee on her kitchen cupboards, never a speck of dust on her shoes. Death is such an unclean thing, she thought. Fit punishment for sinful humanity.

How much she regretted that she had deceived her mother all those years, making her think that she was more devout than she really was. How much she wished that she could pour the news of her salvation into her mother's ears, which were now a hiding place for snails.

Jeannie turned around and looked at the church. Usually the sight of it gave her a lift, no matter how

29

low she had felt. Today, however, the church didn't raise up her soul so much.

Here, during the depths of her breakdown period, was where the grace of Jesus had finally touched her heart. Here, with the help of the Reverend Irving, Jesus had made her see how she had been cutting corners all those years, thinking that she could be a good Christian and a glamor woman too, trying to combine prayer and church attendance with social drinking and putting herself up on a pedestal in flattering clothes for men to admire and possibly lust after. Here, she had finally understood her mother's grief and heartbreak at seeing her cutting corners on the Lord. Her mother had never cut a corner in her life, and she had died, praise God, despite thirty-two years of marriage and children and some very hard times in the city, with a soul as clean and innocent as a little child's.

The tragedy was that her mother had died just a little too soon, and had never seen the miracle of Jeannie's repentance and salvation. Of course, her mother could see it now, from her place among the angels. But still . . .

Her mother's death, Jeannie knew, was God's punishment for her sins.

A gulp of tears came up in her throat, and she choked it back down, and walked hastily out of the cemetery. She would have to start visiting the cemetery after dark again, so fewer people would see her. Otherwise the word might get around in political circles that Jeannie Colter was a little mental.

The tall church doors stood open to the breeze, and she walked in.

The sunlight poured through the tall windows of plain old glass, across the scuffed old oak pews, across the simple pulpit where the Bible and a hymnal lay. On the white wall in back, WORSHIP YE IN GOOD FAITH was painted in black antique letters. The church echoed with gentle swishing sounds—Sister May was up there in the gallery, an apron tied around her bulk, sweeping.

Not seeing Reverend Irving, Jeannie went out again. Along the side of the church, Brother Allan was on his knees, clipping along the bed of orange day-lilies, which bloomed beside the lichened stone foundations. Brother Morris was pushing the old hand lawn mower.

Beyond, in the sunny field, a couple of cars were parked by the new clapboard activity hall that the congregation had funded and built ten years ago, matching its style carefully to the church. Some young people were just going in for a meeting.

Near it was the little old white house where the pastor always lived. Seeing a movement through the window, she headed over there and peered in the screen door.

Reverend Irving was at the oak rolltop desk in his small living room, which also doubled as office and library. His skinny frame sat bolt upright in the big oak armchair as he pecked with his two knotted forefingers at the ancient green Remington Office-Riter. A pile of letters lay by him—he must be writing his column for *Christian Home*.

Reverend Irving liked to call himself the Baptist Ann Landers, and he was no less blunt than the famed woman syndicated columnist, telling his readers how the Word of God applied to their urgent problems of business, love, marriage and bringing up children. Reverend Irving was to the Northern Baptists what John Rice was to the Southern Baptists—the cornerstone of fundamental belief. Except for trips to the Holy Land and across America to speak at church conventions and jubilees, he had spent nearly all his life there in upstate New York. It was all he knew, he said, and all he wanted to know. New York City, he said, was the Devil's playground.

When she knocked on the screen door, Reverend Irving didn't turn. Despite a hearing aid, he was quite deaf. Finally she yelled, "Reverend Irving!"

He turned around creakily, and his wrinkled face lit up with a big gold-toothed smile as he waved her in.

At eighty-two Reverend Irving still had all his teeth
—and, he was fond of reminding people, "all my marbles."

Despite her shouted protests, he insisted on shuffling
into the kitchen and making her a cup of tea. Then he
sat back down and turned up his hearing aid.

"Always turn it off when I write," he said. "Better
concentration that way."

Since Reverend Irving detested small talk, Jeannie
came right to the point. She had made up her mind to
get into politics again, she said. And she was going to
launch her campaign by speaking out against the homosexual rights bill in New York City.

"I've campaigned against just about everything else,"
she said. "It's high time we put a stop to their progress. Believe it or not, Reverend Irving, they *are* making progress. It's hard to believe, but they are. Thirty
cities and thirteen states now have laws like this."

Reverend Irving was shaking his head. "Amazing
that our lawmakers can be fooled by these people.
But then they were fooled by Nixon, so I guess the
pansies can fool them, too."

"I understand that they even have homosexual
churches," said Jeannie. "You know I've been keeping
a file on them all these years, so I know these things.
The arrogance of it!"

Reverend Irving had taken his bamboo cane in his
knotted hand, and was pounding it on the floor, the
way he always did when he started feeling the word
of God inside him. The thumps of the cane marked
out the rhythm of the old, old words.

"Know ye not," he intoned, "that the unrighteous
shall not inherit the kingdom of God? Be not deceived: neither fornicators (*thump*), nor idolators
(*thump*), nor adulterers, nor effeminate, nor abusers of
themselves with mankind (*thump*), nor thieves, nor
covetous, nor drunkards, nor revilers, nor extortioners,
shall inherit the kingdom of God." Then he added, out

of habit, "First Corinthians (*thump*) chapter six, verses nine and ten."

Jeannie's shoulders slumped a little.

"The discouraging thing is . . ." She hesitated. "You know, I have campaigned against so *many* things, and I lost on a lot of them. Off-track betting. Try and take *that* away from New Yorkers. The lotteries. I worked myself to the bone on that one. New Yorkers are gamblers at heart. I had a little more luck with prostitution and massage parlors and pornography. But the forces of evil are very strong. You seize the films and the next day the theater is open again. The only area where I had any real effect, I think, was in child pornography."

Reverend Irving was nodding.

She went on. "New Yorkers seem to feel that, well, an adult can do what he pleases. But to use children like that . . . people are disgusted by the very idea. They are protective of children where they won't be protective of themselves. And that's the key to the homosexual thing, too. Homosexuality survives because they initiate children into it. Keep the children away from them, and they will die. We could put a stop to homosexuality in this country, once and for all, if we cut them off from our children."

Reverend Irving was still tapping with his cane.

"How do you plan to proceed?" he said.

"First of all, to defeat the homosexual rights bill. But that's only the beginning. Then bring back all the old laws. Make it illegal for homosexuals to appear on the street or in public places in women's dresses, or leather, or any of the other shocking costumes they wear. Make it a felony for consenting adults, give them twenty years, the way they do it in some other states. Make it life imprisonment for homosexual statutory rape. Make it explicitly illegal to hire them or rent housing to them, especially in situations where they will have contact with children. And so forth.

New York is a bellwether state, so other states will follow. Carry my campaign to national TV if I have to."

Her eyes were blazing as she rapped out the words.

Reverend Irving was still tapping with his cane as he listened, as if he too were carried away by her grand plan. But when he spoke again, his words surprised her.

"If you do even *some* of this, Sister Jean, it will be a great work," he said. "A great victory for the word of God."

He paused, and the click-click of the old lawn mower came through the open window, and the whispering of the elms by the church.

"*But,*" said Reverend Irving, jabbing his knotted forefinger toward her, "I see that you are not entering into this holy battle with the peace of Jesus Christ in your heart. I see that you are not entering into this holy battle with a love for these sinners."

Jeannie tried to keep her surprise off her face. She had expected total approval from Reverend Irving. But the old man always had a way of surprising you.

"Yes, their sin is the most defiling, the most binding of all sins," said Reverend Irving, warming to his sermon now. "But they are still sinners who can be *saved*. The blood of Our Lord Jesus Christ can save even *them*. We must hate the sin with all our hearts and all our minds. But we must love the sinner, because Jesus Christ has commanded us to love all sinners. He did not say, 'Love thee one another except for homosexuals,' He said, '*Love thee one another, no exceptions, no ifs, ands, or buts.*'"

He fell silent again, his blazing blue eyes boring into hers from beneath his shaggy snow-white brows. (She had always wanted to take a pair of manicure scissors and clip his eyebrows.)

She felt confused and off-balance.

"It's not merely a question," the Reverend went on, "of making it hard for these people to practice their evil ways. That we should do. But we must work to bring the word of God to them, to lead them to the truth and the light. Remember what Jesus said about the lost sheep. And we cannot be bearers of the Word, Sister Jean, if we have hate in our hearts."

They sat silent for several minutes. The cups of tea stopped steaming, forgotten on the edge of the desk.

Finally, Reverend Irving said softly, "And your hatred for homosexuals has little to do with their sin. You hate them because you are anxious for your own children. And you are anxious for your children, *not* because you fear that they will be corrupted, but because you fear that you have failed them."

Jeannie sat with bowed head, crushed.

"*And*," added Reverend Irving, "because of this load of guilt that you carry about regarding your mother. And I've told you a million times, Sister Jean, your mother *is* with Jesus. Your mother *knows* that you are saved."

Far off, over the lawn, she could hear a car engine start up near the activity hall, and the sound of teenagers' voices.

"You know me far too well," she whispered.

Reverend Irving gave a cackling delighted little laugh. "Not nearly so well as God knows you. Imagine how uncomfortable Jesus could make you feel, if He were sitting here in my chair."

Reverend Irving reached for her hand, and patted it gently, with those cool, silky-feeling hands that old people always have.

"Now, Sister Jean, you came here today all fired up with your idea, and you expected me to put a rubber stamp of approval on it. Didn't you? Well, I *do* approve of it. But I don't approve of the spirit in which you are going about it. Now you *have* accepted the Lord Jesus Christ. You *have* repented and confessed. You have been born again. But salvation is not a one-time thing. Salvation is every day, praying and working to enter more fully into the will of God. Salvation goes on from the moment you accept the Lord to the moment you enter into His glory. It's the difference between driving a plane and putting it on automatic pilot. We don't get to Heaven on an automatic pilot."

Jeannie sat drooped in her silk shirtwaist dress. Of course, the Reverend Irving made perfect sense. He always made sense. That was why he was the guest columnist in *Christian Home*. That was why he still spoke at jubilees and conventions and radio stations all over the country.

"Yes," she said slowly, "I'm at my wit's end about the children."

"Have you heard from Lance?"

"He called from Wyoming the other day. I think he calls just to get my goat. He and Linda were at Yellowstone Park. If only they'd get married! And I'm sure he's experimenting with drugs."

"Better no marriage if they'll be miserable later on," said Reverend Irving. "What about Jessica?"

"I had a conference with her teacher the other day. Miss Scott said that Jessica was simply impossible. Disobedient, incapable of concentrating, aggressive to the other children. She is going to hold the child back a year. She still insisted that a psychiatrist should see the child, and that she must be put on Ritalin, or she will disrupt the class next year too. And of course, I will *not* be railroaded into having the child drugged, when it's simply a question of discipline. The question, Reverend Irving, is *what* discipline? Thank God for Steve, my one good child."

A little while later, she was walking back down the flagstone walk to her car. The visit with Reverend Irving, instead of uplifting her spirit, had left her feeling depressed and helpless.

She drove back to 22, swung north on 22, passed the Bel Aire motel.

At Pawling, she took the familiar turnoff to the east, and shortly the car was shooting up along the hairpin curves that led to the top of Quaker Hill. Tires screeched a little on the curves, and the scented air of the woods blew softly through her open window.

Quaker Hill was a choice residential enclave in Dutchess County. In the old days, the area had been settled mainly by Baptists and Quakers. Now it was protected from urban invasion by strict zoning laws and a staunch little landowners' association who fought change and modernity. Its far-flung mansions, and its colonial and Victorian homes, sheltering amid massive old oaks and maples, were homes for conservative-minded people like Lowell Thomas, Norman Vincent Peale and top executives of the *Reader's Digest*.

It was with a feeling of foreboding that she pulled the car into the drive of 11 Ichabod Road, and sat looking at the house.

Ever since she was eleven, this had been the family place. Her father hadn't really wanted a country place, but Cora had come to hate New York City and she had insisted. So he had scraped together his savings, plus a loan, for the down payment on this beautiful 100-year-old house, and the barn and twenty acres that went with it. It was just a little above his means, but—typical of her mother—when her husband made his first million and could afford a more splendid place somewhere else in Quaker Hill, she still said that she was satisfied. She named it Windfall, because of the apples she had found in the grass in the untended old orchard.

The rambling old clapboard house was painted a soft yellow. Big poplars threw a screen of sparkling light and shade across the wide veranda where un-painted wicker chairs invited rest and thought. Baroque scrolls over the windows and the front door gave the place a touch of grandeur. Inside, the fifteen rooms were ample enough to give Jeannie and her husband privacy when they married, and the same to the grandchildren as they grew. Despite Cora's death, it had remained a family home.

Across the lawn to the south, the gnarled old apple trees, now pruned, bore many apples once again, like Sarah bringing forth her child in her old age.

Looking at the house, Jeannie could recall her surprise at first learning that there was something called the country. The wide sunny spaces, the grass, the insects—all terrified her at first. But she got used to it quickly. Even now, though she felt that God called her to stay in the city, she felt deeply drawn to the peace and innocence of this place.

Getting slowly out of the car, she walked up the flagstone path toward the house. Little by little, the feeling of balance that she'd had before talking to Reverend Irving was coming back to her.

Then her dreamlike state was shattered by a fierce ululating Indian war whoop.

She turned, and saw her smallest daughter, Jessica, galloping madly toward her on the black Welsh pony, Jet. Jessica, whom the teachers at the Lerner Day School found too much of a tornado to contain in their classrooms. Jessica was wearing a pair of Steve's too-large jeans, which were strictly forbidden to her, and she was riding like an Indian, clamped boldly to the pony's round back with her little legs. One fist clenched the mane and the reins, and the other pounded at Jet's fat black rump with a birch stick.

"Woo-wooo-wooo-wooo!" Jessica was yelping in the most bloodthirsty fashion she could manage. "Yeeooo-wooo-wooo-wooo!"

Jeannie gave a little shriek as the pony buzzed past her, spraying her with clods of grass and dirt.

"Jessica!" she yelled. "Come here this instant!"

Deaf as Reverend Irving to anything she didn't want to hear, Jessica galloped on across the lawn.

"Jess!" her mother thundered. "Do—you—hear—me!"

Pony and girl plunged off into the orchard, out of sight.

Auntie Mary was standing on the porch. Mary was

her mother's younger sister, who lived here year around and minded the children when Jeannie wasn't there. She was fifty-three, with a sagging face that wore an expression of dour disapproval and helpless disgust.

"A little switching and she'll be exorcised," said Jeannie.

As she said it, a chill went through her. She did believe in Satan—the same Satan who led homosexuals and gamblers and prostitutes to do the things they did.

"Where are the other children?"

Auntie Mary's voice had the tone of a tired politician who was about to write a letter of resignation, effective immediately.

"I just caught Little Cora on the phone, talking to some boy. I don't know where Steve is, but let's assume *he's* not up to some evil, at least. And if you look in Jessica's room, you'll find that before she went riding, she fingerpainted on the wall."

Thirteen-year-old Cora was in her bedroom upstairs, lying across the bed in her swimsuit listening to rock music. The bed wasn't made, and clothes lay everywhere. She had put up posters of wild animals and rock stars. Jeannie slapped her, gave her the usual lecture about neatness and boys, and appropriated her radio.

Later, when eight-year-old Jessica came tramping back to the house, dirty and glowing at her equestrian exploits, Jeannie snatched the birch switch out of her hand, stripped off her jeans and switched the little girl on her bare legs. Jessica, tough as nails, didn't cry. She just fought free and ran out of the room.

Then Jeannie sat down at the kitchen table and cried.

"If it wasn't for Steve," she said, "I'd return all of these children to God for credit."

After she'd had a good cry, she went into the library and sat down at the new white Smith-Corona electric to try and write a first draft of her Y.W.C.A. speech.

As the cab weaved its way through noonday traffic, Bill Laird slumped back on the sticky ripped vinyl seat.

He had told the driver to take him to the Sumptuary, on Third Avenue, and now he abandoned himself to the lurches and skidding stops of the cab ride.

The South Street closing was over, the property was his. But right now it was hard to gloat over it. A New York State governor by the name of Jeannie Colter? he asked himself. It just didn't seem possible. It wasn't just a question of Jeannie being a woman, and of women still being somewhat on the fringes in politics. It was also that Jeannie didn't really have the fine sense of politics, as practiced in New York, to be elected governor and survive a full term. Jeannie was a crusader in politician's clothing, not a politician. And a woman President? Even less possible, in his view.

Still, American politics were no longer the deep safe river they had once been. These days they were full of uncharted white-water rapids and hidden sandbars. Jimmy Carter had come out of nowhere, out of a swing state, and he had ghosted the nation's vote out of Gerald Ford's hands. If Jeannie followed the Carter example, and surrounded herself with sound advisers, and listened to them, and made sound plans, she might at least make it to the State House in Albany. Or at least give her competitors a hell of a race.

On the other hand, there was a ticking time bomb in Jeannie's political future. Namely, her father.

As the cab weaved its way up Third Avenue, Bill slumped back against the sticky seat, his jacket unbuttoned for relief from the heat. He stared out at the city real estate whizzing by on both sides—boutiques, florists, supermarkets, antique shops, delicatessens, synagogues, churches, immigrant activity centers. It seemed like his life was unreeling past him.

Now and then, lately, he was inclined to take stock of his life. He had saved buildings from the city's dim pre-technological past, and had re-connected their graceful spirit into the city's life again. They were buildings in which it was easier to remember that you were a human being, that you carried the burden of history, with its horrors and its delights.

History . . . that was the key to it all, he thought.

He smiled to himself a little. Jeannie, and nearly everyone else he knew in his church, had little sense of history. The Baptists had simply forgotten that in the seventeenth century they had come to the United States to escape bloody persecution in Europe. They staunchly claimed that they stood for religious freedom. Yet, once they were safe in the peaceful landscapes of America, many Baptists had shown a willingness to use their beloved Bible to persecute other minorities, among them gays. In the case of the Southern Baptists, you had to add blacks.

Of course, the conservative Baptists weren't the only guilty ones, he thought.

The Mormons, for instance, were hostile to homosexuals. They were very secure now in Utah, and appeared to have forgotten the fear and loathing which their own beliefs had once inspired on the American frontier. For that matter, the Catholic Church—whose Pope had only recently made the headlines by condemning homosexual practices—had forgotten the terrible days of the human torches and the arena in ancient Rome, and the days of the rack and the stake in Protestant England.

To their credit, some churches—he thought—did remember their own dark days and now extended the hand of mercy to gays: Unitarians, Congregationalists, even the Episcopalians.

And then there were the gays themselves, disunited in peril because they were as human as their persecutors. Being gay did not unify gays any more than being straight made a monolith out of straights. The gay rights movement was forever splitting and regrouping. Some gays were even ready to discriminate against each other in the name of freedom. Some lesbian activists would have nothing to do with the men activists. Many gays of both sexes feared and shunned those who preached what was known as S&M on the East Coast, B&D on the West Coast. And then there were the transsexuals and transvestites who managed to maintain an impeccable dignity despite the unease with which many gays regarded them. He knew some devout churchgoing gays who were shocked if a leather man or a transvestite walked into their church—as shocked as a Southern Baptist would be at a black person entering a segregated church.

At sixty-one, he felt he had seen it all. The single great regret he had was his lack of courage in one thing. With a little more confidence, he could have been a crusader himself. As it was, he was simply William Frederick Laird, noted realtor, who had softened the skyline of one of the hardest cities in the world.

The cab screeched to a stop in front of the Sumptuary.

Bill paid and tipped the cabby, and got slowly out. The noise and oil fumes of the street, and the reek of asphalt melting in the sun, rolled over him.

He walked slowly into the restaurant. He wondered at his slowness today. Staying fit had been his passion for years now. Did this mean he was slowing down, getting truly old?

The Sumptuary was a newer restaurant, already a favorite with downtown publishing people and young executives because it provided gourmet food at modest prices to expense-account people for whom restaurants like the Four Seasons were off limits. It was also a restaurant where he was not likely to meet people who knew him in the business world. The bar, with its heavy dark vine-crusted columns, looked like it had been saved out of a Baroque church just before the wrecker's ball. Farther inside, New Yorkers dined amid the rich glow of tapestries and Oriental rugs on the walls, Renaissance pottery lining the fireplace mantels. A fountain splashed softly out in the skylighted courtyard, amid pots of pink hothouse azaleas.

Marion was waiting, at their usual table on the far side of the fountain. He looked at Bill across the intervening tables with a hesitant smile and a questioning in those blue eyes.

Marion was dressed in his usual dignified style, as befitted one of the top executives for Rolls-Royce in the United States. Bill had seen the navy European-tailored suit many times before, but it still looked store-new, and was set off by a melon-colored silk shirt and a brocaded tie that matched the Renaissance plush of the restaurant. The high fashion and the rich colors gave a solidity to Marion's thinness and to his hesitating walk, the way red velvet and heavy gold jewelry might lend majesty to a crippled Tudor king.

The old red scar tissue could be glimpsed on the left side of Marion's neck, just above the silk collar, and in a patch or two on his left cheek. The scars were from the fierce gas-fed flames of his exploding Lotus that day ten years ago at Le Mans. The helmet had saved his face from scarring—a face that was dry, lean, well-bred and handsome-plain as a thoroughbred horse, that face of impoverished English gentry. The shy blue eyes, the stubborn jaw and the wasted look reminded one of T. E. Lawrence after his Arabian experience.

Fortunately, the flames had missed destroying Marion as a sexual being, thanks to the lightning action of the crews and officials at Le Mans. He had only been in the blazing cockpit for fifteen seconds. But they had seared his torso and one leg with third-degree burns, and he had endured months in the hospital, grafting operations and physical therapy. After that, Marion confessed frankly that he had lost his nerve. But Bill felt that it had taken guts to give up his career as a Class A racing driver, rehabilitate himself, and get into the top job at Rolls-Royce, which was expanding its marketing in the U.S.

Looking across the tables at Marion as he walked through the restaurant, Bill remembered seeing the exploding car on the TV sports news. That was how he learned of Marion's accident. Afterward, it was days before Marion was well enough to reassure him via cable, as none of Marion's associates had known he and Bill were that close. Bill lived out the weeks in agonized frenzy—which he had to hide from his wife, his brother and his family and business colleagues.

"Love is so rare any more," he thought. "When two people manage to find it, it doesn't make sense that they have to pretend they are only friends."

Marion's shy eyes were now squinting up at him quizzically, and he smiled. His glass of white wine was half-empty already—he must have been anxious and gotten there a little early.

Bill sank into the other chair. The waiter was hovering.

Bill pointed at Marion's glass. "The same," he said to the waiter.

Most Baptists believed that alcohol was sinful, but Bill had read the Bible carefully and he had observed that Jesus drank a moderate amount of wine, so he did likewise.

When the waiter had gone, Marion said quickly, "What happened?"

Bill sighed. "Jeannie is about to launch another one of her holy wars."

He told Marion about his breakfast talk with Jeannie. They stopped talking for a minute as the waiter brought Bill's wine, and took their orders. Confused and upset as he was, Bill could hardly focus on the menu. Finally he ordered the Salad Niçoise. Marion ordered the lemon chicken.

"Well," said Marion softly, "you always knew that

she was going to get around to it someday, didn't you?"

Bill sighed again. "She had such a long list of enemies that I kept hoping she'd never get around to it."

"Very ambitious, eh?" said Marion. "I mean, do you really think she has a chance at governor?"

"Not really," said Bill. "But she doesn't know that. Besides, you never know . . ."

"Why not mayor of New York?"

"Because," said Bill, "she knows that being mayor is a dead end. And she knows that being governor gives her a better shot at the Presidency."

Marion gave a low whistle. "*Very* ambitious."

"I think she'd settle for vice-president, or even a seat in the Cabinet. But in the meantime, she'd have a wonderful time running for President, and she'd stir the whole country up with her vision of a moral America."

Marion shuddered slightly.

The food arrived, and they ate it without too much enthusiasm.

"I keep trying to think," said Bill, "where Jeannie learned her phobia about 'perverts.' I certainly never taught her that. Or maybe I did. Maybe I taught her by default, by being silent . . ."

"Don't get off on a big guilt thing now," said Marion. "You never taught her that, and you know it."

"That preacher Irving has had a big influence on her," said Bill, "but I don't think he taught her that either. She had it before she was saved. Besides, Irving preaches that you have to love sinners, all sinners, bar none. Jeannie doesn't love sinners. She'd like to run them all through a big meatgrinder."

The waiter came to get their dessert order, and cleared away their plates. Bill, who always worried about his weight, ordered black coffee. Marion, who had the insolence of a skinny child when it came to calories, ordered the Sumptuary's chocolate mousse topped with whipped cream and hazelnuts.

"Well," said Bill, "what do we do?"

"Nothing," said Marion. He was scooping enthusiastically at his dessert.

"What do you mean, nothing?" Bill felt a little irritated. "You don't seem very concerned."

"I'm not, really," said Marion coolly. But he was smiling a little, and made a little salute at Bill with a big spoonful of mousse, like he was toasting.

"Why?"

"You think she's going to be a problem for *you*. But you're going to be a problem for her. Did you ever look at it that way?"

"What do you mean?"

"Supposing it's revealed that you . . ."

Suddenly Bill realized what Marion was talking about. Of course Marion was right. But it didn't make him any happier to think of the trap that Jeannie would be in. It would destroy her attempt at a comeback, and he didn't really want to be responsible for that.

His shoulders slumped and he didn't say anything more.

"The only thing we can do," said Marion, "is just sit tight and see what happens. Live one day at a time."

"Supposing we come out and you lose your job?" said Bill.

Marion shrugged. "I'm a damn good mechanic. What the hell. I'll get a job in a pit crew."

Bill felt tears stinging suspiciously close to visibility in his eyes.

"I wish I had your guts," he said.

Marion wiped a trace of whipped cream off his mouth with his napkin. "What guts?" he asked. "I didn't say I'd drive cars again. Just fix them."

They paid and left, and hailed a cab.

In the cab, down on the seat where the cabbie couldn't see, their hands groped for each other and clasped hard—Marion's lean long-fingered hand with the red scar on the palm where he'd gripped the scorching side of the Lotus, trying to jump out, and Bill's big broad hand with silvered dark hair on the backs of the fingers.

The cab dropped Marion at the gleaming glass Rolls-Royce office. He gave Bill's hand a last secret squeeze, and got slowly out.

"Have a lovely," he said.

As the cab pulled away, Bill twisted in the seat and watched him limp slowly into the office building, disappearing amid the hordes of New Yorkers ending their lunch hours. There was a lump in his throat like there hadn't been in a long time.

Danny Blackburn shrugged a little at his black leather motorcycle jacket, which was sticking to his broad shoulders in the heat. He rounded the corner of 20th Street and Eleventh Avenue and strode toward the doorway of the Steel Spike Bar. He was off duty, but he didn't dare be without a gun. In his pocket, hidden by the jacket, his .38 Detective Special made a bulge in its pocket-holster.

The bar's entrance did not flaunt itself—a small sign, blacked-out windows, just a wooden door. Across the street were the murky shadows and the studded pillars under the West Side elevated highway where trucks were parked. Beyond lay the waterfront and the sooty old piers. The Hudson River sparkled blue in the distance, looking as if it were unpolluted.

Danny pushed at the door, and walked gratefully into the cool dark interior. After a moment, his eyes adjusted from the glare outside, and he could see the scene so familiar and dear to him.

He had chosen the Spike for a number of reasons. It was one of the few independent non-Mafia gay bars in town. Also, it was well outside his precinct. Both these factors hopefully lessened the chances of his running into a "shoofly." The Spike did not encourage you to push in that door unless you were a man and wore leather and/or denim. Danny was really not sure whether he had become a cop because he liked leather, or the other way around, but he was not one to question himself too much. For Danny, the joy of living, and the risk and challenge of balancing his career on the force with his off-duty life-style, was reason enough in itself.

At this hour, the Spike was nearly empty. That suited Danny fine—it was a third factor that might keep him from meeting a "shoofly." But Lenny was there behind the bar polishing glasses, and the jukebox was playing punk rock.

The place had a dark medieval splendor. Above the bar were masses of glittering trophies won in cross-country races by the local bike clubs, and the ceiling was hung with rich velvet and gilt banners encrusted with the proud names and the heraldry of leather men across the country. DETROIT DAMON AND PYTHIAS, said one, with two clenched fists, or a *sable*. MANHATTAN ENTRE NOUS, said another, with a draped chain *gules*. On the wall, a small sign said, "The dress code of this bar will be strictly enforced." There was a bulletin board with posters announcing beer picnics, dances, bike crosses and personals. On the other side of the bar were wooden rails for the men to lounge against, and unsmilingly display their visual splendor to each other.

Danny slid onto the leather bar stool.

"Hiya, Danny," said Lenny.

The bartender reached for the bottle of Wild Turkey. He knew that Danny never touched anything but Wild Turkey. In fact, one of the few things that Lenny didn't know about Danny was that he was a cop. Fun was fun, but Danny was no dummy—you had to be very careful. You had to trust almost nobody.

Lenny filled the sparkling heavy shot glass. "You're a little late today," said Lenny.

"Yeah," said Danny. "They gave me an extra night

run from Jersey." He had always told Lenny he was a truck driver.

"Armando called," Lenny said. "He's going to be a few minutes late."

"That bastard," said Danny, laughing a little, but feeling a twinge of jealousy.

Lenny must have read his mind, because he wiggled his eyebrows archly and said, "He *said* he got into a big argument with somebody about Intro Two."

"Well, I believe *that*," said Danny. "Armando would argue with Saint Peter about which side he was wearing the key to Heaven on."

Just then the wooden door creaked open again and a great bear of a man walked into the bar.

He was fully six foot five and weighing 220 pounds and dressed in battered black-leather pants and black-leather jacket, and a couple of battered handcuffs. A bunch of battered keys hung from his right pocket, looking like they might fit into the trunk lock of every junkyard car in lower Manhattan. If a bear could walk like a cat, Danny thought, that was the way Armando walked—his father might have been a grizzly, and his mother a great mountain puma.

Armando Ostos was Danny's lover. He was twenty-nine, Spanish American, and the M to Danny's S. He was a bartender in another leather bar a little farther up Tenth Avenue, the Eagle's Nest, where he also doubled as bouncer. Armando could eject a dozen brawling sailors from his bar singlehanded. But those who knew him well saw the quiet, happy, kittenish streak in him. It was this streak of mystical joy, of sunny peace, of pure gold ore sandwiched in a mass of iron, that Danny loved as much as anything. He had met Armando six months ago and he did not ever want to love anyone else again, ever. At least, not right now.

Armando looked at Danny, and under the vinyl visor of his raffishly cocked black leather cap, his eyes took on a mischievous and evil expression, like that of a kitten thinking about killing its first bird. Danny envied Armando's freedom to wear the cap—he wasn't "out" far enough to dare to wear one.

Armando spread his great gorilla arms. "Light of my life," he said to Danny.

Danny burst out laughing. They slid their arms around each other and there, under the dark and splendid banners, they gave each other a lingering kiss. Armando's beard grated against Danny's chin, and he smelled ripe with sweat and booze.

"I was at the Cellblock," said Armando.

This was an after-hours place where leather bartenders often went after they'd closed up their own places.

"I'm sure you were," said Danny, envying Armando's freedom to visit the Cellblock. So far, the Spike was the only leather bar Danny had dared to visit. He was hungry to visit places like the Mine Shaft, but knew he wasn't ready to take the step yet.

"I had this terrible argument with Bert about Intro Two," said Armando.

"I believe every word of it," said Danny.

Grinning, Lenny was busy making a Brandy Alexander. He knew that Armando never drank anything but Brandy Alexanders.

"No, really," said Armando. "Bert thought that the gay rights crowd did the right thing when they threw all the transvestites out of the Liberation Day march. I didn't. I nearly broke his goddam neck."

"It's funny Bert should go along with that," said Danny, "when you think that those straight-looking gays want us leather guys out of sight, too. Nothing freaky around to scare the straightsie-poos with."

"Come to think of it, why *wouldn't* Bert think that way?" said Lenny.

All three men howled at this—Bert was a notorious masochist.

Armando drank his Brandy Alexander down. Then

he cradled his hairy head in mock distress. "For once I have a hangover. Lenny, you got any black coffee?"

Lenny headed for the back, where he kept a coffee-pot on. When a brother bartender asked for coffee, you gave him coffee.

While Lenny was gone, Armando and Danny talked. Every day that they could manage, on their days off or when their work shifts permitted, they met here in this relatively safe place and talked—about their lives, about their past, lovers, about being gay, about cars and motorcycles and guns and dogs, and above all, about St. Francis of Assisi. They didn't live together, so it was the only thing approaching home life that they had. Both of them still valued their independence, and neither was quite ready for the monoga-mous one-apartment bit. Also Danny was a little afraid of moving in with Armando. He had heard of a straight police sergeant who was found to be living with a gay man—just a *friend*, mind you—and the force had quietly busted the sergeant back down to officer. So Danny had his two-room walkup on Lafayette Street and Armando had a basement place on Bedford Street. Sometimes Danny despised himself for still living halfway in the closet. He hungered for more courage. And he knew that someday soon, he would have that courage.

"Seriously, the Intro Two demonstrations," said Ar-mando. "There's gonna be demonstrations. Do you think you'll get sent to them?"

"I doubt it," said Danny. "Unless the whole business gets very disorderly and they send out a call for extra officers."

He hoped not. Using his nightstick on his brothers and sisters was something he never wanted to hear Captain Bader or Lieutenant Mondello order him and Mary Ellen to do. Mary Ellen would wilt at that order too.

"It might get disorderly," said Armando. "I stand

there behind the bar, and I hear the talk. This is the fourth time around for Intro Two. Everybody's getting pretty uptight. Would you believe, there's this dude usually comes in on Tuesday nights who usually tries to proposition me, and last night even *he* was talking about Intro Two."

Lenny came back with the coffee, so they stopped talking about the police force. Then the bartender started slicing lemons for the afternoon.

"Danny," said Armando, "do you think it'll pass this time?"

Danny thought of the talk in the station-house locker room. He thought of his brother (and sister, now) officers out on the streets, pursuing perpetrators, screaming down through traffic, lights on and the yelp going, or bending over to check a wino huddled on the sidewalk. He knew that roughly ten percent of them were gay, and yet the Policemen's Benevolent Association insisted that this was not possible, that there were no gay cops and no *good* gay cops.

"No," he said soberly. "I don't think they'll pass it."

"There's gonna be a lot of unhappy people in this queer's town," said Armando. "Something's gotta give."

"I know," said Danny. "I'll be one of them."

Lenny went in the back to get more lemons, and Danny said softly, "Sometimes I'd like to think I could be a gay Serpico. You know, come out, challenge the powers-that-be, change things. Change them just a little. But . . . forget it. They'd squash me like a rotten tomato, and things would stay just the same."

"In San Francisco they got gay cops out in the open."

Danny shook his head, mimicking the voice of some mythical Bronx politician. "San Francisco is halfway to the moon. This is New *Yawk*, man. This is the Big *Apple*. This is a very *moral* town, man. Take away the massage parlors and the bookies and whaddayuh got? Ya got lace curtains, man."

"You're saying that politically New York is lace curtains?" said Armando.

"That's right," said Danny.

Armando scratched his head melodramatically. "Lace curtains. Hard to believe."

"*Lace curtains?*" said Lenny, coming back in with a grocery box of lemons.

Danny wondered how much Lenny had overheard. But Armando burst out with a perfect roar of laughter. "Yeah," he said. "Danny is redecorating his little apartment."

The three men laughed. For some reason the mention of lace curtains reminded Danny of Mary Ellen and Liv (which was odd, because the two women didn't go in for lace curtains either—maybe some lingering chauvinism made him think it). He dug in his Levi's pocket for a dime to call Mary Ellen, and started to the telephone.

Armando gripped his arm. "Calling someone I know?"

"My decorator," said Danny, grinning. Lenny and Armando howled again.

Mary Ellen answered the telephone. Danny was a little scared of Liv—something spooky about her—but he felt very close to Mary Ellen, even proud of her, and a little protective, which was odd because Mary Ellen didn't need protecting. She was prettier than Farrah Fawcett-Majors, and she worked in uniform instead of plainclothes, and she was a better shot than Danny. Mary Ellen could shoot the eye out of a needle. And why should a regular patrol officer feel protective about a sergeant?

"Hey, partner, see the thing in the paper about Intro Two?"

"Yeah," she said.

"Let's hope the demonstrations are not disorderly, huh?" he said.

"Yeah," she said. "You are so right. We definitely don't want to catch any runs to *that* kind of scene."

His story, then:

"I say," he said, "but you blow-dry your hair like

"That's different," she said. "I'm supposed to have

CHAPTER
Three

The next morning, around eight, Jeannie and her husband were bustling around the bedroom and bathroom, getting in each other's way as they dressed. Sidney was standing in front of the bathroom mirror, blow-drying his hair. His shirt and tie lay ready on the bed. Jeannie stepped into a favorite dress, a white silk shirtwaist with navy polka dots. The high shirt collar and cuffed long sleeves gave it a virginal look.

Then she strode into the bathroom, holding the back of her dress together.

"Zip me up, darling?" She pivoted to present her back to him.

A twitch of impatience crossed Sidney's face. "I'm late already," he said. But he put the drier down without turning it off and zipped up the zipper with a short brusque motion.

Jeannie fixed her eyes on his longish dark hair. "Darling, your hair is hardly long enough to bother with blow-drying."

Sidney picked up the blow-drier, and looked her right back in the eyes. "Do you have an objection to my blow-drying my hair? I mean, do you feel I'm adding to the energy crisis or something?" His voice was mild, yet there was an edge in it.

"Well," she said, "it's so *modernist* to do that."

Sidney laughed. "But you blow-dry your hair, darling."

"That's different," she said. "I'm supposed to have long hair."

"Long hair is God's glory, right?" he said, smiling and turning back to the mirror.

"That's right," she said. "Ephesians, chapter three, verses eight through ten."

Sidney turned and played the blast of hot air over his hair. "Well, then, we'll just have twice the glory, won't we?"

Jeannie strode out of the bathroom, trying to stifle the impulse to be impatient. It was too good a day to get impatient with anyone. If her mother had heard the conversation, she would have said that it served Jeannie right to have married an unsaved man.

Years ago Sidney had seemed like just the right man, to a young bright-eyed actress bent on the most clean and decent kind of career possible in acting. He smoked but he didn't drink—not because he was moral, of course, but just because liquor made him sick. A quirk of his biochemistry, he said. He was a blithe and sunny person, one of those people who almost made you believe the heresy that human beings are good by nature. But her conversion, a year ago, had changed all that. There was no way that Sidney Colter, sunny and good though he was, was going to go to church or adult Sunday school with her. He told her that the guys in the newsroom would die laughing if he went to Sunday school.

Jeannie stood in front of the bedroom vanity mirror, fastening on her earrings. "Of course," Jeannie thought, "I couldn't have married a saved man then, because I wasn't saved myself—was I?"

Sidney shut off the blow-drier, came out of the bathroom, and pulled on his shirt. Despite his love of gourmet food and his encyclopedic knowledge of every good restaurant in New York State, Sidney at thirty-nine still had the lean torso and good shoulders of a college boy. For a moment, Jeannie felt very strongly attracted by him. How wonderful that God blessed loving sex between a man and a women. During the past year, their sex life had suffered because of her breakdown.

Looking at him, she suddenly wanted to make love. But there was no time for love this morning. So she just went over to Sidney, with a whisk of silk, and kissed him gently on the cheek.

"I'm sorry," she said. "I sounded like I was starting a fight."

Sidney, buttoning his shirt, was also reluctant to discuss modernism further. "You're very brisk this morning," he said.

"Oh, I am," she said. "We both came home so late last night that there was no time to tell you yet. But— anyway, I've made up my mind. I'm going back into politics."

As Sidney stood silently before the vanity mirror, knotting his tie, she briefly outlined her plans to him.

"You'll certainly get a lot of publicity," he said, "if you campaign against Intro Two. The faggots in this town are very loud, and very well-organized."

"Well," she said crisply, "we'll be louder, and better-organized. Meanwhile, I'll hope that I can count on the usual help from the *News?*"

"I suppose so," said Sidney. "I'll talk to Bernie." Bernie was Bernard Mankowitz, the managing editor. "But you're forgetting something. I won't be here for a lot of this."

"You won't be here!" she cried. "Where are you going to be?"

"You've completely forgotten, haven't you?" he said quietly, straightening the knot in his tie, looking at her in the mirror. "Next month I'm going to China."

"China?" she wailed. "Can't you put it off?"

Sidney turned to face her, with an expression of sorrowful accusation in his eyes. "Jeannie, I've dreamed of going to China for years. For years I waited for the visa. It's all set. I mean, you don't just . . . *put off* a trip to China."

Jeannie stood, her mind racing. This was something of a setback. Few people knew the ins-and-outs of New York City politics like Sidney did. All over the country, he was regarded as just about the best young conservative political writer in the country. His column, "Fanfare," was widely quoted. He had actually turned down a plush offer to write on national affairs for the Washington *Post* because he was so "hooked on New York," as he put it. It was his lifeblood. More important, it was Sidney's political savvy that had often guided her, so far—Sidney and her father together had helped her negotiate her way into being an honest politician in a city where corruption seemed to be the standard operating procedure.

Sidney stood there, hands shoved into his pockets, with a look of impatience on his face. He was very anxious to be off to the office, so as not to incur the wrath of Bernie, who felt that everyone, even *News* executives, should be seated at their desks by nine sharp.

"I know this throws a wrench in your plans," he said softly. "But I can't help it. Doubleday has approached me about doing a book about China. They're offering me a large advance. I can't afford to blow that kind of money. Especially since we've been living on just my salary for the last year."

Jeannie sat on the edge of the bed, suddenly feeling that her crisp silk dress was already full of wrinkles and smudged.

"No," she said. "I suppose not."

"You do tend to take me for granted sometimes," Sidney added in an even softer voice.

She sighed, feeling embarrassed and humiliated.

"Look," said Sidney, picking up his suit jacket off the arm of the chair, "it's no major tragedy. Your dad is going to be around. He'll help out."

57

"True," she said. "As far as I know, *he's* not going to China."

When Sidney had left, she pulled herself together. No sense letting a little thing like that throw you, she told herself. Today she had a lot to do.

She had started the day with such a blast of energy. The rough speech she'd drafted yesterday sounded good, but it needed the finishing touches by a professional. She had made the rounds of the children thoroughly yesterday, and felt she had whipped things into shape—a long lecture to Jessica on tomboyish riding and a threat to sell the pony. To Cora, a long lecture on the evils of boys and rock music. And a long lovely conversation with Steve that had made her feel better about everything.

At least she had converted Steve, and the boy had changed his mind about what college he would attend. Instead of Harvard, he wanted to attend Brandywine Theological College in Delaware, a Baptist school supported by the American Baptist Convention. He wasn't yet thinking exactly of becoming a preacher, but he was interested in serious study of the Bible. Steve, her beautiful firstborn, her offering to the Lord. How nice that it should all work out just like the Bible commanded.

She took a last few impatient swipes at her hair with the brush. Her hair still hadn't grown long enough to suit her. A year ago, just before her breakdown, she had had it cut in the fashionable Dorothy Hamill wedge, but afterward she understood what a wicked infidel thing she had done. Now it was six inches long, and pretty soon she could get it into a neat little coif. In a few more years, maybe she could wear it in braids across the top of her head, just like her mother had done. That was a very old-fashioned-looking kind of hairdo, of course. But old-fashioned hairdos were just what America needed.

Then she seized her purse, and strode out of the apartment.

Shortly before nine, Jeannie got out of a cab in front of her district office on Park Avenue and 33rd Street. It was the first morning in months that she had not gone directly from her apartment to her father's rooftop breakfast table.

Her office had once been a shoe store that had gone bankrupt. She had chosen that seedy-but-reviving stretch of Park Avenue to enhance her image as a Republican people's candidate who represented all levels of society. As she pushed in the door, she noticed how dusty the bunting was in the display window, and how faded the poster-sized photographs of her were. Worse, they showed her in her infidel stage, with her short bob and a too-stylish dress.

"I'll have to change those photographs," she thought. "They are pretty scandalous."

Inside, the office was brightly lit, but several of the desks were bare. Since her departure from politics a year ago, she had kept only a skeleton staff here. Gertrude Utley, her secretary and a chief aide, was clicking away at her IBM Selectric, typing a few letters replying to ex-constituents who still wrote her about bills and issues. Gertrude was forty-seven, a Baptist of course, a slender wiry woman who favored little knit dresses and coral pins, and had visited the Holy Land three times.

"Good morning, Jeannie," said Gertrude, getting up to brush a kiss on Jeannie's cheek. She gripped Jeannie's shoulders, looked at her searchingly, and smiled. "You're looking good."

Jeannie grinned. "I'm feeling good," she said simply. "I'm going to run for governor."

Gertrude let out a strangled little cry of joy. "Oh, thank God. Thank Jesus. Oh Jeannie, I've prayed so hard for you, I've prayed every way I knew how. When did you decide?"

"Yesterday," said Jeannie. "When I opened up the *Times* and saw all that infidel nonsense about the homosexual bill."

"Oh yes," said Gertrude. "Frightening and distressing, isn't it? I'm certainly glad I'm not raising children, the way the city is today. There are so many homosexuals around."

"Of course," said Jeannie, "I'm not going to announce that I'm in the race yet. I'll do that later, after we dunk that bill in a little fire and brimstone."

Gertrude clapped her hands like a child.

"Oh my," she said, "the place will come to life again. It'll be nice."

Jeannie put her briefcase down on Gertrude's desk and looked around.

The office was crammed with file cabinets—somber dark-green classic files, battered, of every make and size. Those files were the heart of her political career. From the very beginning, as a freshman in Albany, she had made her mark by introducing strong reform bills. And any success her bills had was owed to the in-depth research her people did. She had flooded the legislature with bills—pornography, court reform, prostitution, plea bargaining, drug abuse, conservation—you name it—boldly inviting no one to cosponsor with her, earning the hostility of incumbent Governor Dulles, who resented the popular power she gained. In New York State, the governor held an autocratic power that few other states dared to give their highest office, able to govern by decree and veto. But Jeannie stirred up such popular support for some of her bills that the governor did not dare to veto them.

Other files had yet to be transformed into bills. They waited, their folders close-packed with clippings, chapters from books, surveys, polls, interviews. She had a file there on the budget crisis in New York City, another on corruption in the Port Authority, another on wife-beating. And, of course, her homosexual file, which was about three years old. She had ordered that file begun after she learned several states and cities had passed homosexual laws.

"Well," she told Gertrude, "the first thing I'm going

to do this morning is call up all the old troops and see who is available. I haven't talked to some of them for months. Wonder if Tom Winkler is even speaking to me."

"You'll be wanting to enlarge the staff?"

"Yes. We'll probably get volunteers right away. Meanwhile, could you—who was working on the homosexual file, anyway?"

"Marge Lomo," said Gertrude. "I haven't heard from her in weeks."

"Well, I'll call her and see if she wants to come back. I need a summary out of that file in a few days. I want to know who those people are, where they are, how visible they are."

Almost breathless with haste, Jeannie signed one important letter to Speaker of the House Patton. She and Gertrude discussed and decided a few other things. Then she was off again, hailing a taxi, asking to go to her father's building on East 69th Street.

She wondered how much money her father could be conned into putting in the campaign treasury.

Up in her father's penthouse garden, she strode through the dappled shade of the cherry trees to the table, and kissed him resoundingly on the cheek. In one hand, she was dragging the telephone with its 100-foot cord that usually sat on an end table in the living room.

"Good morning," he said, grinning, kissing her back. "You're in a big hurry this morning."

"I am," she said. "I've been in a hurry all my life."

While he poured her some coffee, she fished her thick black telephone book out of her purse and started looking up numbers. Many of her political people had not heard from her in over a year.

The first number she called was Marge Lomo. Marjorie had only been working part-time since last year, because there was so little for her to do. She smiled at hearing Marge's birdlike voice in the phone. Best of all, Marge was a God-fearing Presbyterian who truly believed in the Bible.

"Marjorie," she said, "I'm going to run for governor. Would you like to come back full-time?"

Marjorie gave a little scream of joy. She said it would be no problem—her last child was off to college, and her traveling businessman husband didn't mind.

Elated, Jeannie kept dialing numbers.

The next calls, however, were more difficult. Her old speechwriter, Jason Richards, was now working for a number of state assemblymen, and he said he couldn't possibly fit her in on such short notice. Her old press agent, Vincent Searls, was also tied up full-time with the mayor's office. Her old pollster was also tied up with someone else.

"Traitors," she said, dialing wrathfully.

Her father watched and smiled musingly, stirring his coffee.

When she called her old campaign manager, however, he responded to the call. Tom Winkler had drifted away from politics into public relations, and had grown disillusioned with it. He agreed to serve in his old capacity.

"Why don't you come into town tomorrow," she said, "and we'll start to make some plans."

As she kept dialing numbers, her thoughts kept turning to money. That was going to be a problem, as Sidney had so aptly said. Even if he did get a large advance on the book, she couldn't very well take all of it for her campaign. Especially when he would get only part of it on signing the contract—the balance wouldn't be paid until the book was done.

She finally finished telephoning, exhausted. The cup of coffee sat there, cold, untasted.

Her father looked at his watch. It was just past ten, not time to leave yet. Wordlessly, he got up and took her cup, emptied the cold coffee into a drain at the corner of the terrace, and poured a fresh cup from the sterling pot.

"Who's going to pay the phone bill?" he teased her. "You or me?"

The tone of his voice was gently teasing, but he had lines and a red look around his eyes. Evidently he hadn't slept well.

"Did the South Street closing go okay?" she asked.

"Yes," he said shortly.

She sipped the fresh coffee. "I've got to start thinking about money."

"You'd better do some serious fund-raising. You'll find that costs have gone up enormously in the year you've been away."

"I'm sure they have," she said. She had an easy feeling now, of moving at full speed through space, at the speed of light, unerringly toward some distant star. "The first thing I'll have people do is go over my old mailing list, and update it, and get out a mailing, and plan some dinners, and so forth. And . . ." She kept her tone bantering, choosing her words carefully. ". . . I might have to hit you for a loan."

To her dismay, she saw a subtle change of expression on her father's face. She couldn't even identify the new expression that appeared on it. She wasn't sure if it was apprehension, or simply a look of adding up his total assets in his head.

"Well," he said, after a moment's hesitation that aged her by at least ten years, "I'll have to think about it a little. Have your Uncle Al sit down and look at the books."

She did her best to keep her cool, to not appear as desperate as she felt.

"But you always bankrolled me before."

"That's true," her father said. "But this time it's a little different. You've caught me a little off-balance. No time to plan ahead much. We're very involved in the South Bronx. And we're very involved on South

63

Street. Very involved in terms of money. And in terms of time."

"Time?" she said. "You mean you won't even be able to advise me much?" A hot wave of panic went over her. "I mean . . . what'll I do without you?"

"Sweetheart, I'm not saying no," said her father. "I'm just saying I have to study it a little. You can't expect the entire world to be at your beck and call the minute you decide to go into politics again."

Bill had watched her dial number after number. Her slender fingers with the pale pink polish and the perfect manicure job had poked extra-decisively at the little lighted push buttons on the telephone. Jeannie did everything with an air of overkill.

He sat wondering how he was going to be able to masquerade his way through the coming months. Thank God that he had had courage enough to hint that he couldn't support her campaign much this time around. But she would make the demand again, he knew. The pressures on him, from both outside and inside, would grow and grow.

The way she was poking at the telephone made him think of a little girl poking at mud-pies to see if they were "done" yet. It was the seriousness of it—those mud-pies were really fruit-and-pastry pies being baked in a real oven. Jeannie had always been so serious about everything she did.

The tragedy was that much in Jeannie's character reflected both her parents. And her parents, over the years, had carried on a silent and undeclared war—a cold war of the heart, a "police action" within their home. This split was faithfully reproduced in the strong conflicting emotions that often threatened to tear Jeannie apart.

Part of the problem had been that he was a liberal modern Baptist, while his wife had been a Bible-believer and a firm conservative. The Baptist faith was being ripped like the Temple Veil. The modernists held that the new scriptural and archeological discoveries showed parts of the Bible were simply myth and history. The conservatives clung doggedly to the idea that every word of the Bible was the revealed word of God. The rift had first split the Northern Baptist Convention. The more conservative churches, disgusted at the way liberalism was infecting the Sunday schools and colleges and seminaries, voted to withdraw from the convention and become independent. Now a similar rift was tearing apart the Southern Baptists.

Those same arguments had echoed in the Laird home—first in the third-floor walkup on Clinton Street in Brooklyn, then in every home after, finally the penthouse apartment here, where the arguments seemed to tear the draperies of Scalamandre silk. The more he insisted that she simply could not ignore the evidence of the fossils that came out of the ground or the Dead Sea Scrolls, the more she retreated into the stark emotion of faith.

"You like to see criminals found guilty at trial, don't you?" he'd yell. "You accept the *evidence* that convicts those criminals, don't you? Well, evidence is evidence, even in religion."

And she would retort in her calm high voice. "It's wicked to compare cops and robbers with the word of God."

The sad part of it was that he had cared for her—her evenness, her purity, her command of herself, the fact that she had never made heavy sexual demands on him. When they had married in 1937, they had been two good kids from Christian families who wanted to do the right thing in life. It all had seemed so simple then.

With the arguments had come the war for possession of Jeannie's soul. Jeannie had her mother's naiveté

65

and her inability to compromise. But she also had her father's energy and his worldiness. On top of that, Jeannie had always felt far closer to her father. Jeannie's mother had hated movies and talked about the Hollywood cesspool. But Bill sometimes said phooey and took Jeannie to a movie on Saturday afternoons— a nice moral movie like Walt Disney's *Snow White* or Bing Crosby in *Going My Way*.

So when, in high school, Jeannie started talking about an acting career, her mother was very distressed and told Bill that he was leading the innocent girl down the path to Hell. Jeannie insisted she wanted to be a nice actress. Cora insisted there was no such thing as a nice actress, that Hollywood dragged everything nice down to its own level. And when Jeannie entered the Miss Subways contest and won it, her mother wept and softly called her an infidel, although the only part of Jeannie's body ever exposed in public was her face, on the subway posters.

The next battle was about Jeannie's education. Cora admitted that Jeannie was a bright girl and felt that she ought to attend a good Baptist college and become a woman missionary. (Good women did not, of course, hope to preach, because that was specifically forbidden by the Bible.) But Bill felt strongly that Jeannie should go to a good cultured school. By then he had made enough money that he moved the family to a nice brownstone on Prospect Park and could afford to send Jeannie to Skidmore, to study acting, and he did.

He was sure that Cora must have discussed divorce with their pastor. He was also sure that the pastor must have discouraged her from the idea of divorce. The pastor was realistic enough to see that, despite her liberal education and her new sophistication, Jeannie didn't smoke or dance when she came home to visit. But when she was a junior, she entered the Miss New York contest, and she won it. Mortified at the idea of her daughter walking down a runway in a bathing suit before thousands of men's eyes, Cora could only turn her face away and weep. Then came Jeannie's near-victory in the Miss America contest, runner-up with her dramatic recital of a modern Iphigenia, and her being signed by Metro-Goldwyn-Mayer in a starlet role, and her engagement to Sidney.

By then Jeannie had learned to sip at a cocktail (never more than two). She tried hard to explain to her mother that she was still pure, but her mother didn't believe her, until she had her examined by the family doctor.

The gentle cold war went on after Jeannie's wedding. Bill liked Sidney—Cora did not. "The boy is unsaved—he doesn't even go to church regularly," Cora said, blinking her soft gray eyes.

As Jeannie's children came, Cora didn't approve of the way Jeannie was bringing them up. "Too much permissiveness. No Bible reading at home." Cora was pleased when Jeannie's acting career crumbled, but she was displeased when Jeannie went into politics. "It is wicked for a woman to teach men, or to hold authority over men." In vain Jeannie protested that she wasn't teaching men, just trying to get them to vote the right way.

In 1976, when Jeannie had her nervous breakdown, Cora was already dying of cancer and high blood pressure. It was in vain that Jeannie assured her mother that now she was saved. Very softly, very bitterly, her mother said, "Just in time for you, and just in time for God. But too late for me. You've helped to kill me."

Then there had been the matter of Bill's slow-growing awareness of his gayness.

He had never been sure if Cora knew about it. He did sense, sometimes, that she suspected something. Sometimes she wept and whispered with terrifying intensity about his "wicked" ways of living, but she never made specific accusations. She came down so hard on Jeannie about an innocent seventh-grade crush on her pretty English teacher, Miss Wilkins, that Jeannie's abilities to have close friendships with other women were badly damaged. As for openly gay men, whom she sometimes saw on the streets of New York, Cora considered them the most infidel of the infidels.

Now that he thought about it, it was possible that Jeannie had learned her homophobia from her mother.

Bill's pragmatic mind led him early to recognize that he liked men better, just as it had led him to see the sense in evolution. But that was in the 1950s, when gay life in New York was still a limbo. A few clandestine visits to bars convinced him that the fear of the police raids destroyed one's dignity as a human being.

Instead, he found his way to the West Side Discussion Group. In those days, the group met quietly in members' apartments, and he became known as "John." He wasn't too surprised to meet a liberal Presbyterian minister in the group, who sat down with him one day and showed him the truth about the Holy Bible. Even today, he could still hear the man's voice, could still see his finger pointing out the passages.

"There doesn't have to be a conflict between your Baptist beliefs and the Bible," the minister had said. "Read the Bible carefully, especially Deuteronomy, Leviticus and Numbers. These are the chapters where God gives all his laws to the Israelites. And you will see that homosexuality clearly falls into what we now call the ceremonial laws, as distinguished from the moral laws. Homosexuality was forbidden to men only—nothing is said about lesbians. Yet adultery, which is clearly in the moral law, is specifically forbidden to both sexes."

As the minister talked, Bill had felt a slow ecstatic brightening of the mind. The Bible called homosexuality an abomination—but it also labeled as abominations the eating of shellfish and blood, the failure to practice ritual cleanliness after childbirth, and the imitating of Canaanite tattoos.

"Think about it," the minister had said. "In the United States we put men in jail for twenty years for sodomy. But we don't put them in jail for twenty years for eating a rare steak or telling fortunes. Yet the Bible says that all those things specifically deserve the death penalty."

That conversation, as much as his first shy sexual contacts with men, was the turning point of his life. Often, when he had arguments with Cora, he longed to tell her that she was an infidel because she loved shrimp cocktails.

Love had come only later.

He met Marion at a quiet little men's dinner party in SoHo, in 1966. Marion was at the peak of his career as a Class A racing driver, and was passing through New York on his way to the Indy. A friend brought him to the party, and all the guests were devastated by the thoroughbred intensity and the blond good looks of the young Englishman, who even then was taking reckless peeps out of the closet. Bill was astonished to find that, of all the men there, he was the one provoking Marion's interest. He drank too much wine, and they talked intensely.

When Marion left New York, Bill recklessly invented a business reason to fly out to Indiana. There, lost in the godless crowd, his ears deafened by the scream of the engines and the rock music, he died a thousand deaths watching Marion drive the Lotus to second place, and knew that he was in love.

He and Marion didn't even go to bed together until three weeks after they met, and a week after the Indy, when they were both back in New York.

He was jolted out of his reverie. Jeannie was dialing again, stabbing childishly at the dial buttons on the phone. Now she was talking to her attorney, George Meers. It seemed that George was delighted at her decision, and ready to help.

He stood up, feeling a little panicked, and picked up his briefcase.

Jeannie moved the mouthpiece away from her lips, and raised her face to be kissed, smiling trustfully.

"I have to go," Bill said, pecking her cheek. "I'll be downtown all day. Maybe I'll see you later."

And he fled.

Four

Bill Laird went striding into his office, carrying his little briefcase with yesterday's closing papers in it.

The deal had been consummated, the money had changed hands. Now, with the aid of federal tax incentives given for private urban renewal, all he and Al had to do was make it work. Today he was going to spend the entire day downtown inspecting his dream.

If it weren't for Jeannie and her cockamamie political venture, it would be a beautiful day.

He strode among the desks, throwing little smiles at his people. "Hello, Jamie." "How's the new grand-child, Mrs. Markstein?"

He stopped at the desk of his executive secretary, Mrs. Voeller, and gave her the papers from yesterday to file.

Then he stuck his head in at his brother's door, and said, "Hi, Al, come on in for a cuppa."

His younger brother Allen looked up from a South Bronx memo he was reading.

Allen was three years younger than he, but he looked ten years older. He was tall, very thin, a little stooped, with a fringe of snow-white hair around his skull and a very shiny pink pate. He had the air of a small-town bank vice-president, and, in fact, he was content to sit at his desk and play with calculators and computers, and figure out all the minute financial and legal angles, and to nitpick and worry. He was the visible Laird partner, the one who sat on the city planning board and was quoted in *Barron's*. He preferred to leave the visions and the creativity to his shyer, less publicly visible older brother. They agreed that they made a very good pair, and in fact they had never had a major quarrel regarding the business.

Now and then they traded jokes about how they were the mini-Rockefellers. "After all," Al was fond of saying, "we're Baptists too, we do a little bit of philanthropy, we've got a tight little family. We've got a little money, and a little real estate, and even a little piece of politics in New York State. The only difference," he'd add, "is that our grandfather didn't get his start selling patent medicine."

When asked what their grandfather had gotten his start at, Al would answer with a perfectly straight face, "Oh, he was a horse thief."

For all their jokes about the Rockefellers, however, the two brothers still felt the weight of their déclassé Brooklyn background. They were not to the purple born, and knew it, and had no pretensions.

For much of his life, however, Bill Laird had had a deep-down worry about his brother. Al was every bit as rigid a Baptist as Cora, every bit as puritanical, and every bit as ready to call something "infidel" if he didn't understand it. For this reason, Bill had felt increasingly remote from his brother over the years, as his inner commitment to being gay broadened. He shuddered to think of what would happen to Laird & Laird if Al found out that he was gay. His brother had a fifty-percent interest in the company.

Al got up and followed Bill into his office.

Like most executive offices, Bill's office made a subtle statement about its occupant. Looking around it, one became aware that the occupant was smitten with old New York, and with the sea that lapped the city's foot. But Bill's intention was less to impress visitors than to charm himself—he worked better when surrounded by the things he loved.

Behind the big walnut captain's desk and the old swivel chair padded in black leather, the tall window framed a beautiful view of the East River. At that moment, an Exxon barge was going upriver toward Bronx Kills, and he could almost hear the cries of the gulls wheeling over the barge's decks. The bold swags of drapery were reproductions of antique blue-and-white linsey-woolsey with the eagle pattern.

In one corner, as a setting for informal conversation, he had two long rosewood sofas upholstered in the blue-and-white eagle fabric. The huge coffee table, made of an old ship's hatch cover, was good for spreading out plans and blueprints. In the corner itself loomed one of the finest old ship's figureheads in private hands—carved by Isaac Poole of Massachusetts, it was from the *Friendship of Salem*. The robed woman, with her prim little hat and her hands clasping a lily to her bosom, always reminded Bill of his wife, who had breasted her way through the storm waves of life with just that same virginal look.

The walls, painted a deep rich blue, displayed the iceberg's tip of his collection of New York paintings and early photographs. His favorite was the Jacob Ryker hanging behind his desk—it showed the harbor and Battery Park ghostly in the moonlight, with a sky swimming in clouds shaped like ships and horses. But there was also the massed display of framed early photographs of downtown New York, among them some priceless Prevost originals from the 1850s. These, too, were only a glimpse of the treasures that lay in his special climate-controlled file—guarded both as treasures and as irreplacable reference material for his work. It was the finest collection of old photos outside of the New York Historical Society. All of the paintings and photographs were, of course, burglar-alarm wired into the wall.

One photograph showed South Street in the days of

the tall ships, with bowsprits thrusting jauntily up over the cobblestoned street, bales and barrels stacked on the sidewalk, and men coming and going from the arched doorways of a stately brick building whose sign read PEAKE & STURGIS. This building, now a gutted hulk, was the one that he had closed on yesterday, together with the block of old stores and tenements that surrounded it. The deal of his dreams—and all threatened now by Jeannie's decision to go back into politics.

The two men followed their morning ritual of going into the small kitchenette and making themselves two cups of coffee from the Mr. Coffee maker and the supply of fresh-ground Colombian blend. (They had started this ritual after the young and liberated Mrs. Voeller announced sweetly but firmly that she would no longer make their coffee.)

Then they settled down on the sofas with their cups of English bone china. As they talked about South Street, Bill asked himself whether he should bring up the subject of financing Jeannie's campaign. He knew Jeannie would ask Al about it herself. It would look strange if he, Bill, didn't talk about it. "Al," said Bill, "not to change the subject, but Jeannie has been asking me about a loan for her campaign. What do you think?"

"Well . . ." Al was thinking. "She already called me last night and talked about it. We're heavily committed right now. But after all, she's our little girl."

Bill felt trapped.

"Why don't you look at the figures and let me know what you think we can manage?" he asked.

"Sure thing," said Al. "It's hard to take in . . . the idea of Jeannie in the governor's mansion, isn't it? But the more I think of it . . ."

After they'd had their coffee, Al went back to his office. Bill signed some letters, looked quickly through some correspondence, made a couple of calls to the company lawyer. Then he headed downstairs again, eager to get to South Street.

He headed his gray Lancia down the East River Drive.

The morning rush traffic had slacked off, and he drove fast, weaving in and out of the traffic. Some people teased him about being déclassé, driving alone like that, when he could afford a limo and a chauffeur, but he replied simply that no, that he preferred driving around the city alone.

He passed the exit for Houston Street. And then there it was, looming ahead: the sign that said "Manhattan Bridge—South Street."

He peeled off the East Side highway, and in another moment he was on South Street, back into another age.

The street, its old cobblestones peeking through the asphalt in places, ran right along the edge of Manhattan Island. It was almost empty of traffic. Old brick tenements and commercial buildings faced out over the water: many were empty, boarded up. A few blocks had been razed, as part of an ill-conceived urban-renewal project—his heart bled every time he looked at these tears in the rich old fabric of that street. Every crosstown street that ran into South Street had a name laden with history—Gouverneur's Slip, Peck's Slip, Catherine Slip, Fulton Slip, Coenties Slip—names of now-vanished piers where the tall ships had tied up.

As he drove slowly down the long, long street, almost at horse-and-buggy pace, he could imagine how it had looked a hundred years ago. There was hardly anything left of all that.

Now, there were some freighters tied up at the newer piers. There were the buildings belonging to the Brazilian Flag Lines, and the Fulton Fish Market. And there was the South Street Seaport Museum, where one lonely great square-rigger, the *Peking*, was tied up permanently amid several smaller vessels, including the old Ambrose Light ship. The *Peking* was a sad sight, with her spars now bare of sails and her gangway charging $1.50 to tourists. Across the street from the museum, a few blocks of buildings had already been renovated by another real-estate concern, with boutiques, apartments and seafood restaurants. The last old building he came to, before he turned around at Battery Park at the foot of Manhattan Island, was the beautiful Governor's Island ferry building built of ornamental iron.

But the times had left South Street behind. The shallower waters of the East River had proven to be treacherous as shipping abandoned sail and took on more tonnage and size. The mammoth freighters and liners now went over to the deeper North River, to the other side of Manhattan Island. South Street had been left in an economic backwater, quaint and decaying.

He turned around and drove back up South Street and stopped at the street marked Catherine Slip. There he parked by the curb. The area was so empty that one never had to worry about parking.

He got out and stood looking.

There, on the corner of Catherine Slip, was his dream house—the old Peake & Sturgis ship chandler and sail-loft building. It and the surrounding block were now all his.

After the close of the shipping era, the building had been used as a warehouse. For years, Bill had looked at the photograph, knowing the building was still intact, hoping for a crack at it. In 1971 the owner, who had known Bill's father, had died, and the property had been tied up in a contested will. Bill had waited out the quarrel, and finally made a deal with the sons and daughters for the entire block of property.

The filthy water, iridescent with the oil from bilge

washings, lapped around the rotting pilings. Off to his left, the Gothic towers of the Brooklyn Bridge loomed over him in the haze. Before him spread the great harbor. Out there in the haze was the far-off Statue of Liberty, and beyond, the Verrazano Bridge.

The impressive old three-story brick building bore no sign now. Its broken windows and gutted interior were scorched from a recent fire, set by junkies, that the fire department had quickly put out. But the tall windows with their neoclassic pedimenta, and the tall arched doorway, had an earthy dignity that spoke of the many seamen and captains who had trafficed in and out.

Ever since he was young, he had dreamed of owning a big house with a view over the harbor. After working all night helping his father with paperwork in Scout Realty, he would walk across the Brooklyn Bridge at dawn to his daytime job as a clerk in a Wall Street brokerage firm. He would always stop halfway across, and lean on the walkway's iron railing to gaze out across the harbor, vast and shining in the morning haze, and try to imagine how it must have looked when it was a "forest of masts." The cops who patrolled the bridge soon learned that he was not thinking of suicide, and they stopped to chat with him.

Now he stood there, half in a dream. A big white Italian freighter was just passing the Statue of Liberty, on her way out to sea. His imagination shot out to her, and he could hear from her rail the hoarse hoot of the buoys, clear out in Ambrose Channel. He could hear the deep thrumming of her engines, and the clang of her bells in the engine room. Now he could see the rolling dunes of Fire Island to the north, as the ship stood out along Long Island. And finally, there was Montauk Light, and the Atlantic breeze was stiff and fresh on his face.

Freedom! Oh, how he had always wanted to go to sea! But he had always been too busy doing landlub-

ber things that he felt had to be done. Maybe now
there would be more time. Surely God wouldn't mind
if he and Marion bought a nice little ketch, and
learned navigation, and did some sailing together. The
deal included the two old piers across the street—he
and Marion would be able to tie up their boat right
there.

Meanwhile, there was this gutted building to find
joy with. It was as mysterious and seductive as an un-
climbed, unnamed mountain in the Andes.

He walked slowly across the street to the high
arched doorway, taking the tape measure and notepad out of his jacket pocket.

The door, of course, stood open and the rusted
metal door hung drunkenly from its rusty crumbling
hinges. He had already hired a watchman, who would
start duty tonight and who eventually would live in a
little trailer in the back.

Inside, his footsteps echoed eerily. The stone floors
and the vaulted ceilings on the first floor were beautiful, though the plaster had long since peeled away,
baring the brick. Before he started measuring, he simply walked around aimlessly, thinking over where everything was going to be.

In the back, there was a large room with a huge
fireplace. This would be a magnificent eat-in kitchen,
where he could feed friends in earthy medieval splendor, while logs crackled in the fireplace.

Another tall arched door opened into a sunny
walled courtyard, where wagons and teams had once
unloaded canvas and other ship supplies.

The paved courtyard was now overgrown with sunflowers and jewelweed, and shaded by a few trees-of-
heaven that had seeded themselves. This would be the
garden, planted formally with old shrub roses to delight Marion. There would be benches, statues, a fountain and formal plantings of roses and herbs, and vege-
tables on the sunniest side.

But today something in the air here troubled him. Every other time he had visited this building, he had felt its peace, its waiting to be recycled into life again. Today Peake & Sturgis was not at peace.

He walked slowly up the worn stone stairway to the second floor. As he ascended the stairs, the uneasy feeling grew stronger. Then it slacked off on the third floor.

Here, under the airy ceilings with their heavy beams, had been the sail loft. Through the broken windows, the sunlight poured on the dirty floor littered with newspapers and junkies' refuse.

He walked slowly over to the windows, and looked out. The Italian ship was now far out in the channel.

Suddenly his chest constricted, and he almost had to choke back a deep and wrenching sob. A number of gay men sought to deny all ties, and traveled from love to love, hoping to find some kind of permanence and security in impermanence, hoping to build a stable sand castle on the sand. But for Marion and himself, the pair bond had been total, like those animals who mate for life, those wolves or swans who are parted only by death. Unlike the animals, however, they had never dared to stake out a territory where they could be at peace. That deep need of a lair, a sanctuary, had been the one need that had marred their relationship. It had always been Marion's apartment at lunchtime or after work. Over the years, Marion had sometimes come to 69th Street for cocktails and dinner, but only as a business associate, never for snatched intimacies, and he had never dared to invite him there while Cora was alive, because he was so sure that she had psyched out what was going on.

When he and Marion had looked at this building together, before contract-signing, they had walked around discussing what room should be where, where the study, where the big bathroom with antique tub and shirred fabric walls. They had stood before these windows, looking out, and suddenly Marion had turned and looked him in the eyes and asked, point-blank. "Then ... you want us to live here together?"

"Well," Bill had stammered in return, "would you be willing to give up your nice little place for this?"

But Marion had answered his question with another blunt question: "Are you really ready for us to live together?"

"Are you?" Bill had parried again.

"I've been ready for years," Marion had said, in a low voice. He stood there in the sunlight, the wet breeze moving his curls, and the strong sunlight picked out ever line and scar on his fine face—picked out every fleck of color in his searching eyes. No doubt about it. Marion was no longer young either.

Bill had not been able to face those searching eyes. He had turned away, and gone to the next broken window, and looked out. A big passenger liner had been steaming slowly in under the Verrazano Bridge —he remembered that detail very clearly.

"I would like to think that I'm ready," he said softly, "but I don't know. All I know is that I want this place. I see myself living here, and I see you here too. I see us waking up in the morning, and looking out these windows at the harbor."

"Is that a real wish?" said Marion. "Or is it just one of those fantasies that make us feel less guilty?"

"I don't know," Bill had said. "I don't know what holds me back. It's not my religion—I've sorted *that* all out. And it's not my profession—self-employed, I'm independently well-off—nobody can take away my job or my money if I come out. It's not even Al. It's ...

"It's Jeannie," said Marion.

"Yes," Bill said.

"Are you worried about what she would think? Or are you afraid of her?"

"Both," Bill had said simply. "I'm afraid of ... of

that moment when she will turn on me like a lioness and call me an infidel."

"But according to your way of thinking, *she* is an infidel," said Marion. He smiled a little. "I notice that every Baptist uses that word about any other Baptist who doesn't agree with him."

"Yes, that's right," Bill had said, shrugging, watching the great steamer majestically heading across the bay, raising her white bow wake, past the Statue of Liberty. "The infidels cursing each other. It doesn't make much sense, does it?"

"My dear Bill," said Marion crisply, "the whole history of humanity boils down to two infidels cursing each other. Sometimes I think that what separates man from animals is *not* that he has a soul, but that he is capable of nasty arguments about religion. Can you imagine two aardvarks arguing about how many angels on the head of a pin?" Bill had started laughing. "Or two elephants arguing about whether Moses really wrote the first five books of the Bible?"

They had both laughed a long time, each of them leaning at his separate window, as the beautiful ship steamed on across the bay and disappeared behind Battery Park, heading for the North River.

Now, standing there alone at the window, Bill remembered this conversation so clearly. It came at him like eerie whispers from the dark corners of the great loft, where the wind had piled up stained yellow newspapers.

He walked around some more, wondering what was troubling him about the house. Now and then he found his hackles bristling. He had felt so good about it every other time that he had visited it. Something was here that had not been here before. He had an ESP about houses and buildings, and sometimes he wondered if he could be a professional sensitive.

He wondered if some muggers were hiding somewhere in the building, waiting to jump him. Now and then he slipped his hand inside his jacket to feel the length of weighted lead pipe that he always carried when scouting out old buildings.

At last, on the second floor, he found it.

In the northwest corner room, as he played the flashlight along the dark wall, he saw an old man sitting on the floor, leaning against the wall, his head tipped over on his shoulder. The man was wearing a ripped old tweed coat; his long white hair was mussed. The flashlight beam also reflected red from two tiny pairs of eyes on the floor beside the man, and from another on his shoulder. Then there was a scuttling sound, and the eyes disappeared. Rats.

Bill froze, his hair rising up on the back of his head. He recognized death instantly. His heart pounded, and sweat sprang out all over him.

He dared to walk a few steps closer, playing the flashlight over the crumpled figure. The man, probably a tramp or a wino, couldn't have been dead more than a day or so, as the smell was still faint. But the rats had already been at work—the man's lips had been eaten away, baring the dried gums and dark-stained teeth. The flesh had been stripped from the hand lying in his lap.

Trembling with revulsion, Bill left the building.

He drove to the nearest pier, and found a public telephone, and called the police.

Mary Ellen and Danny listened to the dispatcher talking about an "unconscious person" found by a citizen in a warehouse on South Street, between Catherine and Peck. She decided she would respond to this one instead of letting her men do it. The reason was simple—it had been a pretty dull shift, and this would not be the first time the precinct had been troubled by goings-on at this old warehouse.

"Cruiser two-oh-four responding," she said into the mike. Danny turned on the flashing red light, and she headed the car down Pine Street toward South.

Two minutes after the radio call, she was screeching to a halt in front of the old brick warehouse. A man in gray slacks and a blue sweat-shirt was standing there beside a shiny gray Lancia which was probably his.

As she and Danny got out of the car, the man stared at her, and at her sergeant stripes. She had seen that stare so many times that it didn't bother her any more. The stare told her that the man wondered if he had been transported into "Charlie's Angels." So she spoke to him in a crisp level voice that would not remind him at all of Farrah Fawcett-Majors.

"I'm Sergeant Frampton," she said. "This is Officer Blackburn. Are you the citizen who called about a dead person?"

"Yes," he said. "I'll show you where he is."

"May I ask what you're doing on the premises?" she asked.

The man hesitated for a moment, seeming a little nervous. Then he said, "My name is Bill Laird. I'm a real-estate man. I just bought this property yesterday, and I was making an inspection. He couldn't have been here long, because I was here with the previous owners just a couple of days ago."

They were walking swiftly into the building.

"Laird," she said. "Uh, aren't you *William* Laird, the developer?"

"That's right," said the man.

Her poker face relaxed into a soft smile.

Danny grinned too, and asked, "You gonna do one of your magic numbers on this place?"

"I hope so," he said, his face relaxing a little too.

Now that Mary Ellen looked at him, she had the vague feeling that she had seen him somewhere before. Not in connection with police work, either. Maybe it was in the newspapers or a magazine. On the other hand, the man kept looking at her nervously as if maybe he had seen her somewhere before too.

"I've bought the whole block," he said. "This build-

ing is going to be my own home, and the other buildings are going to be shops and condominiums. I also
own the two little piers across the street."

"Great idea," she said. "This building has been a
problem. The fire, junkies, you name it. The more you
do, the less we have to do."

"I'm bringing in a watchman, today," he said, "so
you shouldn't have much more trouble."

They had reached the second floor. Mary Ellen and
Danny walked briskly over to the body, and examined
it in the glow of their flashlights without any squeam-
ishness, without touching it. Her instincts told her that
the nervousness of this stately businessman had nothing to do with the death of the old man lying here.

"Looks like an apparent natural," she said. "But you
never know."

"Poor old guy," said Danny. "I've seen him around
the area."

She went back to her car, and William Laird
trailed after her. She spoke into her mike.

"Cruiser two-oh-four," she said.

"Cruiser two-oh-four," squawked the dispatcher's
voice out of the radio.

"Send Homicide to Two-thirty-five South Street,"
she said. "Apparent natural."

When Homicide arrived, Laird had to tell them his
story all over again, and give them a detailed statement. The two detectives scouted the area thoroughly,
poked around in the debris, took notes. They re-
marked that it was odd the man had no small posses-
sions with him, and no empty bottles of booze. But
there were no signs of violence.

"What happens to him now?" Laird asked her.

"Well," she said, "if he can't be identified, he'll stay
in the morgue for ten days, and then the city will take
charge of his burial."

"You don't need me any more, then?" Laird asked.

"You might be called for further questioning," she
said. "But I doubt it."

Suddenly the words came out.

"Mr. Laird, I have the feeling I've seen you some-where before," she said. "Nothing to do with police work or anything," she added hastily, afraid of alarm-ing him. "Just . . . well, you look very familiar to me."

"Really?" said Laird, suddenly a little distant. "I can't think where. This is my first experience with the police."

Humph, Mary Ellen thought. Probably too piss-ele-gant to talk to a common cop. But I know I've seen him. I'll probably wake up in the middle of the night and remember where it was.

As Bill left, the men from the morgue were coming up the worn stairs with the stretcher. By now, two police cars and the morgue wagon were parked in front of his magnificent brick arched doorway.

He got in his car, deeply upset, and drove on down South Street into Battery Park. He was so upset that he hadn't even been able to respond to the good looks of Officer Blackburn. Finding a dead man in his future home was a bad omen. As a man of God, he shouldn't believe in omens. The Bible condemned all manner of sorcery as an abomination. Maybe prophecy was a bet-ter word. The Bible allowed prophecy.

Finally he parked the car near Battery Park, and tried to calm himself by walking around the area.

Ever since he started operating in Manhattan, he had spent whole days—years, now—of his life walking around down here. This was the original New York, the real New York, still defying the steel-and-glass cold-ness that was freezing other areas. With a passion he loved the few old churches that were left here, the few Dutch and Federal houses, the few little parks, the few little cemeteries. In his head he carried men-tal pictures of all the monuments that had been torn down—oh God, so many! Such a loss!

If it weren't for the greed and haste that had always marked Manhattan's growth, this part of town would now rival London for the richness of its antique glories—it would be all church steeples and pillared facades and shuttered windows and tiny parks and paved streets and savory little shops and old piers, and maybe a whole fleet of tall ships standing at anchor forever like at Mystic, Connecticut. It was imperative to save the little that was left. He wanted to humanize New York, and he wanted to humanize the society that now inhabited it.

Suddenly, as he stood in Battery Park, looking out at the harbor again through the sycamore trees, he felt the painful constriction in his chest again.

America had acknowledged all the immigrants who had come pouring up that channel, past the Statue of Liberty, through the now-decaying buildings at Ellis Island—all the immigrants but one. America had never honored the homosexual. The gay sailors who hunted the first waterfront bars, the lesbian governesses who taught the first children of the rich straights. The gays too had come over on the *Mayflower*, had first glimpsed New York Harbor from the decks of the *Half Moon.*

He walked and walked that day, looking at all the old buildings that he had loved, but peace would not come.

He walked down Broad Street. He admired the view of Trinity Church down the long tunnel of Wall Street, its sooty steeple dwarfed between the glass and stone monoliths around it.

Walking was how he had gotten to know New York, and how he had gotten to know himself. Cora, and later Jeannie, had accepted his lonely walking tours as part of his business, as a fit activity for the mad genius of Laird & Laird. He always returned with his notebook full of notes and sketches, and they understood the connection between those notebooks and the money he made. Nevertheless, he had always had the creepy feeling that Cora knew he used those walks for other purposes also. And she was right. They had been his cover.

On his walks he had been free to acquaint himself —intimately yet anonymously—with the gay world, which was so heavily established in the downtown area. On his walks, he had first browsed in gay literary magazines at the Oscar Wilde Memorial bookstore on Christopher Street. Browsing in the Mattachine Society's library on Christopher, he had found a copy of America's first gay novel, Bayard Taylor's *Joseph and His Friend*, published in 1870. It was on one of his walks that he first ventured into a waterfront leather bar, and found that the bartender hesitated at first about serving him the glass of wine he'd ordered because he wasn't wearing jeans or leather. Finally the bartender said gruffly, "Well, you look butch enough for me," and served him. It was on his walks that he made his first shy, fumbling attempts at sexual overtures.

On his walks, he passed corners where hustlers hung out, and found himself backing off from them with a feeling of outraged dignity. How can my society and my religion and my Bible force me to look to prostitution for the only emotional gratification I have? he asked himself. So he stayed largely virginal and kept walking. He visited with gay antique dealers and gay artists and gay restaurant owners and gay lawyers, and always they knew him simply as "John." When he heard of the Metropolitan Community Church, he started attending the services regularly, always sitting in the back, never drawing attention to himself. He was deeply moved by the sermons of the Reverend Troy Pearry (even if Pearry *was* a Presbyterian).

Gradually, he had come to realize that there were two New Yorks. There was the visible New York, the one acknowledged in the history books and the old prints and the bronze plaques and the museums. And there was the invisible New York, unacknowledged anywhere save in the laws that forbade it and the sermons that condemned it. It was that gay and lesbian New York, so complex that few of its own inhabitants knew all its twisting byways, so complete that a person could live out his or her days there and hardly ever speak to a straight person.

He didn't return to his car until late afternoon. This was one day when he didn't have any new notes in his notebook.

CHAPTER
Five

Jeannie had not given her political workers much time. But to their credit most of them had dropped whatever they were doing and had come to their first meeting.

Now they were all sitting around in her large living room. The sunlight poured through the western windows, through the screen of Sidney's palms and orange trees, onto the overflowing ashtrays, revealing air bluish with cigarette smoke, the squashed sofa cushions, and the half-ruined wheel of Camembert cheese and the last dried slices of rye and French bread.

Jeannie scooped up some of the ashtrays and carried them into the kitchen to empty them, wrinkling her nose.

Her old campaign manager, Tom Winkler, followed her, with a small smile on his face.

As she dumped the ashtray contents into the garbage can, he leaned against the large refrigerator and, his arms crossed over his chest, said: "The trouble with you is, you don't really *like* the smoke-filled rooms."

"Ugh," said Jeannie. "I've *never* smoked, and I'll never get used to it, I guess. My mother never smoked, either. It was the one thing that neither of us could stand about my father. My mother always used to tell him that he would never have to go to Hell because he carried it around in his jacket pocket."

"Being a Baptist is easy for you, isn't it, Jeannie? It's your second nature."

Jeannie was at the sink, scouring out the ashtrays with soap and hot water, still wrinkling her nose at the fact that her hands had to be immersed in that ash-flavored water.

"Is that intended to be a dig at me because I didn't put out a lot of booze for everybody to drink today?" she said.

Winkler shrugged pleasantly. "How do you expect me to do my finest work if you don't oil my brain with a little good bourbon?"

Winkler was the kind of tall, slouched man who just missed having a little paunch. His gray hair always had an unkempt look, he never wore his belt in the snuggest hole, and you were sure he might have a shoelace untied. If you didn't know him, you might dismiss him as a slob. If you looked at his résumé, however, you learned about his grim, disciplined, brilliant campaign work for the Rockefellers and for Mayor Shay. He had come to work for Jeannie in 1974 because he was convinced that she could fill the void that the departed Rockefellers had left in New York State politics—a conservative with stature, but a conservative who could do what the Rockefellers hadn't done—reach the people, move the grass roots.

Jeannie knew, however, that he had been shaken by her decision to take a sabbatical from politics last year. He was also worried by what he knew and she knew was her nervous breakdown. He had worked grimly to keep the truth about it from the press, to help her throw up a smoke screen, saying that Jeannie Colter wanted a breather, to be with her family and her husband and her children for a bit, that she wanted to write a book, and various other lies.

Now he leaned against the refrigerator studying her as she bustled about, drying the dripping ashtrays, which were now sparkling clean.

"Jeannie, how *are* you, really?" he said.

"I'm fine," she said. "Really. I've gotten a lot of rest, I've done a lot of thinking. I haven't exactly written the book, but I've made a lot of notes on my thoughts. I've got a whole box of pages in there somewhere. Maybe some editor could put it together into something."

"The last time I saw you," he said, "was four months ago. You didn't look so rested to me then. You looked very strained, very brittle, with an edge like a razor."

"Do I look that way now?" she countered.

"I don't know," said Winkler. "I'm trying to figure out if what I see is your PR, or the real you."

She shot a hard look at him.

"Now listen, Jeannie," he said. "You know as well as I do that I'm good at what I do because I never stick my head in the sand."

She piled the ashtrays on the kitchen table and leaned on it, facing him, her arms crossed belligerently across her chest. It was a pose that state legislators would have recognized as the stance she always took when she was about to make a very heavy speech.

"You're trying to make me feel insecure?" she said. "Trying to tear down what I achieved with myself in the last months?"

He looked her right in the eye and adopted the same pose teasingly. "If you are well," he said, "you *will* be secure. Nothing I could do or say would shake you. I'd find you were like a rock. *Are* you a rock, Jeannie?"

"We'll soon find out, won't we?" she said, slumping a little and dropping her arms.

"Have you seen a psychiatrist?" he said.

"No, of course not," she said.

"Good. They can use that against you. Who *have* you seen?"

"I've seen a lot of Reverend Irving, is about all," she said. "He's been very helpful. Dad doesn't like Reverend Irving, of course."

He swirled the last of his soft drink in his glass. "I have to tell you that this religious business of yours worries me a little. The Rockefellers were church-oriented in their way, but they never paraded it."

"You're going to tell me that I can't be upfront about faith? About believing, about being saved?"

"Politically, it can be a tricky thing."

"The Carters get away with it."

"Yeah," he said, "but the Carters have got a special touch. They may be Baptists, but they have such a velvet touch with it that the *conservative* Baptists consider them to be heathen." Jeannie had opened her mouth, but he shook his head, cutting her off. "Ruth Cater may be a faith healer, but the biggest miracle she works is *not* looking like a religious nut. And Jimmy's beer-drinking brother provides just the right kind of counterweight."

"You're saying I ought to have a beer-drinking brother?"

"Wouldn't hurt," he said, throwing his soft drink down the sink. "Yuk," he said, "I can't understand how people can drink this sugary stuff. Speaking of relatives, where is your dad?"

Her stomach sank a little. She had hoped that Winkler would not notice her father's absence. He had said he had an important meeting with a real-estate biggie. Frankly, it made her suspicious that he should choose to go to a meeting on such an important evening in her life when she had assembled her campaign workers for the first time. Her father had always been one of her best advisers, had always attended these meetings.

"He had to meet with some real-estate guy," she said. "He's had a lot of deals going lately. He finally pulled off the South Street thing. I think if I hear the name 'South Street' one more time, I'll scream. It's all he can talk about."

"Is he going to help with the campaign?"

She sighed and slumped a little more. "I honestly don't know. I already approached him about it. I as-

92

sumed he'd be very excited and say yes. But this time
. . . well, it was a little *strange*. I almost had the feeling
that he was putting me off a little."

Jeannie marched back into the living room, carrying
the ashtrays. Winkler trailed after her.

Shortly after that, they wrapped up the meeting.

"Okay," said Winkler, "I'll write you this long memo
about the strategies I think you should take." He
looked her right in the eye. "And I expect you to pay
attention to it."

The other people were looking at them both, picking
up on the slight tension between them.

"Of course I'll listen to it," said Jeannie. "I'd be a
fool not to."

"Just remember, Jeannie," said Winkler. "Carter set
the model for us all. He got where he is by sound organization and planning. Even when he made some
bad mistakes, the planning saved his ass."

"I'll remember that," said Jeannie, smiling sweetly,
"if and when I make any mistakes. Can you have the
memo to me in a few days?"

"You'll have it by Friday."

"Good," said Jeannie. "And John . . ." She looked at
John Rice, the new pollster, a young man that Winkler
had brought in, saying that he was brilliant.

"I'll get going on the survey right away," said Rice.

When the others had left, Winkler lingered, pouring
himself another glass of soda.

"Tom," she said, "do you still believe in me?"

"Of course I do," he said. "If I didn't, I wouldn't be
sitting here drinking this crap."

That same afternoon, Mary Ellen visited the two
other people on the force that she knew were gay.
She didn't see them in her day-to-day work, so she
made efforts to stay in touch with them. The first one
she visited was an older officer, Sam Rauch, who was
always on duty at Pier 36, on Canal Street.

When she went off duty, she dropped by the A & P

and bought a bag of cat chow. Then she stopped at the White Tower on Canal Street, and ordered two coffees to go and a cheeseburger with lots of onion. You never had to ask Sam Rauch if he wanted a cheeseburger with lots of onion.

Then she drove on along Canal Street and under the West Side Highway, and parked on the worn old cobblestones in front of the pier.

Pier 36 was the limbo of towed-away cars in New York City. When a car was first towed, it went to the modern brightly lit Pier 95 at 36th Street, owned by the United States Lines and leased to the New York Police Department for auto storage. There the Police Department maintained a bustling 24-hour-a-day office always jammed with people desperate to get their cars back. If the car was unclaimed at Pier 95, a tow truck dragged it downtown to Pier 36 on Canal Street. After thirty to sixty days, the registered owner was sent a letter, and if the car was still unclaimed, it was sold at public auction.

Carrying the sack, Mary Ellen strode over mud puddles to the cavernous entrance to the pier. Its towering brick facade was grimy and sooty, its windows broken or boarded up. The only sign of life was the battered sign by the doorway, PROPERTY CLERK'S OFFICE.

She walked along the echoing passageway, as dank and dark as a catacomb tunnel.

The half-mile-long interior was dimly lit by a few high-watt bulbs. She could see the rows on rows of cars, gleaming dully under their dust and grime. She tried to imagine happy ship passengers streaming in and out, luggage crammed with souvenirs, bands playing, baskets of fruit being delivered to staterooms. But she couldn't. Here was nothing but death and decay. The only sign of life was a battle-scarred gray cat with a bobtail, who was creeping shyly away under the nearest car.

As she came up to the office, an ear-splitting burglar alarm went off—she had tripped it via electric eye. Quickly she stepped aside, and the alarm stopped ringing.

On the battered office was a sign: DO NOT LET CATS IN OFFICE—THESE ARE PIER CATS.

Sam opened the office door and peered out. Pulled down over his ears was the red wool ski cap he wore winter and summer. He had his gold shield pinned to a gray sweatshirt—the place was so dirty that Sam never wore a uniform when on duty.

"Hiya, sweetheart, come on in," he said. He spotted the sack. "You're a doll. I didn't get to buy cat food yet today."

In the office, Sam patiently explained to a furious young couple that if they didn't have their car registration with them and if it wasn't in the glovebox of the car, then they would have to apply to the motor-vehicle bureau for a replacement registration, but that in any case, that was not the Police Department's problem, as the car had been locked until the couple had come on the pier, so the registration couldn't have walked away by itself.

"And when we get the registration, then what?" said the young man between his teeth.

"Then," said Sam pleasantly, "you go back to the office up at Pier Ninety-five, and you show them your driver's license and registration, and you prove you're not a scofflaw, and you pay what you owe for storage, and they give you a release card, and then you come back down here, and I release the car to you."

"Fucking bureaucrats," said the girl.

"Filthy language will get you nowhere," said Sam pleasantly.

The couple left in a huff.

Silently, with a grin, Mary Ellen handed him the warm sack of human food.

"You're a doll *and* a sweetheart," said Sam. "If it wasn't for my friends, I'd starve and die of thirst in this lousy place."

The bare little office had a battered old green metal desk in it, and a big ledger. More such ledgers were lined up, dusty, in a cupboard. Sam's paper-shuffling was basically simple. All he had to do was take the auto release cards, and note the release in his ledger, together with the claimant's driver's license number.

Sam was ripping open the sack of cat chow. He went outside and poured the chow into several hubcaps that were sitting around on the greasy ground. At the sound of chow tinkling against metal, cats erupted from among the cars. In a minute, each hubcap had a dozen animals crouched around it, growling, intent, crunching chow in their teeth.

Sam stood watching them for a minute. He pointed at the bobtail cat. "The end of Mr. Ugly's tail finally dropped off. It was all dead."

Only when he was sure his cats were all eating well did he come back and rummage appreciatively in the sack for his hamburger.

His mind was still on the couple who had just left. "They never," he said, "have any idea that you've heard all the stories before. They always think it's worth a try."

Suddenly he said, "Hey, I found Miss Beautiful's kittens. Wanna see them?"

"Sure," she said.

He put down the wrapped hamburger without opening it, reached for his flashlight, and they left the office.

Together they walked down one of the aisles between the rows of cars. Pinshafts of sunlight shone through the rusting metal roof high above, which looked like it had been riddled by machine-gun fire. Along the walls, water reflections sometimes played through holes in the walls. The cars lay lined up like bodies in a mass grave, tilted by flat tires, their batteries dead. They bore license plates from New York State, Tennessee, Arizona, Massachusetts, Oregon, Connecticut, everywhere. They had been abandoned by owners on long vacations, owners who were in legal trouble, owners who owed thousands in traffic fines, owners who had amnesia, owners who had died. The dirt floor reeked with oil.

Halfway down one of the center rows, Sam bent and shone the flashlight into the front seat of a 1973 black Cadillac with wheels and motor gone, that must have been abandoned on a parkway. One of the vent windows was open.

Curled in somebody's tweed coat on the front seat was a longhaired gray cat with white paws. Her three little kittens lay in a neat row, their heads pillowed against her belly, their round eyes gazing solemnly out at Sam and Mary Ellen. They were white with gray spots. It was a shock to see such clean little creatures in this filthy place.

"Aren't they bee-yoo-ti-ful?" said Sam. "They must be about ten days old. Eyes just opened. Pretty soon they'll be out hunting rats like the rest."

"What are you going to do with them?" Mary Ellen asked.

"Dunno," said Sam, his brow furrowing with worry. "The other guys are talking about taking them to the SPCA. I'd take 'em home with me, but I've got three cats already and my landlady would scream bloody murder."

The mother cat made no move to come to the open car window and be petted—Mary Ellen knew she was as wild as all the other pier cats. But there was trust in her eyes, and in the eyes of her kittens, as they all gazed out at Sam Rauch, their protector.

As she and Sam walked back to the office, she thought about Sam.

The tow-truck men and the other cops who worked shifts here made a little fun of him behind his back. They called him the Cat Man because he had adopted the Pier 36 cats. But they never failed to bring him coffee and hamburgers, and they never failed to bring food for the cats. Bags of chow, leftover steak, even

97

Kentucky Fried Chicken arrived regularly at the pier. Those cats lived like kings. If they got sick and Sam could catch them, he took them to the Animal Medical Center. Sam had been very upset when his favorite, a black battlescarred tom named The Panther, was seen with a huge swollen leg after a fight. Sam tried to catch The Panther, but couldn't. The Panther disappeared—probably crawled off in a hole somewhere and died of septicemia. But by and large, the cats were healthy, and when Sam talked about the size of the rats they caught, he spread his hands like a fly fisherman describing a record-breaking trout.

Mary Ellen didn't know much about Sam—he was close-mouthed about his life. But she could read between the lines. He was close to retirement age, a widower who had lost his wife to uterine cancer ten years ago, and now lived alone in a little, railroad-style second-floor apartment on East Eleventh Street. He was Jewish, but not (as he admitted to Mary Ellen) a very "Jewy Jew." He didn't smoke, drink or gamble. Neither did he go to temple. He read every page of the police magazine, *Spring 3100*. He had worked in many different divisions, knew the city like the back of his hand, and loved to tell stories about the good old days when Al Seedman, brother Jew, was chief of NYPD. He had many friends, but they were all on the force.

Mary Ellen knew him for another honest cop—which was not an easy thing if you had brother officers on the take. Time and again, while bringing him coffee she had walked in on the tail end of a conversation where Sam was busy refusing a bribe from some desperate motorist. She wondered why such an intelligent cop had been given a flop—transferred—into this dump. She wondered if he had once been too honest, if he had made an enemy of some dishonest chief up the line somewhere—if maybe he was an unsung Serpico. But he had never talked about it, and she had never dared ask. In so many ways, he was like her father.

Sam was also gay. Mary Ellen didn't know much about that. When he was on the night shift, from midnight to 8 A.M., he was the only soul in that huge echoing place, and he liked to while away the hours of the wolf by reading, with his feet propped up on the little electric heater, and a cat dozing on the desk. One time he had asked her to find his gloves in his locker, and as she fished around in there, a paperback book had fallen out of his jacket pocket. It fell open to the flyleaf, and she clearly saw the library's stamp: the Mattachine Society, which was one of the oldest gay organizations in the city. The book was *The Last of the Wine* by Mary Renault.

Sam saw her notice the flyleaf, saw her change of expression, and flushed—the only time she ever saw him lose his cool.

Quickly she had said, "The Mattachine—hey, that's a good library. I go there sometimes too."

"You do?" said Sam, looking like he was on the verge of a coronary.

After a little more cautious conversation, Sam had been given to understand that knowledge of his library habits would go no further than Mary Ellen. So he relaxed.

Afterward, now and then, they talked about it in an oblique way. Sam never used the word "gay." He had seemed to have come to his self-awareness late in life. He had never—apparently—had a real lover. "Who's going to want an old guy like me?" he scoffed. He avoided bars and most gay organizations, partly because he was still in the closet, partly because he was shy. At home, off duty, he fed his cats, fixed himself some bacon and eggs, lay on the sofa and read books. He could talk about Radclyffe Hall and Willa Cather and James Baldwin and Christopher Isherwood as intelligently as a *New York Times* reviewer, even if his language was somewhat more flavorful. "A bee-yoo-ti-ful book" was his best accolade.

As they walked back toward the office, the alarm rang again. A young hippie type with long lank hair and owlish spectacles was there, with his auto release in his hand, very respectful, probably a kid from a good home who was now working hard to support himself.

Mary Ellen sat in the office looking sadly at the now-cold hamburger while Sam told the young man where to find the car and took his driver's license to start his paperwork.

When they were alone again, Sam turned to a new page in his ledger and said, "Well, I see they're making another try with the bill." By "the bill," she knew he meant Intro Two.

"Yeah," she said. "Whaddya think?"

"Not a chance," he said. "Not in this town." He shrugged. "Doesn't affect me anyway. Freedom is for the kids."

"It *does* affect you, Sam."

As if he hadn't heard, he said, "Tell you what *does* affect me. My library is out of business."

"You're kidding."

"I'm not. The Mattachine went bankrupt, and they are going to auction the books."

Mary Ellen felt a sick feeling in the pit of her stomach.

The alarm went off outside—the kid, coming back, had walked in front of it. When he came back in, he had bad news. His car had a dead battery and two flat tires.

"Kid," said Sam, "the daytime guys have got jump cables for your battery. But flat tires we can't help you with."

He studied the kid's desperate face.

"What if I leave it here till tomorrow?" the kid asked.

"Then," said Sam, "you gotta go through the line at

Pier Ninety-five again and pay another five dollars' storage."

The kid's face reflected an ultimate despair.

"Tell you what," said Sam. "Find a garage around here somewhere and see if they'll come over and fix your flats. If you can get that car out of here by eleven tonight, it's all yours."

"Do you recommend anybody in particular?" said the kid.

"Nope," said Sam. "I can't recommend nobody. The department can't be liable for anything they do to your car." While he talked, one of the cats jumped on the desk and snatched the last piece of his hamburger.

"Okay," said the kid. "I'll walk around and see what I can find."

He left at a half run.

Sam looked for the last of his hamburger, saw the cat eating it, shrugged, and swigged the last of his coffee. "Heard it a million times already. The kid goes on a trip west, right? Loans his car to a friend, right? The friend runs up all kinds of traffic summonses, right? Then the car is towed, right? The kid comes home and finds his car in down here, right? He told me he just paid six hundred in fines that his friend ran up. Heard it a million times."

Mary Ellen looked at her watch. She was supposed to meet Jewel for coffee.

"Sam," she said, "don't you sometimes wish you were seeing a little more action?"

The phone rang, and he started toward it. He tossed his reply back over his shoulder.

"Hey, sweetheart, if I was back on the street catching squeals, who would look after Miss Beautiful and her kittens?"

As she walked back out the echoing passageway, Mary Ellen felt a stinging perilously close to her eyes. She had invited Sam to their apartment for dinner a number of times, but he had always found some excuse not to go. She was sure she knew why. It was not because Sam might have anything against lesbians. Sam was probably afraid he would feel depressed on visiting the home of a happy couple who were settled down. At least, that was her theory. Sam was tight-mouthed about his feelings, so it was only a guess.

The atmosphere of the place overwhelmed her. The rotting pier settling into the harbor bottom, the patches of blue sky glimpsed through its rusted roof. And the outcast cats who lived there, thriving on society's leavings, proud, tough and free.

She hurried out onto the street, gasping for breath.

The sun was setting over the Jersey Palisades. Against the rosy splendor of the cliffs, the long hulk of Pier 36 rose dark and forbidding, like an abandoned cathedral. Pure and white in the last rays of the sun, the gulls flew in slow circles over its roof.

Lighted like a small city afloat, an Italian cruise ship was making its way up the North River toward the glittering new glass ship terminal at 59th Street, where the bands still played and the baskets of fruit still sat in staterooms.

Jewel was already waiting for her in Murphy's coffee shop. She waved gaily, bouncing up and down on her seat a little, as if she were beckoning from the deck of a yacht.

"Hi," she said as Mary Ellen sat down.

Jewel was the most irrepressible person that Mary Ellen had ever known. She managed to make her crisp uniform look as giddy as high fashion, and her body language was so quick that she made her shield glitter like diamonds. This was curious, when you learned that Jewel was a dead shot, and very serious about her police work.

Mary Ellen had known Jewel for two years before they had both entered the Police Academy, and if she had anything like a close friend, Jewel was probably it. Jewel had a Master's in psychology and some social work, and a minor in English Lit, and had been having a hard time finding a job. An only child from a broken home, she was jittery about security. "I want a career that I can count on," she had told Mary Ellen, "and I *don't* want to be in the military."

"Then be a cop," Mary Ellen had told her.

Mary Ellen had persuaded her to enter rookie training with her. Ironically, now that the police layoffs were happening due to the economy, the police force no longer looked so secure.

Jewel had toughed her way through rookie school, but she shortly had to admit to herself that street patrol was not for her. Neither did she want to wind up at some dreary desk job. Then her flair for words came to the attention of Deputy Commissioner Kent and Sergeant Haskins, who were trying to revive the old police magazine, *Spring 3100*. They must have felt that a lovely and literate young policewoman would be just the ornament that Haskins' little staff of six needed. At any rate, Jewel was now Haskins' right-hand person, and brought a life and a sparkle to the magazine that it hadn't had in years. Her crisp in-depth stories about problems and personalities in the NYPD had already earned her the soubriquet "the next Dorothy Uhnak." It was said she could have made old Al Seedman smile. The beauty of this observation was that Jewel never *tried* to make people smile, particularly men.

Mary Ellen often wondered why she had never fallen in love with Jewel. Away from the job, in the safety of the lesbian world, Jewel had written some startling poetry that was published by Daughters, Inc., and was having a good time between lovers. Mary Ellen recalled one mad weekend when several of them had decided to go out to Fire Island. They never went back, declaring that it was too full of men. (They had laughed and screamed all the way out. Jewel was with a girl named June.) At about one o'clock on Saturday night, in the now-famous Island disco, the Ice Palace, Jewel and June had made all the men stop dancing and stare as they let themselves be carried away in a fiery non-choreographed performance to "Macosa." June slowly sank to her knees and pounded on the floor, making the beat that Jewel danced to, and marking the spot on the floor where she wanted Jewel to dance. Jewel was wearing cut-off shorts and a tie-dye halter, and her bushy, glossy, coal-black hair waved loose in the lights. Against the mirrored walls, her body seemed to give off flashes of light, like a pulsar swimming far off in the luminous reaches of forever. She made everyone in the room feel free, unfettered.

How long ago that was.

The waitress jostled two cups of coffee onto the table, almost spilling them. Jewel, her bush of hair now pulled into a neat bun, had a pad open on the table and was scribbling notes.

"I interviewed the chief medical examiner today," she said. "I actually had to go down to the morgue. I had to go into that room where they keep all the bits and pieces, you know, with tags on them. Wow, the smell . . . yes, I'd like something to eat," she said to the waitress. "Do you have some cheesecake?"

"I'll have a piece of apple pie," Mary Ellen told the waitress.

Jewel snapped her pad shut. "Well, guess what the latest rumor is. More layoffs."

"So what else is new," said Mary Ellen.

Something in her stomach clenched. It was not nice to think about layoffs. The Police Department, caught in the coils of New York's slow, agonizing financial death, now and then reacted as the dying monster twitched, and had laid off 3,000 out of its 30,000 cops in three years. One wanted to think that one was indispensible and unlayoffable.

"The Sarge thinks he is going to lose one person off the staff," said Jewel, "but he doesn't think it will be me. They want to save the magazine, and they like the things I'm doing, so . . ."

"Did the Sarge read in the *Times* about Intro Two?" asked Mary Ellen.

"Funny you should ask," said Jewel. "Just this morning, he talked about California and the forces out there that are allowing open gays to be officers. He said that this would happen in the NYPD over his dead body." She lifted her cup of coffee, raising her pinkie as if she were drinking tea. "So I guess I won't be coming out to my boss for a while."

They sat and picked at their pie and cheesecake. It turned out neither of them was very hungry.

"If I thought I would get away with it," said Mary Ellen slowly, "I'd come out, and the hell with it. But I don't know . . . I've talked about it with Danny quite a lot. He doesn't think it's the right moment yet, and I have to agree."

"Supposing you get laid off?" Jewel asked.

Mary Ellen sighed. "I don't know how they could lay me off. They've got that sex-discrimination lawsuit against them; they *want* to get women onto street patrol, into detective school, you name it. I'm one of their Exhibit A's. I'm hoping that I'm safe."

After a moment, she added, "On the other hand, you never know, do you? I've been a little careless sometimes. Maybe they know about me."

"I also heard another interesting rumor," said Jewel. "Haskins and Kent know lots of people in City Hall, see? So they pick up all kinds of political stuff. Jeannie Colter is coming back into action."

"Oh yeah?" said Mary Ellen. "We're going to be out hassling the prostitutes again?"

"Rumor is, she's running for governor."

"Ambitious lady, thinks she can fill Rockefeller's shoes."

"Yeah," said Jewel, "her with not as much money as Rockefeller, and smaller feet, too. And this is the best part of all. She is gonna do another of her big crusades. This time she is not interested in the prosties at all. She is gonna go after *homosexualism*."

A cold little chill gusted down Mary Ellen's spine. "How do you know this?" she asked.

"Haskins had it from Kent, who had it from Councilman Mannie Greenhaus, who had it from Colter's campaign manager. Colter is going to be giving her kickoff speech at the opening of the Y.W.C.A. on Friday, and get this. I am supposed to go over there and cover it for Haskins. He wants me to do a feature on how this kind of crusade affects police work. I'm even supposed to interview the great lady."

"*Homosexualism?*"

"That's apparently what the born-again crowd call it," said Jewel, raising her pinkie again. "I talked to her headquarters to make an appointment for an interview, and that's the word they use. They can't even bring themselves to use the word homosexuality, let alone gay. Haskins has me doing all kinds of research, you see."

"What religion is she?"

"She's a Baptist, but that's neither here nor there. All those conservative religious people are alike, no matter what church they're from. They all hate us. They all interpret the Bible different when it comes to other things, but they all hate queers and dykes just the same. It's the only thing they agree on."

"What else do you know about Jeannie Colter?"

"Not much," said Jewel nonchalantly. "Rumors that she had some kind of nervous breakdown, that she's become a real religious nut, that she and her husband don't get along too well . . ."

"You don't know much, do you?" said Mary Ellen.

Jewel smiled, and then just as quickly her smile faded. "You know," she said, "back in the Middle Ages, there was an inquisitor in Germany named Conrad Something-or-Other. He traveled around Germany on a mule with a little hunchback assistant, and everybody hid when he came to town. He burned more people at the stake than any other single person in those days. Heretics, witches, queers, you name it. They called him The Witches' Hammer.'"

Jewel drank the last of her coffee.

"Jeannie Colter is going to be the Hammer of the Gays," she said.

Mary Ellen tried to scoff it off. "Every other politician in the country makes anti-gay noises . . ."

Jewel shook her head. "You wait and see. This is no ordinary anti-gay person. I've been reading some of her old speeches. She's touched on it now and then. She's well informed. Most of them just make noises about gay men, right? Well, Colter even knows that lesbians exist, and she hates them too. I'll betcha a teacher made a pass at her once, and she loved it, and now she hates herself."

"Well, thanks for cheering me up," said Mary Ellen.

"Sorry about that," said Jewel.

"Too bad there isn't a little button you can push," said Mary Ellen, "to make people like that go away."

"Yeah, really," said Jewel.

The silent bedside clock said 5:30 with its little flip-down numbers. As Bill looked at it, the 0 flipped to a 1. Marion's head lay heavy on his arm, but he knew Marion was not asleep. He knew Marion was there, feeling the tension in both their bodies.

The bedroom looked just the way it had for years. On the opposite wall, Marion's cuff-links and tie-clasp lay on top of the priceless eighteenth-century English highboy, and their clothes lay on the tapestry-covered wing chair. The fireplace was a romantic-looking brick affair with a marble mantel, but it was nonfunctional, and had one of those little gas-burning fake birch-log things in it. The shuttered windows closed out part of the sound of cars floating up from West Eighth Street four stories below.

The fact was, it had been a rather unsatisfactory hour. Maybe he was getting old. Maybe it was silly to think that one could go on with a long love affair. He had always felt a little nervous at having such a good sex life in his sixties anyway.

When the little flip-down numbers said 6:00, he would have to be dressed and going out the door. Jeannie's hastily arranged fund-raising dinner was at eight, and he had to get home to his apartment, and shower, and dress.

"All right," said Marion, "are you going to tell me what's the matter with you, or do I have to ask you?"

"You're not going to approve of what I'm going to say," said Bill.

His arm was going to sleep, and he moved it a little. Marion must have taken it as peevishness and not wanting to be touched, as he sat up swiftly and looked down at Bill.

Bill lay there with his head propped against the thick rosewood headboard of the wide bed, looking up at Marion. Even with the livid burn scars on it, Marion's torso, half-hidden by the sheet twisted around it, had a lean clean beauty to it, a functional beauty, as if designed to offer little wind resistance—like the cars he helped design. He could imagine that body marked also by the caresses of years, overlaid one on the other, like a century of loving hand-rubbed waxing on a fine old piece of furniture.

"Well, I think you'd better tell me," said Marion.

He reached over to the bedside table, pulled a little cigar from a pack, and lit it with his scratched gold lighter. His bent shoulders, his silky blond hair falling forward and the light playing over his chest and hands, made him look curiously young, curiously vulnerable. Bill ached with a tenderness that was not possible to express.

"Nothing to do with you," he said.

"Not true," said Marion crisply. "Anything that spoils our time together is something to do with me."

Bill heaved a slow sigh.

"Today I gave Jeannie a check for ten thousand dollars for her campaign fund."

Head still bent, Marion drew on the cigar, then blew out the smoke slowly, almost wearily. In the light of the bedside lamp, the pale blue smoke curled up past his hair. He shook his head as if in disbelief.

"I haven't a thing to say," he said. "She's your daughter. I can't criticize."

"Now that I've done it, of course, I feel like an ass," said Bill.

He sat up on the edge of the bed, and reached to the wing chair for his shorts.

"Of course you're an ass," said Marion. "She's your daughter, and I can't criticize, but you're an ass anyway. You're gay, and she is going to the governor's mansion over the bodies of gays, and you are giving her money for her campaign fund."

Bill stood up and pulled on his shorts. Suddenly he felt old, ridiculous, out of shape. He felt that he should run a mile a day on an indoor track somewhere, during his lunch hour, and lose twenty pounds.

"I'm sorry you've lost respect for me," he said.

"I haven't lost respect for you," said Marion. "I've just said a truth."

"True," said Bill.

"And you're going to her dinner."

"Marion . . ." He turned to his lover in anguish. ". . . I'm her father. I have to be there."

"How much a plate?"

"Two hundred and fifty."

"So actually," said Marion, "you're giving her ten thousand and two hundred and fifty."

Bill felt himself growing angry—an anger that he knew he had no right to feel, and whose causes he was unsure of. He pulled on his trousers, pushing his shirttails down into them.

"You don't have to give her anything," said Marion. "Why couldn't you just stick with your original story?

That you'd plowed everything into the South Street thing? That you couldn't spare a dime?"

"Because she and Al would know it was a lie, that's why," Bill shouted. "I always gave her money to run with. Now it's the big one, now it's Albany, and all of a sudden I don't have a cent to give her. She'll know it's a lie. She'll wonder what I have to hide."

"Years of us," said Marion, an icy look in his eyes. At that moment he looked as savage and ruthless as the beautiful killer Englishman in *The Day of the Jackal*.

"I can always stop payment on the check," said Bill.

The moment he said it, he realized how stupid it sounded.

"And stop payment on us, too," said Marion.

Seizing his jacket off the chair, Bill turned on him. "What makes you think it's so simple, all of a sudden?"

And then he had left, striding out of the apartment, into the elevator, into the street. With every step his feet were screaming that they wanted to turn around and go back to Marion's door.

Jeannie was dressing carefully. She hoped that the Lord Jesus Christ looked kindly on a woman's dressing carefully for an occasion where her way of looking was important.

A few years ago, she would have sent to the bank for her jewels, and she would have pulled some stunning creation out of the closet. But tonight her jewels were still in the bank—and she had sent all her flashy, immodest clothes to be resold.

She had spent the afternoon at the beauty salon, having her hair and nails done. Now she slipped on a dove-gray chiffon gown with a high cowled neck and long cuffed sleeves, and a lot of little round buttons up the front. It was very modest and old-fashioned looking. Her father kept telling her that she ought to gain a few pounds, but really, she was glad she looked so slender—like a leader with charisma, emerging from a long hunger strike.

She reached to the gold-plated art nouveau jewelry box that had always been her mother's, and opened it. Nestling in the old blue silky lining was her mother's three-strand pearl choker. Her father had bought it for Cora for their tenth wedding anniversary, and it was the only piece of jewelry that her mother had ever liked and worn. The pearls were real, not cultured. The clasp was studded with yellow diamonds.

She fastened the choker around her throat, trying to keep an image of reverence toward her mother. Nevertheless, for just a split second, the thought flashed through her mind that the choker was her mother's dead hand gently encircling her throat, able to squeeze shut and choke her at any moment.

"I have the oddest thoughts these days," she thought. "I really ought to discuss them with my shrink. Of course, I don't have a shrink, and I doubt that Reverend Irving would make much sense out of them. He'd just tell me that my imagination was working overtime."

She slipped her feet into her modest silver slippers with the thick heels, and took her silver kid bag.

There were voices in the living room—her father and some of the others must have come. She swept out of the bedroom, thinking of all the evenings in her life when she had swept out all dressed for the next major step in her life.

Before she went into the living room, however, she detoured into the study where the family altar was, and closed the door.

She put her bag on the library table, and knelt down before the altar (being careful not to harm the fragile chiffon of her dress). For a long moment, she looked at her mother's Bible lying on the altar. Then she put her hands over her face, and closed her eyes.

The altar was really kind of a joke, she thought. The

only people in the family who prayed hard in front of it were herself and Steve. The other children all behaved in an unsaved manner. And then there was Sidney—still not saved after all the years of praying and gentle nagging on her part. She had read thousands of stories in *Christian Home* and *Sword of the Lord* about how good wives had brought their unsaved husbands to Jesus. Those stories, however, always seemed to happen to other people.

In the darkness behind her hands, she prayed.

She prayed for the salvation of her children, Jessica, Little Cora, and Lance out west, and of her husband. She prayed for strength and light in the months to come. Politics are not an easy thing anymore, and she prayed for the wisdom to do the right thing, the wisdom to stand up to her critics. She prayed above all for self-control, and at the back of her mind there was the tiny nagging thought that she was not yet ready to venture into the political arena, that she needed more time, more rest. Yet God was obviously calling her to take up arms against the moral degeneracy that threatened to engulf this city, and this great country of ours. And that was her last prayer—that God open the ears and hearts of everyone in the city to hear her words about homosexualism.

Guffaws of laughter broke in on her prayer.

She touched her mother's Bible, a thing she always did before leaving the house on occasions like this.

Then she went into the living room.

Her father was there, handsome in a dark suit and a wine-colored brocade tie. His face looked just a little strained—she wondered if he would be overextending himself to give her money for the campaign. But of course not—he was always saying that the business was in great shape, and besides, he and Al had always helped her. She had been a little surprised at the small size of the check, but assumed that more would be forthcoming later.

Tom Winkler was there too, and so was Sidney, wearing shirt-sleeves and jeans. Sidney had sworn he had to work on a piece tonight, and he would not be going. She choked back an impulse to feel angry at him.

She swept up to them with little cries and kisses on the cheeks. It was all "You look lovely, my dear" and "Have you got your speech notes."

And then they were all sweeping out through the lobby, and her father's car was waiting in front. No limousines, no pretentiousness. She was to be the people's candidate, remember? to give the people back their moral rights, remember?

And then they were sweeping under the green awning and through the restaurant. She was flanked by protective men, as befitted a good woman, with her shoulders wrapped in a soft white cashmere, fringed shawl. She smiled at the reporters' flashbulbs, and assured herself that God didn't mind this kind of smile, because smiles were supposed to do His work for Him.

And then she was inside, where the room had been reserved and people were already standing by the bar with drinks. The tables had been set with fresh linen and crystal and bowls of daisies, and candles flamed everywhere. This evening would put $2500 more into the campaign checking account.

Jeannie Laird Colter comes out of political retirement.

The assembled Friends of Jeannie Colter were putting down their drinks, applauding.

While the dinner guests were chatting with Jeannie, Bill Laird slipped out to the elegant teakwood public phone booth near the rest rooms, and dialed Marion's number.

Marion answered.

"Marion, I'm sorry," he said.

"You bloody well should be," said Marion.

Then Marion's voice broke.

"Why am I talking to you like this?" he said. "After all this time? How could I . . ."

His voice broke again.

CHAPTER
Six

The glittering glass facade of the new Y.W.C.A. was brightly lit, baring a glimpse of its cozy office facilities and plant-studded lobbies. It already looked full of life, Jeannie thought, as she got out of the car. She had contributed $5000 to the building fund (at a time when she could ill afford it), and now her heart sang as she looked at it.

Instinctively she smiled, just in time for the photographers' flashes.

"Jeannie, give us another smile," called the *New York Post* photographer.

She did find herself strangely nervous, though.

She flashed him that Miss America smile, showing her beautifully cared-for teeth.

In her briefcase was the tenth and final draft of her speech. Phil Murphy, her new speechwriter, had gone over it and suggested a few things, but it was mainly her own words. So much had happened in a week! Back in her office, her other people were hard at work. John Rice was running a big poll. Her direct-mail people were working up a list of names for her first big appeal for contributions. When she'd left, the office had been full of life, phones ringing, typewriters clicking; after she had finished her speech, the place would be a madhouse.

Behind the police barricades, there was a crowd—larger than she had expected and a lot of women in it. Her PR people had been busy generating interest, hinting at a major announcement. Many women stood excitedly in the crowd—working women, housewives, the kind of women who had idolized her as they had never felt able to idolize Bella Abzug, who was so loud and so leftist. They were waving at her, calling out, "Hey, Jeannie!"

It was a brilliant sunny day.

The main doors were draped with bunting, and across them was the red-white-and-blue ribbon that she would cut.

The podium was flanked with cases of red, white and blue carnations, and faced down the broad concrete steps to the garden plaza in front of the building. There, several hundred chairs were already crammed with spectators. The standees spilled back onto the street, where the police barricades were set up, and several cops were directing traffic.

As she walked toward the chairs where the dignitaries would sit, behind the podium, she felt herself soaring toward a new and untrodden pinnacle of her life.

The ceremony was short and simple. The Reverend John Markis, of the First Presbyterian Church on Queens Boulevard, read a prayer. A choral group sang some hymns, their voices sounding bravely pure and a little thin through the raunchy din of the daytime traffic. Then various dignitaries—the president of the Y.W.C.A., someone from the mayor's office—said a few words.

Finally it was time for the key speech. The master of ceremonies was saying:

". . . So it is my great pleasure to introduce to you a great Christian woman who has served with honor in our state legislature—and who has gone on record as a tireless crusader for decency in this great city of ours, and in this great country of ours. I give you . . . Jean Laird Colter!"

As Jeannie stepped to the podium with her type-written pages of speech, the crowd's applause was almost drowned out by the throbbing thunder of a Port Authority helicopter flying overhead.

She stood very straight and tall before the microphone, her eyes searching the crowd, and waited for the helicopter noise to die away.

She crossed her arms over her chest.

One thing was wrong with that crowd. Her father was not there. During the past few days, he had made a big show of being busy with architects and contractors and blueprints, talking endlessly of the renovation of the old brick apartment houses on Catherine Slip, next door to his future house. Only Uncle Al was down there in the first row, grinning up at her proudly.

Finally the street was quiet, and she began to speak, her amplified voice ricocheting off the facades and the windows of the brownstone buildings across the street.

"My fellow Christians," she said, "today we celebrate..."

She started in a low key, speaking of the new Y.W.C.A. itself, and what it would mean to New York City—fit bodies and fit minds for thousands of decent young Christian women. Then she slowly broadened her focus, speaking of the resurgence of Christian faith across the country, and the moral problems in the great decayed urbanopolis that was becoming typical of America today. When she began to speak of homosexualism, she caught the fire and the cadence of her best speeches, and her strong voice rolled over the crowd like an ocean breaker, sweeping everything before it.

"At this very moment," she intoned, "we have before our city council a bill that would grant specific civil rights to the worst element in this city of ours—the homosexuals. A bill that would grant them the right to work wherever they wish, to live wherever they wish. It is curious that these homosexuals should ask for total access to our world, for in a sense they already have it. They *are* everywhere. They *are* legion."

Her voice cracked out over the crowd like a whip. Even the cops on the street were listening to her.

"It is no secret that our city has become one of the homosexual capitals of the United States. The city is riddled with their unsavory meeting places—their bars, their bathhouses, their stores where they cater to each other's perverted tastes. And yet on top of this, they ask for *freedom*. The freedom to teach your innocent children in any school in the city. The freedom to work side by side with your God-fearing young sons and daughters on any job in the city. The freedom to live next door to you in any neighborhood of any borough of this city. In other words, the *freedom* to make the acquaintance of your sons and daughters, and to seduce them into the homosexual way of life."

She was aware of the TV cameras zooming in on her, the reporters scribbling notes, checking their tape recorders to make sure the tape reels were turning. They knew the beginning of a Jeannie Colter attack when they saw one.

". . . And so I urge you to let the city council know how you feel about this bill. Write them, wire them, telephone them. Urge the unions or organizations to which you belong to speak out. If you are in any doubt as to how to contact them, call my office or drop by, and my friendly staff will do anything they can to help you . . ."

She was very excited now, her body vibrating all over, and her clenched fist hammered at the air, in a gesture that people knew as her trademark. A hundred flashbulbs went off, capturing that raised fist in a blurred still. Now she was back on the stage, devouring the audience with a passionate monologue, feeling a personal relationship with every person in the house —back on the spotlight stage in the Miss America contest, rocking the place with her modern rewrite of Iphigenia about to be sacrificed by her father (and why the judges had awarded her the runner-up spot and not the Miss America crown for that, she would never understand as long as she lived).

The crowd was applauding wildly, cheering. A stout woman, poorly dressed, with a baggy sweater—she looked like a Grand Central Station charwoman— came rushing up with a tiny bunch of daisies that she had probably bought from a sidewalk vendor, and shoved them into Jeannie's hand. She took them, smiling, clasped the woman's hands, kissed her on her damp cheek, trying not to notice the woman's sourfish smell of sweat, and said, "God bless you."

The reporters were racing for telephone booths.

Then Tom Winkler came up with a young policewoman who carried a notepad. "This young lady is scheduled to interview you for the police magazine," he reminded Jeannie.

"Oh, yes," said Jeannie, trying to disguise her disapproval of the girl's uniform. She didn't think the Police Department was a good place for women. "Why don't we go inside and sit down?"

In the precinct station house, Danny Blackburn caught the tail end of the Colter woman's speech as he came through the locker room.

PO Benny Forbes had a little transistor radio in his locker, and he always tried to catch the news if he was around. Mary Ellen had the day off and Danny had been put with Det. Martin Garapullo on an undercover assignment because of a shortage of detectives. He was unshaven, dressed sloppy and dirty like the type of bum who hangs out in warehouse areas, hoping to find an oil drum to make a fire in, and a dry corner to sleep in. The two of them had been trying to come up with information on some truck hijackings. It had been a discouraging day, they had come up with nothing, and Danny wanted to report to his chief and take a shower and go off duty and have a drink.

As Danny walked by the radio, he heard the deep thrilling voice. ". . . They *are* everywhere. They *are* legion . . ."

He stopped and Martin walked on.

"Who's they?" said Danny.

"Fags," said PO Benny. "It's Jeannie Colter. She's back in action, and she's going after the fags."

"No kidding," said Danny, trying to look totally unconcerned. At moments like this, one's training and discipline, especially in UC work, came in very handy. He was sure that his face did not betray anything but cynical amusement.

"That dingdong broad went after the prosties," he said, "and they're still in business."

Trying to look weary and unconcerned, he went slouching on, heading for the chief's office.

Behind him, he heard Forbes say to Mullan, "Well, we're gonna be a little more busy after this. Lotsa action around the faggot bars. Pansies getting beat up. Maybe close a few bars down. Fun, huh?"

Downtown, on South Street, Bill Laird had made the excuse to the contractor that he had a luncheon engagement. He headed out to the street where his car was parked.

He sat slumped in the car and snapped on the radio just in time for the twelve o'clock WNBC news. Just as he'd expected, the station aired a few sentences of her speech.

Jeannie's powerful voice filled the car, that voice that could fill a huge auditorium like the Mormon Tabernacle Choir. "I urge you to speak out against this dispicable bill . . ."

Bill snapped off the radio, started the engine, and drove aimlessly on down South Street, under the

Brooklyn Bridge. Finally he pulled over and parked by the water, near the Seaport Museum.

He stood watching the gulls glide over the oily East River and the white steamy smoke rise from the stacks of the Con Ed power plant on the opposite shore. He felt sick to his stomach.

And I paid for that speech, he thought.

He wanted to call Marion, but he didn't dare. Marion would give him no sympathy.

So he wandered aimlessly onto the museum dock, hardly noticing when the girl in the ticket booth said, "Hello, Mr. Laird." He actually bought an admission ticket to board the *Peking* and climbed slowly up the gangplank of the great silent square-rigger.

Beneath his feet, the huge steel hull seemed to echo like a cavern. The empty masts and spars towered over his head, never again to feel the good lashing wet of a North Atlantic storm. He walked slowly aft, hands dug into his pockets, and leaned on the starboard rail near the stern. He looked out at the wide blue reaches of the harbor, at the far-off hazy towers of the Verrazano Bridge, at the Narrows leading out to sea. He had a lump in his throat, so it was surprising that a few tears did not roll down his cheeks—tears as salty as that sea of freedom he would never reach.

If anyone was watching him, they would imagine that he was standing there thinking of another Save-Old-New-York project.

Mary Ellen did not hear about the Colter speech till she came home from grocery shopping.

When Mary Ellen reached the apartment, shortly after seven, Liv was in the kitchen making one of her exotic and nameless Swedish-American-hybrid casseroles, and she said over her shoulder, "There is this lady on the television making bad speeches about gay people. I saw it on the six o'clock news."

Mary Ellen made a slight face. She went into the tiny kitchen, put the sacks on the table, hugged Liv from behind, and reached around her with one hand to filch a tidbit from the casserole.

"Is her name Jeannie Colter, by any chance?" she asked.

"Yes, that is the name," said Liv, grinning, making like she was going to spear Mary Ellen's hand with her cooking fork.

"Jewel told me Colter was going to do that," said Mary Ellen.

Liv turned around in her arms and aimed the cooking fork at Mary Ellen's chest. "Ah," she said, "so you have seen Jewel." She was still grinning, but Mary Ellen was not so sure she was still amused.

"Look," she said, "Jewel is an old friend, nothing between us, a sister officer. I've told you that a million times. I had a cup of coffee with her at Murphy's Coffee House the other day, and she told me all the gossip from City Hall."

Liv was still smiling, but now more softly. She played the cooking fork gently, teasingly, over Mary Ellen's throat.

"Jewel is lovely," she said. "Very lovely."

"I know Jewel is lovely," said Mary Ellen. "I've seen the long, long line of her lovers. But I'm not standing in that line. Understand?"

"If you are unfaithful to Liv," said Liv, "Liv will put you in her casserole, and *eat* you!"

The two of them started laughing. Mary Ellen grabbed the knife from the chopping board, where a few bits of onion still lay, and the two of them had a mock sword-fight around the kitchen, gently parrying and thrusting with their little weapons, and saying "Aha!" like pirates.

This was the joy of coming home to Liv. This was the joy of knowing her, of always being surprised at the rich train of things that came out of her head, at her fantasies and her sweet nonsense. Loving Liv

122

was never the same two days in a row. Every day you always started from the beginning, but always with a feeling of sweet security. Ingmar Bergman's movies (which she had seen on television) would—the later ones, anyway—have you think that Swedish women were grim and Gothic and a little unbalanced. But if Liv was Bergman stuff, she was *Smiles of a Summer Night,* not *Silence.* If Liv was a northern forest, she was that forest in springtime, teeming with animals and insects and strange little wildflowers.

Later that evening, however, as they ate the casserole and petted Kikan and watched TV, it struck Mary Ellen that the lady making speeches intended to take Liv away from her.

They turned to the ten o'clock news report, hoping to get an in-depth coverage of the speech.

Sure enough, the screen switched from the newscaster to a live clip showing Jeannie Colter taking a pair of scissors and cutting the striped ribbon across the doorway of the Y.W.C.A. Then Colter was at the podium, shaking her fist and saying, ". . . They *are* everywhere. They *are* legion."

Mary Ellen felt the mirth go out of her, replaced by the sudden pouring-in of a cold anxiety. As a police officer, she knew very well that the actions of public persons often prompted actions by private persons, and that these actions often ended up on the books of the New York City police precincts, and in the hospitals and the morgue. Every action that made a public splash spread its psychological ripples across the city.

She looked at Liv, who was munching a mouthful of casserole, gazing at the TV set, her face bathed in the bluish light. Kikan was sneaking up to eat from Liv's plate. Liv's expression was that of an innocent beyond the reach of Jeannie Colter's speech.

"It's a pretty violent speech," Mary Ellen said.

Liv shrugged. "Yes," she said. "But it is only words."

Mary Ellen shook her head. "Not true. Words make people do things. What she is *really* saying is, get the perverts out of this town."

She went to the telephone and dialed Danny's number. He didn't answer, so she called the Spike Bar. Danny was there, of course, and he sounded pretty drunk.

"We're gonna be responding to scenes caused by that bitch," said Danny thickly. "Matter of fact, couple sergeants—at roll call, right?—coupla sergeants were already briefing the guys to pay extra attention to the bars. Ya know, beatings and stuff."

"*They* don't give a damn if gays get beaten."

"Yeah, but they don't want things to get out of hand, either," said Danny. "Captain Bader, right? Says that nobody beats up *nobody* in his precinct. Says if straights beat up faggots, or if faggots beat up straights, they *all* go to the tank."

The next morning, Jeannie sailed up to her father's rooftop breakfast table with an armload of newspapers.

"It's wonderful," she said. "It's on the front page everywhere, even the *Times*."

Her father had a lot of blueprints spread out, and seemed unduly engrossed in them.

"That's wonderful, sweetheart," he said. "Congratulations."

He reached for the phone and called up one of his contractors, and had a long conversation about the plumbing in the Peake & Sturgis building.

Feeling decidedly deflated, Jeannie sat down, poured herself coffee, and ate several croissants, still flaky and melted-butter-fresh from the patisserie on Lexington Avenue. After all the intense activity, she was actually starved.

When her father hung up, she said, "You know, I have the distinct impression that you don't give a damn."

Wearily her father removed his glasses and polished the lenses, then put them back on, and looked at her through them.

"Jeannie, for God's sake," he said. "It's been the dream of my life—my *entire* life—to get my hands on a major piece of real estate on South Street. I've got an awful lot on my mind right now. You can't expect me to drop everything and just . . . go on the campaign trail with you. You're a big girl now. You go on and run for governor, and I'll give you my blessing and whatever financial help I can afford, but I can't be involved in what you're doing."

"You mean you might donate some more money?"

"We'll see," he said evasively.

"Uncle Al gave me a personal check of his yesterday," she said proudly. "Five thousand dollars."

"That's very good of Al," said her father, already picking up the phone again.

Jeannie sipped her coffee with growing irritation, listening to him talking to a boat manufacturer downtown, inquiring as to prices and extras and so forth on a twenty-foot fiberglass cabin cruiser.

The families of political figures were *supposed* to be supportive and helpful of their candidates. In the filing cabinet of every American's memory were heartwarming photos of the wives, children, et cetera, of the Kennedys and the Carters and the Rockefellers. But her family seemed to be different. Only Uncle Al and Steve seemed to care. Her other children were ingrossed in their heathenish pursuits, and her father was childishly engrossed with his building blocks, and her husband was engrossed in his book and in China. And her mother was in the grave.

When her father hung up, she said, "You're buying a *boat*?"

A small smile came to Bill's lips.

"Did you know that, among other things, I own a *pier* down there? Two piers, in fact. Old ones. One of them is in bad shape, but the other is pretty sound.

I want my own little boat to get around the area in, inspect things from the water. Part of the project is going to include a little marina for pleasure boats. Hopefully these boats will be owned by the people who are hopefully going to rent my apartments."

Jeannie shook her head.

"I think you are having your second childhood," she said.

A spark of anger raced through her father's eyes.

"Is there anything wrong with that?" he said.

As the days passed, however, Jeannie forgot her aloneness. She was caught up in a swirl of events of her own making.

Her immediate objective was to bring about the defeat of Intro Two in the city council. She plunged into lobbying, calling up city council members, inviting them to lunch, talking, haranguing gently. A couple of them owed her political favors, and she now made it plain that she was calling up the IOU's, in the form of their vote against the bill.

In this she was not alone. The local dignitaries of the Catholic Church, the benevolent associations of policemen and firemen, the teachers' union, various other unions, were all putting the heat on the city council.

Jeannie was shocked, however, to find how powerful the homosexual lobbyists were. They were battle-hardened from all their experience in Washington and other major cities around the country. They were politically sophisticated. They sang a siren song of human rights, and kept harping on the fact that many states and major cities in the United States had passed similar homosexual rights bills. They painted a picture of New York City languishing in a Middle Ages of repression and bigotry, while the rest of the country sailed on into the bright sunlight of liberty.

The city council, caught in the middle, squirmed uncomfortably.

One day Harrison Hotchkiss of *The New York Times* asked her: "Jeannie, why are you coming out against gays only *now*? Intro Two has been brought up before."

"Because," she said tartly, "on the two previous times when Intro Two was voted on by the council, I was very busy fighting pornography and massage parlors. And, if you'll check the record, you'll find that I did speak out against Intro Two. Since then, the homosexuals have made tremendous inroads. I now regard them as a major threat, and I am now mounting a major campaign against them."

"You vowed that you would run porn and sex parlors out of the city," said the reporter. "Have you vowed the same about the gay people?"

"Let's put it this way," she said crisply. "If there were no homosexuals in New York, the quality of life in this city would be that much higher."

For the first time now, she felt the weight of homosexual opinion in New York.

Her office had already taken hundreds of phone calls from outraged homosexuals. Most of them gave their names, a few of them didn't. The mail carriers started delivering whole bundles of letters written by these people. Some of these, too, were anonymous, but most of them were signed.

On the sidewalk outside her campaign headquarters, members of the National Gay Activist Alliance were picketing. They carried signs like OFF OUR BACK, JEANNIE. There were rumors that a march was being planned, which would parade thousands of homosexuals past her Park Avenue office so that she could see how many there were.

On the more serious level, she was surprised at the number of city and state political figures who were sympathetic to the homosexuals. They contacted her by phone and letter to let her know they thought her actions were deplorable. A couple of them had the audacity to remind her that she owed *them* political favors.

Most upsetting of all were the threats. A few times, Gertrude Utley picked up the phone and found an anonymous caller telling her that if Jeannie Colter didn't shut up, her office would be bombed, or something might happen to her children, or the like. Gertrude was fairly hardened to kook calls, but there was something about these calls that shook her.

Jeannie notified the Police Department about these threats, and the office was put under close watch. Early one morning, the police arrested a young homosexual with a spray can who had just written JEANNIE THE SCREAMING BEAUTY QUEEN across the office windows. One of the staff got some stain remover and hastily removed the graffito.

Even *The New York Times* seemed to take their side and came out with a cautiously worded editorial that maybe it was time for the city, and the country, to face up to the civil-rights question here. Jeannie contacted the *Times* and told them she thought *that* was deplorable.

In the first week after her Y.W.C.A. speech, she found herself the target of what she regarded as more vicious abuse than in all the years of her political career rolled together.

On another front, her campaign for governor went ahead. The result of John Rice's first poll was very encouraging. It showed Jeannie with a 20 percent popularity margin over Milt Kossin, the most likely Democrat to run, and a 10 percent margin over the republican incumbent, Governor Grant Clark.

The first direct mailing went out. Part of it went to 10,000 well-to-dos on her list, with a letter calculated to tickle their egos, appealing for $100 each for the campaign fund. The rest of the names were hundreds of people of more modest means, who were appealed to as the salt of the earth, and who hopefully would give what they could. Her goal was to raise a million dollars, and the money was already rolling in.

Tom Winkler was planning for her to stump the state speaking in every major city, speaking on every local radio and TV station they could cover, speaking to women's clubs and firemen and American Legionnaires and church groups and farmers' co-ops, and everything and anything they could line up in New York City and all across the state. Go to the grass roots. Get the people to feel that you're their next-door neighbor. Get the people to feel that they'll have one of their own in the State House in Albany, for once.

"You ought to quit wearing such good clothes," said Winkler. "Put all that Bergdorf-Goodman stuff in the closet for a while, if you'll pardon the expression, and go buy a few things at Korvette's. You want to look like the nice lady down the block who drives her own children to school."

"You're right," said Jeannie, and she obeyed him.

Last but not least, Winkler persuaded her to finish up her book, and give it a catchy political title. So she spent an hour a day polishing it and dividing it into chapters. A contract to publish it in paperback was signed, and the book would be out as soon as possible.

Danny and Armando were sitting in a quiet corner of the Spike Bar, talking. They kept their voices low, so that Lenny wouldn't hear.

"There's definitely going to be trouble in this town if the bill gets voted down," said Armando.

"You mean a riot?" said Danny.

"I mean a riot," said Armando, "that might make Watts look like a nice quiet bridge game."

It was noon, the bar was empty, and Danny was still off duty. Armando didn't go to work 'till later in the day.

"How do you know?" Danny asked.

"I know," said Armando. "The gay activist hotheads

are planning a big demonstration on the day of the vote, if the bill is defeated. And a lot of nonpolitical people are going to get sucked into it, and things are going to get out of hand. The anger in town is incredible. I can feel it rolling across the bar at me, every night."

Danny could feel his shoulders slumping. He and Mary Ellen had talked about this eerie contingency so often—the possibility that someday they might be ordered to raise their sticks or draw their guns against their own brothers and sisters. Rioting was inexcusable. But they had no way of condemning the anger that might feed that riot because each of them lived with that anger. Danny knew that Mary Ellen felt the same way.

Danny knew that the lie he was living almost didn't seem worth it.

A week later, Bill Laird was there when Jeannie Colter made her second major anti-gay speech.

He had sensed that Jeannie was becoming suspicious of him. So he had decided—very much against his better judgment and his instincts—to attend.

He sat there in the front row, wearing his best navy suit, arms crossed across his chest, and listened to Jeannie's attack. Before coming here, he had had a quarrel with Marion over his plans to attend. "You've never been a father," Bill had yelled at his lover, "you have no idea how torn I feel." This time, however, it had been Marion who walked out the door. And, in the past, there had been the time when he could not conceive the very idea of yelling at Marion, brave Marion, who had lain moaning in agony in the hospital hoping he would come.

The short speech was at a press conference held at Jeannie's headquarters. The place was crammed with reporters and TV camera crews. Halfway through the speech, he was amazed to see her haul out a list of names.

"I have said that homosexuals are everywhere," she said, her voice cracking through the room, "and I know whereof I speak. My staff and I have been paying close attention to this question for some time. These people are a spiderweb whose strands reach into every area of life in our country. They reach into the ranks of our city officials, our law-enforcement people, our teachers, our businessmen, even our religious leaders. We must put away the old myth that homosexualism is confined to the theater and the dance and interior decoration. It is found in all walks of American life today, at every level. It is there"—she stabbed at the air with every word, for emphasis—"*because . . . we . . . have . . . permitted . . . it . . . to . . . be . . . there.*"

Pausing for effect, she adjusted her glasses and picked up her list, looked at it, then scanned the audience with her burning eyes.

"I have here," she said, "a list of one hundred names. I am not going to *read* this list. And it's by no means a complete list. But it is a list of homosexuals *of both sexes* who can be found at every level of life in our city. These are *not* open homosexuals. There are many of those in New York, and some of their names are probably known to you. No, these people on my list are known as homosexuals only to a few. You would be very interested to know the positions they occupy in our city."

Bill sat there stunned, feeling exactly as though a crane-load of something weighing three tons had swung and smacked straight into his stomach. And that something was fear. He wondered if his name or Marion's name was on that list.

And then he realized what Jeannie's intention was. Any closet gay of position and power listening to her was *supposed* to feel that fear.

He pulled himself together. She couldn't possibly know about him and Marion. He had been too careful. If Jeannie knew, she would have attacked him about it long ago.

131

But whose names *were* on the list?

An excited buzzing went through the room. When her speech was over, the press people present literally sprinted for the nearest telephones. They badgered her for the list, but she refused to show it to them.

After the press conference, Bill could not contain his curiosity about the list, and he invited Jeannie, Sidney and Winkler up to his apartment for a cup of something.

While the housekeeper, Ann, was making tea and coffee, they all sank into the sofas. Jeannie was looking very pleased with herself, with the big rock that she had just hurled into the pond that was New York. Her eyes were sparkling. Sidney, however, looked grim, and Winkler looked noncommittal, sitting on the edge of the sofa and cracking his knuckles compulsively.

Sidney looked at Jeannie. "I can't believe your list number," he said bluntly. "The cheapest McCarthyite trick in the book."

"Yes, but it worked, didn't it?" she said gaily.

"It plunged the country into ten years of fear and stupidity, if that's what you mean," said Sidney.

Jeannie sat up, realizing that Sidney was serious, "Darling, you're supposed to be a conservative. You're supposed to approve of getting rid of people like that."

Sidney stood up, hands in pockets, and looked down at her from his six-foot-two height. "I'm for *dignified* conservatism," he said.

"Sidney!" she said, really distressed now.

"Good night, Mrs. Republican," Sidney said, and walked out of the room. They heard the hall door close.

"Well, I never . . ." said Jeannie, gasping.

Winkler went into the kitchen for a glass of water, and Bill followed him.

"Did you advise her to do that?"

Winkler was filling a glass of water at the sink. "As a matter of fact, I didn't," he said. He popped a tranquilizer into his mouth, and washed it down. "I advised her against it."

"She may have made a grave political mistake," said Bill.

Winkler shrugged. "I know," he said. "She may scare people enough to get Intro Two voted down. But this may come back to haunt her, as far as the governor's race is concerned."

Bill went back into the living room. Jeannie was sitting alone there, amid all the Chippendale antiques and brocade draperies, looking very beautiful and very lost. The list of names lay on the coffee table in front of her.

Bill sat down by her, and put out his hand toward the list.

"May I?" he said, as casually as possible.

"Sure," she said, shrugging, not looking at him.

The list was a Xerox of names and addresses in the New York area and New York State, arranged in alphabetical order, in two columns, starting with Leonard Berkowitz, 85-23 259th Avenue, Floral Park, Queens, to Mr. and Mrs. Andrew Christoff, Silver Lake Way, Syracuse, New York. Scanning quickly, Bill did not see his name anywhere, nor Marion's.

"Who the hell are these people?" he said.

"Don't curse, Dad," she said. "It's not Christian. They're just a page from my mailing list. But there *are* people like that out there. Everywhere."

"I'm shocked," said Bill, though inwardly he was a little relieved.

Her lovely brown eyes, fringed with just a touch of mascara and eye shadow, turned toward him in anguish.

"Oh, Dad, not you too?" she said. "Doesn't anybody understand?"

"Listen, sweetheart," he said, "your list is a lie. But

133

it *also* isn't Christian to hate quite that much. Why do you hate those people the way you do?"

Her eyes stayed fastened on him, and he was sucked back into her childhood, when she was the most appealing and infuriating child he could imagine, and he would have walked through machine-gun fire for her.

"I hate them because the Bible says to hate them," she said simply, "and because Mother said to hate them."

"Your mother?" he said, feeling that three-ton weight of fear cargo swinging into his stomach again. "What did she know about things like that?"

"Nothing, I imagine," said Jeannie. "She just hated them on general principle. She always warned me against them."

Bill's instincts told him that Jeannie was telling the truth. Cora had turned the child against homosexuals in general but had never dared to breathe a word against her own husband. A strange loyalty, that, considering the tensions that they'd lived in during the last years of Cora's life, when he was sure that she knew about Marion.

Bill took Jeannie's hand and patted it. "Now, Jeannie, tell me the truth," he said. "Did any woman ever, uh, make a pass at you?"

She raised her deep dark eyes to his again. The pupils were wide and dark, with some emotion that he could not know.

"Oh no," she said. "I never even let women be *friends* with me, I guess that's why . . ." She seemed to search for words. ". . . why I don't have any women friends, never did. The only woman I could ever be close with was Mother."

Suddenly she was sobbing against Bill's shoulder.

"I have to make up with Sidney," she said against his jacket sleeve. "I can't live without him. And I can't have our marriage break up while I'm running for office."

Late that same night, while she was working on the night shift, Mary Ellen and Danny found themselves responding to a radio run that turned into a wild car chase. Real life being what it is, and police work being different from the movies or TV, neither of them had ever participated in one of these theatrical affairs.

They had been driving east along Houston Street, when they heard the squeal on the radio. A patrol car a little farther downtown had spotted a wanted car, a maroon Chevy with the license plate 371-HEX, and had called for assistance, saying the car was heading onto the north ramp of the FDR Drive, and was heading north.

"Cruiser two-oh-four responding," she said into her mike as she tromped on the accelerator and Danny flicked on the lights and siren. Their tires squealed, and they flew along Houston Street and went screeching into the north entrance ramp just as the maroon Chevy flew past them at seventy miles an hour.

As her squad car peeled onto the FDR Drive, it fishtailed a couple of times, but Mary Ellen skillfully straightened it out and roared after the Chevy. In her rearview mirror, she could see behind her the flashing red light of the patrol car that had sighted the Chevy. She and Danny knew the Chevy didn't have a chance —patrols farther uptown would be flocking to every entrance ramp of the FDR Drive, setting up roadblocks.

The Chevy had no more speed, and quickly she and Danny drew even with it. The driver, a white man, tried to sideswipe her.

Suddenly, at 34th Street, the Chevy swerved off the FDR Drive and onto an empty little service road that ran along the water, to service some Port Authority buildings. Reacting quickly, Mary Ellen also whipped onto the service road.

Shortly she and Danny drew even with the Chevy, and forced it right into a great pile of sand and gravel, where a few city-owned cement mixers stood. She braked their own screeching, skidding car to a stop.

Instantly, she and Danny fell out, service revolvers in hand. The Chevy driver and his woman were also scrambling out.

"Police," Mary Ellen yelled hoarsely. "Don't move!"

The woman was floundering in the sand pile. The man, shaken up and jelly-kneed, went for his own gun, but then he stumbled in a pothole and fell flat on his face. His gun went spinning off across the pavement. Mary Ellen and Danny were on him in a second, and had him handcuffed before he could get up.

Just then, the other squad car came screeching to a halt behind them. Back up the FDR Drive, Mary Ellen could see the flashing red lights of other cars responding to the scene.

The sand-covered woman scuffled briefly with the four police officers. Shortly both fugitives were lined up by the squad cars, frisked, handcuffed, and read their rights. It was two good arrests, and Jewel would probably get to write up the chase briefly in *Spring 3100*. The red lights bathed the waterfront area in an eerie pulsing light.

One of the other male officers grinned at Mary Ellen and said, "Hey, Cuffs, that's what I call cuttin' 'em off at the pass."

Back at the station house, Mary Ellen and Danny were able to bask in the pleasant notoriety of the moment. They were patted on the back and kidded a lot.

"Hey," said Lieutenant Mondello, "if you two make such beautiful music together as *cops*, just think of the symphony when you get *married*." The whole place broke up into hee-haws and honks of glee.

Captain Bader, however, had more class. A tall heavyset man with a sad expression, he lived in Yonkers with his wife and two children. Mary Ellen had always liked him—partly because he never gave her any sexist nonsense. He let her do the job, and then he expected her to do it well, or else.

"Nice work, Mary Ellen," he said warmly. "One of these days, you'll be taking my job away from me."

When Mary Ellen went home that night, she had a glow that she hadn't felt for weeks.

Liv was already home, and had cooked some spaghetti with clam sauce.

"You are in an excellent mood," Liv said.

"*Excellentissimo*," said Mary Ellen, hugging her. The day's work had almost made her forget about the rumors of a gay riot.

They kept hugging each other all during dinner and had scarcely finished the last mouthful when they felt impelled to adjourn to the bedroom.

Their bed was an invention of two busy working women—a queen-size mattress and box spring that stood right on the floor. It was covered with a lush blue-velour fitted slipcover that was sensual to the body touch, and easy to pull off and wash. Even the pillows and the quilt were covered in blue velour. Liv had sewn duplicate velour sets in gold and bronze-green. To make the bed, all you had to do was plump the pillows and fold the quilt, and the bed was neat as a sofa.

They had a lot of fun undressing each other, playing with each other's hair and nipples. Finally their jeans were in two heaps on the floor and they were sprawled tenderly on the velour bed.

At first they both giggled a lot. Then suddenly they got very serious, and Liv said softly, "Draw me."

This was a child's game that Liv loved. They had made it into something passionately tender and adult. Bending over her, Mary Ellen was the "artist." With one finger, she gently traced the outline of Liv's face, then her eyebrows, eyes, nose, lips. Everywhere that she "drew," she left a kiss.

Next, shifting down along Liv's body a little, she "drew" Liv's neck and shoulders, and finally traced her finger tenderly along Liv's arms and each of her fingers.

137

Liv fondled Mary Ellen's head as she kept tracing and kissing.

"Oh, draw me, looove," she said.

"Draw me more."

"Draw me, draw me."

Afterward, Mary Ellen lay listening to the sound of deep gentle breathing as Liv drifted off to sleep, but she was too keyed-up to sleep.

It would have been nice to describe the day's work to her father. She didn't give Liv all the details, as she never wanted to worry her. But her father would have smiled in appreciation, maybe even laughed at her imitation of the fugitive falling on his ass.

Her father, Ed Frampton, had been the quintessential New York cop. An honest cop, too—never on the take, as far as she knew. More important, her father had raised her after her mother died, when she was ten. She had grown up at horse races and poker games and gun-club rifle ranges, surrounded by cops, sitting on her father's lap, listening to the men talk about hunting and fishing and guns and perpetrators.

He taught her to shoot early—gun games at carnivals, clay pigeons, targets, you name it. He gave her a .22 rifle, later a Winchester, .3030, and taught her the care and respect that goes with responsible gun ownership. Her father was a peaceful man, and in all his years as a cop, he had never killed a man. He was very proud of that. On summer days off, they would drive up to his little cabin on a wild ten acres in southwestern Massachusetts, and have fun shooting the Kentucky rifle and a few other fine old guns he'd pinched pennies to collect. The guns were still up there at the cabin, which was hers now. Her father had planned carefully—a neat will, money in the bank for ready estate-tax payment. He was always saying that you never knew when lightning would strike. And strike it did, just one month before mandatory retirement, when she was a senior at NYU. A fleeing suspect, a junkie with a record, shot him dead on the sidewalk at 125th Street and Amsterdam.

Lying in bed, Mary Ellen could feel the tears rising in her throat, and she swallowed them back.

Ed Frampton's funeral had been one of the best attended police funerals in recent years, and she had felt the weight of the officers' sympathy—they remembered her as the little curly-headed girl who had sat on his lap and cut the cards, and now they saw her as the motherless, fatherless, daughter left to bury that flag-draped coffin and face the world, alone.

She struggled through her senior year because she knew he would have wanted it. By then there was talk of sexual integration in the NYPD (Washington, D.C. and some other American cities already had women officers on street patrol). She applied to the Police Academy and was accepted. She was the first woman sergeant in Manhattan. One reason she had advanced, she was sure, was that she was Ed Frampton's daughter. Captain Bader had known her father pretty well.

Her father had never known she was a lesbian. All that came after the junkie's bullet. But she was sure she could have told him, and she was sure he would have been finally able to accept it. His philosophy had always been: my daughter right or wrong. He had never pushed dating and marriage at her. The only thing he had pushed at her were education and a career—"neither of which your poor mother ever got," he'd add.

Suddenly Mary Ellen became aware that Liv was lying with open eyes, looking at her.

"Your thoughts are so noisy," said Liv, "that they woke me up."

"Loud as sirens, huh?" Mary Ellen turned over and embraced her under the quilt.

Seven

The next morning, Jeannie was not too surprised when she got a visit from the police commissioner of New York City.

Benny Manuella, commissioner since 1976, was not a stranger to her. She had gotten to know him during her antiporn and anti-massage-parlor crusades. She knew that he had come up through the ranks. Above all, he was very protective of what he regarded as his underpaid, overworked police force. Up till now, Manuella had always been very cooperative with her reform efforts.

That morning, however, he was visibly disturbed at the statements she'd made at the press conference.

Gertrude Utley showed him in, and the two of them talked in her office at the campaign headquarters, with the door shut.

"I understand," said Manuella, "that you have made some allegations about homosexuals in the New York Police Department."

She looked at him with her eyes wide and steady, though her stomach was just a bit nervous.

"I did not make any statement to that effect," she said.

"At the press conference yesterday, you had a list of names," he said. "You implied that some of these names are members of the NYPD."

"No." she said. "I don't believe I implied that at all."

They had settled into the deadly word game, looking each other in the eyes. Jeannie wondered if Manuella could sense her nervousness. Cops were like sharks—they could smell blood a mile away.

"Well, could you enlighten me as to exactly what you did say?" asked Manuella.

"I'd be happy to," she said.

She made a show of fishing in some folders on her desk and pulled out a copy of the statement that she'd read to the press yesterday. "Here is what I said. All I said was that homosexuals are found on some police forces in the country."

He read her statement swiftly, but she knew that he did not miss a single word. Then he looked at her silently for a moment.

"Mrs. Colter, let me put it this way. Do you have any information about homosexuals in the NYPD?"

"Not at the present time."

"And supposing you were to come into possession of this kind of information?"

She looked him right in the eye. "I would campaign to have these people exposed and fired. I do not believe that homosexuals are fit to be law-enforcement officials. By their very nature, they are in violation of the law."

His eyes bored into hers. She knew now that, however cooperative Manuella had been in the past, he was on the verge of becoming an enemy of hers.

"Mrs. Colter, this list of names . . . may I see it?"

All at once she realized what a trap she had set for herself. If she did give him the list, he would burst out laughing, and she would be the laughing stock of the whole country by tomorrow. Her mind raced to pull together the right words.

"I'm sorry," she said, "I can't give you the list."

"Supposing I decide that you are withholding information from the police, Mrs. Colter? New York State still has a sodomy law on the books. You would be withholding information on lawbreakers from me."

She drew herself up, and the correct words poured into her mind, strong and clear. Surely it was with God's help.

"Oh, I did not allege that these people have broken the *law*," she said. "I don't pretend to know what they do in their bedrooms. My information is simply that their life-style suggests what may be a homosexual orientation."

They were silent for a moment, Manuella's eyes holding hers.

He made a small smile. "Very good, Mrs. Colter. Very good." He gently brandished the statement. "May I keep this copy?"

"Certainly," she said.

He got up to leave.

"And, Mrs. Colter . . . if you *do* come into possession of any information on homosexuals in the police force, I presume that you will contact me first, before you do anything else."

She smiled her Miss America smile at him, and got up to escort him to the door.

"Certainly," she said.

When he had gone, she shut the door, collapsed into her chair and broke into a sweat.

That same day, Mary Ellen checked in with Jewel and Sam to find out how they felt about it.

At Murphy's Coffee Shop, Jewel was enraged.

"That holier-than-thou bitch," she said. "I'm so mad I can hardly type. And I'm supposed to do this dynamite little feature on the Scuba unit . . ."

At Pier 36, Sam just shrugged, but Mary Ellen could tell he was a little nervous.

"I watched her on TV," he said. "She's a spooky broad. I got this creepy feeling that she knows where I borrow my library books."

"What's happening on the Mattachine books, anyway?"

"Dunno," he said. "They had a helluva time saving them. They had to move out of the building, right? So they threw the books in boxes and took 'em somewhere. The auction is supposed to be next week. Wonder if anybody will buy them."

But Sam didn't want to talk much about that.

"Hey," he said, "wanna see Miss Beautiful's kittens? They're getting so big. 'Scuse me, I should say *Miz* Beautiful when I'm around you, right?"

The next day was Sunday.

As the city still reverberated with his daughter's sayings and doings, Bill quietly spent the early morning at his office, doing some papers. Then he took his notebook, the one he always took on his walks, and told Al he was going downtown to do some poking round.

He got into his Lancia and drove across town to the First Presbyterian Church on Seventh Avenue, to attend the Sunday services at the Metropolitan Community Church.

As usual, he parked the car several blocks from the church. He was dressed in old jeans and a cheap-looking shirt, and left his glasses in his pocket, because with them off, he looked quite different.

He slipped into the church at the last moment, just as the congregation was singing the first hymn, and sat in the very last row, alone.

Every Sunday it never failed to amaze him—the contortions he had to go through in order to attend a worship service where he felt truly at home.

The Metropolitan Community Church had now spread to many U.S. cities, and even abroad—to Canada, Australia, England. While a number of straight churches now had their gay splinter groups, the MCC was still one of the largest, oldest and best-organized of the interdenominational gay churches. They

143

enjoyed a good relationship with the First Presbyterian, which allowed them to use their premises. Bill had once heard the First Presbyterian minister (who was straight, of course) lament the fact that the gay congregation was larger and more active and gave more money than his own.

Yet Bill wasn't truly at home, was he? He had never dared to make friends at the MCC, had never dared to attend the coffee hours or the seminars, had never dared to become involved in the MCC's activities. And of course he always came alone because Marion preferred to attend the evening service held by Integrity, the gay Episcopal group, at the Episcopal church on lower Fifth Avenue. There was no gay Baptist group, as far as Bill knew, and often he wished that somebody would start one.

Thanks to his hiding in the back as "John," and to his avoidance of publicity as William Laird, Bill was sure he had never been recognized here. At least, he hoped and assumed he hadn't.

He sat gazing fuzzily at the pulpit, for he could hardly see anything, and listened to the sermon. It was an okay sermon. But Bill hungered to hear the Word of God preached as only a gay Baptist preacher could have preached it. Hurling gay lightning bolts from the gay Sinai!

First the Reverend Martin Erickson said: "Once again, a reminder that our general conference is being held in Washington, D.C., two weeks from now. If you haven't planned to come, please think about it. It will be a blessed and exciting time to worship, and to share ideas and experiences, with our brothers and sisters from all over the country. In the back of the church, we have flyers available ..."

Then he launched into the sermon.

Predictably, the sermon was about Jeannie Laird Colter's attacks on the gay community, and on Intro Two. The preacher deplored, of course, all the things that Jeannie Colter was saying and doing. But he also deplored all the violent talk that was flying around town, among gays. He deplored the threatening phone calls and threatening letters that Jeannie Colter had received. He deplored the talk of a riot, of trashing and burning Jeannie Colter's headquarters "Acts like this," he said, "will only confirm the straight world's mistaken opinion that gay people are criminals."

The preacher wound up by saying: "The city council will be voting next week. I have been in touch with the National Gay Activists Alliance, and they tell me that we are still short six votes to get Intro Two passed . . . So please do make your opinion felt by the City Council, but in a peaceful and Christian way . . ."

As he listened, Bill felt his head coming out of joint. He stopped paying attention, and started looking distractedly around the church.

Five rows ahead of him, he noticed two young women together, very much the pair of lovebirds, sitting with their shoulders pressed together. Something about the crisp blonde curls of the one on the right, something about her straight back and almost military air was familiar.

Then, when the congregation rose to sing the final hymn, she turned as she rose, searching for her hymn book on the seat beside her. He saw her face.

He recognized her instantly, even without her uniform hat. It was the woman police sergeant who had come to Catherine Slip when he found the dead tramp. Good God, a woman cop, here in this church, looking so cozy with another woman, could mean only one thing. When Jeannie talked about gays in the Police Department, she might know more than she let on.

In all his years of furtive churchgoing, she was the first person he had run into who would know him, in his other life, as William Laird, real-estate man and developer.

Hopefully, she had not noticed him, being engrossed with her lovely blonde friend.

145

Shaking with fright and confusion, Bill got up and left the church while the congregation was still bellowing out the last verses of "A Mighty Fortress Is Our God."

Even as he walked out, he cursed himself for his fear.

With his glasses back on, he sat in the car for a while, feeling like he was on the verge of tears.

Finally, he drove downtown, to do his usual cover-up sketches. He wandered around the Wall Street district, so empty on Sundays, and went to Trinity Church. The services were over, the church was empty.

He wandered around in the churchyard, looking at the sooty old tombstones, and wishing that his bones were moldering under one of them.

In the church, Mary Ellen and Liv stood together, singing "A Mighty Fortress" together at the tops of their voices. Now and then Mary Ellen sneaked a glance at Liv because she liked to study her lover's profile when she sang. Liv had the wholesome abandon of a child singing a Christmas carol, showing her tonsils, cocking her head to one side.

When the Reverend Erickson preached the sermon, it was—or course—about the Jeannie Colter business.

Mary Ellen sat there listening, trying to make some sense out of it. The Reverend Erickson had picked out various quotes from the Bible to show that gay people had to love their enemies, and to pray for them.

Mary Ellen sat there trying hard to digest what he was saying. She knew very well that Jesus had talked about loving thine enemies and turning the other cheek and so on. But the very mention of Jeannie Colter's name stirred up a witches' caldron of resentment on her stomach. The Bible talked a lot about revenge and outraged anger too. "Revenge is mine, saith the

Lord." "And they took them out and stoned them," and so on.

What we need, she said to herself, is a gay Joshua who will march around the straight Jericho, and blow a trumpet, and make the walls come a-tumbling down.

When the service was over, Liv said, "What is this general conference?" She added wistfully, "I have never been in Washington, D.C."

"I wanted to go to the general last year," said Mary Ellen, "but it was in San Francisco, and I couldn't afford it. Maybe we should go . . . get away from the witch hunt for a while."

"Oh, I would looooove that," said Liv. "We could drive down there, no?"

They were walking slowly down the aisle toward the back of the church, arms linked, jostled happily amid the congregation. At the church door, the Reverend Erickson was shaking hands.

Mary Ellen reached out to the pile of flyers and took one.

Eighty miles north of New York City, Jeannie Colter was attending the 11 A.M. worship service of the First Baptist Church in Pawling.

She sat in the first row of pews, on the right. With her were Auntie Mary and Steve. The smaller children had gone to Sunday school, and her father was down in New York. These days he came up to Windfall less and less—he was so engrossed in his South Street thing! If it weren't for Steve, so straight and tall for seventeen, with such a good head on his shoulders, she would have felt totally alone.

Behind her back, she could sense the sympathy— condescending and otherwise—of the congregation. *Poor brave woman . . . coming to church alone all these years . . . unsaved husband who rejects God . . . maybe she doesn't pray hard enough for him . . . I've heard rumors that their marriage is on the rocks . . . shocking.*

147

Things had not gone well at home that morning.

Little Cora had asked if she could go to the movies with a boy. Jeannie had said that no, she couldn't, that she was too young. Cora had retorted that all the girls her age were wearing bras, so that wasn't too young to go to movies. Jeannie had retorted that wearing bras and going out with boys had nothing to do with each other, and that Cora had nothing to put in a bra, in any case. Cora then retorted that she knew girls her age who were already sleeping with their boyfriends. Jeannie had been horrified that her daughter was able to talk about it so easily, let alone that she was in contact with girls who were doing it. She had retorted, just for that, Cora wouldn't be going to the movies with anybody.

"It's everywhere," she moaned to Auntie Mary. "It doesn't matter what you do. It's like a smell that you can't get rid of, no matter how many windows you open."

Then there was Jessica.

Yesterday, before Jeannie had driven up, the little girl had disappeared off the property completely. Auntie Mary had panicked and called the state police. Eventually the little girl was spotted, nonchalantly riding her black pony along a back road in the direction of the Connecticut state line. The police loaded her and the fat little pony into a van and brought them back to Windfall. Jeannie had spanked the girl and sent her to bed without dinner, but she was beginning to have the feeling that all this was just an exercise, that Jessica was beyond hearing her.

"I'm not supposed to *have* children like this," she said to herself. "I'm supposed to have good children."

Then Lance, her eighteen-year-old and oldest son, had called from Las Vegas. He and his girl friend were having a good time playing the dollar machines, and they had paid for part of their trip with a $700 jackpot. They had actually been smart enough to walk out of the Sands with their winnings.

"Good for you," said Jeannie dryly.

Now, with the morning sunshine slanting strongly through the tall glass windows of the church, she tried to put it all out of her mind. Many of the congregation had come up, before the service, to tell her what a blessed thing she was doing to the homosexuals, that it was high time somebody did it.

"You ought to do it all over the country," Sister Ethel had said to her. "New York isn't the only state with this problem."

Sister Ethel was right. It occurred to her that she ought to carry her fight against homosexuals to the national level. She had already been invited to tape a segment for "Sixty Minutes"—why not keep hammering away on the big talk shows, etc? It would be a start, long in advance, on her campaign for President, if she went that far. The problem was that Tom Winkler had warned her against doing anything like this right now. He had even warned her to limit her anti-homosexual activities to New York State. "You want to be remembered for a lot of edifying things," he had said, "not for just one rather unsavory thing."

Now Reverend Irving came slowly to the pulpit, using his cane.

The morning sunlight fell strongly across his snow-white hair, across the rims of his horn glasses, as he stood and gazed out over his flock.

Then he preached a fiery sermon against homosexuals, using a lot of quotes that Jeannie didn't even recognize. How wonderful the Bible was—a mine of riches! The congregation vibrated with approval. Reverend Irving asked them all to pray for the city council, to pray that they would vote the right way.

After the service, she visited alone with Reverend Irving in his study, while her security people waited for her.

"It's Sidney," she said. "I'm at my wit's end. If I weren't a Christian women, I'd say that my marriage was on the rocks."

149

"Your basic problem, Sister Jeannie, is that intellectually you know what God's ideal woman is like, but emotionally you cannot fit yourself into that pattern. Am I right?"

"I suppose so," she said wearily.

"Deep down," he said shrewdly, "you are one of those bossy women. You really feel that women have the right to preach, and to lead men."

"No, I don't," she said. "Politics isn't preaching."

"Now, Sister Jeannie," he said shrewdly, "don't argue with me because I know you too well. You have let your short hair grow out, and you are not playing the beauty queen any more, and you wear modest Christian clothes, and you are stirring up a nice fuss down there in New York City, but that is not the same thing as obeying your husband in all things, the way God has commanded you to do."

"*Obey* him?" she said. "He isn't even saved yet."

"Perhaps if you tried obeying him," said Reverend Irving, "he would be saved. Perhaps he is waiting to see that example from you."

"I'm not sure that's the kind of woman that Sidney ever wanted," she said a little sourly.

Danny and Armando celebrated the Sabbath in their own way.

In the early evening, just before the little St. Francis of Assisi Church on Wade Street closed for the night, the two of them slipped in and quietly walked down the aisle.

The church was nearly dark; and the scent of incense lingered in the air. The only light was from the flickering sanctuary lamp, beside the altar where the Blessed Sacrament reposed, and from the banks of candles flickering, row on row in their glass holders on the big metal racks.

They headed for the side altar where the image of Saint Francis stood. They knelt down at the altar rail, side by side, and gazed up at it.

In the flickering light from the banks of candles, the plaster image of Il Poverello almost seemed to be alive. It was a fine old piece of Victorian sculpture, showing the saint with eyes rolled up in ecstasy, his hands spread to show the stigmata in them. He was surrounded by Franciscan brothers and by wild animals, who seemed to share in his rapture. Brother Sun stood behind his head. Sister Moon rested below his elbow. Doves and sparrows perched on his shoulders, gazing up at his thin radiant face. At his feet stood a wolf, with head lowered humbly toward the saint's feet, as if to lick the holy wounds.

The two men knelt close together, arms touching, in total silence.

This was something that they shared, a feeling that they had never been able to share with any other man. It was something quite remote from, and distinct from, all the unsmiling business in the bars, and the flamboyant exteriors of black leather G-strings with padding to make your basket bigger, and handcuffs jangling from your belt. When each of them discovered that the other shared his feeling for this, it was the thing that cemented their relationship. It was not something they paraded, even in the gay community. They both felt uncomfortable in the gay churches, because they knew they were not properly understood, that they were shunned and whispered about.

Anyone who saw Armando behind the bar at the Eagle's Nest, mixing drinks with deft speed, laughing, joking, playing the role of the handsome-gay-bartender-sex-object would not recognize him now. Armando gazed silently up at St. Francis, silent, his large hairy hands folded on the altar rail, in a manner as still as a trance.

Almost in a dream, Danny himself was recalling the guilty pleasure that he felt in parochial school in the Bronx when he read in the prayer books about the torments of the martyrs, and the joy with which they gave themselves up to the spears, and the hot coals, and the teeth and the claws of the wild beasts. He was enthralled by this fusion of pain with love. Once, when he was thirteen, in his innocence he tried to find words for confessing this guilty feeling, but the priest simply didn't understand, and brushed his words aside. "It's not a sin, my son, to be edified by the stories of the holy martyrs," the priest had said.

When he met Armando, six months ago, it took several weeks, and a number of rather ordinary lovemaking sessions, with rough games and other things, before they began to trust each other and to haltingly reveal their innermost desires and to move to satisfy each other truly.

"The thing is," Armando had said, "I've been laughed at too many times. So . . . you can understand why I never run a personal ad in Trader Dick or anything . . ."

After a few minutes, they both got up, dropped their money into the offering slot. Each of them slowly lit a candle, as if beginning a magic rite.

Then they slipped out of the church and walked swiftly to Armando's apartment.

There, they did not even speak, in order to keep the trance-like mood that they had carried away from the church.

Armando's little basement apartment was a homey clutter of cheap antiques, half-starved plants, battered old prints and oil paintings, worn Oriental rugs, books, souvenirs, afghans thrown over armchairs and sofa. Through the back, by the tiny bedroom, a door went out into a tiny back-court garden. Here, surrounded by a high palisade fence, there was one gingko tree, a lot of ivy and privet bushes and a few hanging plants. At a table and chairs under an awning, Armando could relax with friends on a warm evening.

The bedroom was so small that there was room for little else but the king-size bed and mattress on the floor.

Without speaking, they lit a couple of candles and undressed. Their bodies threw huge flickering shadows on the wall papered with stained old Chinese landscapes.

Fifteen minutes later, they were well into what they had to do.

Armando lay spread-eagled on the bed, held rigidly in position by four iron chains and manacles, which were bolted solidly to the corners of the bed. In the candlelight, his face and limbs glowed with sweat, and his burly barrel chest heaved up and down with uneven panting breaths. His eyes were fixed on the ceiling, unseeing yet seeing. Special large pins were thrust through his nipples, from which thin rivulets of blood ran down his sides, thinned by sweat, to stain the rumpled sheet under him.

Danny lay beside him with the next pin, devastated at being both the instrument and the witness of this passion. There was no desire to hurt Armando, or pleasure in it. He was the flaming angel. He was almost God, willing it to happen and knowing it so intimately. There was envy, too—he had hungered to know the feel of it, but once a year he had to pass a police physical, and there could be no suspicious scars or recent wounds on his body.

Now and then, the slow progress of the rapture wrung a moan from Armando. And when the flaming seraphim bathed his fiery lance in Armando's heart, the big man uttered a long muffled cry that Danny had to hope the neighbors didn't hear.

Needless to say, they couldn't to this every night, or even once a week. It had to be reserved for the now-and-then, and it had to be built up to over a period of time. The choice of time was partly dictated by the practical considerations. It had to be when neither of them was working a shift at that time of day.

Afterward, they lay embraced, stuck together by the drying sweat, blood and semen, looking into each other's eyes in the light of the guttering candles. Armando's eyes saw clearly now, and they had the limpid look of a little child.

For the first time, Danny spoke, but in a very low voice, almost a whisper.

"You're the dream that I don't dare to dream."

Armando's feverish lips moved, but no sound came out.

In a few more minutes, they were falling asleep. Through the little door, they could hear the stillness in the little garden, the ivy sending new tendrils into the old bricks, the leaves breathing on the gingko tree, the wings of the moths beating in the dark like the wings of seraphim and cherubim.

As he drifted off, it occurred to Danny that he had not thought about Jeannie Colter or the riot rumors for approximately five hours.

Eight

As Mary Ellen had feared, the crime reaction to Jeannie Colter's anti-gay campaign was not long in coming.

As she and Danny drove around they were extra-alert to the radio dispatcher. With every passing day, they were more and more frightened of the idea of being assigned to break up a gay riot. But they were determined to respond to any scene that sounded like it had a remote possibility of being connected with violence against gays. They hardly even dared to sign out for a few minutes to snatch something to eat.

So far, nothing of that nature had involved them when they were on duty.

But they heard things around the station house, from the officers and from their chief. They also heard things from Jewel, who seemed to know everything. There had been a definite increase in assaults on gays during the nighttime hours, especially in areas of the city where there were a lot of gay bars. The assaults were usually on gay men. Rarely did straight punks think to beat up on lesbians.

Then, a few days after Jeannie's second speech, it happened.

At midday, a call went out for assistance from a precinct farther uptown. There was a big fire at a midtown theater on Sixth Avenue and 44th Street.

"Cruiser two-oh-four responding," she said into the mike. Danny flipped on her lights and siren, and they bored their way through the midday traffic.

The block between Sixth and Seventh was a mass of fire engines and police cruisers arriving, a sea of flashing red lights. There were the usual gawking spectators getting their cheap thrills. The smoke and flames were rolling up from the theater, already making an angry dark pillar above the area.

The moment Mary Ellen saw the name of the theater on the scorched marquee, she felt sick to her stomach. It was the Apollinaire, a theater specializing in all-male gay porno films.

"It's gotta be arson," said Danny. He had voiced the thought that went through Mary Ellen's head just then.

Splashing through puddles, showered by soot and falling sparks, they helped control the crowd, direct traffic, and interview witnesses.

The badly shaken manager, Jim Stratford, said that the theater had been about to open for its 12 noon showing, the first of the day. He, the cashier and a scrubwoman had barely escaped with their lives. When the fire was out, the arson squad moved into the still smoking building. They found that a rear entrance had been forced. They found the gasoline cans, and telltale signs of arson: walls blackened in a special way where the gas had burned so fiercely.

"An amateur job," sniffed one of the arson squad men to Mary Ellen. "No finesse at all."

That night, as she sat at home with Liv eating dinner, they watched it all over again on the evening news. Liv even swore that she could spot Mary Ellen in the shots of the scene.

"Why are you so depressed?" Liv wanted to know. "It was just a place where they show dirty movies."

Mary Ellen shook her head.

"I'm not crazy for porno films," she said. "I don't defend them as freedom of speech. I don't think I'd even be crazy about porno films about *women*. But that's not the point. The point is, that people only burn down the *gay* theaters that show porn."

"Is that really true?" Liv insisted.

"Ask any police department in any big city," said Mary Ellen. "The arson rate for gay theaters and gay bars is higher than for straight bars and straight theaters. For chrissake, on the West Coast, gay discos and gay bars are *always* burning down."

Liv was gazing at the TV screen, where the smoke-and-flames scene had just shifted back to the newscaster at his elegant big desk, which looked like the console of a spaceship in "Star Trek."

"At work," Liv said, "people are talking a lot about Jeannie Colter. I hear all the talking. But I don't say anything . . ."

Jeannie Colter was watching the same TV broadcast, as she sat at her dressing table blow-drying her hair. She had a dinner lined up with city council member Ervin Blakey, whose vote she felt she could swing if she frightened him enough.

As she watched the smoke and flames rolling up from the burning theater, a deep thrill rushed through her. It was like something from the Bible, like the final day of the cities of the plain when the Lord rained His destroying fire on those who defied His word. Reverend Irving would have been able to come up with a thousand Bible quotes about fire.

"Probably some arsonist with a finer moral sense than most people," she thought. "I hope they don't catch him. If I dared, I'd burn down every theater like that in this town."

Several days later, Bill was saddened when a smaller all-male theater downtown on the Bowery, the Grecian, was also gutted by fire. This time, witnesses recalled seeing a man fleeing from the vicinity.

Quick radio work by the police caught him a few blocks from the scene. He confessed to setting both fires, and was booked.

Now Jeannie's critics were accusing her of creating an evil climate in New York City, a climate that made open season on gay people and anything connected with them. Jeannie, who had responded to the pickets and other gay harassments by hiring a few security people, had an answer to that. She said that she regretted the crimes themselves but that, in a way, the crimes represented the feelings of New York City's decent law-abiding ordinary citizens. "The average person does not want these places in town," she insisted. "My mail is running ten to one in favor of cleaning this element out of town."

Bill was sad for a number of reasons.

One was: he and other city historians knew the Grecian as a stately—if seedy and rundown—example of an early 1800s theater. He had a number of photographs and sketches in his bank of files, from when the little marquee stood in the shadow of the old El, now also gone.

This city's sign must be Scorpio, Bill thought. It is forever devouring its own tail.

As the days passed, however, Mary Ellen learned that Jeannie Colter's verbal violence was affecting gay women too.

One afternoon, at Murphy's Coffee Shop, she heard from Jewel a wrathful story of vandalism. The victim was a lesbian news-magazine, *Women*, that had been launched six months before. *Women* was now being quietly sold on some newsstands in the city, alongside such New York–oriented gay male magazines as *Michael's Thing*.

"They broke into the printer's during the night," said Jewel, her voice tremulous with anger. "They completely destroyed the new issue. It had just come from the bindery and was ready to be shipped. They ripped up a lot of copies and poured oil and paint on the rest. And then they trashed the type that was already set, for the issue after that."

Mary Ellen felt a little ill.

"*And*," Jewel added, "the perpetrators had to have some inside help. Because the printer had other jobs in the shop—non-gay stuff—but none of *that* got touched."

Mary Ellen sat weighted with sadness. The incident had happened in the West Village. She wondered whether the precinct there was working hard on the case.

Then, one night, as Mary Ellen and Danny drove down a street in their patrol sector, they saw a young woman in jeans standing on the corner, frantically flagging them down.

Something about the woman told them "lesbian." With a screech of tires, they pulled over.

The young woman pointed into the narrower crosstown street, to a small neon sign.

"The bar there," she panted. "Some guys trashing it . . ."

Just then, on their radio, the two cops heard the dispatcher assigning a run to a bar address on that street, to two of Mary Ellen's squad, PO Stewart and PO Mooney. She could see the flashing red light of their car three blocks away, coming from the west along the crosstown street.

"Cruiser two-oh-four responding," she said into her mike.

Three men came sprinting out of the bar, saw her and headed west. She wheeled around the corner, parked with a screech near the bar. She and Danny got out running, hands on their guns. The scout car coming east cut the fugitives off neatly. The men were drunk and didn't resist much. It all happened with much noise of feet pounding on the sidewalk, and not a shot fired. The four officers collared the three fugitives.

The bar's modest green neon sign, PORTHOLE, hung over a neat basement entrance. It was a new bar on this quiet residential street. The brick and brownstone fronts had been painted, and flower boxes installed by a block association.

But inside the bar, chairs and tables were hurled around, broken bottles everywhere, and the mirror behind the bar was broken. The jukebox was still playing. Balloons and crepe streamers from the opening still decorated the glittery ceiling. A few stunned women were standing around.

On the floor in front of the jukebox was a scene of the purest horror that Mary Ellen had ever witnessed since she had become a cop.

An older heavyset woman with a butch haircut knelt there, holding a younger woman in her arms. The young woman's face was a mask of blood, and her little cotton madras shirt was soaked with blood. She had been assaulted with a broken bottle, which now lay on the floor. Most of her nose and part of one cheek were sliced away, baring her teeth and her nasal passages. She was holding her head dropped down, so that the bubbling blood would not run back down her nasal passages into her lungs.

Mary Ellen wanted to cry out, to cradle the young woman in her arms, to say, "My sister, my sister."

Beside her, Danny was blanched, silent, staring at the scene.

So Mary Ellen just said, "Good God," and sent Danny out to radio for an ambulance.

The owner of the bar was a woman named Leslie Forbes. Looking over the wreckage bitterly, she said: "We opened a month ago. The building owner leased to us. But the block association has given us nothing but trouble, saying we ruined their neighborhood and so on. It was a mistake. Those three guys . . . neighborhood types, hanging around, insulting the women. Tonight they came in here drunk and talking about Jeannie Colter . . ."

The screaming ambulance came and took away the mutilated girl. The three men were brought in, handcuffed, and were identified on the spot as the perpetrators. The women witnesses willingly made statements. The men were white middle-class and had families in the block and would certainly suffer some of the consequences, at least, of their drunken rampage. In a few minutes the wagon took them off to headquarters for booking.

And the moment came when Mary Ellen and Danny had to wrap things up, get in their car and leave the scene, all without daring to identify themselves as a sister and a brother to the women there.

Later that night, as they continued their patrol, neither of them could shake away the memory of the mutilated face of that lovely young woman—a living skull, a mask of blood. They couldn't even talk about it.

Mary Ellen wished that she had already known what the three men had done when she saw them running, so she could have shot at least one of them. But shooting people wasn't so simple, if you were a cop. TV series to the contrary, you were temporarily suspended if you fired your gun, until it was determined if you had really needed to fire. Her father wouldn't have fired, even out of anger. But then her father had never known oppression.

As she and Danny drove the empty streets, lined by gloomy warehouses, the bars closing up, the gas stations darkened, even the East Side Highway only lightly traveled, she passed the hour of the wolf mulling over a dull and aching anger that was growing inside her.

It made Mary Ellen sad and angry to see that the poisons preached by Jeannie Colter were even reaching the sunny Liv. Sometimes Liv was depressed and brooding when she came home from the post office.

It was Liv's first encounter with anti-gay hostility in its most naked American form. Since her own coming-out, she had lived lapped in the joys of lesbian love, and of fellowship in the gay community. So far, her civil-service job had been only a neutral experience.

But one night in the kitchen, bending over to put a clean dish of cat food on the floor for Kikan, Liv said, "There is this woman who works next to me who has always been very *very* nice to me." Something in the jerkiness of how she bent down gave away the tension and upset in her nervous system. "She tells me all about her family and her children. She is always trying to make dates for me, with nice young men there. But ever since this Colter lady is making so loud about the gay people, this lady is saying not so nice things about gay people, in her very nice way. She thinks they should all be put in concentration camps."

She sat heavily down on a kitchen chair, and watched Kikan eat.

"Every day I have to listen to her now. She thinks the Colter lady is wonderful. She says she is the best thing to happen to America since Richard Nixon. And of course she thinks that Watergate was nothing, that Nixon was . . . how do you say . . . ah, yes, like in the gangster movies . . . *framed*. Every day she is quoting from the Colter lady, what she reads in the newspapers or hears on the TV."

The teakettle was whistling, and Mary Ellen got up to turn it off and make them both a cup of Sanka with milk and sugar.

Then slowly they climbed up the stairs toward the roof garden.

It was a hot night, and it seemed even hotter up there, where the brick chimneys and tarpaper roofs seemed to hold the heat of the sun. The petunias blooming in the milk boxes made a heavy, almost exotic, scent in the air. The full moon rested over the Palisades, looking swollen and feverish.

"Look, Liv," said Mary Ellen, trying to lighten the moment, "the moon is gay and some redneck punched it in the face."

Liv shook her head as they sat down.

"It is something in America that I cannot get used to," said Liv. "It is the violence. In Sweden we are not even allowed to see violence in the movies or on TV. Sex and violence. Americans are obsessed with them. At home, we do not love these things for their own sake."

They sat drinking their coffee in the heat of the night, the sweat shining on their limbs.

"Today," said Liv softly, "I could not stand it any more, with this lady. I said to her, you think *I* am a nice person, right? She said yes. I asked her if she would want me put in a concentration camp? She said no."

Mary Ellen closed her eyes, knowing what was coming.

"So," said Liv, "I said, but you *should* want me put in a concentration camp. And she said, 'Why?' She was very surprised, right? After all, in America they wouldn't put nice people in those camps."

"So," said Mary Ellen, "you told her that you were a lesbian, right?"

"Yes, I did," said Liv.

"And of course the nice lady is a big tattletale, so now you're afraid that you'll lose your job."

"How did you know that?" said Liv.

"Just a wild guess," said Mary Ellen grimly, "based on my years of police work."

"I am sorry, Mary Ellen. But I couldn't keep the words back any more."

"For chrissake, don't apologize for coming out! Especially to me! What was her reaction?"

Liv was shaking her head in a puzzled way.

"I expected her to be very shocked. To be very *very* angry. So I was very surprised. She said, oh, you poor poor child . . ."

Mary Ellen found herself whooping with laughter.

"My God, one of those kind," she said.

"She was talking about the Jesus cults, and how

163

there are these people who kidnap Jesus people and
. . ." Liv searched for the word. "De . . . de . . ."

"De-program them?" said Mary Ellen.

Liv's face lit up. "Yes! De-program. And she said
there ought to be an organization that would kidnap
gay people and de-program them. She said that I obviously was brainwashed, that I really wasn't a lesbian
at all, that I was a nice girl . . ."

"Oh, they could always de-program you in that concentration camp she is talking about," said Mary Ellen.

"You know," said Liv morosely, "sometimes this
lady—her name is Mrs. Whalen—she talks so much
about how nice I am, how *very* nice, that I think she
would like to have a date with me herself."

Mary Ellen was torn between falling out of her
chair laughing, or kicking a chair off the roof with
anger. One of the things she loved most about Liv was
her naiveté. It always took Liv a long time to figure
out something that Mary Ellen, hardened from street
experience, knew instinctively. Part of the fun of
knowing Liv was seeing her pick her way, in her slow
wide-eyed manner, toward one of these realizations.

"I'll bet she envies you," said Mary Ellen.

"Oh, yes! She envies me because I am so very young
and so *very* beautiful, she says. She is in her forties,
and looks like a package of mushrooms that sat very
long in the refrigerator. She likes my hair the most.
One day it came undone, and she wanted to braid it
for me."

Mary Ellen made a face. "And I suppose you let her
do it."

"Oh, no," said Liv. "I went to the women's room and
did it myself."

"Well, you picked a fine time to come out," said
Mary Ellen. "With all the rumors running around the
department about layoffs, I don't know how long I'll
have *my* job."

The moon, that celestial victim of assault and battery, was sinking slowly behind the Jersey Palisades. Kikan had come up from the kitchen and washed her face and paws. Now she prowled around the tiny garden, sniffing the flowers, hopping on Liv's lap to check out her cup of cooling Sanka and take a tentative lap at it. Liv petted her cat; but her face had a brooding absent look—the face of the angel who was the only witness to the first crime committed in the Garden of Paradise.

Looking at her then, Mary Ellen saw her in the context of history.

Liv was such a devout Lutheran, far more devout in her church than Mary Ellen was in hers. She had somehow fitted her gayness in with the Lutheran doctrine of sin. Today she had imitated Luther, and bravely, very bravely, she had nailed her own pesonal theses on the cathedral door of America.

On the morning that the city council was to vote on the homosexual bill, Jeannie waited anxiously in her office. Sidney was going to call her and let her know how the vote went.

Actutally, she wasn't too worried about the vote. Two weeks had passed since the homosexual bill had been introduced, and she had spent that time in a whirlwind of lobbying.

The 43-member New York city council differed from many other city councils, in that more than half of its members did not work full-time at it. For this, the city council periodically came in for harsh criticism from both the liberal and the conservative press. The council met twice a month, and a bill introduced at one session would be voted on at the next meeting.

As a longtime political person in New York City, Jeannie knew exactly how the council functioned. You couldn't do anything without having an understanding with the council's Democratic majority leader, who was now Ed Bloomfield. Bloomfield controlled every-thing—committees, agendas, even (it was said) the number of wastebaskets in meeting rooms.

So, naturally, her first move had been to meet with Bloomfield.

A strange meeting, that. He, representing the Dem-ocratic party, which had always held such total power in New York City. She, representing the Republicans, who forever yearned after power in New York City. In this case, however, Bloomfield's power was bal-anced by the fact that Jeannie knew something about him that had come out of her file. She knew that Bloomfield's son, a nice-looking, college-age boy, hung around a lot at the homosexual bars and disco-theques in town.

During the meeting, she calmly and sweetly told him how concerned she was at the possibility that the Intro Two might pass. She knew that he knew her as someone who would not rest once she got a campaign going. Without actually saying so, she managed to give the subtle impression that if the bill were passed, she would call for investigation of the city council members who had voted in favor of it. She would expose, she hinted, any moral conflicts of interest that might have affected their vote—say, a homo-sexual relative.

Bloomfield didn't let on that he understood exactly what she was getting at, and he even said that he wanted to just think about it. But she had the feeling that, when he left the meeting with her, he was wor-ried about what she would do.

She had spent the rest of the two weeks putting the heat on other selected council members.

One of them, Charles Stratton, made his living in city real estate, so she had gotten to know him through her Uncle Al. Charles actually lived in Westport, Con-necticut, and had attended only nine out of twenty-four council meetings in the last year (for which he had been very much criticized). Nevertheless, he agreed that the bill was cause for grave concern. He promised that he would make the effort to attend, and vote no. So—maybe—that was another vote.

Her tactic, as it had been with Bloomfield, was to get people to cooperate by frightening them—in a genteel way, of course. Nobody, not even a part-time council member, wanted to have his personal morality questioned in this way.

Actually, Jeannie thought to herself, a little fear of God might do the council good. She had to agree with the liberal press on that one—the council should work full-time, and they should take a more active role in city politics, instead of letting Bloomfield do it all.

So, she waited that morning in pleasant anticipation of the result of her lobbying.

In about a month's time, after the Intro Two thing had faded from people's minds a little, she intended to make a public announcement of her intention to enter the gubernatorial race.

If she *had* decided to run for mayor of New York City, all those things would have been reforms to be tackled by her. And with relish. Make the council meet once a week, make it work hard, for instance. End corruption, put the city on a paying basis. Unfortunately, she had long ago realized that being mayor of New York was a political dead end. It was only for someone who felt so wedded to city politics that he or she didn't have state or national ambitions. The failure of John Lindsay's bid for a role in national politics was proof of that. The liberals were right on that one too—New York City was about to go down the tube, and the mayor, whoever he or she was, was about to go down the tube with the city. It was a job for a masochist.

Just before noon, Gertrude came in and said, "Sidney is on the phone. He's at City Hall."

She seized the phone. "Sidney, it's me."

"Congratulations," he said.

She grinned. "What was the vote?"

167

"Thanks to you, nearly the entire council was at the meeting. The gay bill went down thirty-two to seven."

But there was an edge in his voice that disturbed her profoundly.

"What's *your* problem?" she said.

"Well," he said, "to be honest with you, I've been hearing about your tactics. I have to tell you—like with the list of names the other day—that I really don't like them much."

"You're naive," she said. "This is not one of those times when you talk nicey-nice to people and promise them the moon."

Sidney was laughing, a dry laugh of disbelief. "You're calling *me* naive?"

Jeannie sighed to herself, and slumped in her chair. These days her conversations with him always went like this. She recognized vaguely that she had a habit of leading with her chin, but she always saw it as standing up for the right thing.

"Forget it," she said.

"No, I won't forget it," he said. "I'm leaving for China in ten days and, frankly, your tactics are all too totalitarian. All too similar to the country I'm going to visit."

"Sidney!" she said. "That's hitting below the belt."

"Don't deny it," he said. "For years I've heard you say how great it would be to be governor, and rule by decree, like Rockefeller did."

She made a last-ditch desperate effort to follow Reverend Irving's advice, and submit herself to him.

"You want me to get out of politics? Just be a house-wife?" she said.

"Don't be crazy," he said. "I would never force a wife of mine to make a decision like that."

When they had hung up, she sat there brooding. Her pleasure at the vote was dimmed by the argument with Sidney.

She wondered if he was going to China in order to be as far from her as possible, for a while. She wondered if the thought of divorce was crossing his mind. Being unsaved, he could certainly think of divorce, and she couldn't stop him. She wondered if he had been running around with other women.

Gertrude put her head in the door. "You'll want to make a statement, won't you?"

"Yes, of course," she said, sitting there with clenched hands.

Danny heard the news while he was sitting alone in the Spike, nursing a finger of Wild Turkey. It was noontime, and he was waiting for Armando to come. Four other patrons were drinking at the other end of the bar.

Lenny had a transistor radio in the back of the bar, and it crackled out the twelve o'clock news.

"The gay rights bill was voted down by the city council today," said the WNEW newscaster. "This is the fourth defeat for the bill now famous as Intro Two. The news of the defeat was greeted by a storm of protest by gays and their supporters in the city . . ."

Sitting there slumped over, Danny felt the weight of the handgun in his pocket. It was like the millstone, dragging him to the bottom of the sea.

He was so alone, sitting there at midday like a tired businessman or an old drunk. He didn't dare to go steamin' and gleamin' in crowded discos at midnight, with a thousand men doing the Bionic Boogie all around him. He didn't even dare to have dinner with Armando publicly in a restaurant—they had always eaten at home. Wouldn't it be nice if Armando could pick him up at work, and the guys in the locker room could yell, "Hey, Danny—Armando's here!" But that was a dream. Not even Martin Luther King's kind of dream. It was a dead dream.

At four that afternoon, he and Mary Ellen would go on duty. It was no rumor now that a giant gay demonstration was going to happen at Colter's headquarters that evening, while he and Mary Ellen were on duty.

Colter's headquarters were in the next precinct up-town. But if those guys couldn't handle the riot, and called in other precincts for help, then what?

Danny figured that the usual figure of 10 percent gay, applied to the U.S. population as a whole, also applied to the NYPD. Which meant that, in Manhattan, dozens of other police officers, sergeants, captains, etc., were secretly feeling the same dream and doubts that he was. He did not have to know these hidden police gays personally—he did not have to know their names. He knew their feelings to the full, and that was enough to link him with them.

His hand tightened on the glass of Wild Turkey.

The men at the other end of the bar were leaving. They were big husky outdoor types, beautiful men. Two wore machine-faded Levi's, and the third, a blond, wore his daytime everyday bagged-out black leather pants.

As they tramped by Danny, the blond man stopped and put his hand on Danny's shoulder and said.

"The word is out, brother. Walk by Jeannie Colter's office at eight tonight."

Danny looked gloomily up at them from his drink. He sincerely hoped that the blond didn't decide to grope him. If he did, he'd find the off-duty gun in his pocket.

"Walk by?" he said.

"Yeah," said the big leather man. He was weather-beaten, looked about thirty-five—a ranch type, maybe a fugitive from the West.

Danny went into his simpleminded trucker's act.

"Well," he said, "I've heard a lot of wild talk about violence. I'm not so sure this looks good to the straight folks up at the big plantation house. Know what I mean?"

The blond man's hand tightened lovingly on Danny's arm, but respectfully did not slide any farther down. It was not a moment for groping.

"No violence," he told Danny. "Some of us have de-

cided to be there as enforcers. You see, we think that
the folks up at the plantation house ought to see our
power. But we also don't want to dirty our hands
with that bitch's blood. So it's gonna be a *walk-by*,
brother. Understand? Anybody gets out of line, we
take him out."

The big man winked at Danny.

"See you at Thirty-eight and Park, brother," he said.

The three men walked on out of the bar, with that
muscle-bound semi-bop that not even a black brother
from Harlem could duplicate.

Danny looked at Lenny in disbelief.

"Yeah," said Lenny, "I guess there's been a lot of
controversy about this thing tonight. Some people want
it to be noisy, some people don't. But the organizers
have realized they'll turn out more gay people if
they advertise it as a peaceful thing."

Danny thought about it a bit more, feeling a single
ray of light shining into his dread. Then he went to the
telephone and called Mary Ellen.

She was home, housecleaning and about to take a
shower and get ready for work.

He told her what the three men had told him.

"You and me have been through the whole thing a
million times already," he said. "We don't dare call
in sick, right? Every gay person on the force is going
to be tempted to call in sick today, and they'll be
watching whoever does. If we're on duty, and we get
assigned a run to this affair, we can't sabotage our car
or something, because they'll find out, right? So . . ."

Mary Ellen's mind was already a jump ahead of
him. You had to hand it to her—she was a brave smart
girl.

"So you're saying that we go if we have to," she
said. "You're saying we should take the chance."

"That's just what I'm saying," Danny said.

"It's a big chance," she said.

"What isn't?" he said.

"If your big tough friends keep things quiet,
171

that's great," she said. "But if things get ugly, then we're right there in the middle of it."

"What the hell," he said. "We can fake. Wave your stick around. Make it look like you're going for the money. Look," he said, "you know I'm a gambler at heart. And I know *you're* a gambler. Your dad would bet his last hundred bucks on a hundred-to-one shot, right?"

Mary Ellen started to laugh.

"All right," she said. "We'll gamble. I just hope that these three guys you talked to are on the level."

"See you at work, sweetheart," Danny said.

Bill heard the news about the 32-to-7 vote while he and his brother Al were out on the harbor in the new cabin cruiser, *South Street,* a 25-foot fiber glass Marine King.

He and Al were sitting about one hundred yards offshore, in the channel, and they had cut the motor to drift a little, look at the shoreline, and talk. It was a muggy day, a real scorcher, and both he and Al were in shirt sleeves. A thick haze hung over Manhattan, and the Jersey shores had a far-off mysterious look.

Casually Bill flipped on the radio, and tuned it to WQXR to catch the noon news broadcast. After all, they both wanted to know how the vote had gone.

Al was talking about the possibility that the city would back off on the urban-renewal project in the South Street block next to theirs, owing to cutbacks on funds. If that happened, he said, Laird & Laird might be able to get a line on the property.

Bill listened, nodding and asking the right questions out of pure habit, but his ears were tuned to the radio.

Then he heard the *Times* station's news broadcaster saying in his crisp cool voice:

"Today the New York City Council voted down the so-called gay rights bill, now famous as Intro Two. The bill would have made it illegal to discriminate against anyone in housing, employment, insurance and

172

other areas because of sexual preferences. The vote was thirty-two to seven. This makes the fourth time that Intro Two has been defeated."

Bill felt a little sick to his stomach, sitting there in the heat, with the sun beating down on his head. The rotten-seaweed and sewage smell of the harbor clogged his nostrils.

Uncle Al grinned proudly.

"Good for Jeannie. I'll bet Jeannie is tickled pink," he said.

"I'm sure she is," said Bill, trying to look happy himself.

They discussed the vote briefly, then went back to discussing their life passion.

". . . trouble is," Al was saying, "that the city already demolished one building in that block. So it's debatable, whether we could . . ."

Bill sat there and kept on talking to Al as if his mind had been put on automatic pilot.

His imagination wiped out the image of Al sitting there, and replaced it with the image of Marion, smiling, hair blowing in the salt breeze.

A memory came back to haunt him, of the day of the tall ships in New York Harbor, during the Bicentennial. Some friends, the Scribners, had invited him and Al to sail around the harbor with them in their 35-foot ketch that day. He had contrived to get Marion invited also, and—as a cover—one other good friend of his and Al's.

The little ketch had tacked gracefully around the harbor, its modest sails overshadowed by the tall masts and the clouds of canvas, on the visiting sail ships from all over the world. They were careful to give the old-time monsters all the right of way they needed. From water level, they waved cheerfully up to the crew on the *Nippon Maru,* and the *Deutschland,* and the *Enchantress,* and the *Flying Cloud.* They had eaten a picnic lunch on board, and drank a little wine.

Bill would never forget the sad magic of that day —being out there in the harbor with Marion, so close to freedom, yet unable to look at him as he would have liked, or talk to him the way they would if they were alone.

Now, listening to the WQXR newscaster reading the baseball scores, he felt that the city council's vote had set the seal of finality on his freedom. It would never happen. He would never have the courage.

Mary Ellen arrived at the station house with the coppery taste of fear in her mouth.

As a cop, she had learned to live with fear long ago —ordinary fear. But today, it was more than fear. It was the clear knowledge that the next few hours might catapault her safe, meaningful life into the unknown.

The station house was buzzing with talk about the gay demonstration. Openly, the men and women there expressed nothing but contempt for the "pansy parade," as PO Bronsky called it. But Mary Ellen wondered how many of them were feeling the same secret nervousness that she felt.

She and five other sergeants were called in to see Captain Bader immediately.

Bader was sitting at his desk, wearing dark circles under his eyes and an air of disgust with the whole world.

"You and your squads are being assigned to the Colter headquarters area," he said. "They've asked for our help up there. It looks like it's going to be big, very big. You'll have all the crowd-control backup we can get."

Mary Ellen knew what this meant. It meant mounted police, Mace, tear gas—the works.

"The Colter people are apparently shitting a brick," Bader went on dryly. "They didn't realize what a hornet's nest they've stirred up."

He was scanning reports on his desk.

"Funny thing, though. We've had a couple of anonymous phone tips that we're going to have a little help from some of the demonstrators. If we see any big tough motorcycle types out there, we're supposed to handle them with kid gloves, because they're supposed to be on *our* side. They apparently don't want a riot either."

Bader looked at all of them broodingly.

"At any rate, I want you to make it very plain to your squads that I don't want to hear *any* complaints about unnecessary police brutality. If things get out of hand, use your heads *first*. Is that clear?"

As the sergeants trooped out to roll call, she heard one of them say, "Didn't the Hell's Angels say they'd keep order at a rock concert a few years ago? And some guy wound up getting stabbed to death . . ."

At her roll call, Mary Ellen stood crisp and straight in front of the rows of uniformed men, who were sprawled in their chairs taking notes. The men had learned the hard way that she didn't like comments like "Isn't she pretty today." They were all business, taking notes and weighing her words.

"The brass say *no* brutality," Mary Ellen told them. "And I will have to emphasize that to you gentlemen."

She didn't even trade looks with Danny, who sat with head bent. She could only guess at the turmoil of feelings going on inside Danny's crisp blue jacket.

And then, all too soon, they were on the street in front of Colter's headquarters at 38th and Park.

It was after seven. A light summer rain was falling.

The area already teemed with "walk-bys," and with police, and TV camera crews with their sound trucks, and photographers, and curious onlookers. Mounted police sat on their big bay horses, whose necks and rumps glistened in the rain.

The police had thrown up yellow wooden barricades around part of the block where the Colter headquarters stood. Lights burned brightly in the Colter office. Mary Ellen could see some of the Colter people in there, trying to pretend they were working, glancing nervously over their shoulders at the street outside.

Unfortunately, since the office faced out on Park Avenue, the police could not block off the entire avenue—especially since it was still the tail end of the rush hour, and the traffic was still heavy.

So the police were simply making the marchers keep to the outside of the barricades.

Mary Ellen stood in front of the yellow barricades, sweltering in her slicker, repeating, "Move along, please. Just move along."

She was amazed at the size of the march. Gay people were pouring into the area from all directions. They walked swiftly and silently and purposefully, as if they were going to work. There was little to distinguish their manner from the rush-hour masses which had filled the streets an hour or two before—except that all of them signaled their gayness in some way.

They hoisted signs such as WE PROTEST COLTER'S CRUELTY TO GAYS. They wore T-shirts lettered with things like "Closets are for clothes." They raised their fists. Little groups sang "We Shall Overcome." Several groups carried huge banners with the names of gay churches.

The leather men were very visible. They must have turned out in force from all over the metropolitan area—a grapevine just as fast and efficient as the police force's radio. Many of them were in full dress—unsmiling, forbidding, impressive in their full regalia—their black leather caps and broad black chain-draped shoulders looming above the crowd.

Mary Ellen stood there at the barricades with her heart in her mouth. If things got out of hand, that crowd might crush her like a dead dry leaf. She felt smothered by the smell and feel of thousands of excited angry bodies pouring past her.

"Move along," she kept saying if anyone paused.

Not far away, Danny had his back to the barricades too, and was actually keeping up an unsmiling banter with the crowd. "Move on now. Just be free and do your thing, that's okay. But keep it quiet. We don't want anybody to get hurt ..."

Mary Ellen wondered if Colter was there in the office. Probably not. That woman probably didn't have the guts to face the people she had destroyed with a vote.

Mary Ellen kept moving them along too. She kept her hand away from her gun, and tried to keep an expression of friendly disinterest on her face.

Now and then she could see the leather men go into action. Down the line, a couple of hotheaded kids were about to mix it with the cops. The leather boys swooped in like eagles and the kids found themselves being whisked out of the crowd and scolded by their own kind. The cops watched unsmilingly.

Suddenly, from the mob closer to her, someone heaved up a Molotov cocktail. It went flying over Mary Ellen's head. The thrower's aim was short, however. The bottle splashed harmlessly into a pool of flame on the empty sidewalk in front of the headquarters. A cop quickly put it out with a foam-thrower.

As Mary Ellen's nerves reacted to this with a hot rush of their own, she saw a disturbance in the crowd, out there where the bottle had been thrown from. Just a ripple, like when a big trout comes flashing to the surface to snap an insect. She saw a couple of leather caps and broad backs moving away, and someone being pushed between them.

She pretended not to see.

It was the longest night she had ever spent.

And sometime during it, a young lesbian leaned out of the crowd at her, said "Woman pig," and spat in her face.

Mary Ellen controlled herself with clenched hands. She looked the lesbian directly in the eyes and said, "Sister, you don't know me."

The lesbian flushed, understanding her meaning, and moved on hastily.

After midnight, the crowd started to taper off.

When they finally went off duty, Mary Ellen and Danny dragged themselves to Mary Ellen's apartment.

Liv was waiting up for them, drained with worry. Switching from channel to channel, she had caught glimpses of the "walk-by" on the evening news. She sat the two exhausted cops down at the kitchen table, and poured two strong cups of coffee.

Danny slumped down in his chair.

"I'm fed up," he said.

Mary Ellen propped her elbows on the table, put her head on her hands, and closed her aching eyes. She could still feel the girl's spit on her face.

"Was Armando out there tonight?"

"No, he wasn't," said Danny. "We had a discussion about it. Not a fight, you understand. Just a discussion. He said he wasn't going to go because he sincerely believes that somebody should take Colter out."

"Hard to blame him for thinking that," said Mary Ellen, getting up and fishing in a kitchen drawer for the aspirin bottle. She took two. "On the other hand, the guys who *were* there got you and me off the hook, didn't they?"

"Yeah, sure, *this* time," said Danny. "What about *next* time?"

"Look," said Mary Ellen, "you want to come out? Come out. And start job-hunting right away."

Liv sat listening to them with her eyes full of pain, stroking Kikan on her lap.

"I like being a cop," said Danny. "But I like feeling good about myself too. I don't like the way I feel anymore. Everybody at the Spike thinks I'm a truck driver. Well, I might as well be one. Better be a truck driver and free than what I am now." Mary Ellen started to speak, but he kept talking. "Look, I'm not passing judgment on you. You're carrying on this family tradition, and it's harder for you to think of giving it up. Me, the only tradition I have is Danny Blackburn."

"I'm not trying to stop you," said Mary Ellen. "Go ahead and try it, and see how far you get. I don't like

178

how I feel either, and I have to find my own way. But I support you one hundred percent, whatever you decide."

The next day Mary Ellen went through her usual routine of visiting with Sam and Jewel.

At Pier 36, Sam bit into the cheeseburger she brought him. He wasn't too interested in hearing about the walk-by. He said:

"You lose one, you win one."

"What do you mean, Sam?" she asked.

"Well," he said, "the city council voted my rights down, right? But I got my library back."

"You mean the Mattachine books are safe?" she said.

He grinned. "The Church of the Beloved Disciple got some money together and bought the whole library. They're fixing up a room for the books. Soon as they've got them catalogued, people can go up there and start using them again."

As usual, Sam escorted her to the stripped Cadillac to show her how Miss Beautiful's kittens were coming along.

At Murphy's Coffee House, Jewel was bitter, and hardly able to talk about the vote. She hadn't been sent to the walk-by. But she hadn't dared to join in as a protester either.

"The rumor is," she said, "that the Police Department did its usual lobbying number, and leaned on the council to vote against the bill. And of course that Colter bitch didn't help us much."

Jewel bit savagely into a Danish.

"And another rumor is," she said, "that five hundred cops are gonna be laid off pretty soon."

Mary Ellen felt a giddy rush of nervousness. She tried to tell herself that they wouldn't dare lay her off.

"Seems somebody made a few mistakes in the city budget," Jewel said. "The money to pay the salaries of these five hundred police officers is just not there.

My boss is so upset about it," she added, "that he's hardly said a word about the gay bill."

At home that night, Danny dropped by and visited with her and Liv for a while.

Danny was deeply depressed, but full of news.

"Armando says the latest talk is a city-wide gay boycott. The walk-by was so successful, I guess it went to their heads."

"Do you think it will work?"

"Dunno." Danny shrugged. "It worked for the blacks in Alabama. Mainly because they organized a lot of car pools and stuck to it for ten months or something. Here . . . I don't know. Armando says one guy came up with a brilliant idea. To organize co-ops that would buy things for gay people out of town—cigarettes, booze, groceries, everything. That way gay people wouldn't pay the city sales tax."

"Then New York *would* go broke."

"Probably," said Danny. "But sooner or later the city is going to go broke in any case."

It was just two days later that Mary Ellen received the curtly worded notice that she was being laid off the New York City police force.

Nine

Mary Ellen and Liv were stunned. They sat at their kitchen table, and Liv read and reread the notice while Mary Ellen sat with her arms folded and stared at the wall.

"But Mary Ellen, what will you do?" Liv finally asked.

Mary Ellen could hardly talk.

"Well," she said in a stifled voice, "there are probably two alternatives. Sometimes they offer you a substitute job as a corrections officer. Or you can move to another city and get a job on another police force." After a moment she added, "And I don't want to be a corrections officer."

Liv sat silent. She reached across the table and held Mary Ellen's hand, which lay inert in hers, unable to respond.

"I can't believe it," said Mary Ellen. "I'm the only woman patrol sergeant in Manhattan. I've done good work. This is gonna make them look very bad in court, when the women's lawsuit gets there. They *have* to have me around. So . . . why? Why let me go?"

"Maybe," said Liv, "that nasty Colter lady knows what kind of person you live with?"

Mary Ellen shook her head. "There were rumors of layoffs before Colter started making her noises."

Once Liv had voiced the idea, however, it was hard to shake off.

When she knew Danny was off duty, Mary Ellen called him. He wasn't home. She called the Steel Spike.

"Yeah, he's here," said Lenny. "He's drunk and mad as a bull. He got laid off his truck job."

"Is Armando there?"

"Yeah."

"Have Armando bring him to my place, and we'll calm him down."

Mary Ellen's head was reeling. The monstrous suspicion was becoming a possible certainty. She called Jewel.

Jewel's flat, half-choked voice coming over the telephone wires told the story.

"Guess what?" she said bitterly. "I'll be going to work in Murphy's Coffee House as a waitress."

Inside Mary Ellen's head, the stunned state of shock was rapidly giving way to pain and anger.

"Listen, Jewel, there's two others who bought it. Me and Danny Blackburn. I have this creepy feeling about the whole thing. Danny and his lover are at the Steel Spike. Why don't you come over to our place?"

Jewel said she'd come.

Now Mary Ellen's thoughts turned to Sam Rauch. What about his job status now? Sam had probably never done anything more gay than visit the Mattachine library. But she decided to check Sam out. Before Jewel, Danny, and Armando came, she'd have time to race over to Pier 36. If Sam was still working, he'd be on duty by now.

She drove fast down the West Side Highway. She parked in front of Pier 36's gloomy doorway, and walked in. As she came up to the office, the usual alarm shattered the air. A strange officer came out.

Her heart sank.

"Miss, we close at four o'clock," he said.

"I'm a PO," she said, pulling her shield and ID out

of her pocket. "I'm a friend of Sam Rauch's. I usually bring him coffee."

"Oh," he said. "Well, Sam's not here."

"Is he sick?"

"Nope," said the officer bitterly. "Laid off."

Deeply depressed, Mary Ellen drove back home and phoned Sam's house. He was there, of course.

"So they told you, huh?" he said.

"Sam, how could they do this to you? You're only two years from retirement."

"Well, I gotta say, they *are* retiring me at full pension. But you know what worries me? I went by there to get some personal stuff and say good-bye to the cats. And the daytime guys, they had moved the car that the kittens were in. Miss Beautiful was looking all over for them. There's a thousand cars in that dump, she'll never find them herself. They're still little, and they need her. They'll die . . ."

Mary Ellen closed her eyes. The cats were Sam's personal variety of tunnel vision.

"Sam," she said, "there's two sisters and a brother been laid off, and I'm one of them. You understand, Sam?"

"You mean the others are . . ."

"That's right."

"Well," said Sam dubiously, "I'm no activist, I got my pension and everything, so why should I beef already?"

"Sam," she said, "come over to our place. Please. It's a moment when we all need each other. And maybe I'll get your kittens for you."

"Okay," said Sam. "I'll be over."

When she hung up, Mary Ellen went down to the building's basement and found a stout J&B whiskey box. She and Liv cut a few little air holes in it. Then Liv stayed behind in case the others came, and Mary Ellen got into the car again, and drove back down to Pier 36.

"I just talked to Sam," she said to the officer on duty.

183

"I was going to adopt those kittens that are around here in one of the cars. Would it be okay if I took them?"

The officer looked at her thoughtfully, and for a moment she was afraid he would say the kittens were city property. Finally he said, "I guess it's okay. The guys was talking about sending them to the SPCA anyway. You know which car they're in?"

"It's a stripped black Cadillac, license plate 598-GBO," Mary Ellen rapped out.

The officer checked his ledger. "It's way down at the end, in one-thirty," he said.

They walked down there in the dark, playing a flashlight beam along the cars. Finally the light picked out the number 130 painted crudely on the wall, and the rusty Cadillac back against the wall, behind a Volkswagen bus. Then the light played on the white kittens who were frantically jumping around inside, yelling with hunger. When Mary Ellen opened the door, the kittens scurried under the seats. It took her ten minutes to pry them out. The kittens, half-wild, made little spitting noises, like tiny firecrackers going off.

She drove home in triumph, with the kittens yowling and scratching and scrambling frantically in the box.

Danny arrived, held up by Armando. Then Sam came. His face lit up when he saw the box and heard the kittens screaming.

"You're a doll *and* a sweetheart *and* a damn nice woman," he said to Mary Ellen.

They were a curious group—three women, three men, and four screaming kittens in a box. Liv made coffee for all, and Danny sobered up a little. They turned the TV on, and the six o'clock newscaster talked soberly about the 500 cops that had been laid off, and the Policemen's Benevolent Association's objection to same.

The cupboard yielded some powdered milk, and

Sam mixed it up nice and thick. He said regular milk would give the kittens diarrhea. In their box, the three tough little kittens crowded around the dish, lapping, slurping, sneezing, blowing bubbles, till their sides bulged out.

"Aw-right," said Sam, "what do we do with these little monsters?" He glared around at everybody. "These here kittens are not going to the SPCA."

"We'll take one," said Liv grandly.

"Okay, I'll take one, too," said Armando.

"What the hell," said Jewel, "I'll take one. Isn't this hysterical? I've never owned a cat."

The group sat around the table and talked about their situation. Danny and Mary Ellen were sure they had been fired because they were gay. "They must have known all the time," Danny said.

Jewel and Sam were not so sure. "The rumors of layoffs were around a long time," said Jewel. "It's just a coincidence."

Danny was adamant. "Sure, they could have been planning to lay people off. But when this Colter thing blew up, they got the idea to lay off any suspected gay people at the same time. This way, nobody would know but them. It's a brilliant idea, really brilliant."

Sam, shy at the new place and the new company he found himself in, drank a beer and didn't have much to say.

The next morning, at her father's breakfast table on the penthouse roof, Jeannie opened up *The New York Times* and said, "O-ho!"

"What?" said her father, from behind a copy of a book called *Lost New York*, with a photograph of the old Penn Station on the cover.

Her father was really in a mood this morning, Jeannie felt lucky to get his attention at all. She wondered if she could get him to talk to Reverend Irving. The trouble was, her father didn't like Reverend Irving much.

"The Police Department has laid off five hundred officers," she said.

"More crime on the streets," said her father, not taking his eyes off the book. "Not a very smart decision."

"I wonder," said Jeannie, "if any of them were homosexuals. They couldn't all be homosexuals, could they? People say there are ten percent homosexuals in the population. The police force is around twenty thousand now, right? Five hundred would be something like two percent homosexuals. They'd have to lay off two thousand . . ."

"I doubt if any of them are," said her father, looking a little far away, as if he were sad about all the beautiful buildings that had vanished in the city. "Al was saying there are rumors of layoffs. The city is going to be laying off a lot of other people, not just police officers."

"But it's kind of strange, isn't it?"

"What?" he said shortly.

"I mean, it's coming just a couple of days after the council voted down the bill." She grinned. "Now if I were Police Commissioner Manuella, and I knew about some homosexuals in my department, and I'd been letting them just go along and do their jobs, and if suddenly I was scared of what Jeannie Colter might say, and they were going to lay off police officers anyway—why, I'd . . ."

Her father didn't answer, turning the pages of his book as if searching for one particular photograph.

"Dad," said Jeannie, "you are in a mood. In fact, you've been in a funny mood for days. I've never seen you like this."

Her father put the book down, and looked her straight in the eyes.

"I am a little overworked," he said, "and I am also tired of hearing about homosexuals. For a month now, I have heard nothing but homosexuals at the breakfast table. I think it's high time we found a more uplifting subject for conversation."

Jeannie felt wounded, and a little contrite.

"I suppose you're right," she said. "I do tend to get carried away sometimes."

The days after the police layoff were strange ones.

Mary Ellen felt dazed by the loss of her job. It still wasn't real yet. Later on, she knew, would come the deep depression and the feeling of being adrift.

She got sympathy calls from Captain Bader, and from several men and women on the force. "Cuffs, I can't believe it," said Bader. "I can't believe they'd let you go. The decision came from higher up."

The PBA was angry, a shrill last-ditch anger after so many layoffs, and it was lobbying on behalf of the laid-off people and their families. Mary Ellen wondered if it would now come out that a few of those laid-offs were the dreaded "homosexualists," who were therefore not entitled to share in the benefits of the PBA's lobbying. But nothing was said. She was still not sure why they had laid off the NYPD Four, as they now called themselves, or that they even knew any of the Four were gay. Still, it was odd. She, and all three of the only other gays she knew in the department, no longer had jobs, and the Colter vote in the city council was just a few days past.

Meanwhile, she and Liv were still worrying about Liv's status in the post office. Moreover, none of the four had been offered jobs as corrections officers, while other laid-off cops had.

However, the days passed, and Liv was not harrassed or fired.

Finally Liv said, "Mary Ellen, I cannot believe this, but Mrs. Whalen hasn't said anything to my boss. I'm sure of it."

"That figures," said Mary Ellen. "She thinks you are so young and beautiful, why is she going to get you fired?"

Mary Ellen did not sign up for unemployment. Her father had despised the welfare system and had brought her up to think poorly of it too. She got right out on the streets, job-hunting. Two days later, she had a job as a waitress in a women's restaurant, Ouika's, on Ninth Avenue and 14th St. It was better than nothing.

She felt so naked—stripped of her uniform and her gun and her beautifully maintained car. Of course, she still had the uniform and guns at home, since they were hers. But without the shield and the ID, they were junk. If the PBA didn't get her reinstated, she would have to sell them. She could see the ad in *Spring 3100* now:

WOMAN'S UNIFORM AND EQUIP: Fits 5′ 9″, 135-pound frame, all leather goods, cuffs; 38 S&W 4″ barrel Service Rev. Laid off. Will sell separately. 469-5503 evenings.

The other members of the NYPD Four dealt with the employment problem each in their own way.

Jewel said the hell with being a cop. She wrote herself a beautiful résumé, based on her reporting experience at *Spring 3100*, and she landed a $12,000-a-year job at a small New York publisher.

Sam had his pension, but he also had the problem of how to fill his days. He wound up going over to the Church of the Beloved Disciple every day to help catalogue his cherished books. Just handling them was apparently a balm to Sam's wounded soul.

Mary Ellen secretly wondered how well he would get along with the spiritual-and-art-minded group of men who ran that little old gay church. To her surprise, Sam reported to her that he was getting along with them just fine.

One day just out of curiosity, she went over there with him. The church was now located on 23rd Street, between Ninth and Tenth Avenues, and was the only gay church in the city that actually owned the real estate where it operated. They walked around in the modern Gothic chapel, very moved, looking at the stained glass windows, at the columned high altar rich with color and gold leaf.

Sam said he had been very impressed when he first saw it.

"Nobody would let those fellas have their own Gothic cathedral. So they built their own. They made every inch of this place with their bare hands," he said. "It's their own Saint Patrick's. Never seen anything like it in my life."

She spent an hour in the library room upstairs, drinking coffee with Sam and a couple of the deacons. The famous collection of books, having survived its "Perils of Pauline," now reposed on many new shelves on four sides of the room. Sam was cataloguing the books, and weeding out a few mavericks that had somehow gotten stuck in.

"This one here is a black sheep, for instance," he said, pulling out a biography of Harry Truman and throwing it scornfully on the long library table in the middle of the room. "The only book about 'Give 'Em Hell Harry' that should be in this place is Merle Miller's."

The deacons cracked up laughing. Mary Ellen could see that they all adored Sam, adored his curious blend of street-wise tough guy and sixty-year-old naiveté.

She could also see that Sam was getting his first closeup look at long-time male love relationships. Two of the men who ran the church had been together all their lives. Sam was obviously touched by this, though by no means sure that he could make a start on relationships this late in life.

While she was sitting there, Mary Ellen was also struck for the first time by the importance of those books. She had never been much of a bookworm herself and had always dismissed Sam's rage for reading as part of his cop-out.

The deacons impressed on her that this was one of three major gay book collections on the East Coast, another being owned by a famous activist and still another by an anonymous private collector. And there were rumored to be two important libraries on the West Coast.

Mary Ellen touched the backs of the books gently, realizing she was in the presence of something larger than life, almost holy. The books were an effort by gay people to rebuild their history, which had been shattered by the persecution of the Jeannie Colters back through the ages. They ranged from serious works on psychology to current bestsellers to cheap awful unliberated paperbacks of the 1950s, to august Victorian tomes of poetry, bound in leather and published in England.

"It's like our Library of Congress, see?" said Sam, showing her a first edition of Walt Whitman's *Leaves of Grass*. "Or like that library in . . . where was it? Alexandria, I think it was called. All kinds of books of history and philosophy written on sheep hides, in the old days, right? Somebody burned the place down, and the world was never the same after that."

Mary Ellen left the church feeling a little happier than she had in days, feeling that Sam had at least made a start on finding his niche.

But when she got home to the empty apartment, the small glow about Sam faded.

Liv was at the post office. Mary Ellen puttered around the apartment, washed the breakfast dishes, gathered some laundry to go to the laundromat. She even went up to the rooftop garden and busied herself picking faded blooms off the petunia plants. She didn't have to go to work at the restaurant till six.

Suddenly wave after wave of memories of her father assaulted her.

She remember his passion for playing the horses. On nice Sundays like today, they would take the bus out to Aqueduct or Belmont, and her father would sometimes parlay fifty dollars cash into several hundred by the end of the day. He said he had figured out a very original system for beating the track, and he didn't make too many bets for fear the track would find out. During the week, he sometimes went to one Off-Track Betting office, and sent Mary Ellen to another OTB office to place another bet. In their apartment, her father had stacks of computer cards sitting around. He didn't have a computer, so he did all the calculations himself. The worst thing you could do to her father was knock over his stacks of cards. Whatever the system was, it worked, and over the years her father put away a nice nest egg. He paid taxes on it scrupulously, because "it's for my little girl," he told Mary Ellen. The racetrack money had gone to pay the estate taxes on the place in Massachusetts. It was now hers, and she had not visited it since his death. For the first time, she felt the wish to go there, almost a wish to reopen the infected wound of her father's death and let it bleed healthily.

Oh, those happy larcenous Sundays with her father at the track, sitting in the cheaper seats, yelling their horse home, celebrating with steak and eggs if they won.

She sat on the edge of the velour bed, and sobbed as if she were still at his funeral, seeing his brother officers carry his coffin out of the church.

The anger rose up between her teeth like a sour black vomit, from somewhere in her guts that she still didn't know.

Slowly the anger was taking her over, like some raging demon with a long Hebrew name, straight out of the Bible.

CHAPTER
Ten

It was the Fourth of July weekend, just a month after
Jeannie Colter had made her first speech against the
gays.

It was a little past midnight on Saturday night—a
hot sultry summer night with a threat of sudden rain
in the air.

Danny came out of Armando's apartment feeling so
good that he wasn't ready to go home and go to bed
yet. He didn't have to worry about being fresh for
police duty anyway. For the moment, he was living
off his small savings, and reading job ads in the newspapers—and he was having a good time.

Danny Blackburn, ex-cop, had come out.

The shock of having lost his job was starting to wear
off. When he was a kid, he had been a bad boy over
there in Queens—one of the bad boys of Howard
Beach. He had done a lot of things that the cops had
never caught him at, like smoking dope and shooting
speed and taking joyrides in cars he didn't own and
even a few small burglary jobs.

But finally he had realized that all those small-time
punks he knew were going nowhere. Ten years from
now, they would still be hanging around in the same
bars and poolrooms, or in the same parking lots, looking to cop a hit of methadone from the same tired

small dealers. Danny had realized that the cops who chased them were a way he could better himself.

So he had decided grandly to be a cop, and give the police the benefit of all his knowledge of bad boys. But now the cops didn't want him. Okay, that was cool. He would find something else to do with his life. He wasn't sure exactly what, at the moment.

Meanwhile, since his layoff, he was busy burning all his bridges behind him.

The NYPD might offer him a corrections officer job. They might even invite him back on the force—a few laid-off officers had been reinstated in the past. But Danny was beyond caring about this. The hell with them. He was getting his first taste of total freedom.

He had visited every bar, bath, and after-hours place in Manhattan—anywhere that the big strong men hung out. He had not gone to these places at noon, when they were half empty, but at the midnight hours. He had been a little unfaithful to Armando (though not much). Armando, not possessive, was amused. The hell with the shooflies. Let them see him.

Danny had even gone to the Treasure Chest and bought a leather cap just like Armando's. (He had driven the store crazy, trying on everything in the place.) He even toyed with the idea of buying a pair of those black leather chaps that bared your buns, but he couldn't afford them.

But he did collect a bunch of old keys from around his apartment, and proudly hung them on his left hip. The hell with the shooflies.

That day, Armando had had the day off. Danny had gone to his lover's apartment about noon. They had a rather ordinary but very emotional session in the bedroom. Then they went out to the Men's Club, and had a big steak dinner and a few drinks. Then the two of them toured various bars on Barrow Street. All eyes turned toward them, and Danny knew that he and Armando made a very impressive pair.

Then they went back to Armando's apartment, and had another session, and talked about moving in together.Then they fell asleep.

Danny woke up about two, and knew that Armando was finished and would sleep clear through.

So he got dressed and put on his jacket and his new hat and his bunch of keys. He felt strangely happy. He didn't have a job, but at least he had a lover, and he was very happy about that. He'd survive, somehow.

Out in Armando's garden, he could hear the gingko tree and the ivy leaves rustling in a delightfully unsettling breeze. Off in the distance, over the noise of the occasional passing car and a stereo in the neighboring apartment, he could hear distant rumbles of thunder. A summer thunderstorm was blowing up.

Out on the street, on an impulse, he decided not to go home yet. The night was young, and he was so beautiful.

So he headed for the Spike, for a night-cap.

He walked swiftly, feeling an eerie little rush as he walked down the long blocks of darkened warehouses.

It had been years since muggers had tried to jump Danny. Matter of fact, the last time he was mugged was during his bad-boy days. He was hanging around a supermarket parking lot in Howard Beach just about this time on a Saturday night, looking to cop a nickel bag of grass from one of the local small-time dealers, and three boys mugged him, and beat him up, and robbed him of the five dollars he had in his pocket for the dope.

At the Spike, he enjoyed himself enormously, considering that none of the guys in the place seemed worth being unfaithful to Armando with. He leaned unsmiling against the bar for a while, and let himself be admired from a distance. He had an interesting conversation with Lenny, who told him all about his boyhood in Wyoming. He had three shots of Wild Turkey, and one on the house from Lenny, and when he left the place, he was riding pretty high, with the black leather cap cocked at a rakish angle over one eye.

Outside, he could see the thunderheads coming over the Palisades, all lit up with fantasies of pale orange and pink and yellow lightning. The wind blew as fresh across the river as he could ever remember it, and it actually carried from somewhere a scent of grass and trees across the Hudson to the sleeping city.

Danny turned the corner of 21st Street and started east toward Ninth Avenue, whistling tunelessly.

There was a big feeling inside him, of Saturday-night good times going back over the years—good times in the little clubs and discos of Long Island, when he still thought he could get to like girls, good times in red-neck bars in the shadow of the elevated in Queens, where his innocent face helped him to hustle a little pool, playing for quarters against straight left-over-beatnik types in black leather jackets—good times that taught him everything he knew about people and about the streets, and that had stood him in such good stead on the force. Good times hanging around people who were fencing stolen goods and dealing coke and playing numbers and hijacking trucks—even people who smuggled seed clams in from the South Shore towns—never getting into serious trouble himself, (Well, a couple of scrapes as a juvenile, but never as an adult, a felon) because he was too fond of his family to hurt them, but always on the edge of trouble, always knowing what was going on.

Danny knew that he had done well on the force, and he was convinced he would get another chance to give society all his knowledge of bad boys and how they got to be that way.

A small part of his mind wasn't drunk, however, and told him that these thoughts were fantasies. He had always sent part of his check to his parents, who still lived on 257th Avenue in Howard Beach. His mother had already phoned to ask why his last couple of checks hadn't come, and he had to break down and tell her the truth. She had begged him to come home, and look for a job out in Queens, but he had said no, that he had a line on a couple of jobs in Manhattan. His mother had been crushed. She said his father had always been so proud of his career on the force, after the grief he gave them when he was such a punk in school.

He walked with long strides, feeling the storm at his back, sniffing the air.

Suddenly he was aware that he was being followed.

He whirled to face them in the shadow of a darkened warehouse and some dusty closed-up shop windows. If this had been TV, now, he could have disposed of them with a couple of karate chops and kicks. But it was real life, and there were five of them, with lengths of weighted pipe and chains. He didn't have his off-duty gun any more. All he had was a bunch of keys and four Wild Turkeys.

His cap fell off as he punched one, then another. He tried desperately to grab one of the pipes, so he could defend himself. The last thing he heard was one of them panting, "Motherfuckin' queer," before a weighted lead pipe crunched down on his skull.

They kicked him and stomped him for several minutes. Then they left a scribbled note lying on his chest, and walked hurriedly away.

Just down the street, a car's headlights glared into life, and the engine started. The five men all got in, and the car drove quickly away.

Danny lay crumpled and twisted against the sooty foundation of the warehouse, right by the dusty corrugated truck doors. The cap lay upside down on the sidewalk about six feet from him.

The storm squall came slowly across the river, peppering the broad reach of water with heavenly buckshot. It slowly blotted out the Palisades, so that the lights of the faraway apartment towers along them glowed fuzzily in the dark, as if out of focus. The raindrops spattered on his bloody hair. As the sidewalk wetted, thin wavering threads of dark red began to spread away from his head.

A couple of days later, Mary Ellen got a phone call from Armando, just before she was leaving for work.

"Have you heard from Danny?" he asked. "Or seen him?"

"No," she said. "Why?"

"Oh, I don't know ... it's funny, but he's been out job-hunting every day, and usually we get together afterward, like at my place if I'm off, or he drops by my bar. And if he can't come, like if he's sick or something, he always calls. But yesterday and today, he didn't show, and he didn't call. And he's not home."

"I can't help you," said Mary Ellen. "I haven't heard a thing."

She was just getting ready to walk out the door when the phone rang again.

Armando's voice had the sound of an animal's death rattle in it.

"Mary Ellen, it's right in the newspaper," he said. "It's right there in the *Daily News*, in black and white."

Mary Ellen felt her heart give a deathly rush in her chest. Even before he said the words, she knew what they would be.

Armando's voice was breaking.

"Apparently he went to the Spike after he left my place. I was asleep when he left. According to Lenny —the cops were down there interviewing guys, right? —Danny had several drinks, then left. They jumped him just around the corner, and they beat him to death ..."

Stunned, Mary Ellen stopped at a newsstand and bought a copy of the *News*. Her fears were confirmed. In death, Danny's cover was blown in rather spectacular fashion, right on the front page.

EX-COP SLAIN NEAR GAY BAR

The story inside read:

> Late last night, a laid-off police officer, Danny Blackburn, was found beaten to death just around the corner from the Steel Spike, a well-known downtown gay bar. Two weeks ago, Blackburn had been laid off, along with 499 other officers.
>
> The body was discovered by a passing motorist, who called the police. The 24-year-old Blackburn was pronounced DOA at a city hospital. The identification was made from the dead officer's wallet.
>
> Lenny Marks, a bartender at the Steel Spike, told police that Blackburn had been there earlier in the evening, and that he was a regular visitor. A black leather cap, of a type often worn by the regular clientele of these bars, was found near the body.
>
> Also found with the body was a note scribbled by the unknown assailants. The note read, "One for you, Jeannie." Police believe that the note refers to Jeannie Colter and her campaign against the homosexual-rights bill recently voted down by the city council.

Numbly, she threw the newspaper into the next city trash can.

As she walked on down the street, toward her waitress job, her mind played a strange trick on her.

It seemed like she was back in the precinct station house, still a cop, and she was seeing and hearing the reactions of the police officers all around her.

She had to read the report that one of her own squad members had made—they had been given the radio run for the "unconscious person" on 21st Street. At roll call, she was not given a "wanted" to read regarding Danny's assailants, as there had been no witnesses. The only thing the police had to go on was the scribbled note.

The atmosphere was strange. Had Danny not been found near a gay bar, with the telltale leather cap beside him, the station house would have been seething

with the usual rage when a cop—even a laid-off cop—
is killed. As it was, everybody was talking about it—
but no one was showing emotion, either out of fear of
showing sympathy or out of lack of sympathy altogether.

"Just goes to show you," one PO said in Mary Ellen's hearing, "those queers can fool anybody. Lookit
Danny, the most masculine kind of guy you could
imagine, and he turns out a crud, a real skell . . ."

Mary Ellen's own need to keep quiet almost choked
her. She still had her own cover to think about, her
own job to protect.

She wondered how many other closet gays on the
force were feeling as she was.

Finally she was out on the street with a new partner, driving west on the first blocks of her patrol.

Suddenly the emotion burst the iron bands that had
wrapped around it. She sat at a stoplight, her chest
heaving spasmodically and violently under her uniform jacket, her mouth open, her eyes blurred. A
thread of saliva was dripping from her chin. She didn't
care whether her new partner saw her cry or not.

She was dimly aware that she was crying all over
again for her father.

And then she was dimly aware that she was not
sitting in her squad car at all.

She was walking down the street to her waitress
job. She was crying openly on the street, where everybody could see, just like one of those typical New York
psychopaths who talk to themselves on the street.

That was when she realized that they weren't psychopaths at all. They were just human beings whose
last protective layer had been peeled off bloodily, and
who were transmitting the noise of grief that could not
be shut off.

Bill sat glumly on a heap of old tires in the large
immaculate downtown garage where Marion always
serviced his car.

No more Formula 1 racing cars for Marion. He didn't even test-drive cars for Rolls. And his personal car was a rather sedate sports model, a new one, manufactured by the company he worked for. The Rolls 100 was up on the lift, waxed and polished to a fault, and Marion, wearing a crisp blue grease-monkey suit with only a couple of smudges on it, was doing a wheel-balancing job. The whole garage was brightly lighted, scattered with assorted foreign cars in varying stages of repair and so clean that you could have done open-heart surgery there.

Bill had just finished telling Marion about the death of the police officer, Blackburn. He had arrived at the garage just before noon, and he and Marion had adjourned to the corner beef 'n burger joint for some lunch.

There, in a corner booth, over hamburgers deluxe and fries, while the waitresses clattered all around them, Bill had talked compulsively, and Marion had listened without saying a word.

"Maybe if I'd come out, years ago, I could have educated her about all this, when her mind was more pliable. Maybe even if I'd come out to her when she started doing all this campaigning, I could have put a stop to this whole thing. Maybe if I hadn't given her that money . . . maybe that kid would be alive today . . ."

"Maybe," said Marion.

He seemed curiously unsympathetic.

"I suppose," Marion added, "that you feel guilty enough to go to the funeral."

"That's the sad thing," said Bill. "It was in the papers this morning that his parents aren't even going to claim the body. It's still at the morgue."

Marion stopped eating, and leaned his forehead into one hand, and closed his eyes. His lips seemed to form the word "God."

"In other words, his parents aren't too pleased," said

Bill. "Apparently they never had an inkling. They're working-class Catholics. Danny was their only son, so . . ."

Marion pushed his plate away.

"Those fries are pretty greasy," he said.

"The papers said that his lover and some friends at the MCC are trying to claim the body," Bill said. "So one way or another, I guess he'll get buried in some kind of style."

"How does Jeannie feel about all this? I mean, whoever did it, did it for her, right?"

Bill shrugged. Those fries *were* pretty greasy. They were sitting there in his stomach, feeling whole and unchewed, like a logjam.

"Well, she's not exactly jumping for joy. But she does feel that he asked for it, of course. Her attitude is, if he hadn't gone to that bar, if he hadn't been living in filthy sin, it wouldn't have happened, right? And she sympathizes with the parents totally."

They had paid and walked out of the place, and back to the garage.

Suddenly Marion had said, "I'm sorry to be talking like such a prig. I've been very hard on you the past couple of weeks. After all, I'm not marching up Fifth Avenue with a banner saying 'gay is good' either."

A flicker of joy had lit Bill's mind briefly.

But now, while Bill sat on the tires, Marion went back to work on the car. He worked with the absorption of the professional who knew what a car would do at 164 miles an hour. A half hour passed, and Marion didn't say more than a few words to him.

The fact was, their relationship seemed to be in an unprecedented crisis. Here they were, planning the living spaces within that handsome brick-and-stone shell down on South Street, and meanwhile they were hardly getting along. Quarrels they had had, but always they made up quickly. Was it possible to lose your lover in your sixties, after years of happiness together? After all, these days, straight people in their sixties broke up and got divorced.

Bill tried to imagine living alone in the house on Catherine Slip.

"Well," he said to Marion, "this doesn't seem to be the time and the place for visiting."

Marion, who had been working with head thrown back, arms stretched up toward the under parts of the car, drew his arms down and looked at him with the veiled look he always used in public.

"I'm glad you came," he said.

But he seemed to say it with almost an air of formality.

"I guess I'll head back downtown," Bill said. "I'll call you later."

"Please do," said Marion.

"How about dinner?" Bill was almost afraid to ask, as if it was a first date.

"It depends," said Marion, "on how late I am here. I've got to do a few other things."

"Well, I'll call you, and we'll play it by ear," said Bill.

And then he was out on the street, away from the roar of gunned engines and the clang of tools on the concrete floor.

He walked back to his own car, numbed by a dread so great that it was hardly a feeling—rather an overwhelming fact that was collapsing over him, like one of those "white seas" that sometimes overwhelm a ship in the lonely quarters of the seas.

Mary Ellen waited for the police to contact her.

She knew that they would talk to her. If they were going through the barest motions of solving Danny's murder, they *had* to talk to her, as part of their canvassing. After all, she had been Danny's partner.

If they hadn't known she was a lesbian before, they might find out now.

Of course, she and Danny had always been careful. They had never visited gay places together. After their first meeting at the MCC, they had never gone to the gay church together. But still . . . she waited now to see if their routine investigating would turn up her true sexual identity.

To her surprise, it was not some detective who came to see her. It was Captain Bader himself.

He showed up at Ouika's Restaurant late one night, about an hour before closing time. He was dressed in plain clothes. He sat down at a table alone in a corner. The dark circles under his eyes were still there.

Her stomach clenching with nervousness, Mary Ellen went to wait on him.

"Could I talk to you when you get through with work?" he asked. "Just a few routine questions about Danny, if you don't mind."

He had a drink while he waited.

When the restaurant was closing, he and Mary Ellen sat quietly in the corner. The cook sent out a couple of dinners from the kitchen. Bader looked suspiciously at the soybean croquettes and the strange salads, but manfully tried them.

"I'm ashamed," said Bader, "that my people didn't give you more aid and comfort when Danny was killed."

Mary Ellen shrugged sadly, and could not eat.

"I did hear a lot of talk about 'Poor Mary Ellen, that skell taking her for a ride, using her for his cover.' That kind of crap."

"You don't have to tell me," said Mary Ellen hoarsely. "I know exactly what was said. And who said it."

Bader looked around the restaurant. "How are you doing?"

"Okay," said Mary Ellen. "This is just temporary. When I pull myself together, I'll find something better."

"Mary Ellen, I want you to know that Danny's file hasn't been stuck in a back drawer somewhere. The department is moving to find his killers."

"I'm glad to hear it," she said faintly.

"Yesterday there was a similar assault near another bar. Same MO. Same kind of note left on the body. Fortunately the victim is still alive. He's in a coma. But if he ever comes out of it, we're hoping that he can identify the assailants."

Unable to help herself, Mary Ellen felt the blinding tears running down her face again. They ran silently, without a sob or a drawing of breath.

Bader rubbed his hand over his face, evidently distressed at the sight of her tears.

"Mary Ellen, do you have *any* information on who might have beaten Danny?"

She shook her head.

"If you learn anything, will you come to me with the information?" he persisted gently.

She nodded, unable to speak.

He studied her awkwardly. She had the impression that he was on the verge of reaching out and patting her hand, but he didn't. He just sat there, silent for a few minutes.

Finally he said, "Mary Ellen, I want you to know how very sorry I am that you're gone. And I'm sorry that Danny is gone. He was a good cop, and a damn nice kid."

She looked at him dumbly through her tears, and managed to nod.

Later, when she was home having a last cup of coffee and bathing her burning eyes, it occurred to her to wonder about Captain Bader. He could have questioned her at her apartment, but he hadn't. At the apartment, he would have noted the one bedroom, and the one bed. He might have seen Liv. It was lucky that he hadn't gone canvassing to Bedford Street.

She wondered if Bader was one of the real hard-core closet cases in the department. With his high rank and all his citations and his good pay and his family, he'd have a lot to lose. So a guy like that wouldn't come out to anyone.

In any case, she couldn't help noting his delicacy in the matter—his not questioning her at home, his not questioning her in detail, his sympathy for Danny. And by questioning her himself, Bader had made sure that no one else would talk to her. With Bader's report in the files, the police would probably consider the matter closed.

Jeannie Colter faced the TV news cameras.

Something like outraged indignation was going on inside her. But she maintained her calm exterior, as she mentally rehearsed the prepared statement that she had memorized.

The death of this obscure patrolman had certainly become a cause célèbre in the city. The mush-headed liberals had the nerve to say that Blackburn's death was her fault. The liberals and the homosexuals were making a martyr out of someone who didn't deserve to be one—an unsavory character, with a record as a juvenile, who had been beaten to death by some misguided thugs (probably drunk) in an unsavory neighborhood.

What was there to glorify in that?

She was also very jittery, and in the back of her mind was the memory of how soothing a cocktail had been. She pushed the thought away.

There had even been a rumor that the parents of the immoral young man were planning to sue her for a million and a half dollars. Quickly she had had her attorney contact them, and it turned out that they planned no such thing. In fact, they seemed as outraged about Danny Blackburn's hidden homosexual life as she was.

The problem was that the men who beat Blackburn to death, and thousands of others like them, had no legal means to express their anti-homosexual feelings.

After all, they had rights, too. They had the right to live in a society uncontaminated by this element, to send their children to schools free of homosexual teachers, to live in neighborhoods where there were no homosexuals carrying on.

In centuries past, society had a more clear-cut method of dealing with homosexuals. It put them in jail, or in insane asylums—it even dared to mandate the death sentence against them. And when you considered that in some countries, people had been hanged for stealing a loaf of bread, hanging homosexuals didn't seem severe by comparison.

All these thoughts poured through her mind. They were what she *really* wanted to say.

But, with whatever experience she had gained in her ten years in the New York State political arena, she knew that she couldn't express herself in this way. She had to water it down.

The TV crews were setting up in her district office. NBC, ABC and CBS had all naturally wanted to know what her feelings about the Blackburn murder were. So she had agreed to hold a press conference and make a statement.

Tom Winkler was very unhappy about the whole business. He had just retained Hart & Straus, a Boston firm who had successfully handled the media affairs of several winning candidates. He had mumbled something about how Hart & Straus would have their work cut out for them.

She had dressed carefully for this appearance. TV had always been her strong point, and she knew it. She was wearing a simple black dress with a little white Peter Pan collar and short sleeves with white cuffs, that one of her staff had jokingly called Camp Revival. Her hair was simply done. A bare minimum of makeup. Missing would be her famous beauty-queen smile. She wouldn't dare to flash it at such a somber moment—but she could make people remember it.

Tom Winkler was going around mumbling that he felt that things had gotten way out of focus. He had written her statement for her, saying he hoped this would get things back on the track again. He had mumbled that he was sick of hearing about homosexuals. Funny ... her father had said that.

"Mrs. Colter, are you ready?" asked a man from one of the film crews.

"Any time you are," she said brightly.

The fact was, even Steve was unhappy about the Blackburn business. Steve was a very sensitive boy—rather oversensitive about violence, in fact. He refused to watch television because it upset him. And so, the other day, Steve had said something about Blackburn that had really shaken her up.

The bright lights were shining on her. Under her crisp little dress, the heat of the lights was bringing out a fine sweat on her limbs.

She trained her eyes on the camera lens so the viewer would feel she was looking directly into his or her eyes and making personal contact with her dark eyes that she had tried to use to such good effect in the "good girl" roles she had played in films.

The cameras were rolling. One of the crew men signaled to her to start speaking.

"I *deplore* the fact that Blackburn was beaten to death. I would deplore it whether it was done in my name or for no reason at all. In general, I deplore violence. It is one of the things I have always stood for in politics. I deplore crime in the street, and the easy violence that seems to plague our society, and it's one of the things I will work for if I am elected governor. I hope that the men who killed Blackburn are caught, and punished to the fullest extent of the law."

She spoke slowly, intensely, yet naturally, letting the full timbre of her voice find its way through, without theatrical speechifying.

The fact was that Steve had upset her greatly with his comment. She had called Windfall to find out how everything was, and to say she would definitely be coming up there for the weekend. Steve had gotten on the phone and asked her what she thought of the Blackburn thing.

She had said, "Well, it's like a drunk who walks in front of a car and gets killed. If he hadn't been drunk, he wouldn't have gotten in front of the car in the first place."

She had said it lightly. Perhaps she had counted too much on Steve's faith, and too little on his youth and sensitivity.

He had said, "But Mom, that sounds like you're excusing what those men did."

"Darling, that's not so."

"Mom, those guys beat a guy to death, and they did it because of things you said, and I bet they'll do it again."

Later that day, after the press conference, Jeannie and Tom Winkler and a couple of her other aides were driving up Route 684 toward Pawling.

Jeannie was driving with her usual panache, and Winkler had one hand braced defensively against the dashboard, as he always did when he drove anywhere with her. The others were in the back, silent. All her staff were feeling a little off-balance right now.

"By the way, what's the latest on the Blackburn thing?" she said.

"The parents claimed the body," said Winkler.

"Oh, they did? What made them change their minds?"

"The fact that the gays were trying to claim the body."

"Tom, don't call them gays," she said, a little irritated. "That's *their* word. Don't tell me you're sympathetic to them."

"I'm not," said Winkler. "But I find the word homo-

208

sexual a little cumbersome, and I'm not going to waste any more energy saying it."

"So there's going to be a funeral after all " she said.

"No. No viewing. A short service, and straight to the cemetery. No one but immediate family allowed. Masses said for his soul. And that's it. I gather a few policemen wanted to attend—not in uniform, of course. But the family said they didn't want anyone there. No reporters, nothing."

Winkler gazed glumly out the window.

Jeannie looked at him briefly, then switched her eyes back to the highway.

"I think you're over-reacting to this whole thing," she said.

"I am," he said, looking back at her intently. "I think it's a disaster. Fortunately, you handled it as correctly as possible. But it's still a disaster. The voters will now remember you as someone whose political activities cause violence. And of course, deep down, I know damn well that you don't care about the kid's death at all."

"Pooh," she said.

He turned to face her on the seat, so agitated that he actually took his hand off the dashboard.

"Jeannie, I think you're way out in left field with this gay thing. I think you're overdoing it. People are going to associate you with this alone, when they go to the polls. They are going to associate you with something that they think is ugly and distasteful."

"I bet we can do a poll and prove you wrong. And I've always campaigned against things that are ugly and distasteful," she said sharply. "People are going to remember me for massage parlors and pornography. Is that so bad?"

Winkler was almost yelling now, too.

"Well, I'll tell you what I think, in case you're interested in my twenty years of experience running campaigns for people who hold much higher offices than you do!"

"All right, tell me," she said sarcastically.

"I think you ought to forget about this gay business, and start talking to the voters about the cost of living, and consumer problems, and taxes, and some other down-home issues. You got the Intro Two defeated, what more do you want? Take my advice and drop it, Jeannie. If you get elected governor, you can try to get the laws against gays stiffened up, if that's what you want to do. But do it *later*, in a context of caring about the other concerns of voters. I don't think they are really truly concerned about it. They are concerned about putting their kids through college, and . . ."

"I disagree," she said sharply. "I think they are very concerned. I think the whole issue frightens them to death. I think it's a great way to get their attention."

"But Jeannie, the big scare issues of yesterday . . . where are they? What did they accomplish? Where is George Wallace? Where is Senator McCarthy? Where are they? Tell me."

Jeannie was silent. She found she had no answer to Winkler's questions.

"Jeannie, I believe in you," he said, lowering his voice a little. "I believe in your integrity and your energy and your toughness and your stubbornness and your intensity. I feel those are very marketable political products right now. But goddamn it, you are also wrongheaded and fanatical and bigoted and you don't have too much common sense."

"Thanks a lot," she said.

"As of right now, I am taking more hold on this campaign. I have been giving you too much leeway. We're not running an anti-gay Ku Klux Klan here. We are running for governor. I am having some major speeches written for you that are going to put this whole thing back into perspective, and *right now*."

She sighed.

"All right," she said.

"If it doesn't get back into perspective," he said, "then I won't feel like wasting my time on it. Do you understand, Jeannie?"

She understood all too well. If she and her campaign manager had a falling out, and he went around saying things like that, it would be bad publicity.

"All right, all right," she said.

They reached the spot where 684 narrowed down and became old Route 22. After a discreet silence, one of the aides, a new kid named Burt Haddleigh who had worked for the mayor, spoke up from the back seat. He had an idea, he said, about something new that Jeannie could speak out against, that would get people's minds off the gay thing.

"Tell me about it," said Jeannie, looking at him in the rearview mirror.

"Well," said Haddleigh awkwardly, "er, you may think I am nuts . . . but Manny Schwartz of Brooklyn has introduced a bill in Albany that will put a ten-percent tax on pet food and vet care for pets. The tax money will go to, uh, clean up after, uh, dogs on the streets in the bigger municipalities. Now, this is going to accelerate the rate of abandoned animals, because people won't be able to care for them. So . . ."

Jeannie had been about to cut the kid off irritably, but with his last sentence, she began to see what he meant.

Winkler's mind was miles ahead of them all.

"That English vet," he said, "what's his name, Herriot, sold millions of copies of his books. People are pushovers for animals, right? And why should pet owners be discriminated against that way? I can see Jeannie being photographed visiting shelters, and going to bat for old people who can't afford to keep pets . . ."

"It's not a big idea, really," said the aide, growing

braver. "But it will show people that Mrs. Colter cares about the smaller issues like that . . ."

"I like it," said Jeannie to the aide. "Write me a memo on it."

For the moment, the storm had blown over. They all felt charged with a new sense of purpose.

CHAPTER
Eleven

It was shocking, Mary Ellen thought, how fast a dead friend could disappear out of your life, if you were gay.

Danny had been whisked away into the eternal blue without giving his friends any of the comforting rites that society afforded to straight people. His parents had the body removed from the morgue to an undertaker in the Bronx. They told the press that none of Danny's "depraved associates" would be allowed at the brief church service, or in the huge Bronx cemetery where Danny was laid to rest amid hundreds of rows of thousands of tombstones. So neither Armando nor any of Danny's friends sat in the church and heard the comforting words of the Catholic priest about the resurrection and the life. They were also denied the catharsis of crying at Danny's graveside.

Mary Ellen found that Danny's death had lodged in her throat like a lump of bread too dry to swallow. And, she told herself, she had been only Danny's friend. Armando must feel a hundred times worse.

The condolences that Armando had received had been "off the books," so to speak. No nice notes from relatives saying "if only I could find the words" and all the other funeral folk-ways which became precious when you were denied the right to them.

However, within itself, the gay community had reacted heavily to Danny's death—not just in New York,
but all over the country.

The gay newspapers ran editorials about it. For a
week or so, picketers outside Jeannie Colter's headquarters carried signs such as COLTER PREACHES MUR-
DER and BLACKBURN'S BLOOD IS ON YOUR HANDS. That
Sunday, at the MCC, Reverend Erickson preached to
a packed church and wrung muffled sobs from his congregation with a fiery sermon about the able young
police officer, cut down in the flower of his youth just
as he was finding his way out of the closet. Reverend
Erickson also managed to get in a few digs at some
gay Christians who had hardened their hearts to Danny's death because he was into S&M.

"We are our brothers' and sisters' keepers," he thundered, "*regardless* of what their life-style is."

As the MCC general conference in Washington,
D.C., got underway, the MCC board decided that
the candlelight march to the Lincoln Memorial,
planned for Friday night of the conference week,
would be turned into a gigantic memorial service
for Danny Blackburn and others who had died violent deaths back over the years of the gay liberation
movement.

Mary Ellen and Liv, seeing how Armando was suf-
fering, tried to persuade him that they all ought to go
to Washington for the Friday march.

"It won't be his funeral," she told Armando, "but
it'll be the next best thing."

She had been afraid that Armando would start
drinking a lot. But Armando had learned too much
discipline as a bartender to drown his grief in booze.
He trudged to work at the Eagle's Nest every day,
went through the motions behind the bar, drank no
more than usual. The big man, an underground celeb-
rity overnight, didn't make plays for his customers'
sympathy. He was silent, with fixed eyes, beyond
reach, like a wounded animal. The men crowding into

214

the bar quickly learned that he didn't want to hear their condolences. He didn't even accept the larger-than-usual tips they left.

Finally Armando said he would go to Washington. This was on Thursday night. Sam and Jewel decided they would go too.

Friday afternoon, the five of them drove down to the capital, Mary Ellen and Sam and Liv in front, Armando's bulk and tiny Jewel wedged into the back of Mary Ellen's Vega wagon.

It was for occasional trips like this that Mary Ellen put up with the hassles of keeping a car in New York, getting up at odd hours to move it to another parking place. Her father had always kept a car. Besides, she told herself, someday she might want to start going up to the cabin in Massachusetts again, and she and Liv would need the car to get there.

In Washington, they just had time to check into their cheap hotel. Then they hurried to the First Congregational Church, which was hosting the MCC general conference.

Mary Ellen looked around in astonishment at the hundreds of people streaming into the big modern brick church. It was the first time she had ever attended a gay convention of any sort. It hit her that Jeannie Colter was right about one thing. "We *are* legion," she thought. "We *are* everywhere."

The big church was packed—it didn't seem possible to shoehorn another body in. The balcony, laden with gay humanity, seemed in danger of collapsing. The organist, an older man wearing a Lambda pendant, was playing a stately old hymn, "Jesu, Joy of Man's Desiring," on the big pipe organ. But despite the solemnity of the music, a joyous bustle filled the air—people running around talking about MCC politics, talking about the growth of MCC abroad, passing out hymn sheets, greeting old friends.

Since there was standing room only, Mary Ellen, Liv and Armando inched their way along a side aisle

215

toward the front. Then Reverend Erickson saw them and came quickly to escort them to extra chairs put hurriedly at the front for them.

Mary Ellen looked out over the sea of gay humanity, and a lump lodged in her throat. Joyous, bra-less lesbians in T-shirts and clean jeans, older women in knit dresses and sensible shoes, young and middle-aged men in faded jeans and silver jewelry, old men in business suits and gray hair—whites, blacks, Puerto Ricans, Japanese-Americans, Hawaiians, Canadians, Australians, Europeans . . .

When the service began, the organ crashed into the opening chords of "Washed in the Blood of the Lamb." That mass of humanity came to its feet and roared out the hymn like she had never imagined it could be sung. Cold chills went racing up and down her body. All around her, arms were raised high in the air in the evangelical gesture of affirmation. She found herself raising her arms too.

The sermon was given by a forty-year-old lesbian preacher from Oklahoma, Alice DeBolt, who was on the MCC board.

Striding back and forth on the dais, wearing a man-styled beige suit and cowboy boots, carrying her mike on its long cord, DeBolt presented a fiery sermon on gay liberation in the best tradition of tent revivalism.

"Every one of you here tonight," she shouted, "is a Moses! Every one of you can go home, to your cities, to your towns, to your schools, to your families, and you can say, *'My people are in slavery here!'* "

"Amen!" sang out many people in the crowd.

"You can go back to those Pharaohs where you work, where you live, all over the country, and you can say to them, 'Let my people out of the *bondage* of ten thousand years!' "

"Amen! Hallelujah! Right on, sister!" more people shouted.

"And above all—" She paused, one clenched fist frozen in the air, "those brothers and sisters who live in New York, you're gonna go home and say to Jeannie Colter, 'Let my people go!'"

The whole church erupted with a roar of amens and hallelujahs. Everybody surged to their feet with their arms thrust in the air.

Mary Ellen glanced at her companions. Armando seemed to be scarcely reacting to all this. He was just sitting there, staring straight ahead. Sam was all eyes, with a "gee whiz" expression on his face. Jewel and Liv had both let themselves go, shouting and singing at the tops of their lungs.

After the service, everyone flooded out of the church to where hundreds of pre-ordered taxis were waiting.

In half an hour, the thousands of conference-goers were massed by the reflecting ponds in front of the Lincoln Memorial.

Thousands of white candles were passed out and the MCC leader, Reverend Troy Pearry, gave quiet instructions for the march. Candles flamed to life everywhere in the dark, until the area around the pool was a sea of tiny flickering lights. Ahead lay the Lincoln Memorial, bathed in floodlights in the soft summer night. A few tourists walked up and down the long flight of steps. Mary Ellen noted the D.C. police also standing on the steps. The march was a legal one, and Washingtonians had learned with a sour surprise, from smallish items in the city press, that a major convention of gay Christians was being held in the nation's capital, and that these gay Christians planned a candlelight march on that bastion of straight liberty.

Shortly the long column was winding toward the Memorial, singing "We Shall Overcome," and soft slow hymns. People walked four or six abreast, sheltering their candles from the soft summer breeze. All the ebullience of the church service was spent. Everyone was serious, faces lit by the candles.

Mary Ellen and Liv walked by Armando, their arms around him. Sam and Jewel were right behind.

A few tourists stood watching the column pass with non-hostile looks. "They probably think this is some leftover anti-war group," Mary Ellen told herself. But when the marchers reached the verse, "Gay and straight together," the tourists hardened their faces and turned away.

Suddenly Armando spoke softly.

"What?" said Mary Ellen.

"Think of the marches into the catacombs . . . thousands of people winding with torches—" His voice broke off.

Now the fiery column was flowing up the steep steps of the Memorial, up, up, past the D.C. cops who stood watching with bemused or poker faces.

The great statue of Lincoln towered over them, floodlit from above, pensive, brooding. Mary Ellen wondered if Lincoln would have really understood the gay problem. They massed around it, candles half-burned now, everybody's hands and clothes wearing cooled drippings of wax.

The Reverend Pearry came forward and spoke. Tall, powerfully built, with jet-black hair and beard, and glowing dark eyes, Pearry had all the charisma of a true religious leader. The crowd hushed the moment they saw him.

His voice rang out in the soft night, so strong that he didn't need a mike.

He spoke of how it was better to light a candle than to curse the darkness. He said that enough candles had been lit tonight to shine into the darkest corners of America.

"We gather here tonight in a loving memorial for those brothers and sisters who have gone from us, and who suffered and died because of the crushing burden of guilt imposed on gay people by our society . . ."

A quiver of feeling rippled through that rapt crowd. A few people said soft amens.

". . . We want to remember Jim Forsythe who took

218

his own life in Louisiana . . . we want to remember Janet Margolies . . . remember Rudy Frink . . ."

Then Mary Ellen was moved to hear Pearry saying, ". . . We remember Danny Blackburn, the New York City police officer who was a member of MCC in New York, and who was beaten to death last week by a gang of thugs claiming to be inspired by the anti-gay statements of former New York State Senator Jean Laird Colter . . ."

Armando put his face in his hands, and his shoulders started to shake. Liv put her head on Mary Ellen's shoulder and started to sob. Blinded by her own tears, Mary Ellen saw Lincoln swimming in that sea of flame, as if he were being burned alive in it.

". . . And we wish to remember in our prayers the lovers who were left behind, alone and desolate at these deaths, the helpmates whom our society considers that it does not have to comfort . . . we wish to remember Armando Ostos, Blackburn's lover, who is here with us tonight . . ."

Then broken voices began to shoot up, like sad sky rockets, from the dark mass of people, as others began calling out names of dead gays whose sorrow they had personally witnessed. "Marcy Coleman," "my brother Bill" . . .

A wrath of the ages was filling Mary Ellen. Moses had not let the Pharoah off easy. Neither, for that matter, had God. The Pharaoh had been punished for his crimes against the Israelites. All the firstborn in the country slain by the angel. Plagues. Rains of blood. Clouds of locusts that ate up all the crops. But Jeannie Colter was getting off very easy. Instead of death and tears, she was getting fan mail and publicity for her campaign for governor, and invitations to be on TV talk shows.

"That woman ought to be made to pay for what she's done," she thought. "God ought to come up with some special avenging angel, just for her."

219

And then two people, a man and a woman, were carrying the great green wreath with its black bow. They were laying it at the feet of the departed, sad-faced, stoop-shouldered President who had signed the Emancipation Proclamation for the slaves.

The next day Bill read about the candlelight march in the *Times*, as he sat at the breakfast table with Jeannie.

He should have been in Washington, carrying a candle. But even MCC attendance in New York was out for now—as long as that blonde girl cop who knew him as William Laird was hanging around the MCC.

Of course, Bill didn't comment to Jeannie about the march. And she didn't comment on it to him because she wasn't reading the papers. She was busy telephoning to the state speaker of the house, trying to line up his support in the gubernatorial race.

Yesterday he had presented Jeannie with her share of his New York Telephone Co. bill for that month. It came to $638.59. Jeannie had been quite miffed that he expected her to pay it.

Later that morning, Jeannie sat with Gertrude in her office, briefing herself on the news, and read in the *News* about the candlelight march in Washington.

She stared, amazed, at the photographs—the river of lights flowing up the steps of the Lincoln Memorial.

"If I was in the District of Columbia," she said, "they wouldn't even have gotten a *permit* to do that."

Gertrude was looking over her shoulder. "Lincoln must be turning over in his grave."

Jeannie was reading the article in the *Times*.

"Gay Christians," she said. "Humph. The very idea is preposterous. Christians are supposed to *love*. Homosexuals don't love anything. They hate. They hate the opposite sex. They hate their parents. They hate

220

their society and their country. They hate God. And of course they hate anybody who tries to keep them from doing the filthy things they do. Like me, for instance."

A couple of days after the Washington march, Armando called Mary Ellen at home in the afternoon.

Mary Ellen had gotten up about an hour before. It was hard to get used to not having a job that you loved. She was standing restlessly in the kitchen in a T-shirt and shorts pouring herself a cup of coffee when the phone rang. Liv wasn't home from work yet.

"Are you alone?" Armando asked.

"Yeah. Why?"

"I want to talk to you about something," said Armando. "Just wanted to make sure you were alone. I'll be right up."

In five minutes, the buzzer rang, and she pressed the button to open the door downstairs. She heard him coming heavily up the five flights of stairs. He was carrying a small sack of groceries.

Something in his manner made Mary Ellen pay close attention.

"What's up, Armando?" she asked. "Let's go up on the roof."

"No," he said. "Somebody might see us."

So they sat at the kitchen table, and Armando slowly unpacked the groceries, laying them ceremoniously on the table. A quart of milk, a loaf of bread, a jar of peanut butter, a half-pound of sweet butter . . . and a gun.

A Beretta automatic complete with a silencer, and a clip with eight rounds of ammo in it.

Without a word he laid the gun on the table between them.

Mary Ellen stared at it, feeling her hackles bristle.

Armando looked her in the eye.

"A lotta people," he said, "would like to see this

221

Colter lady get hers. If somebody doesn't stop her, she's going to take away all the ground we've gained, right? She's going to hurt a lot of people, right?"

Mary Ellen was looking at the gun, mesmerized.

"But most of all, you and me, right? Because of Danny. Me because of you-know-why, and you because you're a cop, and I know how cops feel when other cops get killed. And don't tell me I haven't read your mind."

Mary Ellen actually couldn't meet his eyes. She got up and went to the window and stared out blankly, at the sooty old brick wall of the next building just four feet away. A little shadow flashed on the wall as a pigeon flew over the roofs.

Armando went on: "I took the liberty of getting the gun. I won't tell you how. Suffice it to say that I know bartenders who work in the Mafia gay bars. From there it's no problem to get a piece, because even in the Mob we have got brothers and sisters, right? And they have got their own reasons to not like Jeannie Colter, because she cuts in on their own action, right?"

Mary Ellen turned around and leaned against the window, looking at the gun.

Her bare feet, the little kitchen where she and Liv had made a year of breakfasts, the still-unmade velour bed in the bedroom, Liv's antique cat figurines on the bookcase in the living room, Kikan and Sam dozing on the sofa—all shone in a strange new light, a cool steely light that seemed to be reflected from the Beretta on the table.

She tried to make a joke of it.

"I should turn you in for conspiracy to commit Murder One," she said.

Armando went right on looking her in the eye and talking in his low level voice, so he was not taken in by her joke.

"I'd do it myself," he said. "But I'm an incompetent when it comes to stuff like this. I'd probably shoot myself in the foot. And I'd probably get arrested before I could pull it off. But you're a cop, right? You know all the angles. And you're a dead shot. Danny told me how the whole NYPD used to talk about what a terror you were on the pistol range."

"You're wrong about the angles," she said. "I know all about cops who thought they could commit the perfect crime. Shake people down, deal confiscated dope, whatever. They're in the slammer now."

"The point is, you know better than me," he said. He shrugged. "Maybe you'd rather use your own gun."

"No," she said quickly. "That'd be stupid. The last gun I should use is one I used on the force."

The minute she said the words, she knew that she was seriously considering this thing.

"Now here's my next idea," said Armando. "*You* do it, and I say *I* did it. I mean, I don't care what happens to me now. The best thing I could do with the rest of my life is go to jail because of Danny."

The idea of Armando deliberately going to jail horrified Mary Ellen. All her education in life was built around the idea that going to jail was an awful thing. She sat back down at the table. She picked up the gun, checking to see if it was loaded. It wasn't. She examined the silencer, which was a fancy new European type she had never seen.

"Armando, didn't you ever read any police novels?" she said. "Supposing they find my prints on the gun?"

"They won't," said Armando. "After you do it, you'll come straight to me and we'll wipe your prints off, and put my prints on it, and the gun will be at my place. They know Danny is gay now, right? So the first thing they'll do is look for Danny's lover, right? I've got the motive, right? So they'll come looking for me, and they'll find the gun at my place. And of course I won't mention your name. So . . ."

Mary Ellen hefted the gun gently, aimed it at the wall, pulled the trigger. The Beretta was Italian-made, a nice elegant precision-tooled weapon. Not your cheap American-made Saturday night special.

The mob didn't fool around, did they? She checked to see if the serial number had been taken off. It had. But in this case it wouldn't have mattered if the serial had been there in blinking neon lights.

"Armando," she said, "have you ever been in jail?"

"Yes, as a matter of fact," he said. "I did six months for soliciting in California. I lived in L.A. then. Made the mistake of making advances to an undercover guy."

"So you know that jail is not a nice place," she said.

"It's better than being free when Danny is locked in the grave," he said. "And there's plenty of action in jail, anyway."

"But Armando, you're religious. And Danny was religious. Don't you think it's wrong to kill? You know I'm religious. Don't you think *I* might not want to kill?"

He shook his head. "Danny and you and I are religious as far as our own thing goes. But for the rest . . ."

She shook her head, knowing he had described her own religion exactly.

"Armando," she said, "you are the most masochistic masochist I ever met."

He grinned.

After Armando left, Mary Ellen sat fondling the gun.

She had to admit that it was a pretty good plan Armando had thought up. But then not every person who conspired to commit a homicide was willing to take the rap, the way Armando was. She was still horrified at the idea of his sacrificing himself but part of her mind said that this had to be accepted, that she had to respect Armando's point of view.

She had told Armando that she would make her plans by herself, and that for her own protection she would not inform him of the details, but that he would be told when to rendezvous with her and the smoking gun.

She had another cup of coffee, sat with her bare feet up on the table, and played with the gun, and thought.

It wouldn't be too easy. Colter had already been harassed and threatened so much that she probably had a lot of security people around her. The best way to learn the holes in the security net would be to watch Colter a lot. But Colter was out of town half the time, traveling around the state. And how could Mary Ellen travel around after her without Liv suspecting something? If Liv knew the truth, she would be horrified.

And of course there was always the possibility that she'd figure out a better way than shooting Colter. She wondered if she'd get scruples at the last minute. After all, she'd never actually shot another human being.

Then she smiled to herself.

She had just thought of the near-perfect solution to the problem of reconnoitering Colter.

Meanwhile, Liv would be home soon—she had better hide the weapon.

In the bottom of her closet were two boxes of mementos relating to her father—stacks of old *Spring 3100s*, photos taken at police picnics, even a mounted head of a 10-point buck that her father had shot, and that Liv couldn't bear to see hung on the wall. Mary Ellen hid the gun deep in one box, under several pounds of magazines. Liv never went near those boxes.

That night was Sidney's last night in New York. The next afternoon he was flying to Tokyo, and from there to Peking.

In those last days before Sidney left, Jeannie's physical need of her husband had increased in direct proportion to her apprehension about his going.

She had almost reverted to her old beauty-queen self. She actually went to Saks and bought a lovely new nightgown and negligee, very modest, but boldly printed in art-nouveau flowers. She made sure she was ready for bed when Sidney was, with no political work to delay her. She was lounging around the bedroom, smiling, bathed fresh, lightly misted in cologne, her hair brushed loose, no cream on her face. She left the phone off the hook.

But Sidney came shambling in, shucked his jacket, said how tired he was, went into the bathroom and took a shower. He emerged wrapped tightly in his white terry cloth robe, and sat on the edge of the bed and smoked a cigarette (which he knew annoyed her) and repeated how tired he was from all the briefings and all the last-minute running around town for vaccinations and letters of introduction to People's Republic officials.

Shortly he lay toppled against the pillows asleep, before she even turned off the light.

He had done this to her every night for weeks. And every night Jeannie had lain there in the dark, wide-awake, her body screaming with need for him. The need was almost a pain. It made her body rigid, it clamped on iron vise on the back of her head and around her shoulders, it throbbed in the small of her back.

In vain she turned this way and that on the bed, hoping to brush her hip or breasts against him in such a way that he'd wake up and make love to her.

She remembered how good things had been, once upon a time.

The fact was, their lovemaking had been a lot better back when she was the beauty queen and he was the ambitious young political reporter. Good juicy love, nearly every night, sometimes twice a night. Things had even stayed good when she had started feeling the nervousness, when she had started doing a fair amount of social drinking. Even when she realized that, from a given Friday night to a given Monday night, she had been half-boozed the whole time.

But when her mother died, she stopped drinking,

stopped cold. Now she was lucky if Sidney performed his conjugal duties one or twice a month.

The deep nervousness had stayed there all the time, and being saved hadn't helped it, and the change in Sidney's attitude to her hadn't helped either.

The irony was that the Bible didn't forbid married people to enjoy each other in bed. God had made man and woman for each other. Those poor homosexuals didn't know what they were missing.

What really frightened her was that men's sex drives supposedly slacked off when they got older, and women's sex drives got stronger as they neared their forties. What would happen if Sidney stopped having relations with her altogether, and she was left to deal with her itch of desire herself? There could be no masturbation, of course, and no adultery. No relief at all. Then what? She couldn't believe that Sidney had slacked off simply because he no longer found her attractive. Good heavens, she broke her neck to make herself attractive—even now, with her more modest way of looking.

That last night before China, after Sidney fell asleep, she was sure she was getting a taste of the future, and she was sure she couldn't stand it. She was also aware that she was very nervous. If she was this bad now, how would she be in the last frantic weeks of the gubernatorial race next year? She found herself thinking of a nice little glass of sherry to calm her nerves.

She started to cry.

Sidney woke up. She hoped he would feel sorry for her, and enfold her in his arms.

"Do you have a problem?" he said crossly.

"Yes, I do," she sobbed.

"What is it?"

"You're going away for two months tomorrow, and I want us to make love. It's been a month since we've made love."

"Jeannie, when will you learn that I can't make love

227

when I'm tired? And when you put the pressure on me, I can't make love either."

She got up out of bed, and dragged around the room in the dark, crying with deep gagging sobs.

"Good God," said Sidney from the bed. "Am I supposed to feel pity for you, or what?"

When she heard that, she knew it was no use. So she went to the kitchen, cried some more, and made herself some hot milk. Then she took an extra blanket from the linen closet, and settled down on the flowered sofa in the living room, with the TV on.

Finally she fell into an uneasy sleep, her body aching with tension.

She had a dream.

In the dream, she was cleaning out a closet, and found some old clothes of her mother's—wonderful 1930s blouses with rhinestone buttons on them, crepe dresses with dozens of tiny buttons up the front. She was trying them on with cries of joy, flinging them right and left. Then on the top shelf she found a magnificent old hatbox that said SAKS FIFTH AVENUE. She opened it up. Inside, amid the soft tissues, nestled a magnificent hat made of iridescent bird feathers, with a pearl hat-pin stuck in it.

Underneath the hat, as she lifted it up, was her mother's head. It was quite nicely mummified, with the dry-looking silver hair done in the braids her mother had always worn.

The reek of lavender sachet from the box seemed to linger in her nostrils even after she had shuddered awake.

The next morning, Sidney finished packing, checked his documents, made a call to a Mr. Field in the State Department, confirmed his reservations with Northwest Orient Airlines, and called a cab.

"Do you want to go to the airport with me?" he said.

"No," she said.

"An eye for an eye, huh?" he said.

Without answering, she dialed Tom Winkler. His line was busy.

"Okay," said Sidney, "if that's the way you want it. Give my love to the kids. And be easy on them while I'm gone, okay?"

From the second-floor bedroom window, she watched him throw his suitcases into the trunk of the cab, with the muscular ease of a high-school boy. From the street, he looked like he was a handsome and dewy twenty-two.

The cab drove off down the street.

At that moment, she was sorry. She envisioned herself catching a cab, following him to Kennedy Airport. She could still catch him there, and walk with him past the security checkpoint, right to the gate, and kiss him good-bye before he boarded.

But she didn't. She called Tim Winkler instead.

"It's going to be something like undercover work," said Mary Ellen to Liv. "Only I'll be doing it for gay people."

In the glow of the single lamp, they were naked on the velour bed. Liv was sitting in the lotus position, and Mary Ellen was lying on her side before her, studying Liv's face just a little anxiously.

"I'm going to go to work for Colter, find out about her plans—bills she's sponsoring, and so on," Mary Ellen went on. "She's going to be doing a lot more anti-gay crap. We have to know about it."

"Like being a spy," said Liv.

"That's right," said Mary Ellen. "And of course it's all for a good cause. But it does mean that I'll be away sometimes, when Colter goes out of town. So I want to tell you about it, so you won't think I'm out running around or something . . . so you'll know where I really am and what I'm doing."

"Are you doing this for some organization?"

"No, just for me, right now. Some organization might

229

want my info later, of course. And let's face it—it'd be a paying job for me too. I don't dig being a waitress."

Liv sat looking gravely down at her crossed legs. In the soft lamplight, her breasts cast deep shadows across her firm belly. Her fleece, so clean that the hairs had golden highlights, parted to show the labia, and the red pearl of her clitoris. She had been brushing her snowy blonde hair dry, and now it spread in a white shining mantle across her shoulders. But she was thinking hard, looking like a child trying to decide why two and two couldn't be five. One hand lay limp on her thigh, the other lay on the rumpled velour with the hairbrush loosely clasped in it.

"I do not like all this," she said.

"What?" said Mary Ellen, her stomach clenching a little.

"I do not like politics, and spying."

"But that's the way life is," said Mary Ellen. "You don't approve of the things people do to *us*, do you?"

"No, of course not," said Liv.

"You don't like the way people talk at the post office where you work?"

"No . . ."

"We're going to have to do a little political stuff to get things changed," said Mary Ellen.

She did not like lying to Liv. She did not like having a secret from Liv. She wondered if the satisfaction of getting rid of Colter was worth having to lie. Risking the loss of Liv was definitely not worth it.

"Let's face it," she told herself. "I am not your typical assassin or hit man, am I?"

Liv moved her shoulders suddenly as if she were cold, and clasped her arms around herself. "I do not like the way I feel," she said, tossing back her hair.

Mary Ellen knew then that Liv wasn't able to truly read her thoughts. If she were, she would go straight to the closet and find the gun. At that moment, she knew that Liv's ESP was pretty good, but not as accurate as the cross-hairs in a gun-sight.

Neither of them felt like making love, so they turned out the light.

Lying awake in the dark, Mary Ellen thought of her father, and Danny, and Sam, and Jewel, and Armando crying, and she realized all over again how angry she was.

Twelve

Rumors drifted out through New York political circles that Jeannie Colter planned to seek the governorship. All this while, she was busy building the organization that would carry out her campaign.

After many phone calls and breakfast meetings, she put together a twenty-one-person statewide Citizens for Jeannie Colter for Governor committee. These people were active Republicans around the state whose abilities and loyalties she knew—around them twenty-one field offices would be built. The office in Manhattan was now her campaign headquarters. Actually, she would have liked to transfer her headquarters out of that evil city, and up to Pawling. But for image purposes, and out of a desire not to offend the many voters in greater New York, she left it there.

As a result of diligent fund-raising, the money was coming in. She had $500,000 in the campaign account. Of course, she was spending it rapidly, so money would continue to be a crisis.

Volunteers were starting to come to the Manhattan office, hoping to work for the Colter organization. It was heartening to see how many of them were staunch young Republicans. During the 1960s people had formed an image of young people as liberal or leftist, irresponsible and immoral. Not so. She felt flattered to have attracted such solid young people.

For instance, just yesterday, an unusual young woman had come in to the Park Avenue headquarters, and wanted to work for Jeannie as a personal bodyguard.

She told Gertrude her name was Mary Ellen Frampton. She was one of the police officers just laid off by the New York City Police Department. As a recommendation, she gave the name of Captain Mark Bader, in the police department.

Gertrude had been somewhat amazed and taken aback at the idea of meeting a female police officer in the flesh.

But Mary Ellen seemed like such a soft-spoken efficient person, dressed so modestly and quoted so glowingly from the Bible that Gertrude had picked up the phone and called Captain Bader. The police captain had described her as a hard worker, a no-nonsense type, and added, "Incidentally, she is a crack shot, and a black belt in kung fu. I'd think she'd be most valuable to Mrs. Colter."

So Gertrude had spoken to Jeannie about it, the next time Jeannie was back in New York, fresh from speeches upstate.

Jeannie, too, had been intrigued, and had had Gertrude telephone the young woman for an interview.

Part of her felt that it wasn't proper for a woman to work in a police force, or carry a gun. But part of her —that part of her that Reverend Irving called "bossy," that refused to submit to men, that broke fellowship with the true-blue all-out fundamentalist Baptist types —that part of her that, in her more lucid moments she recognized as unsaved and infidel, that part of her found Mary Ellen intriguing.

Mary Ellen walked softly into Jeannie's office and sat down with the easy grace of someone who was very fit.

She was wearing a little white short-sleeved blouse,

a denim skirt that came below the knee, white golf socks with little pompoms on the back, and faded blue sneakers. Her hair was neither short nor long, and looked like it was naturally curly. It framed a lovely fine-cut face with a strong jaw and wide gray eyes. She had a look of gun-metal coolness and confidence; without these, she would have been a vapid kind of TV starlet pretty.

"So you want to work as a *bodyguard*," Jeannie had said.

Mary Ellen smiled cheerfully. "I read the newspapers, and I would imagine that you need one," she said. "I'm sure you already have some security people. But you need more than that. You need a personal bodyguard."

"Why?" said Jeannie.

"I would imagine that certain people write you threatening letters, and make threatening phone calls and so on," said Mary Ellen.

They looked each other in the eye for a long moment.

Very good, Jeannie thought.

"It would involve a lot of traveling," Jeannie said.

"That's okay," said Mary Ellen. "I'm not married, and I'm unemployed."

"Why me, in particular?" asked Jeannie.

"Because I am very struck by the things you say," said Mary Ellen quietly.

Jeannie studied her, tapping her pencil on the desk.

Then she tried a classic thing on her interviewee.

"Tell me," she said, "if you died today, do you believe that you would go straight to Heaven?"

"Oh yes, I do," said Mary Ellen, with such quiet fervor that suddenly the shivers were chasing up and down Jeannie's spine.

"You accept the Lord Jesus Christ as your Savior?" she said.

"Oh yes," said Mary Ellen.

"Are you a Baptist?"

"No, I'm a Presbyterian, actually. But I believe in the Bible. My dad and I used to read the Bible together." She paused a moment, then added, "My dad was a cop."

"Oh?" said Jeannie, the shivers still chasing. "Is he still on the police force?"

"He's dead," said Mary Ellen. "He was shot and killed on duty, in Harlem."

"Oh dear, I'm sorry," said Jeannie.

Suddenly she felt that she could understand why this young woman, who obviously loved her father deeply, would want to be a policewoman.

Still testing, she said, "You must be very sorry you were laid off."

"Well, no actually," said Mary Ellen. "The force is tough for a woman, really. That's why I thought of being your personal bodyguard. Men politicians always have men bodyguards, right? Well, it's really more *proper* for a woman to have woman bodyguards. I mean, supposing somebody tries to crack a shot at you in the ladies' room?"

Jeannie was delighted. The girl had given all the right answers.

"All right," she said. "We'll pay you three hundred dollars a week, plus all expenses. I presume you can start tomorrow?"

Mary Ellen left that interview with Colter just a little shaken.

She had gone into it with open eyes, coldly, knowing that the Colter organization would surely check with the New York Police Department about her. If the NYPD—above all, Captain Bader—had known she was a lesbian, and if they had laid her off for that reason, they would surely tell the Colter people about her "deviant tendencies."

Of course, there was always the possibility that the NYPD would not admit to having had any gays in its true-blue ranks, not even to Jeannie Colter. They might fear further investigation. And if there was anything that Commissioner Manuella feared, it was outside investigation and interference in his department. Surely Manuella wouldn't want a Knapp Commission-type affair with sexual overtones.

But the most likely possibility was that the NYPD would tell Colter that Mary Ellen Frampton was a lesbian—if they knew it.

"Now is the moment," Mary Ellen had thought, "when I find out if this is why I was laid off."

Instead, to her surprise, she had learned from Utley and from Colter that Bader had praised her to the skies, and said he was sorry she was gone.

So what did this mean?

It meant either that the NYPD, in a panic about the discovery that it had harbored at least one homosexual in its ranks (Danny), was frantically covering up, and denying the presence of any others. It meant that Bader himself might be gay, and covering up for her if he knew she was lesbian. Or it meant that the NYPA had *not* known that she was a lesbian, and had therefore laid her off for economic reasons. And it raised the question of whether *any* of the NYPD Four had been laid off as gays.

As she got ready to start her bodyguard job with Colter, Mary Ellen tortured herself with these thoughts.

If she hadn't been laid off as gay, then why was she going ahead with her plans to kill Colter?

But after she had spent several days in the midst of the Colter people, and heard all the casual anti-gay talk, especially the constant stream of colorful homophobic statements from her new boss, she found herself choking with anger all over again.

The fact was, she still had plenty of reason to kill Colter. Danny, her partner, her kid brother, was dead because of this woman. Many innocent people were being hurt because of this woman. Even if Mary Ellen herself had an only questionable claim to having been hurt, she could still act on behalf of all the millions of aggrieved gay people in the country whose lives would be touched, and seared, by the Colter poison.

Bill was walking along a downtown street during one of his peregrinations. He passed an antique shop and saw a soup tureen in the display window.

It was one of those small shops that have a small stock of choice stuff—everything in immaculate condition and nicely arranged. The window also displayed a silk Ghiordes prayer rug, a couple of little French inlaid tables, sterling candlesticks, Dresden bisque figurines, a nice ivory miniature portrait of a lady.

The tureen looked like an original piece from the old Staffordshire pattern Fair Winds. It had been done from copper engravings of harbor and sea scenes in the great ports of the time: New York, London, and Canton. This dish showed a splendid view of New York Harbor and ships at anchor in the roads. It was such a fine old pattern that modern copies were being sold in the supermarkets now.

He went in. The owner was tending shop, a very pleasant slender brown-haired man in his thirties who seemed to be gay, which made it all the more perfect.

"I'm interested in the Staffordshire tureen," Bill explained.

"It's an entire set," said the man. "Just about complete. I've got the rest boxed in the back. Would you like to see it?"

Bill knew enough about antique china to know that a close-to-complete set was a rarity, and also very expensive. He also knew that Marion adored old Staffordshire.

He helped the owner carry out the three boxes. The china was carefully wrapped in old newspapers that told of Watergate and Son of Sam. The men unpacked selected pieces—dinner plates, sugar and cream pitcher, teapot, serving dishes, cups and saucers. Aside from a chip here and there, the china was in beautiful condition.

Bill mused over the scenes etched on the pieces, getting lost in them. Work was proceeding apace on the Catherine Slip house. The men had started on a general clean-up and the plumbing. The place needed a new roof, new windows, new shutters. He was hoping to move into it by fall. But, with supply shortages and the usual other construction delays, a more realistic date would be in early winter, maybe Christmas.

He pictured Marion and himself celebrating Christmas in their own house. A magnificent pine tree in the living room, covered with antique ornaments. A fire crackling in the great new fieldstone fireplace. A roast goose, or maybe game, and champagne. Friends dropping in. Yes, it would be interesting to see which of their present friends would drop in for drinks, if and when he and Marion ever managed to come out.

Their relationship seemed to be stymied by a kind of coldness. Bill knew that it depended mainly on himself, on his attitude to Jeannie, to break the stalemate.

Sometimes Marion seemed to forget that he was Jeannie's father. But Bill found it was impossible to throw over a lifetime's love and concern just because he wanted to lead an open life. For instance, he was terribly concerned at the threatening letters and phone calls that Jeannie had received. Maybe some emotionally disturbed or angry gay person might try to harm her or the children. And Bill knew that, no matter how much she might have taunted someone into doing it, he would be grief-stricken if something happened to her. Because life was not a simple thing at all, not the strictly black-and-white thing that Marion thought it was.

Yesterday she had told him, chortling, that she had just hired a bodyguard—a young former policewoman. A bodyguard! Bill's stomach had done a sick-scared plunge. Jeannie had even considered wearing a flak vest, though she said the bodyguard said that flak vests were no defense against a head shoot.

Tenderly he set the last cup and saucer on the counter.

"How much?" he said.

"A thousand dollars for the set," said the man.

Bill hauled out his checkbook and his card. "Would you have the china delivered to this address? It's going to be in storage for a little while, so please repack it carefully."

The man studied the card. "Are you *the* William Laird?" he asked, delighted.

Bill wasn't listening—his mind had drifted off to Marion again. Buying the china was one of those motions of making white magic, of trying to make a thing happen. If he bought the china for their future life together, maybe he and Marion could get back to the old feeling again.

"What did you say?" he said, looking up from his checkbook.

Mary Ellen and Liv were driving up Route 7, north through Connecticut, along the Housatonic River. Her father's old place was on the river, just over the Connecticut-Massachusetts line.

Mary Ellen was driving the Vega, and she looked over at Liv, then back at the road. Kikan and Sam were in a cat carrier in the back—Kikan was asleep and Sam was yelling his head off.

Liv was definitely unhappy about things. She sat there looking straight ahead, her hands folded with uncommon prissiness on her shorts-bared thighs. Mary Ellen was positive that Liv did not know anything about the Beretta hidden in Mary Ellen's knapsack, yet Liv was unhappy with something in the vibes that she picked up from her lover.

Mary Ellen let her thoughts range back over the past couple of weeks.

Aside from Liv, other things were going pretty

well. She had settled into her job, and she was adjusting to the pace, which was more frenetic than her old patrol job. She did not have regular weekends off, but she would have agreed days off. Liv was going to spend two weeks' vacation at the cabin, as she was yearning to be in the country, and that was just as well —Mary Ellen had given the Colter organization her real address, and she didn't want them nosing around there and finding she lived with another woman.

As to the salary, it was more than she had earned in the police force. She had felt financially reckless enough to stop by that antique shop on Christopher Street and work out a payment-plan deal with them about the primitive cat painting. Liv's birthday was coming up, and Mary Ellen was hoping that the gift would soften Liv's unease.

She was learning things fast about Jeannie Colter's life, and about the organization, and saw that there were several situations of which she could take advantage. She hadn't talked to Armando yet, because she was still unsure which situation was best to exploit.

One thing was sure, though: she doubted that her faith in the American political system would survive the close exposure to a political campaign. It was all as phony and as stagy as a nightclub show—the speech-writing, the advertising, the polling, the carefully managed PR. Other candidates probably didn't do things any differently. Where was truth, where was sincerity? It all made her sick.

Now and then, she felt uneasy in her resolve to end this woman's life. But then she saw or heard something in the Colter office that showed her, once again, how all this phoniness was being used against gay people, and she got angry all over again, and eager for the kill.

She had the gun hidden deep in her knapsack, and she was driving very carefully. She knew very well how the police sometimes pulled cars over for traffic violations, and then went on to search without warrants.

"Well, we're getting there," she said.

They were now in Massachusetts. Mary Ellen turned off Route 7, onto a road called Furnace Woods Road. They went winding up the bluffs that overlooked the Housatonic River, higher and higher, among the crags of rock and the clumps of birch trees, and beech, and mountain laurel.

On the top, Mary Ellen looked for the little hidden drive, and finally saw it. She remembered the way as well as if it were yesterday. One tree by the drive still had the board nailed to it, where her father had hung one of the No Hunting notices that posted his land.

She turned into the drive, which was just a tiny dirt road. They drove slowly through the sun-splashed woods of birch and aspen. Mary Ellen had a lump in her throat—it was just as beautiful as she remembered it.

Liv had roused from her lethargy. "I loooove it," she breathed. "Oh, it is like the place where we used to spend the summer when I was a little girl . . ."

The woods opened out into an immense wild meadow. To the west, the meadow sloped away to the edge of the bluff, and they could see the blue river far below, and the bluffs on the other side, and the ancient rounded mountains rolling softly away into the hazy horizon. To the east, on the high side of the meadow, she could see the cabin on the edge of the woods.

As they neared the cabin, Mary Ellen strained her eyes, anxiously looking for signs of vandalism. But the windows were unbroken. As they stopped the car, she could see the padlock on the front door.

She stopped the car, shut off the engine—and started to cry.

For the first time in days, she felt Liv's arms around her, warm and comforting.

"You must cry," said Liv soothingly. "It is very good to cry, no?"

After she'd dried her eyes, they got out of the car.

The "cabin" was actually a small old hillbilly-like farmhouse. It had a front porch where one could "set a spell" in a rocking chair if one wished. The clapboard was very weathered, peeling off, and the little brick chimney was crumbling at the top. It was shaded by big old white birches, bent and broken by winter storms. A few straggling irises still grew by the porch. Off against a nearby hill, Mary Ellen could see a mound of moldy weathered hay—the remains of the pile of baled hay where she and her father used to fix targets for target-shooting.

She unlocked the padlock, and they went in.

Everything was pretty much as she and her father had left it: the ancient wicker and leather furniture in the living room, the old painted table in the kitchen, the hand-pump right by the sink which went clankety-clank and drew sweet water directly up from the well under the house.

Liv kept clapping her hands with delight, transported back into her own childhood. They unloaded the car.

The first thing Mary Ellen did, when Liv was out doors, was to check in the padlocked chest in the bedroom, where her father had kept his gun collection. The guns were all there, the Kentucky rifle, the 1868 Colt .45, the buffalo gun. Quickly she put the Beretta and the ammo clip in there, and padlocked it again.

From here, it would be easy for her to get to Pawling. Because of the summer heat, Jeannie Colter was concentrating her activities at Windfall right now, and the staff was jokingly calling it "the summer White House." Here also, she would be able to do a little target-shooting—though she couldn't take a chance on firing the Beretta until it was aimed at Jeannie Colter.

Meanwhile, she would just try to relax.

She and Liv scoured up the kitchen, arranged the groceries (there was no refrigerator, so they would have to drive often to town). They got out the dusty old kerosene lamps, cleaned them and filled them, and hauled in firewood for the fireplace. They swept and dusted the bedroom and made up the bed (whose mattress smelled just a little musty).

Liv was in a state of almost feverish excitement, asking all kinds of questions. "Are there any berries to pick?" "Are there any deer or other animals to see?"

Mary Ellen suspected that Liv, too, was covering up her nervousness.

The next day, Mary Ellen drove almost to Hartford, Connecticut, to make a phone call from a pay phone at a rest area along the highway.

She dialed Armando's number in New York City.

When Armando answered, she said. "Okay, I've got it all worked out. Don't write anything down, okay? Just try and remember everything."

"Okay," said Armando. "I was beginning to think I'd never hear from you."

"You're going to think this is a little strange, but the best place to hit her is at her church some evening."

"If *you* don't think it's strange," said Armando, "then *I* don't think it's crazy. But why the church?"

"Well," said Mary Ellen, "Colter is one strange lady. The other people on the staff tell me that she has this thing about her mother, and I believe it. Her mother was super-religious, right, and now Colter feels guilty, because her mother died before *she* got saved. Her mother is buried in the churchyard down here at the First Baptist Church. It's right off Route Twenty-two just south of Quaker Hill Road—you won't have any trouble finding it, because there's a sign right on the road. So every evening Colter goes down to the church yard there, and she mopes around her mother's grave. I mean, she goes down there *late*, when there usually isn't anyone around—sometimes after midnight."

"Sounds pretty weird," said Armando.

"It is weird," said Mary Ellen. "I guess she does it

243

course she always takes me with her, because she knows it's a tricky situation."

late because no one will see her at that hour. And of Armando started to laugh softly.

"Now," said Mary Ellen, "here's what you have to do. Next week is a week that she's not going anywhere to make speeches or anything. She told me she's tired, and she wants to take a few days off. She's going to be staying there at Windfall. I want you to come up here and stay at the Bel Aire Motel, which is right on Twenty-two, between Quaker Hill Road and the church. You've got to be seen locally."

"I don't have a car," said Armando.

"Rent one," said Mary Ellen. "The point is, that you're on record here. I won't be able to call you from Windfall, to tell you exactly what time we'd be coming down. You'll have to watch out the motel window for the car. You can't miss it, it's a brand-new white Lincoln Continental. When you see that car go by, you jump in your car and drive to the church. We'll be in the churchyard. You park near the cemetery. If you were shooting from your car, you'd be able to hit her from there. I'll make the hit with gloves on, toss you the gun quick, and you grab it and get the hell out."

"Then what?" said Armando. "How do the police figure out it's me?"

"Very simple," said Mary Ellen coolly. "I'll call them up and in a panic tell them Jeannie is shot, give them the description of your car and the plate number. If they're quick with the radio work, they'll get you before you get back to the city. And you'll have the gun with your prints on it. So . . . you're on."

"Beautiful," said Armando.

"Just make sure you hold the gun in your hand the right way, *after* I give it to you," said Mary Ellen. "Your prints have to be all over it, but *some* of them have to be in the right position for firing the gun."

"I understand," said Armando. Then he added, "Christ, it's really simple, isn't it?"

"It's simple because you *want* to get caught," said Mary Ellen bluntly. "I *don't* want to get caught, you understand. If either of us screw up, we both go to the slammer, and I won't appreciate that."

"No, no," said Armando fervently, "the last thing I want is for you and Liv to get screwed up."

"Just one more thing," said Mary Ellen. "Starting Tuesday, I want you at the Bel Aire Motel, and I want to know you're there, but I don't want to make any calls. So whatever car you have, make sure it's in front of your room, and put three pieces of clothing in the back window, one white, one red and one blue. Got that? That way, I can see it from the road, and know you're there."

"Okay," said Armando.

"Now," said Mary Ellen, "if for any reason I decide to abort the whole thing at the last minute, and you're already sitting there in your car by the cemetery, I'll give you a hand signal. I'll raise my hand twice like I am scratching my head. Got that? When you see that, you just sit quiet, or pretend you're asleep and she and I will just get back in her car and leave. Then we'll try for the next night."

"So, she's a pretty strange lady, huh?" said Armando.

"Yeah," said Mary Ellen. "In fact, sometimes I think she is going to crack up. I guess she had a breakdown before, too. I wonder if all politicians are as crazy as she is, when you look behind all the PR . . ."

That night, Jeannie had a hard time sleeping. Usually she always fell right into a deep sleep at Windfall.

When she finally did sleep, she had another bad dream.

She dreamed that she was walking through the little cemetery back down at the church. It wasn't a dark and scary night. The sun was just going down, and the shadows were long.

She walked slowly among the tombstones, and saw

245

that each one was fitted with a small radio speaker. And out of each speaker came a human voice. Some of the tombstones were singing in high clear jabbery voices, like a tape being played at a higher speed. Other voices were calling in a wordless alto or tenor monotone . . . "ahhhhhh."

She listened to the voices, and felt a deep thrilling fright.

Finally she came to her mother's tombstone. This one, too, had its little speaker, covered with a sparkly tweed fabric. But the sound coming from it wasn't a voice. It was like faint radio static, as if sunspots were playing havoc with the reception. There was a little tuning dial on the tombstone. She reached and twisted the dial. For a few minutes, nothing happened, no matter how much she fiddled with it.

But suddenly the static stopped, and the reception was clear. She listened intently. The tombstone was broadcasting, she knew. She knew someone was there. But she couldn't hear anything.

She bent, and put her ear up to the speaker.

Suddenly she heard it. Heavy breathing, slow and uneven, like when someone is making a threatening phone call but doesn't want to speak.

She woke up bathed in a cold sweat. She sat in the kitchen wrapped in her art-nouveau negligee, drinking a cup of hot milk and afraid to go to sleep again.

Whenever Mary Ellen returned to the cabin, she found Liv in a skittish ecstasy of enjoying the place.

Often Mary Ellen worried about leaving Liv alone there. She tried to instruct Liv in the use of the guns, but Liv wouldn't touch them. "If anyone comes here," Liv said firmly, "I shall *blaaaast* them with my white magic."

They had more or less mastered the art of cooking on the old wood-burning range in the house, so often Liv would be out sawing and chopping wood. Her arms and legs were browner by the day, and her hair bleached flaxen by the sun. Or she would be coming up from the lower meadow, carrying a pan full of wild blueberries, the two cats scampering ahead of her.

With the berries, Liv baked pies and tarts and other things. "If you are here," she teased, "you can eat them with me. If you are off spying on that nasty lady, I will eat them myself. I loooove blueberries."

Their lovemaking left a good deal to be desired, however.

On the few days that Mary Ellen managed to get to the camp, their experiences together were splashed with both the sun of happiness and the moving leaf-shadows of sadness.

Liv's birthday came, and Mary Ellen had driven down to the city to make the final payment on the painting, and bring it up.

They had a mellow evening of kerosene lamps softly glowing in the living room, and steaks grilled in the fireplace. Liv opened the glittering package that Mary Ellen had wrapped with awkward care.

When Liv saw the painting, her mouth fell open in that childish way that Mary Ellen loved.

"How . . ." she began.

"Don't ask," said Mary Ellen. "Just enjoy."

Liv was studying the painting, which did indeed look like Kikan. "I *know* how," she said. "You bought it with the money that the evil woman gave you, and you are earning that money because you are spying on her."

Liv studied the painting longer.

"On the other hand, I know you bought it because you love me." She suddenly put the painting down and put her arms around Mary Ellen. "And I love you, too," she added, "no matter what happens."

On another day, Mary Ellen stacked up a dozen bales of hay that she had bought, and cleaned some of the old guns, and practiced target shooting. The cats hid in the house. Liv put her hands over her ears, and finally seized her berry pan and left. Mary Ellen had never realized how intensely Liv hated guns. She wondered how Liv had ever managed to accept her work as a police officer.

As she sighted in the Winchester .3030 and put bull's-eye after bull's-eye into the target, and felt the gun's good kick against her shoulder, the echoes rolled off down the meadow like summer thunder. She realized that she was finally facing up to her grief for her father, exorcising it, by visiting this place that they had enjoyed together, handling the guns that they had treasured and fired together.

On still another day, Sam, the kitten, met with an untimely end.

The little pier kitten had already grown big and feisty, eager to explore the strange sights and smells of the woods and the meadow. Kikan, by contrast, was happy to sleep rolled in a ball on the seat of the old wicker rocking chair that the two women had stood on the porch.

One evening, just before bedtime, Sam scooted out of the screen door into the dark. Liv followed him out with the kerosene lamp, and tramped around, and called and called. She could hear the mischievous kitten scampering about in the bushes, but he would not come to her. After an hour, she gave up and came in.

"He'll come back," she said. "He's only a baby, he won't go far."

But a little later, they heard the kitten give one short scream out in the woods. Liv went scrambling out again with the lamp, calling desperately. The woods were silent.

They never saw Sam again.

"A bobcat probably got him," said Mary Ellen sadly, "or a fox."

When they told Sam Rauch about it, he said philosophically, "Hell, he went down fighting. He's a pier cat, right? And he had a good life while it lasted . . ."

Sometimes Mary Ellen didn't sleep well. She lay awake at night tormenting herself about what she'd committed herself to do. Supposing Armando screwed up somehow? Supposing he had a flat tire on his way from the motel to the cemetery, or lost his appetite for assassination, and she was left there with the smoking gun in her hand. Supposing . . . She was not kidding herself that the two of them had planned a perfect crime. As far as ordinary homicides went, she knew that between 60 and 70 percent of the homicides committed in New York City every year went unsolved. This was something that the police knew, and the general public generally did not know. However, in the case of a public figure like Colter, the pressure to find the killer would be tremendous, and the police would not rest until they had canvassed the whole state and followed every lead.

She knew that she would be questioned. The police would know that she had been at the scene, ostensibly as Jeannie's bodyguard. The police would also eventually discover that she knew Armando, and that she was gay, and it might come out that she had been laid off from the force because she was a lesbian, and they would see that she had a clear motive for wanting to get Colter. Her only safety lay in the fact that Armando had an even more compelling motive—a dead lover. And Armando would have the murder weapon, and it would be covered with his fingerprints. The tire tracks of his car would be found at the scene, he would have a clear shot at Colter, and the opportunity to make a getaway while Mary Ellen ran to Reverend Irving's house and called the police. Above all, Armando would confess. As long as Armando confessed, she was safe.

And how likely was Armando to keep his promise to confess? Very likely, she felt.

But there was always the off-chance that something would get screwed up somewhere—that Reverend Irving would come over unexpectedly from his house, or that some other undesirable witness would come on the scene at the wrong moment.

The part of her that seethed with hate and anger warred with the part of her that wanted only to live quietly, to love Liv, to work at something meaningful, to be free.

And still another part of her mind had begun saying quietly that there must be another way to get Colter —another way besides pulling the trigger of the Beretta.

Jeannie Colter had impressed her as a human being whose nerves were stretched to the breaking point. The woman had a problem marriage, problem children, and—it seemed—a problem squaring her domineering personality with the stricures of her religion. On top of that, she was running for governor. The strain would be too much. If left to herself, Jeannie Colter might just harmlessly self-destruct.

As Mary Ellen fell into restless sleep, she would be telling herself all these things.

But the next day, when she would get up and rejoin the staff for the day's work at Windfall, she would hear or see some mind-blowing bit of anti-gay prejudice from someone at the place, and she would feel disposed to use that gun that still lay padlocked in her father's chest, awaiting its moment.

One day she was idly glancing at a copy of one of the national tabloids lying around the Colter office. Jeannie had given them an interview.

Mary Ellen read the article, and thought she'd vomit.

The headline read: JEANNIE COLTER LIVES IN FEAR.

The reporter went on to paint a colorful picture of the Colter family beseiged by hordes of vicious and violence-minded homosexuals. Thousands of hate letters and hate calls came in every week. Both the Colter houses—the town house and Windfall—were wired with all kinds of burglar alarms, and connected with the closest police departments. Jeannie herself wore a special beeper on her belt, which would beep the police if she were assaulted.

Mary Ellen knew, better than anyone, that none of this was true.

Jeannie *was* somewhat perturbed at the threatening letters and phone calls she'd received, but they were fewer than the paper claimed. Tom Winkler had told her that the amount was nothing out of the ordinary.

"Any rock star," he said frankly, "gets that many in a week."

Mary Ellen also knew that the security precautions were exaggerated. There were guards at both properties, but not as many as the paper stated. And there was certainly no police beeper.

In fact, Jeannie, perhaps discouraged by what Mary Ellen had told her about flak vests, had actually decided against a lot of security paraphernalia.

"Why should I have to live like that—under guard in a free country?" Jeannie had said. "Why should I have to protect myself like that? I haven't done anything wrong. God will protect me."

Yet she had seen fit to portray herself, to this reporter, as that poor lovely woman who was just trying to clean up the country and protect her family and other people's children from being perverted, and whom those awful homosexuals were persecuting.

Mary Ellen threw the newspaper down in disgust.

"For that lie alone, lady," she thought, "you ought to get a bullet between your eyes."

CHAPTER
Thirteen

Jeannie continued to have bad dreams.

Somewhere she had read (maybe it was in the *Reader's Digest*) that you dreamed during your REM sleep, and that the amount of time you spent in REM sleep increased when you were in a state of tension or anxiety. She had also remembered reading that, if you drank or took pills, that tended to decrease your REM sleep below what you needed—which was why people on pills or booze got even more upset about life.

She tried discussing her dreams with Reverend Irving. But she found that he didn't have much to say about dreams.

"I have this feeling that my mind is trying to tell me something," she told him, "but I don't know what."

"*God* is trying to tell you something," said Reverend Irving one time.

Another time he said, "Dreams are vanity." And he pounded with his cane and intoned, "Knowest thou not this of old, since man was placed upon earth, that the triumphing of the wicked is short. He shall perish forever like his own dung: they which have seen him shall say, Where is he? He shall fly away as in a dream, and shall not be found: yea, he shall be chased away as a vision of the night."

She was puzzled.

"But, Reverend Irving, God sometimes uses dreams to tell people things. He sent dreams to the prophets. Daniel . . ."

"And false prophets *pretend* to revelations in their dreams," intoned Reverend Irving.

She left the old man with a queasy feeling that, in a few respects at least, Irving was out of touch with reality.

"After all, what can you expect?" she told herself. "He's old as the hills."

She decided that she would not interfere with whatever her mind was trying to work out. She chased away the temptations to take just one little glass of wine, just one wee Valium. "All I need is to get more nervous," she thought. Bravely she drank a cup of warm milk every night before going to bed, and slipped into her bed wondering what new thing her subconscious mind would come up with that night.

One night, however, she woke up shuddering and terrified to the marrow of her bones. She wondered if she was going mad.

She was so frightened that she went into the living room and turned on the TV. Feeling morally unable to watch a movie, she sat there trying to watch a late-night talk show. But she could not wipe away the memory of the dream, and it would haunt her for days afterward.

In her dream, she had found herself in the balcony of a huge auditorium, high above and far from the stage. The place was dark, and she could sense rather than see an immense crowd in evening dress. On the great bare stage, dramatically picked out by a single spotlight, was a woman's figure.

Slowly she found herself drawing near the figure. It was like she was a camera doing a slow zoom.

Pretty soon she was close enough to see that it was Miss America standing there. The figure's crown sparkled in the spotlight, it carried a trophy, and it was

253

holding a mike with a long cord and singing sweetly, "Don't Sit Under the Apple Tree With Anyone Else But Me."

Jeannie found herself going closer and closer.

Finally she was close enough to make out all the details.

The woman was wearing an elaborate rhinestone crown and high-heeled rhinestone shoes. She had on a sweeping floor-length cape covered with red and blue stripes and silver stars. Her bathing suit was made of the same patriotic-looking fabric. A tall silver trophy rested across one arm. She was wearing silver lamé gloves.

And she was dead. She was a frail shriveled thing, not quite a mummy, because the flesh was rotting all along her skinny limbs, and hanging in moldy pieces off her face. The nose had caved in, and the lips had melted away. The front of the bathing suit hung obscenely loose where the breasts and the pubic mound should have been. Underneath the glittering crown, her matted white hair was stuck to her skull and neck. In the sockets of her skull she had two giant rhinestones that glittered like lizard's eyes.

Jeannie found herself zooming in still closer. She realized that, with three or four more feet, she would be forced to touch the thing. She struggled. She felt frozen, trapped.

Suddenly she became aware that she was screaming. And then she had yanked herself into the safe dark of her bedroom.

Now she sat staring at the TV set.

"Like a vision of the night," she said softly to herself.

Maybe she only thought that she was saved. Maybe she was kidding herself. It wasn't that she believed God to be unmerciful, or Jesus to be unforgiving. But she began to fear that her regeneration was only skin-deep, that there were still poisonous things deep in her soul that resisted the goodness and the forgiveness of the Lord. Perhaps she had been an infidel too long to change.

She got her mother's Bible from the family altar and thumbed through it. She came across a passage in Jude that terrified her. Jude had written to his congregation, scolding them about converts who did not strictly keep the faith. She closed the Bible with a snap, those dread images flapping away like great birds into her mind.

> *Angels which kept not their first estate, but which left their own habitation, he hath reserved in everlasting chains under darkness.*
>
> *Clouds they are without water, carried about of winds*
>
> *Trees whose fruit withereth, without fruit, twice dead, plucked up by the roots*
>
> *Raging waves of the sea, foaming out their own shame*
>
> *Wandering stars, to whom is reserved the blackness of darkness for ever . . .*

"Am I one of those angels?" she cried out to herself. "Am I one of those clouds? Those wandering stars?"

The next time she saw Reverend Irving, she tried to talk about this latest dream with him.

But he seemed to have little patience with her, and cut her off short.

"Sister Jeannie," he said, "do you believe in the Lord Jesus Christ?"

"Yes, I do, but . . ."

"Do you accept him as your Saviour?"

"Of course. I did, and I do . . ."

"Then stick to that, and forget the rest. Throw your dreams out with the garbage."

That day, Bill decided that he would give in to Jeannie's pleadings and go up to Windfall for a visit.

Actually, she hadn't pleaded. She had spoken to him sharply about it. She seemed to be very much on edge lately.

"Your grandchildren haven't seen you for weeks," Jeannie had said. "Jessica adores you. And she's starting to ask me if Granddaddy doesn't love her any more."

He felt deeply discouraged about the way his own affairs had been going. They had run into a hitch on connecting the Catherine Slip house into the sewers. Some of the hardwood flooring he wanted was delayed in shipment. And to top things off, Marion had been less in touch with him over the past few days. If Bill called him, he said the same things as always. But he called Bill less often.

Bill's weariness and depression was evident even to Al, who had gruffly observed, just yesterday, that maybe he needed a little vacation.

So that morning, Bill had climbed into his Lancia and headed upstate to Pawling.

When he arrived at Windfall, Jessica came flying up from the pony barn, screaming, "Granddaddy! Granddaddy!"

She flung herself at him like a little wild animal, clinging and hugging with her skinny little arms, with a strength that amazed him.

Naturally she made him come with her to the pony barn and see Jet. The pony stood knee-deep in fresh straw, groomed and pampered almost to death. He had given Jet to Jessica as a birthday present last year, and, to his surprise, Jeannie had objected—she didn't think it was seemly for girls to ride horses, though he suspected that she envied Jessica's ability to fly over the earth on that pony.

He sat with Jessica on a bale of straw, and Jessica talked to him jerkily, sullenly, holding onto his arm till he thought she would bruise him.

"I want to come live with you in New York," she said.

"Oh?" said Bill. "Don't you like it here any more?"

"Mommy doesn't like me any more," said Jessica.

"Oh now, I don't think that's true," said Bill. "Your mommy is pretty busy right now, but I think she's—"

Jessica cut him off in the most abrupt adult style. "Mommy talks about God all the time, and about my Grandmommy."

Bill smoothed the little girl's hot silky hair gently. Jessica had a little purple bruise on her forehead, as delicately tinted as the petal of the anemone.

"Did you fall off Jet?" he asked, touching the bruise.

Jessica shook her head.

"Well, how did you get such a bump on your head? Did Jet run under a tree with you?"

Jessica kept shaking her head, with the air of a child keeping a secret, but so sullenly that it gave Bill a creepy feeling. He knew Jeannie's impatience with the children, and wondered if she'd hit Jessica harder than she meant to.

He went up to the house, and in through the kitchen door. Auntie Mary was in the kitchen with the cook and one of the staff women. The three of them were making potato salad and hamburger patties, obviously to feed a horde of people who hadn't much time to eat.

Bill had never been too fond of Mary—she had all of Cora's faults, and none of her virtues. He was aware that Jeannie was fond of her, mostly because she admired Mary's strictness with the children.

"Where's Little Cora?" he asked Mary.

"Upstairs," said Mary shortly.

Bill started up the back stairs, but Mary said, "Wait, I'll have to go with you." When they were alone, going down the hall upstairs, Mary said, "I have to unlock the door."

"Unlock the door?" said Bill incredulously. "You mean she is locked in her room?"

"If we didn't lock her in," Mary said grimly, "she'd be running after boys. She is a boy-crazy little monster,

257

that's what she is. A seething caldron of sin at the age she is . . ."

Bill couldn't believe his ears.

Mary unlocked the door of Cora's room. The room was stripped of all the posters that Bill remembered. He could understand Jeannie not liking posters of rock stars, but even the cheerful animal posters were gone. The radio and stereo were gone. The room was bare and deathly neat as a nun's cell. Cora was lying on the bed in her bathing suit, facing the wall, her limbs bathed in sweat. Mary went back downstairs.

Gently, Bill sat down on the bed beside her.

"How long have you been in here?" he asked.

"Since last night," she said in a low voice.

"They brought your supper up here?"

Her body shook with a bitter soundless laugh. "They didn't bring me *nuthin'*."

Gently Bill pulled her into a sitting position. She sat drooping like a wilted flower, clutching his hand. Finally she bent her head and put one cheek against his hand.

"I'd like to run away," she said in a low voice. "But I know awful things happen to kids that run away. I don't want awful things. But I don't like it here. Ever since Daddy went to China, Mom has been pretty weird."

She raised her head, and looked into his eyes with a strange intensity. "I wish Mom wasn't saved. I wish she was an infidel like everybody else."

He shook his head disbelievingly, and stroked her hot dry little hand.

"You aren't saved, are you, Granddaddy?"

"Listen, Cora . . ." He spoke to her as if she were an adult. ". . . Cora, there are two kinds of people who are saved. Some of them become wonderful people, and the others, well, it kind of goes to their heads . . . Heaven only knows what the Lord Jesus thinks of the second kind . . ."

He kept talking with a terrible urgency.

"Cora, your mother shouldn't be doing these things. But I don't think your mother is well these days. Now if I let you out of your room, will you promise me that you won't run away or do anything like that? And I'm going to make things better for you. Do you promise, Cora?"

"I promise," she said, closing her eyes. "Just get me a drink of water, please, Granddaddy?"

Bill went downstairs like a tornado.

The whole downstairs, so elegantly furnished with colonial antiques, seemed to have turned into a shoddy political office of some kind. Jeannie and Tom Winkler and the whole bunch of them were there. Most of them were madly stuffing envelopes, and Jeannie was on the phone talking to someone. Tom Winkler looked angry.

When Jeannie hung up the telephone, Bill asked, "What's happening here?"

"Well," said Jeannie in her brightest, most brittle, most nervous voice, getting up and coming toward him, "it's a little fund-raising mailing that—"

Tom Winkler cut her off. "It's another bunch of anti-homosexual crap," he said. "Over my dead body," he added.

"Oh come on, Tom, it's nothing to do with me, or my campaign, it's just . . . ."

"Some people want to start a national anti-homosexual organization, and Jeannie isn't going to participate in it," said Winkler, furious, "she's just going to raise them a little *seed money*, that's all . . ."

"Now, Tom, really—" Jeannie started to raise her voice.

"Before you people get into a big discussion," Bill said, "Jeannie, could I speak to you for a minute?"

He motioned Jeannie upstairs. When they were in the hallway, Jeannie noticing the taut expression in his face, said, "What on earth . . ."

Bill opened the door of Little Cora's bedroom. "You will *not* do this," he said.

"I will if I please," she flared at him. "How would you like a fallen thirteen-year-old grandchild?"

They were speaking in low voices so those downstairs wouldn't hear.

"This is *my* house," he said, "and you will not abuse my grandchildren in *my* house. Do those people downstairs know what is going on?"

"No, of course not, they—"

"I'll bet not. If they knew, they'd drop you and your promising political career like a hot potato."

"I'm their mother and—"

"If you lock up Cora once more, or if you hit Jessica once again, as God is my witness, I will cable Sidney in China and he'll be on the next plane home from Peking. You know damn well, my dear, that you wouldn't dare do these things as long as he is around."

"He wouldn't . . ."

"You bet he would, my dear, and he might even divorce you and sue for custody of the children, and you might even lose them! And then we'll see if you'll be governor of New York!"

"Don't you 'my dear' me," she hissed. "Where do you get this 'my dear' stuff, anyway? You sound just like some faggot."

There was no stopping Bill now. "You get down on your knees in front of your famous family altar, my dear, and ask God to shine His flashlight into your heart, and see if you like what you see there . . ."

"You dare to judge me," she raged, "and I always knew you were an infidel of some kind, with your sneaky ways lately, not giving me any help with the campaign, running around the city all the time, it's pathetic to see a man your age chasing after *skirts!*"

It left them shaking, and drenched with sweat—the worst quarrel they ever had.

Jeannie turned on her heel, and went back downstairs to where her staff was working away. Bill marched straight down to the kitchen, and poured a glass of milk for Cora, and made her two peanut-butter sandwiches. His hands were shaking so much that he could hardly butter the bread.

Auntie Mary tried to interfere, muttering something about how the Bible said that children should be punished, and he turned on her: "If I hear one word about the Bible, the whole bunch of you will be out in the street, and you can burn your Bibles to keep warm."

When he went back upstairs to Cora, he sat on the bed and watched her wolf the sandwich and chug-a-lug the milk.

"Granddaddy," she said with her mouth full, "hey, you can level with me. Is that true what Mom says, that you chase women? You can tell me, Granddaddy, I won't tell anyone, I promise."

She grinned at him with that disarming too-grownup way she had.

Bill grinned back tautly.

"If I *did* chase women," he said, "I'd tell you. But I never chased women in my life, and that's God's truth."

"Okay," she said, shrugging pleasantly, "just asking."

When Bill went back downstairs, Jeannie was on the phone again, to some party person in Syracuse, the envelope-stuffing had been finished, and most of the staff had gone outside to barbecue themselves some hot dogs and hamburgers. Only a few of Jeannie's political workers were still sitting around—and one of them was the young woman he had seen at the MCC church service on that Sunday morning weeks ago.

A sensation that was more than fear, a nameless terrible sensation, crashed into his chest.

There was no mistaking her. He had seen her twice. Once at MCC. And once at the South Street house, when she had worn the uniform of a New York City police officer and bent over the dead tramp so briskly.

He went into the library, closed the door, and sat down to think for a few moments. He distractedly pulled out a book titled *The Upper Crust* filled with photographs of old New York City mansions, and tried to think things through.

He had better not panic. He had to handle this carefully. There was every possibility that she had not seen him at MCC. Or she had seen him in passing, and did not connect him with the man she'd met at the South Street house. It was only a slim possibility, because police officers usually had a keen memory for faces.

He decided that he would test the wind and see if she seemed to connect those two men.

So he left the library, and went out onto the lawn.

As he walked toward her, he was thinking. What was she doing here, anyway? If she attended MCC, she had to be a lesbian. What was a gay person doing in the Colter organization? There were three possibilities that his logical mind ticked off right away. One, she believed in Jeannie's politics in non-homosexual areas, and simply wanted to work for her. Two, she was a plant put there by some gay activist group, who wanted inside information on Jeannie's anti-gay activities. Three, she intended to harm Jeannie or the Colter organization in some way.

Out amid the gnarled apple trees, the staff were all grouped around a couple of redwood picnic tables. They were talking shop quietly, as smoke drifted up from the barbecuing meat.

The young woman was sitting with Jeannie and her speech-writer at one of the tables, and he put a little food on a paper plate and joined them.

"Well, Ms. Police Person," he said to the young woman, "we meet again. What a nice surprise."

The young woman grinned, without a trace of alarm. "Yeah, I told Jeannie how we met. Pretty crazy, huh?"

Jeannie didn't speak to Bill, stabbing furiously at her hamburger, not eating much.

"Whatever happened to the old man's body?" Bill asked.

"I have no idea," she said. "Usually the officers at the scene never find out the end of the story, because they're running to other scenes."

"So how come you're not in uniform?"

"I was laid off," she said. "So I was looking around to find some other place where I could, uh, keep from putting my light under a bushel."

Bill looked at Jeannie. "Is she good, Jeannie?"

Jeannie shrugged. "She made us think of things we'd never thought of before. For instance, somebody sent a package with T-shirts for the children. Jessica was about to put one on, and Mary Ellen stopped her. Turned out the T-shirt was treated with acid."

Bill shuddered.

"Well," said Mary Ellen dryly, "I don't think that little kids should get hurt for what their parents do."

When Jeannie got up to talk to Tom Winkler, Bill said quickly to Mary Ellen, "I'm sorry to be so inquisitive, but I have to ask what you're doing here."

"Huh?" said Mary Ellen, who had been watching Jessica galloping around on her pony. The expression on her face had hardly changed, but suddenly she had a subtly guarded look.

"I'll be very frank with you," said Bill. "I happen to know what church you belong to in New York. And it's not the Antioch Baptist Church either. So I have to ask you again, what are you doing here?"

She stared at him, and answered without hesitating: "I don't understand what you mean. I needed a job, and it seemed like a good bet."

"Did the Police Department know you belonged to that church?"

She shrugged. "I have no idea. I doubt it. We were hearing rumors about layoffs long before Jeannie started making her noises."

"But it's odd, Mary Ellen, a member of your church here . . ."

"Not really," she said. "Look, I happen to think that in *that* respect, Jeannie has done more good than harm. She's made the whole country talk openly about something they didn't want to talk about. And that's good. And in other areas I do admire her politics so ..."

Jeannie had had a short violent argument with Tom Winkler, and was coming back, walking in the foot-stomping way she had when she was angry.

So Bill broke off the conversation with Mary Ellen.

Later that afternoon, it clouded over, and a couple of swift violent line storms came over. Everybody sat in the house, feeling claustrophobic. Tom Winkler had apparently quit as campaign manager. A couple of the staff were writing long memos about it. It looked as if everything was falling apart.

The conversation with Bill Laird had left Mary Ellen in a stormy state of mind, though outwardly she kept her cool.

How did he know that she belonged to MCC? Was he so protective of his daughter that he made a habit of checking out everybody who worked for her?

She kept asking herself if this had blown the whole thing. And she wasn't sure it had. She had already discussed with herself the certain knowledge that, if the plan worked out, the police would find out she was gay. She had given Bill the answers that she had rehearsed with herself in case anyone in the organization found out she was gay. Had this really changed things? Not really.

Armando had been at the Bel Aire Motel since Tuesday. Today was Thursday. She had driven past the motel yesterday on an errand, and had seen a dark-green 1974 Pinto with a red T-shirt, blue sweater and white T-shirt piled in the back. She had brought the Beretta and the silencer down from the cabin a couple of days ago, and had them hidden in the small powder room where she slept, right off Jeannie's room.

Tonight would be the night, she was sure. She could feel it in the air. Jeannie had been happily busy with the plans for the new anti-gay organization, and for a couple of nights, she had actually not visited the cemetery. But the way things were going, she would surely go there tonight.

Hearing them talk about going national with the anti-gay thing had whetted her anger to a new sharp point. All over the country, thousands more people were going to be hurt because of this woman. She would focus and direct the homophobia in American society as it had never been focused before.

Jewel had been right. Dear Jewel, who was now so safely removed from the whole thing, working quietly at her publishing job. Jewel, who had called Jeannie Colter the "Hammer," using the name of a medieval kingpin who had caused terror and death wherever he went.

Someone was needed, to break that Hammer on the anvil of divine justice.

Jeannie woke from the dream, gasping and drenched with sweat. She lay there trying to shake off its dread spell. She had had the Miss America dream again.

She looked at the bedside clock. It was nearly one o'clock.

She felt the usual compulsion to visit the church grounds.

She got up and banged on Mary Ellen's door to wake her up.

"Okay," said Mary Ellen sleepily, "be right with you."

You had to hand it to the girl—she was very good-natured about getting up in the middle of the night. Maybe she realized—as Jeannie now dimly recognized—that these trips to the church at night were

265

screams for help, and she was not yet sure what she wanted to be saved from.

Fifteen minutes later, they were driving down Quaker Hill.

Mary Ellen clutched the dashboard as Jeannie took the big car screeching around the hairpin turns. We'll *both* get killed tonight, she thought. She had the Beretta and the silencer in her big suede over-the-arm bag. She had already slipped the ammo clip into the gun in the bedroom.

Her stomach was clenching uneasily. All the rationalizations of what she was about to do, and all the objections to it, had returned to haunt her mind in these last minutes. Ten minutes or so from now, she would be guilty of a homicide.

She wondered if everybody who did things like this had second thoughts at the last moment. Some killers probably didn't—the psychopaths. They probably spent the last minutes as cool and detached as if they were about to spray cockroaches with insecticide.

They passed the Bel Aire Motel. The room was dark in front of the dark-green Pinto. Armando had better be awake. Maybe he had left the room dark so that he could see the road better. She definitely would not fire until she saw that Pinto coming up the drive to the church.

She thought of Liv, deep in her warm and innocent child's sleep at the cabin, sleeping grandly on her back with her arms spread out to the world, the way she always did. If she and Armando goofed this thing up, she wondered if Liv would stay true to her, visit her in jail.

Jeannie gunned the car up the little church drive, parked it in the gravel parking lot, and shut everything off. They got out of the car.

It was a very dark moonless night, sultry and close. The church, which looked so small in the daylight, seemed to loom larger in the dark. So did the two immense elms in front of it.

First Jeannie had to go through the whole charade, as if she didn't know why she had really come here.

She said, "Now you wait here. I am going up to visit Reverend Irving."

While Jeannie walked off in the dark, Mary Ellen looked nervously down the drive. No headlights coming yet. She fitted the silencer to the gun. The spent bullet casing would fly out on the ground somewhere. That was okay—the police were supposed to find it.

She hoped that, this time, Jeannie wouldn't actually wake Irving up. The old man probably wouldn't appreciate this much. Jeannie had told her that, when she was first saved, she used to come down here late at night and talk about Jesus with him, so maybe all this was less crazy than it looked. Maybe the old man went to bed earlier now.

In a minute Jeannie was back, wearing a long face. "He's asleep," she moaned. "What'll I do? I need to talk to him."

She went over to the church. It was locked tight—Irving always did that, for fear of vandals. Jeannie shook the door with futile rage, and the rattle echoed hollowly inside the church.

Mary Elled stood silent. Still no sign of Armando, damn it. The fucker *was* asleep.

Jeannie came back from the church. "Well . . ." she said, sounding like a lost child.

She started off toward the cemetery, her raincoat wrapped tightly around her, walking with unsure steps over the grass. Mary Ellen followed. If the voters could see this, she thought, they'd be amazed. She wondered how many politicians had a crazy side like this, a closet craziness that no one but a few aides and intimates ever saw. After all, Nixon seemed to have lost some of his grip on reality in those last days in the White House. And she could think of others . . .

She followed, her hand in her bag, holding the gun hidden under the flap of the bag. In another minute— zip! zip! and the Hammer would be dead, killed by one million of her victims, past, present, and future, all their uneasy spirits crying out from the grave for revenge, one billion gay ghosts haunting the corridors and bedrooms of the castle of Western civilization.

Where the motherfucking Jesus was Armando?

They went into the little cemetery. Nothing very spooky about it—a lot of gravestones crowded together in the dark, like empty cardboard boxes piled up in the back room in a supermarket. Mary Ellen had always yawned through graveyard scenes in horror films.

She leaned against a tall Victorian marble angel as she watched Jeannie wend her way among the graves a little farther. The smell of wet grass and moss was fresh in her nostrils. Her brain was very clear, like a dark crystal receiving powerful signals from a far star and transmitting them to an atomic-powered computer for earthlings to read.

Jeannie sat down on the edge of an eroded colonial headstone, and stared at her mother's grave, clasping her raincoat tightly around her.

Down the drive, by Route 22, she could see the headlights of a car slowly turn in. It was about time. But she waited to make sure it was the dark-green Pinto, and not another car.

Her hand slowly drew the Beretta from her bag. With the silencer, it looked long and menacing in the dark, like one of those ray-guns they used in sci-fi films.

Jeannie Colter had less than sixty seconds to live.

Jeannie didn't even notice the car coming—she was crying.

The car definitely had the silhouette of a Pinto as it rounded the corner of the trees and came slowly into the parking lot. The headlights played harshly over the cemetery, back-lighting all the graves and the bent figure of Jeannie Colter.

Now, Mary Ellen thought.

And then an important thought came through the dark crystal.

It was one of those thoughts that you got in police work, when you wondered why you hadn't thought it before, but once you had thought it, you knew—with all the power of your hunter's instincts—that it had to be the correct and only thought.

Bill Laird could know that she attended the MCC with her lover . . . if he had been there himself.

Quickly she slipped the gun and the silencer back in her bag, and latched the bag shut.

Armando had parked the car close to the cemetery, shut off the lights, and leaned his head against the window, pretending to be asleep.

Slowly she walked toward Jeannie Colter. Now a hot sweat was breaking out all over her, as she thought of the close call she had had. Liv, everything, so close to being lost forever, when there was a better way to do it.

Jeannie had stopped crying, and was searching in her handbag for a handkerchief.

"What's the problem?" Mary Ellen asked.

"Oh . . ." Jeannie found something, and blew her nose. "Tom has quit, and some of the others are mad at me. My dad . . . No one seems to understand."

"Understand what?"

"That the homosexual thing is special. That I can't give it up. That I've been called to do it."

"Why do you hate the homosexuals so much?"

"Wouldn't you like to know?" Jeannie said, getting up, brushing off her raincoat. "I guess we'd better go home."

As they walked past the car, Mary Ellen could see Armando sitting slumped in there, pretending to be asleep. He must really be puzzled. Mary Ellen gave the agreed-upon abort signal. She reached up twice and rubbed her head.

"Wonder who that is, in that car?" said Jeannie.

"Looks like he's asleep in there," said Mary Ellen. "He was falling asleep at the wheel so he pulled in here to take a nap."

Fifteen minutes later, they were back at Windfall.

They sat in the empty kitchen, not talking, and Jeannie made herself a cup of hot milk, and Mary Ellen poured herself a cup of bitter leftover coffee. Jeannie looked haggard, with dark circles under her eyes.

When Jeannie had gone upstairs to bed, Mary Ellen sat in the kitchen writing a note.

Dear Jeannie,

I guess it's one visit too many to the cemetery for me. Anyway, the craziness around here is beginning to get to me too. So effective immediately, I won't be working for you any more. Please send my last few days' pay to my home address in New York.

Sincerely,
Mary Ellen

Softly, as the house full of people slept, she packed her few things, got in her car and left.

Dawn was just breaking over the rolling wooded hills. The clearing skies bared streaks of blue. She breathed deeply, feeling a great relief. All of a sudden she couldn't imagine why she had agreed to go along with such such a cockamamie idea.

She stopped at a rest area where there were public phones, and called Armando.

He was awake and very angry.

"What's the hell's going on?"

"Armando, I've called it off. There's a better way to stop this lady. Better than a bullet."

"What do you mean?"

"I'm sorry," she said. "It'll mean that you won't be able to go to jail for Danny. That'll be something you'll have to work out for yourself. But you gotta realize, I had to work this out for myself, too, and I was the one pulling the trigger for you. And when I realized that there was a better way, I just couldn't do it."

"You're not making any sense," he said.

"Armando, I've just found out something interesting about her father. I think he's gay."

She crossed the Housatonic River at Kent. The little old iron-girder bridge was deserted. On the other side lay the sleeping resort town with its Victorian houses and its little country-cabin motels. She stopped in the middle of the bridge, and put up her car hood, and pretended to fiddle with the engine.

She looked carefully to make sure no cars were coming, then quickly she whipped the Beretta out over the side. It fell, winking, and made a little splash in the smooth green current. She whipped the silencer out at a different angle, and it made a smaller splash about fifty feet from the first.

Fourteen

A few mornings later, at about 11 A.M., Bill was working in his office when Mrs. Voeller buzzed him and said, "You have a call from a Miss Mary Ellen Frampton."

Bill's stomach fell with fright. He knew that the young woman had quit Jeannie's staff.

He picked up the phone. "Yes?"

"Hi, this is Mary Ellen Frampton," she said. "I think you remember me."

"I do indeed," said Bill. "My daughter was furious when you quit without notice."

"Well," she said. "I have to admit, the whole thing was starting to get to me a little. You know, I found myself stuffing envelopes for an organization that I didn't approve of, and I suddenly thought, 'This is ridiculous.'"

Bill's stomach was churning. At least the girl had sense enough to disguise her talk, in case Mrs. Voeller was listening.

"What do you want?" he said bluntly.

"I want to talk to you," she said. "You see, I figured out how you know about me. You know because you went there yourself."

Bill was silent for a moment, trying to collect himself. He had feared this moment for so many years that, when it finally came, he hardly knew how to handle it.

"I suppose you want money from me," he said. "Well, I—"

She cut him off in her cold cop voice.

"I don't want money from you, Mr. Laird. I want us to talk heart to heart like a brother and sister in Christ. You and I have something pretty urgent to discuss."

He sat there for a long long moment.

"Mr. Laird?" she said.

"All right," he said heavily. "Are you free for lunch?"

"I'm free any time you are. I'm back in the city, and I'm unemployed."

"Meet me at the Sumptuary at twelve-thirty," he said. He gave her the address.

Then he called the member of the city planning board with whom he'd planned to have lunch at the Four Seasons, and he postponed it.

Mary Ellen and Liv had closed up the cabin and returned to Manhattan on Sunday afternoon.

Liv still cried when she thought of Sam the kitten but she was basically happy with the time she had spent there, and with what she felt was a new atmosphere between herself and Mary Ellen.

"I don't know exactly what it is," she said. "But I know that it is better. Maybe you needed to go to the cabin, Mary Ellen."

Mary Ellen had to agree. Of course, Liv would never know—she hoped—the reason for the shadow that had passed over them, unless Armando was so uncool as to tell Liv. But in some mysterious way, the whole affair had vented all her anger, drained all her bitterness. For the first time since her father's death, she felt at peace.

Armando was mad at her for giving up the plan to "terminate" Jeannie Colter.

273

She had told him bluntly, "If you want to kill her, you'll have to do it yourself. But look—isn't it better to try it this way? So maybe the whole country will see her giving up her homophobic crap of her own free will. They gave us a martyr, right? They gave us Danny. Is it really smart of us to make a martyr out of her for them? I don't think so. I don't think either of us was thinking too clearly right after Danny was killed."

She had sat with Armando at the Eagle's Nest for a couple of afternoons, when the bar was empty, and talked to him a lot about all this in a low voice. Finally, grudgingly, Armando saw her point.

So, on that Tuesday noon in August, she headed for her lunch with Bill Laird with a relatively light heart.

When she walked into the Sumptuary, Bill Laird was already waiting for her, in the sunny area around the fountain, in the back. Poor guy, she thought, he's really anxious and shook up.

She sat down, and the waiter took her order for a drink.

There was an awkward silence.

Abruptly, she said, "Look, I know you think I'm going to try to blackmail you. Well, I'm not. I just . . . you saw me at the MCC, so you have to be gay, right?"

Bill was silent, staring at his glass of wine. He didn't deny it.

"And that's none of my business," Mary Ellen went on, "except that your daughter happens to be very anti-gay. It's possible I lost my job on the force because they knew I was gay and they were afraid Jeannie would have them investigated. There were four of us, two lesbians, two gay men, who got canned off the force, all at once."

Bill had one hand over his eyes.

"Plus," Mary Ellen said softly, "I was a close friend of Danny Blackburn. *And* his partner on the force."

"Oh my God," said Bill.

"So my question is . . . I mean, obviously you're not

274

out, and Jeannie doesn't know a thing about you, and I'm just curious to put it bluntly . . . how do you feel about all that?"

"I don't feel too good," said Bill brusquely.

Mary Ellen looked him in the eyes earnestly. "Bill . . ." Unconsciously she had slipped into the easy familiarity of the gay church brethren, where status and age barriers disappeared and everybody was a first name. "Bill, you could stop her. And you're the only one who could stop her."

"I know," said Bill. "I've known it for weeks, every hour of every day."

"If her own father came out against her . . . her own father . . . maybe people would begin to understand gays better. And she'd have to stop doing what she's doing. It would de-fuse her completely."

Suddenly Bill said, "Now I've got a question for *you*. What were you doing working on Jeannie's staff?"

Mary Ellen was silent a moment. Then she said, "I'm going to be very honest with you. Three years ago, my dad was shot and killed on duty. I became a cop mostly because of his example and because he was an incredible guy. My mother is dead. I'm an only child. Aside from my lover, the police force is all I have. And suddenly, because of Jeannie I'm off the force, right? And then suddenly, a guy who is a brother cop and a very dear friend is also dead, right?"

She paused again. "Bill, I was going to harm Jeannie in some way. I changed my mind, and that's all you need to know."

Stunned, Bill stared into those frank gray eyes of hers.

Suddenly, with the force of a blow, he felt her steely courage and her honesty. He found himself admiring it hopelessly, and loving it, and not at all shocked at her confession. After all, the other day he had been within a hair of wringing Jeannie's neck when he found out how she'd been treating the children. He felt a surge of fatherly affection for this singular young woman.

"Tell you what," he said. "Let's get out of here. I want to show you something. I'm not hungry, and I don't think you are either. We can get a bite a little later."

They paid for their drinks (she refused to let him pay for hers) and got in a cab.

"The corner of South Street and Catherine Slip," he said to the cabbie.

The house was buzzing with activity. The courtyard in the back was full of parked trucks and vans whose tires had smashed all the sunflowers flat. Men were working on the roof. More men were inside, working on the plumbing. Inside, on the first floor, was the precious flooring which had finally arrived— magnificent pecan planks for the whole house, tenderly covered with tarps. New windows sparkled in the stately facade flanked by new shutters. In the arched doorway, the old crooked metal door had been replaced by a stout wooden door rich with heavy hinges, just like the one shown in the old photograph.

They walked around in the house.

"If I ever get up the courage to come out," he said, "my lover and I are going to live here. If not, I guess I live alone."

In the South Street house, he found it easier to talk about it. They walked all around his new neighborhood, and he pointed at things, and talked, and told her the story of his life. They walked down the waterfront, smelling the rank smell of the river. They walked around on the Seaport Museum docks, and gazed up at the masts of the *Peking*, and Mary Ellen talked about her life too.

They wound up in one of those dark little seafood restaurants, near the Fulton Fish market, and got a little smashed on white wine, and ate baked halibut fresh off the boats.

Mary Ellen laughed, her cheeks a little flushed. "I'll tell you *one* thing about the last couple of months of my life. I never used to know anything about gay men. I sure have learned a lot. More than I ever wanted to know."

"Oh, I never knew anything about lesbians either," said Bill. "I've learned a lot in the last two hours. It's a shame that we're always two worlds apart." He leaned back in his chair, realizing that he was a little drunk—far drunker than even a liberal Baptist should be. "You know, another crazy dream of mine . . ."

"Dreams are not crazy," said Mary Ellen.

"Okay, another dream of mine is to start a gay Baptist caucus in town. It's there crying out to be done."

"So do it," she said. "What are you waiting for? Do it, and invite Jeannie to your first service."

"I'd rather be boiled in oil than do that," said Bill, trying to signal the waiter for some coffee, so they could start sobering up.

"You've got the perfect place for it," said Mary Ellen. "That little place on the corner there, right by your house. That used to be a shop or something." She giggled. "You could have your own storefront church."

"That's not a bad idea," said Bill.

"Liv and I'll help you. That is, if you'll accept the help of a renegade Presbyterian and an imported Lutheran."

Bill threw back his head and laughed, a cathartic laugh that seemed to vent some of the tensions of the past couple of months.

"Seriously," said Mary Ellen, "call Reverend Erickson and have it announced at MCC next Sunday. Do the same for MCC in New Jersey. Run an ad in the *Voice*. Liv and I can go around and put up notices. We'll rent chairs. What kind of an altar do you need?"

Bill leaned across the table toward her, with a mock-serious look.

"Before we go any further, my dear, I have to know

277

just one thing. If you died today, are you sure you'd go to Heaven?"

Mary Ellen was grinning through her glow of wine.

"I'm more sure of it than I ever was in my life," she said.

"Good," said Bill, grinning widely. "Because I can't possibly associate with infidels."

Later that day, Bill called Marion at home.

"I know I've been, uh, nothing to admire for a while," he told Marion. "But all that's going to change. If you can find it in your . . . heart to appreciate the change, I'd like . . . to see you."

Marion must have been struck speechless—he was silent for a moment. Then he said, "Bill have you been *drinking?*"

"Yes, I have," said Bill. "I just got drunk with a very lovely uh, lesbian who has made me see the light of God's truth. It's amazing what three glasses of uh, wine can do to a man."

Marion was laughing.

"Bill, you have no idea how funny you sound. I've never seen you drunk, and I don't want to miss it. Where are you?"

"I'm at Sloppy Louie's, on South Street. My lovely friend just left, because her lover will be home from work. Why don't you . . . take a taxi over here?"

Fifteen minutes later, Marion was getting out of a yellow cab in front of Sloppy Louie's.

As Bill watched Marion walk stiffly toward him, he realized all over again why he loved Marion. Laughing reckless Marion, the idol of the Grand Prix circuit, who was brave enough to drop out into a quiet and mundane life. Marion, who was brave enough to admit he was chicken. Marion, gay, though kissed by a thousand beautiful women as they handed him trophies. Only now, he felt, was he feeling the force of

Marion's courage in his life—and this was through his decision to come out.

The two men walked slowly south along the waterfront, into the deep shadow under the Brooklyn Bridge, then out into the sunlight beyond again. Bill managed to convey to Marion the information that he was organizing a little Baptist caucus in the store on the corner of the South Street block, and that he was going to invite Jeannie.

"You mean you're not going to tell her beforehand?" said Marion. "You're just going to have her come and find out . . . like that?"

"That's . . . right," said Bill.

"What do you think she'll do?" said Marion.

"Probably tear me limb from limb," said Bill. "You must meet Mary Ellen. Wonderful girl. Wish I'd had a daughter like that. She's got Jeannie's guts, and she's got all the common sense that Jeannie never had. I'm supposed to go to their apartment for dinner some night next week. You must come with me."

His toe hit a crooked place in the concrete, and he nearly fell flat on his face.

"Are you sure you're all right?" said Marion anxiously. "Do you want to sit down somewhere?"

"No, I want to walk and look at the ships," said Bill violently. "I imagine Jesus had one too many before He went to the garden to pray. Don't you think? Do you want to walk with me and look at the ships?"

"Of course," said Marion. "What made you think I wouldn't."

"I was beginning to think that you didn't want to look at ships with me any more," said Bill.

"Well, we'll look at ships all you want," said Marion.

For the first time, Marion publicly slipped his arm through Bill's, and they walked on down the waterfront together.

A little farther on, Bill celebrated his first step toward freedom by hanging over a piling, right by one of the slummy old piers, and vomiting his lunch into the oily waters of the East River.

Jeannie got out of the cab on the corner of Catherine Slip and South Street. The street was brightly lit, but almost deserted. The warm wind brought a strong sea smell from the East River.

She looked around. It was actually the first time in her life that she had ever set foot on South Street. Farther down she could see the floodlit masts of a big sailing ship. That must be the Seaport Museum that everyone always talked about. Several cars were parked along the street, among them her father's Lancia.

It was a little scary here. The gentle rain spattered her face, and she wrapped her raincoat around herself as she walked toward the corner building. The tall old shutters were closed, but she could see the lights inside. The door stood open just a crack.

As she mounted the step, she could see about two dozen people sitting on metal folding chairs inside. On the other side of the room was a handsome old counter, hardwood-and-glass cupboards to the ceiling—this must have been a store one hundred years ago. She glimpsed someone standing up behind the counter, holding a book open.

Arrested by the voice, she stopped by the door. It was her father's voice. He seemed to be reading from the Bible, from Revelation.

". . . Behold," he was saying, "I have set before thee an open door, and no man can shut it: for thou hast a little strength, and hast kept my word, and hast not denied my name."

She smiled a little. It was nice to hear her father's voice reading the Bible.

But as she stood there a moment longer, her smile faded.

Her father stopped reading, and a discussion started.

". . . so we can only be sure this applies to gay people if we are sure all the stuff in the Old Testament doesn't apply to us," said a man's voice.

"In other words," said a woman, "if we *believe*, if we accept Jesus Christ in this spirit, then that door is open . . ."

"Right," her father was saying, "because if we have faith in Jesus Christ, if we accept Him, then He couldn't possibly throw that faith away . . ."

Jeannie felt as if some heavy chilled fluid had been injected into her veins, forcing out all the warm blood. The people in the room were homosexuals who felt that the Bible did not condemn them. And her father was in there with them. What in God's name was he doing there? By rights he should be preaching the Word to them, telling them that they were doomed to fall in the lake of fire if they didn't stop practicing their special kind of sin.

"But," somebody else said, "supposing we believe? And supposing we are wrong? And when we die, God says, 'Too bad for you, kid, I never did like queers . . .'"

The group inside laughed a little.

"But the straight believers have the same problem," said Bill. "In the long run, nobody can know for sure. All we can go on is simple faith . . ."

Jeannie stood there, feeling the blood draining down out of her brain, feeling like she was going into shock. The sea smell clogged her nostrils, and she thought she was going to gag.

Her father was in there talking with these homosexuals like he was one of them. How was it possible? Her father, so big and masculine, married to her mother for 32 years.

Her mind still couldn't take it in. She decided to go in and investigate further, before flying off the handle and maybe making a fool of herself.

She shoved at the door. It flew open with a bang— someone must have recently oiled the ancient hinges —and hit against a chair in the last row. The smell of the harbor rushed past her into the room. On the counter, the two candles guttered as the breeze hit them.

Everyone in the room turned around to look at her.

Bill had been waiting for her to come in, with every nerve in his body vibrating. He had heard the cab pull up outside, heard the car door slam, heard her footsteps, heard her pause outside the door.

Then the door flew open, and she stood there, looking curiously like a little girl, in her flat shoes and her belted trench coat, and the little paisley silk scarf tied over her head. He recalled that, for a thousand times in his life, he had dreaded the moment when she would stand looking at him with that look in her eyes that he saw there now.

Just a little shakily, he laid the open Bible down on the rich wood counter, not closing it.

"Hello, Jeannie," he said. "Come on in. This is the Bible study group that I mentioned."

She walked a couple of halting steps into the room, her hands clenched deep in her pockets, and looked savagely around.

"What is going on here?" she asked hoarsely.

The people in the room were staring at her. It was just beginning to dawn on them that former State Senator Jeannie Laird Colter, now a candidate in the gubernatorial race in New York State, and famous, yea, notorious for her pitiless pursuit of moral reform in the state, was standing there in the open doorway.

"Well," stammered Bill, "as you can see, this is a little Bible study group. It's not quite a service. We're not really ready for that. We don't have a real preacher, and we're just feeling our way ..."

"A *real* preacher?" she burst out. "What would a real preacher be doing here keeping fellowship with these infidels? What are *you* doing here with these infidels?"

Bill put his shaky fingers on the pages of the open

Bible, as if to reassure himself with the touch of its cool pages.

"Well, Jeannie, I am here because I am one of these people."

She came striding angrily toward him, then stopped suddenly and glared around at all the members of the group. They glared back, all of them a little blanched with apprehension. Bill saw that she noted Mary Ellen was there. Sam and Jewel, whom he'd also met, were there, but she wouldn't know those two surviving members of the NYPD Four.

"Look," she said harshly, "if this is some kind of joke—"

"It's no joke," said Bill, "and it's time that you finally knew the facts."

The blood was rushing back to her head, into her lungs. The heat and redness of it almost suffocated her. Her eyes fell to her father's hands on the Bible.

"Then you have no right to touch that book!" she cried out.

She lunged at him to grab it.

Marion, who was leaning against the counter to one side, reached to grab her arm. Quick as lightning, she grabbed one of the old candlesticks and swung it at Marion with terrible strength, nearly hitting his head

With gasps of dismay, the group were on their feet. The burning candle fell down against the counter, against the old wood. "Quick, put it out," screamed one of the women. Bill felt his heart snap painfully, envisioning his entire South Street property in flames like in an old movie.

Sam, meanwhile, had grabbed Jeannie as her wild swing made her lose her balance. Mary Ellen twisted the candlestick out of her hand. One of the other men dived with his jacket, and jabbed it several times against the counter, snuffing out the tiny flames that had started.

Jeannie was wrestling pitifully with Sam and Mary

283

Ellen against the counter, screaming, "Infidels! Infidels!" Tears were running down her face.

Finally Sam had her grimly braced against the counter, and she went limp, with her head hanging. All the gay Baptists stood anxiously watching her.

Then she slowly raised her head, and looked into Marion's eyes. He gazed back, calm, impassive, a T. E. Lawrence gazing at her out of his own personal desert of pain and risk.

"Jeannie," said Bill softly and shakily, "the gentleman you're looking at is my lover. Meet Marion, Jeannie. Marion, meet my daughter Jeannie."

He looked out at the group. "Would somebody shut the door?"

One of the young men shut the door.

"Brothers and sisters, sit down again," he said. "I think the fireworks are over now. I apologize for my daughter's behavior. Please forgive her. I am sure you can understand the shock she is feeling . . ."

Mary Ellen loosened her hold on Jeannie, and she twisted away from the young woman with a baleful wounded look at Marion. For a moment Bill thought she was going to rail at Marion about how he had come as a traitorous guest to the Laird house while her mother was still alive.

Then she turned around, and looked at Bill full in the eyes.

As long as he would live, he would never forget that look.

"Jeannie," he said in a low voice, "I am very much at fault for not having told you sooner. I did not have the courage to witness to the truth. But I have it now."

"So I see," she said in a strange animal tone.

Slowly, with cautious rustling sounds, the little Bible study group were sitting back down in their metal chairs. They could not take their eyes off him and Jeannie.

Bill shrugged a little and spread his hands. "If your conscience tells you that you have to go on campaigning against gay people, then go ahead. But I have to tell you that you and I will break fellowship on this one point. And I will oppose you. *Publicly.*"

She turned away, but he already knew, from her expression, that her very political mind was already coming to life, considering the ramifications of all this.

"There is no way I can undo the harm I have done," he said. "I gave you a campaign donation, and you used some of that money to campaign against the Intro Two and defeat it. My lack of courage touched the lives of innocent people that I did not know, and harmed them. But from now on it will be different. Among other things, I will campaign openly for Intro Two next time around, and maybe next time we'll get it passed."

She turned around and looked at him again. "In other words," she said sarcastically, "you are trying to blackmail me into stopping my reform movement against homosexuals."

"Call it anything you want," said Bill. "What people are going to see is the curious spectacle of the daughter calling her own father an infidel. When the public sees you on one side, and me on the other, they can hear both sides of the story."

She shook her head disbelievingly, and put her hand over her eyes.

"I must be dreaming," she said.

"Why don't you sit down?" said Bill. "We'll go on with our discussion. If you want to join in, feel free. After all, didn't Jesus debate with the elders in the temple?"

Marion, always the soul of English chivalry, brought a chair and put it behind her. She looked daggers at him . . . then she looked at Bill . . . and then slowly she sat down.

Feeling as if he was about to faint, Bill picked up the Bible again, his hands still shaky. Let's face it, he thought, this is too much excitement for an old man like me.

"Let's see now," he said, "before we were interrupted, we were talking about faith . . ."

He flipped a page, looking up at them again. Swiftly his gaze touched the gaze of every brother and sister in the room, then Marion's. Marion had a small smile on his face, but his eyes wore the old tender expression that Bill had not seen there for some time. Finally his gaze touched Jeannie's.

She sat there somewhat awkwardly on that infidel chair, in that infidel room, amid two dozen infidels, looking at him with that deep and disbelieving hurt in her eyes. And that was when he learned how much his daughter loved him. She might never accept him, might never understand him. But on the strength of less love, she would not be sitting there now. She would already be standing out on deserted South Street, angrily waiting for the occasional cab to come along.

As the Bible discussion went on, Mary Ellen sat with her eyes riveted on those fatal two—the homophobic daughter and the gay father.

For one of the few times in her life, a geniune religious emotion shook her. She had come so close to robbing those two of their necessary confrontation. She had come so close to robbing the world of whatever courage and understanding that might flow from that clash of theirs.

Yet she had had the undeniable reasons to take the gun in her hand. She, too, had had the right to a confrontation—a very private one with herself.

Looking back on it now, it shook her to the depths to see how it all had happened.

For one of the few times in her life, she really said a prayer. There in that dusty old store, with no altar and no minister, just the knocked-over candles and her friends and her lover and the Bible lying on the scarred store counter, she uttered within herself a wordless and passionate thanksgiving for her deliverance.

In that moment, she saw herself pressing, freer than she had ever been, toward a full future that was yet unrevealed.

Fifteen

It was a beautiful August day.

On the rooftop garden on Bedford Street, the petunias and begonias had bushed out in full bloom, spilling over the edges of the milk crates. The canvas awnings were a little more sun-faded than they had been two months ago.

Mary Ellen and Liv sat drinking their morning Sanka, watching Kikan strolling lazily around on the decking. Sam's little kitten ghost seemed to be somewhere around. Mary Ellen stretched out her long bare legs in the sunshine luxuriously.

She thought of Sam Rauch, and smiled. The other day he had said wistfully, "I wish there was a gay synagogue." Mary Ellen had told him there was one, Beth Simchat Torah. It met on the West Side somewhere, and was supposed to be a joyful group of people. Sam's jaw had fallen on hearing this. But then he'd said softly, "I always wanted to be a cantor . . ."

Armando had disappeared. He had quit his job, taken his pier kitten and a few things, sublet his apartment, and gone. He had said good-bye to no one, not even Mary Ellen. Mary Ellen felt an enormous sadness on thinking of the big man. He would probably spend the rest of his life wandering the country, looking for another Danny—"seeking and not finding."

At the same time, she was a little relieved that Armando was gone.

Another disappearee was Captain Bader. She had called the precinct to say hello to him. They told her that Bader had quit the force. He had taken a job in private life, and had moved his family to the Midwest somewhere. The men had been sorry to see him go. In the precinct's news column in *Spring 3100*, they had wished him luck.

Mary Ellen sat there in the sunshine, thinking of the tall heavy captain with the dark circles under his eyes. She knew she would be haunted by him too, wondering what his truth was, and how he had lived with it.

But then there was Jewel—always a joyful truth. Jewel was now assistant editorial director at her little publisher's. She was working on another book of startling poetry that they planned to publish next spring. It would be Jewel's literary debut with a "straight" house.

"Well," Mary Ellen said to Liv, "so what do I do? Do I look for another colorful job as a bodyguard? Or do we move somewhere else, so I can try to get hired as a cop again?"

Liv shrugged pleasantly.

"It is your life," she said. "You should not ask me. It depends on how much of a policeperson you feel you are."

"I was born to be a cop," Mary Ellen said. "It's bred in the bone, blood will tell, as my dad used to say about the horses. I *am* a cop."

"Then we should move somewhere else," said Liv.

"We could try California, huh? We could try one of the cities there, where they allow open gays on the police force, huh?"

"I would looooove to see California," said Liv, grinning. "And I will liberate the post office there."

Mary Ellen waved at the neighboring roofs covered with broken glass, soot and pigeon shit. "Bye-bye, Big Apple, hello Golden Gate."

But a lump rose in her throat. This was her father's city, the streets he had patrolled, the OTB windows where he had placed his bets, the bars where he had played poker with her on his knee.

Liv read her thoughts.

"Every day we say good-bye to something the day before," she said. "Someday we have to get used to saying good-bye."

"Except to you and me," said Mary Ellen.

"Yes," said Liv, smiling, "that is the one exception."

Up on East 69th Street, Jeannie slumped in the wrought-iron chair, her half-full juice glass forgotten on the table.

She gazed out over the East River, thinking over a thousand things that she had already thought over a thousand times in the last few days.

She had made a colossal ass of herself, for sure. To make everything perfect, an AP photographer had caught her slapping Jessica in the driveway at Windfall, and the photo had gone out on the wire services. People still criticized her for the famous list of homosexuals. They were those little political mistakes that would take a long time to live down. Fortunately, she was young and tough, and she could plan as far ahead as necessary. Nixon had made mistakes, and he had come back to be President, forget governor. Carter had made the mistake of admitting to *Playboy* that he lusted after ladies—they would never let him forget that—yet Carter had become President. Slapping Jessica around in public was surely not going to keep her from being governor of New York. She would have to make sure Sidney didn't try to divorce her.

She moved her eyes to her father, who was sitting across the table, hidden behind his copy of *Barron's*.

The matter of her father was different, however.

At first she had wept, gnashed her teeth, railed, called him un-Christian names. But by some mysterious power, the very next day, when she woke up, she put on her clothes and came over here, the same as usual. She wanted to talk to him, to understand how this monstrous thing had happened, how it had been hidden from her all these years, how she had been too stupid to see it. It didn't mean she would approve of her father's sin, of course. But after all, he was her father. One didn't break fellowship with one's father.

It would all take some more time to sort out. But, then, she needed a little more time anyway. She hadn't been ready to go back into action yet. Her nerves weren't steady enough, and she had a lot more thinking to do. She was beginning to understand those dreams she'd had. That dead woman in the beauty queen's clothing was not Satan, nor her mother, nor even herself!—but the fears and terrors that still stood between her past and the person that she could be.

Tomorrow was another day, as Scarlett O'Hara had said in that famous novel.

Funny she should be quoting that notorious lady to herself. Scarlett O'Hara was such an infidel, and a beauty queen.

Behind his copy of *Barron's*, Bill could feel his daughter's silence. Her thoughts were so loud that it was like gears grinding.

But he didn't say anything. He was letting her ask all the questions, shape the discussions herself. She would have to sort it out for herself, and he wasn't sure that it would lead to a meeting of their minds. She still got pretty violent when Marion's name was mentioned, and she swore that she would tear that depraved queer to bits if he set foot in Bill's house, that queer who had seduced and defiled her father. Bill had smiled a little on hearing this. It certainly was a change from her insistence that dirty old men seduced innocent young boys.

Still, she had showed up here for breakfast the next morning, which surprised and pleased him.

She was also talking about disbanding her political organization. It's possible that she felt she couldn't win with her father being openly gay. He also had the feeling that she would cease and desist from her moralistic crusading for a time.

He put down his paper and said, "More coffee, sweetheart?"

"Yeah, I guess so," she said.

He poured her a cup, then settled back and looked out over the harbor.

In a few months, if all went well, he and Marion would be moving into the house on Catherine Slip. He didn't know if she would come all the way down there for breakfast, especially with Marion there, but . . . time would tell.

He had already had one painful conversation with his brother Al. Al had taken the news much harder than Jeannie had—he wasn't even speaking to Bill, for the moment. Bill wasn't sure whether their business and family relationship would survive this crisis. All he knew was that, from now on, he had to live just one day at a time.

He looked out over his terrace railing at the harbor. He could almost make out the masts of the *Peking*, far down there in the haze.

And out past the Brooklyn Bridge, he could see a snowy-white ship, a freighter or a cruise ship, making her way slowly out across the harbor, toward the channel. His spirit followed it with a powerful surge, out past the Verrazzano Bridge, out past the long low horizon of Long Island, out past the Montauk Light.

He had lost count of the ships he had watched in the past. And he had already lost count of the ones that he and Marion would watch—white ships with every inch of canvas crowded on, making their way boldly out to the open sea.

292

ABOUT THE AUTHOR

PATRICIA NELL WARREN was born in Helena, Montana, and grew up in Deer Lodge on her father's historic Grant-Kohrs ranch. She began to write when she was ten, was encouraged by her parents and, as a freshman college student, won the *Atlantic Monthly* College Fiction Award. As an adult, she learned Ukrainian and has written three books of Ukrainian poetry that are regarded as among the best contemporary work in that language. In 1971, under the pseudonym Patricia Kilina, she published her first novel, *The Last Centennial*. This was followed by *The Front Runner* and *The Fancy Dancer*. She is a long distance runner, one of a group of women athletes who forced the Amateur Athletics Union to change its discriminatory track-and-field policies, and has been a staff writer for *Runner's World*. As a book editor for *Reader's Digest Condensed Books*, Patricia Nell Warren has been a leader among female employees in the attempt to gain equal rights. She is a resident of upstate New York.

THE NOVELS OF
PATRICIA NELL WARREN

In just a few short years, Ms. Warren has become a major selling author with three highly acclaimed novels. (She wrote her first book, THE LAST CENTENNIAL, under the pseudonym Patricia Kilina.) Ms. Warren has been hailed for "her compassionate insight," and "the poignancy and conviction with which she details the emotions, aspirations and ways of life of gay people."

THE FRONT RUNNER
The breakthrough novel. Billie Sive, a young long-distance runner is trained for the big time by a small college track coach, Harlan Brown. Billie not only becomes America's Olympic hope, the idol of the nation's youth, but he falls in love with the coach. This compelling story reaches a startling climax at the Olympics.

THE FANCY DANCER
This novel was greeted with enthusiasm— "Warren possesses the rare knack of putting the reader under the skin of the gay male. Her characters are warm and real." A young priest, in a small Montana town, befriends a brawling drifter. During counselling their friendship turns to love. The priest is thrown into conflict about himself and his obligation to the Church.

THE BEAUTY QUEEN
A timely change of pace. Jeannie Laird Colter is a beautiful woman yearning for political power. In her campaign for Governor she mounts an anti-homosexual crusade which has an unexpected effect on her personal life. A blistering story of a woman blinded to the love of others because she can't see past her own fear and hate.

(All Patricia Nell Warren novels are now Bantam Books, available wherever paperbacks are sold.)

Explore the Other World of Sexuality

Fiction

☐	12852	**The Fancy Dancer** Patricia Nell Warren	$2.50
☐	12526	**The Front Runner** Patricia Nell Warren	$2.25
☐	13016	**Rubyfruit Jungle** Rita Mae Brown	$2.50
☐	12341	**Trying Hard To Hear You** Sandra Scoppettone	$1.75
☐	12054	**The Man Without A Face** Isabelle Holland	$1.50

Non—Fiction

☐	11162	**The David Kopay Story** David Kopay & Perry Deane	$1.95
☐	11702	**Lesbian/Woman** Del Martin & Phyllis Lyon	$1.95

RELAX!
SIT DOWN
and Catch Up On Your Reading!